LOST & FOUND

A Novel

By

Alexandra Y. Caluen

LOST AND FOUND

The Playlist

Breakaway – Kelly Clarkson

Always a Woman to Me - Billy Joel

Still Crazy After All These Years – Ray Charles

Rainbow Connection – The Carpenters

Keep Holding On – Avril Lavigne

Natural Woman – Aretha Franklin

It Is You I Have Loved – Dana Glover

I'm Going to Go Back There Someday – Rachael Yamagata

Bird on a Wire – k.d. lang

Never Tear Us Apart – INXS

"And I don't want the world to see me
'cause I don't think that they'd understand
When everything's made to be broken
I just want you to know who I am."
'Iris'
Music & Lyrics by John T. Rzeznik

LOST & FOUND

Contents

CHAPTER 1

January 2003

Always knew I would end up here, Sacha thought. He was braced on his elbows to hold his face off the bricks of the building's back wall. Feet apart, skirt rucked up to his waist, and a stranger up his ass. Thanks to the drugs, the thought didn't trouble him. Half an hour ago, he'd been dancing in the bar. Fifteen minutes ago, counting his tips and tucking the money securely into his g-string. And then the rough voice and rough hands in the filthy bathroom, suggesting they go outside where the air was a little more breathable.

It wasn't the first time Sacha had let someone do this, though the alley was the least pleasant venue for it so far. It was only the latest in a long string of numb, progressively-less-excusable encounters that kept him more or less off the street. When he wasn't high, his downward slide felt unstoppably swift. There was only one likely outcome. So he stayed high whenever he could.

He'd been so full of hope and dreams those first few months in Los Angeles. He was getting hired, on average, for three out of five extra gigs. He'd found a tiny apartment – not small by New York standards, but small for L.A.; at least it had a private bathroom – and a place to park his car. There was a dance studio he could afford, not far away, and if the other dancers there were intimidating at least it was another place to get leads for jobs. He had enough money to last a year if nothing bad happened.

But six months in, an uninsured driver ran a red light. Sacha's underinsured car was totaled. He'd walked – well, limped – away from the accident, through some freakish good luck, although in retrospect he sometimes thought he'd have been better off if he'd been killed. That was typically when he went out to turn a trick and score some drugs. Because without a car in L.A., the only jobs he could get to weren't in any branch of the entertainment industry that led to stardom. And with an education that had prepared him for nothing but life as a performer, those jobs weren't in any branch of any other industry that led to prosperity. His current job had led him into this alley.

"Take it easy," he said, hazily aware of force, too much, too hard.

Then there was a hand on the back of his neck. "Shut up." A final thrust, a throb, a grunt. Rough withdrawal. The hand on his neck turning him away from the wall and giving him a shove.

Sacha went down to his knees. The pavement bit in. He caught himself on his hands in time to save his face. "Fuck! What was that for?"

"Little bitch," said that rough voice, the one that had sounded almost appealing in the bar when the Ecstasy and the popper were fresh. The used condom went splat on the pavement. Then the hand again, gripping, and another hand at his shoulder. The snick of a blade, a stinging pain to add to the others. *Oh*, Sacha thought. *This is it then.* The fear was a physical thing, a sick surge through his gut.

And then the hand groping at his groin, for the money that was all the money he had. "No!" It was a reflex.

"Hey! Get off her!"

"Shit," said the rough voice, and the hands went away. Sacha heard fast footsteps retreating behind him, and others approaching. His heart was pounding.

"Hey," that other voice. Faintly accented. Sacha couldn't place it, didn't really care. He wasn't sure if he was grateful for the intervention. Wasn't sure if what happened next was going to be an improvement. "Can you stand up?" A hand under his shoulder, another around his upper arm. He let himself be helped to his feet. He was shaking, nauseated, weak from hunger and the still-surging terror. He towered over the other man. "Oh."

Now he'll leave, whatever. Sacha said, "Thanks. I'm okay." The glare from the streetlight at the end of the alley was painful. His eyes weren't quite focusing.

"No you're not." Jesús looked at the emaciated person he'd thought was a woman. He didn't know how the guy was even standing up. "Give me a second." He moved the guy back enough to lean on the wall, tugged the skirt down, noticing the wad of cash in the g-string and thinking, *What a mess.* He went down the alley to the waiting car. "Boss, not a girl. Really fucked up. Bleeding in three places."

"Get him in the car."

Jesús was more than a little surprised. They'd picked hookers up in alleys before, or rather found and assisted hookers. Jerry always tried to help. They both knew that most of the time, the meal or money or job he offered wouldn't be enough to get someone off the street. Drugs nearly always won. This one looked so far gone ... but Jerry was the boss, and Jesús owed him, so he didn't question it. He went back down the alley, put the hooker's arm over his own shoulders and an arm around his waist, and walked him down to the car. He was stumbling, not too surprising with those five-inch heels on. Shaking, too, also not surprising. "Do you need to go to the emergency room?"

Sacha might have laughed. He made some kind of sound, anyway. It certainly wasn't 'yes.' They got to a car, a big black SUV with tinted windows. He hesitated. The short man said, "It's okay. Step up."

Sacha stumbled up and into the car's back seat. There was another man there, and yet a third in the driver's seat. "Are we going to a party?" he said through his teeth, which seemed to be chattering. The short guy fastened his seat belt. There was just enough rationality to think *hope I don't bleed on this seat.* Maybe the cheap pleather miniskirt would save that situation, at least.

"No," said the man on the back seat with him. "You sure you don't need the ER?"

Sacha shook his head woozily, risked another question. "Got anything to drink?" A moment later a plastic bottle was in his hand. Sacha drank all the water, gasped a little, and said, "Thanks."

"Do you have somewhere safe to go?"

Another almost-laugh, bordering on a sob. Sacha hadn't been asked anything like that since he left home. "Can you take me to New York?" There were the tears, the ones he hated, the ones he tried with every cigarette, every drink, every pill, every cynical thought to repress. He couldn't go home. He couldn't tell his parents what he'd allowed to happen.

Jesús heard it from the front passenger seat, tears stinging his own eyes because all he could think of now was his own brother. His brother, who Jerry had saved years ago, now a successful businessman in Mazatlán.

Jerry didn't ask any more questions. They went to his house, his big safe gated house in the Hollywood Hills. Once there, Jerry and Jesús spoke for a few minutes while the hooker sat passively in the back seat and the driver waited patiently for instructions. He owed Jerry too, for almost the same reason as Jesús. In a few minutes they got the hooker out, walked him to the guest house, took him inside. Jesús thought there was no chance they could safely leave him. He was either going to pass out and drown in the tub, or hang himself from something.

It took both of them, him and Martin, to get the guy stripped. Even though he wasn't wearing much of anything, certainly not enough for a fifty-degree night. Jesús cleaned the makeup off his face. They got him showered, and then wrapped in a spa robe. Into bed, with some snacks and more water on the nightstand. He was basically catatonic. "I'll stay with him," Jesús said. Martin nodded, and went to help Jerry get ready for the night. Jerry didn't need that much help anymore, but both of his helpers were there for whatever he needed. That was the kind of guy he was.

Sacha woke up with a pounding headache, a sore ass, sore knees, a sore neck, and profound disorientation. He was mostly sober, which accounted for the headache. He couldn't exactly remember what had happened the night before, but assumed whatever it was accounted for the sore ass. The rest of it seemed trivial. He didn't move for a few minutes. Instead he looked around, trying to figure out where he was. His gaze landed on a short Latino sitting by an open pair of French doors on the other side of the room. "Hey."

The other guy looked over. "Hey yourself. How you feeling?"

Sacha shrugged. It was an unanswerable question, and the answer was probably irrelevant anyway. "Where am I? Who are you?"

"I'm Jesús Zapata. You're in my boss's guest house. We found you on Hollywood Boulevard last night about a second before some guy put a knife in your throat."

"Oh." Sacha thought about that for a few seconds. There was a lot to unpack. He'd always remembered his bad decisions before. "Thanks. I think."

"Want some coffee?"

"God, yes." Sacha moved then, sitting up and swinging his legs out of bed. He felt a little light-headed, knew he was probably hungry, as usual couldn't really tell.

Those scraped knees, those skinny legs. "You should eat something. When's the last time you ate?"

"I don't know."

Jesús headed for the kitchen. "Any food allergies?"

"I don't think so."

"What do you want?"

"I don't know."

Anorexic? Jesús wondered. They had to find this one, they couldn't find somebody with just one problem. Jerry was going to feel like a failure when they lost him. He didn't say anything. Opened a package of King's Hawaiian rolls, put four of them on a plate, split them open. Used a spoon to spread one with butter, one with jam. Then folded a slice of cheese into another, a wad of prosciutto - the only meat in the guest-house refrigerator – into the last. During the night, he'd removed anything that needed a knife to prepare, and then he'd removed all the knives. The guy didn't look much less doomed this morning than he had when they found him. The only really hopeful thing was that he didn't have any track marks. He looked terrifyingly young without the makeup. "What's your name?"

"Sacha. Sacha Lebedev."

"What kind of name is that?"

Almost a smile. "Russian."

"You're from New York?" Jesús took the plate and a cup of coffee - with cream and sugar; this kid needed every calorie he could get - over to the bed and placed them beside the untouched snacks on the nightstand. Sacha hadn't moved after swinging his legs out. Jesús figured he wasn't sure he could stand up, and didn't want to risk it. "How long have you been in L.A.?"

Sacha shook his head slightly. He couldn't remember mentioning New York, but he must have. Or maybe he still had an accent. "What's the date?"

"January thirteenth, two thousand and three. It's not a Friday," Jesús added, to see if the kid had a sense of humor.

Sacha smiled, but it was bitter. "Then I've been here exactly eighteen months. I didn't come here to turn tricks."

"Yeah, nobody does. Can you eat?"

Sacha looked at the food. Picked up the coffee, sniffed it. "Wow." Took a sip. "Wow. This is not the kind of coffee I've been drinking lately." A bigger sip, savoring it, swallowing with appreciation. Then he picked up the buttered roll and took an experimental bite. "God, this tastes good."

"Do you not eat because you don't like to eat, or what?"

"I don't eat because either I'm high or I'm working or I can't afford to," Sacha said with his mouth full. "I didn't come here to take drugs, either."

7

"Yeah, I hear there are plenty of those in New York."

"I'm not gay," Sacha said, for some reason he couldn't have explained. Maybe it was the complete lack of judgement, and feeling like he deserved it. "There was a bad minute, and I made a bad decision, and before I knew it this happened." The way Jesús was looking at him, Sacha figured he knew. Maybe somebody close to him had a similar experience. That moment of quiet desperation when somebody not too repulsive says, if you'd do this I'd pay you, and it seems like an acceptable solution. Even though you know it's temporary, and you know you've put your foot on the top of a slippery slope, but you tell yourself you can keep your balance anyway. Sacha didn't know how the gay guys did it at all. He always thought, for them, it should have been part of love. It must have hurt so much more. The fact that he never tried to enjoy it made it the very tiniest bit easier to stay outside it. He'd quickly learned to distinguish physical reaction from desire. Some men wanted that reaction, and would work hard for it, and then pay him more. If he faked pleasure, sometimes a lot more. Others only wanted to get off. "Did my face get messed up last night?"

"No, you're still beautiful." Jesús had been watching the kid think. Now he watched the startled blink, the almost-smile. It was a slight exaggeration to call him beautiful, but if there were some flesh on those bones it would be true. The kid had short sandy hair and a face that was mostly eyes. "Did you come out here to be an actor?"

"Yeah. Or model, or dancer. I'd done some of all those things back home. Got lured out here by a promoter and a big stupid dream." Everyone except him had thought it was stupid. When they realized he truly meant to go, they'd said so. Sacha wished he had listened. He'd never be able to look his father in the eyes again.

"How old are you?" *Older than eighteen, please.* Jerry was running enough of a risk bringing him home, which was a first. It was more than enough of a risk cruising the boulevard looking for people to save. Jesús minded his own business, but that didn't mean he didn't care about Jerry's. So far, nobody had gone running to TMZ to say hey, this Hollywood guy picked me up. But then, Jerry wasn't that well known outside Hollywood, and it would have been whoever's word against the three of them anyway.

"Twenty-three. I have a degree in dance. I'm a good actor. I can sing like a dream, according to that promoter." Sacha shrugged again. It didn't matter. "But I can hardly type, and I've never tried to run a cash register, and I'm dyslexic so I get numbers mixed up all the time anyway. I had a car and it got totaled. I was injured, I couldn't get to any jobs, and I was too proud to ask my parents for help. Too confused and scared to go looking for anyone else's help until I was so fucked up nobody wanted to offer. So thanks. Thanks to you and your boss. What's the catch?" He had to assume there was one. He was relieved at getting all that out so flatly.

"I haven't spoken to him yet today," Jesús said. "I don't think there's a catch. Someone did him a solid back in the seventies, kept him out of big trouble. He's always trying to pay it forward. He saved my brother, a few years back." The food was gone. "I would give you some more but I think it might be better for you to wait a while."

"Probably, yeah. What should I do?"

"What do you want to do?"

"I don't know. Lie in the sun and pretend I've been rescued?" Pretend he was back home at the beach, that the daylight outside was where he belonged.

Jesús made a why-not face. "You can do that. There's some clothes. Tee shirts, warm-ups, nothing fancy." He regarded Sacha for a minute. Maybe this one could be saved after all. He didn't talk like someone whose brain was fried. The blue-gray eyes in that almost-feminine face were wary and intelligent. "If you promise not to drown yourself or hang yourself I could go talk to the boss, see if he wants to talk to you."

"If I'd wanted to kill myself I could have done it a thousand times," Sacha said. "Not wanting to face life isn't exactly the same thing."

That was true. Jesús nodded, and left him alone. Sacha watched him go, saw the glitter of sun on water outside, thought amazed and hopeful thoughts, and stood up. Sore, weak, still hungover. The headache had backed off a little. The food was staying down. He went to the bathroom. There was a cut on his neck, about an inch above his collarbone. He didn't remember when or how that happened, but he was prepared to believe Jesús. He found a tee shirt and warm-up pants, got dressed. Found a beach towel. Drank more water. Fixed himself another cup of coffee, and went outside. The grounds – no other way to describe this, it wasn't anything so pedestrian as a 'backyard' – seemed to go on forever. There was a wall around the perimeter. Big mature shade trees. Rose bushes in profusion, bird feeders under the trees. A big patio of grow-through pavers, around a

10

sparkling pool. Sacha arranged himself on a lounger and closed his eyes.

Jesús found him still out there, now in the shade, an hour later. "You awake?"

Sacha squinted up at him. "Yeah."

"The boss wants to talk to you."

"Okay. Where did my clothes go?" All he'd been able to find was the slim wallet he'd had tucked inside the padded bra, and the wad of cash. "Did you throw them away?"

"No. They're clean, if you want them."

"I don't, honestly, but I might need them again someday." Sacha really didn't ever want to go back to that bar, or any bar where he'd have to dance for money, or fuck men for money. This princess moment couldn't last, though. "The wig, too." It wasn't an especially good one, but even a cheap wig wasn't that cheap.

"Well, let's go see Jerry. Maybe he can help you figure out a way not to need those."

Sacha thought, afterward, that he'd never understood the word 'surreal' until that day. Jerry Morgenstern, a TV and movie producer, the kind of producer with an office full of awards and a multi-million-dollar house in the Hollywood Hills, offered him six months to get clean, get organized, and figure out what he wanted to do with his life. Six months to live rent-free in the guest house, and help with any job training he wanted. Sacha had to suspend disbelief early on because there was absolutely no reason for this man not to be sincere. If he wasn't sincere, he could have left Sacha in the alley for the next guy with a knife. And in exchange Jerry wanted …

11

nothing. Or, more accurately, he asked for nothing. Nothing except an honest effort from Sacha, no visitors, and no drugs. Not even cigarettes.

Within a month Sacha was detoxed. Within two, he'd finished a course of antibiotics, and had a chart full of clean blood tests to show for it. Jerry gave him a laptop. Sacha learned to type, to do internet research, to write business letters. He started helping Jerry in the home office, and was happy to do it. Everything was words, not numbers. He had never felt quite so competent. He wrote, cautiously, to his parents and let them know he was doing well. Told them something true, which was that he had a safe place to live. Told them something sort-of true, which was that he had a job. And simply lied about everything else.

In the spring, Jerry started coming out to the pool with his therapist. Sacha fetched and carried for both of them. After a few sessions, he'd overheard enough to know about the car accident, about Jerry's broken back. The therapist said Jerry should have been in the water all winter, why wasn't he working out, whatever. Jerry said, "Because I tried one time and had to call Martin to haul me out of the pool. It was humiliating and it hurt."

"I told you you should have retrofitted some steps in here," said the therapist, not very constructively. The only way into the pool was to sit on the edge and drop in, or go down the ladders. For Jerry, the new, heavy-duty ladder at the shallow end was the only way out. Sacha had seen how the therapist managed that.

Before he could stop himself, he said, "I know how to swim. Could I learn how to help?" The therapist looked him over doubtfully. Sacha was four inches shorter than Jerry, and at least sixty pounds lighter. "I'm tougher than I look."

Jerry snorted. "That's for sure." That was all he said. His face gave nothing away.

The therapist stared at them both for a few seconds. "If I teach your godson how to help you in and out, will you promise to do your exercises every day?"

Godson, Sacha thought with total surprise, hoping his face was as blank as it needed to be. Well, of course Jerry needed a cover story for the people who came to the house. Martin and Jesús had been with him for years, there was an ever-changing cast of kitchen help, but this brand new young man would have raised some questions with anyone else.

"Yes." Jerry's tone was impatient. "I will do the goddamned exercises every day."

"Okay fine. What's your name?"

Sacha gave it a second, to see if Jerry had given him a fake one, but Jerry didn't say anything. So he gave his name, changed into a tee shirt and swim trunks, and got in the pool.

He learned; Jerry exercised; and by the end of June, Jerry didn't need him anymore. Not for the pool, anyway. The therapist congratulated them both, and suggested if Jerry's godson hadn't chosen his major yet, he might consider physical therapy. "You've got the right personality for it," he said.

Sacha appreciated that. He spared a moment to consider how his life might have been different if he'd studied therapy to begin with, instead of dance. But it wasn't really relevant; there was no point in looking back. "Thanks." Then he thought, *wait*, because he hadn't been able to come up with some course of study that would lead to permanent, full-time employment without dooming him to life in a box somewhere. "Is there some kind of therapy I could do without going to college? Because, you know, college." He made an 'ugh' face and the therapist actually laughed.

"There's massage," he said. "You don't need a college degree for that. It's six to eight months, and a lot of practice hours."

Sacha knew his face was hopeful when he looked over at Jerry. Jerry said, "If that's what you want to do, I'll fix it with your parents."

"Thanks, Jerry. They always listen to you." They were both such good liars.

At the end of the first six months, Jerry said, "Do you want to stay another six, so you can finish that course?" Sacha said he would. They were all getting along. Sacha was doing well in the course. He was also learning – from Jerry – how to analyze a script, how to turn a screenplay into a shooting script, how to break down a scene. It was fascinating, every bit as absorbing as learning how to act had been. Jerry told him they could put this on Sacha's resumé as an internship. Sacha constantly looked for ways to thank him, because he was not good at taking a 'thank you.'

It was four men in the household, but not in that big house. Jesús lived in, and had a girlfriend who lived in Silverlake. Martin lived with his wife not far away, in the Fairfax district. Jerry went out on occasional dates, which never seemed to involve sleepovers. He went to industry parties with women who didn't seem to be 'dates,' exactly. Sacha didn't ask; it was none of his business. He stayed in the guest house, gradually picking up more skills and taking

14

care of more business for Jerry. They didn't have a formal employer-employee relationship. Sacha didn't know what, exactly, their relationship was. He only knew that day after day, week after week, something was growing between them. It was more than simply trust, on Jerry's side. It was more than simply loyalty, on Sacha's.

He brought in the mail one day and found Jerry pacing, as he often did, to relieve the pain in his back. "Are you all right? Can I get you something?"

"Hey Sacha. No, it's just the usual." Jerry had given Sacha a little more detail about the car accident that broke his back, as well as his second marriage. Sacha privately thought of that second wife as That Bitch, because who leaves a man when he's just been told he might never walk again? He watched and waited. Something told him there actually was something Jerry needed. The older man took a drink from the glass on his desk, full of what might have been ice water but was very likely gin and tonic. Then he sighed, looked away, and said, "Can I ask you a couple of personal questions?"

"Of course."

"Like, really personal. Not in here."

Sacha blinked. The only rooms he'd been in, even after all this time, were the kitchen, the home office, and the den. The den was Jerry's private retreat, not a place for what it seemed might be a disturbing conversation. The kitchen wouldn't be private. "The guest house?" he ventured.

"Would you mind?"

"Jerry, for God's sake, it's yours. Mi casa literally is su casa." That got half a laugh. Sacha felt this veering toward something he'd half-feared from the beginning. For a while he'd almost stopped wondering about it, because Jerry was clearly uncomfortable being handled. He'd worked hard to master the ladder. Sacha's hands on his back, or under his arms, made him flinch. He'd never asked for one of the training massages, though everybody else in the household stood in line.

Sacha didn't say anything else, only turned and went out. Jerry followed. He must have been bringing his drink, because Sacha could hear ice cubes rattling. *He is nervous, and this is probably that.* Sacha took a deep breath. Whatever Jerry wanted, he'd have to deliver. At least he genuinely cared for him. It wouldn't be the same. He tried to keep breathing, to keep himself calm.

In the guest house, Jerry seemed even more ill at ease. Definitely not wanting to say something, desperate to say it anyway. Sacha said it for him. "Jerry, you saved my life. Anything you need, I will do for you." Still not a word. "Do you want to sleep with me?"

"No." Instant answer. Not making eye contact. "What do you know about me?"

Not enough. "Personally? Only that you've been married twice and don't have kids and don't have a girlfriend, even though you are rich and nice-looking and one of the best men in the world." A glitter of tears. Sacha took a step closer. "Jerry. Are you gay?"

"Yes. I hate it. I don't want to be." Eyes closed, barely breathing. "Tried not to be. And now I couldn't even if I wanted to."

"Jerry. Sit down. Tell me." And he did, he lowered himself into one of the rattan chairs and told Sacha more, told him everything, about the accident and the rehab and the long, painful recovery. About

16

learning to walk again, but never coming all the way back.

"I'm impotent. I always will be." Jerry's glass was empty. Sacha went to his kitchen, found his own bottle of gin, fixed another drink. Handed it to Jerry, watched him take a mouthful and swallow it. Knelt beside him and put a hand on his thigh. Jerry squeezed his eyes shut again.

"How long has it been since anyone touched you?"

"I can't remember." Jerry gazed down at Sacha now. "I'm a dozen years past twice your age and I know you're not gay. This is gross, I shouldn't be here, you don't deserve this."

"Jerry, please. I would be dead if not for you. That is not an exaggeration. You've given me so much. I've learned so much from you. In a few months I'll be qualified for a career that I'll enjoy. That I'll be good at. I will do absolutely anything for you." It was sincere. Easier to be so, now that he knew whatever Jerry wanted wouldn't include that one thing. "Can I touch you?"

"I can't get an erection." Jerry's voice was very low.

"But would it feel good?" A sound of assent. *All right, then.* Sacha stood up, went to lock the doors, then returned. He knelt down again and ran his hands up the insides of Jerry's thighs. Looked up at his face and said, "Let me say thank you." Heard the intake of breath, saw the pained, unwilling desire, and looked away. This was no time to confront, or to seduce. He unzipped Jerry's pants, somehow knowing only a hand would do. Fellatio would be so far over the line of 'too much,' too much of what Jerry feared, or even hated. Sacha was grateful, because this way he could think of it as therapy.

For a few minutes there was no sound except Jerry's breathing. Sacha concentrated almost clinically on the touch. He'd given more hand jobs than he could remember during that twelve-month death spiral. This was the first time he'd felt and heard a response that didn't include an erection. "Can you ejaculate?" he asked softly. Another sound of assent. "Do you want that?"

"God, Sacha." It wasn't agreement, exactly, but it certainly wasn't a 'no.' Sacha looked around for a moment to locate the ottoman. He hooked a foot into the rattan and pulled it over so he could position it with his free hand. Got off his knees, seated himself, and leaned his face against Jerry's. Skin to skin, feeling and hearing the instant response. That helpless reaction opened a floodgate. He was swamped with gratitude, appreciation, respect. *He needs me, I can help him, maybe I'm the only person in the world who can.* It was so good to feel he could help someone. Be of use to someone. He brushed his face against Jerry's like a cat. Not a kiss, only that light touch, his breath against Jerry's neck, and now his free hand in Jerry's hair. Cupping the back of his head. Making love to him, because he loved him. Jerry's breath quickening, harsher, almost a word with each exhalation. Sacha kissed his neck. Jerry's body jerked, and it was over. "Oh Christ."

They sat quietly for a moment. Then Sacha rubbed his face against Jerry's again, kissed his mouth, and got to his feet. Went to wash his hands. When he turned around, Jerry was standing up, pants zipped. His glass was empty again and his expression was unreadable. Sacha thought that one of two things would happen now. Jerry would ask him to make this a regular thing, or Jerry would ask him to leave. He was a prominent man. He wasn't out. He didn't want to be the way he was, maybe felt he couldn't afford to be open about his desires. Even in California, even today.

What Jerry said was a surprise. "You didn't have to kiss me."

"I wanted to."

Jerry crossed the room in a rush, the fastest Sacha had ever seen him move, and hugged him. "Thank you." Sacha held him tight. After a minute Jerry laughed under his breath. "That was so not what I meant to say, or do." He moved back a little. "I have to go to the Emmy Awards. I was going to ask if you would come with me."

Sacha's eyebrows shot up; his poker face was nowhere near good enough for that. "As your date?" He didn't think the godson cover would hold up. "If you do that." He stopped. He didn't need to finish the sentence.

"I know, but." Jerry made a God-help-me face and stood away. Awkward, scared, but no longer near panic. And not angry, as Sacha had half expected. He'd only had one prior experience with someone closeted, and it had gone very wrong. That man was furious about being gay, and took it out on Sacha. He hadn't been able to work for a week. Jerry, who could yell with the best of them and who could have taken Sacha apart with his bare hands, only looked a little sad. "I hadn't figured that out yet. The world thinks I like women."

"You'd rather it did." Sacha thought for a minute. "What if I were a woman?"

"Eh?"

Sacha almost laughed at the completely confused expression on Jerry's face. "I used to do a pretty good job passing as female." He was healthy now, but still slim. His body had always looked good in a dress; he had won a fundraiser drag pageant two years in a row in college. Tanned, sleekly muscular, and not too tall. Six feet, when he had three-inch heels on. And his facial hair was light. "Let me put something together and you can decide if you want to try it."

"You would do that?"

Sacha shrugged, one shoulder, with a tip of the head and a sly glance under his eyelashes. He knew it was feminine. Lowering his chin a little meant most people only noticed his eyes, not his neck. When he wore lipstick, when he had long hair, in an eye-deceiving gown … it might work. It would call on all his dance and acting and vocal training. It would be proof that he really did have talent, that the Hollywood dream hadn't been entirely insane. It would be a middle finger raised against everybody who'd made Jerry feel less-than.

And: "It might be fun."

CHAPTER 2

February 2015

Charlie looked around the room again. She'd already gotten a zillion great shots for the charity's website. They were making a fuck-ton of money at this casino-night fundraiser, and everybody was dressed to kill. The big honcho, Jerry Morgenstern, was across the room with his date. Maggie Eisenstein, as always. Tall, blonde, glamorous, and devoted. Charlie caught the eye of the event planner and sidled over to her. "So Louise. Why aren't they married?"

"Like I know?"

"I Googled after that second round of shots and I see all these pictures of them together, going back a dozen years."

Louise said, "He got screwed in his second divorce. Maybe the pre-nup was a thousand pages and Maggie said, eh, the hell with it." Charlie laughed. "They don't even live together, as far as I know."

"And you would know." Louise knew everything about everyone. If she ever wrote a tell-all, there would be no bodies left buried. Of course, she wouldn't be able to publish it until she was dead because the instant it hit the shelves she'd be dead anyway, smothered under a heap of lawyers. Charlie watched Jerry and Maggie for another minute. He was in black tie, in the wheelchair that had made an appearance at last year's Emmy awards. She was talking to another industry bigwig, holding a glass of champagne in one hand. The other rested on Jerry's shoulder, little finger touching the side of his neck. So intimate, so loving, Charlie felt a little choked up. But they were about to start the auction, so she got ready for another round of photos.

An hour later, Charlie spotted Maggie coming out of the ladies' room and heading for the balcony. Her dress swung from her hips, swirling around her ankles. The event room was incredibly loud. So many people, so many drinks, so much-too-big of a band, and hot as hell. Charlie drifted along in Maggie's wake, for no reason that she could have articulated, and fetched up beside her at the ornate railing. Maggie was leaning over it, only a few degrees, face angled to catch the ocean breeze. Charlie put her back to the wind and faced the room. "Having a good time tonight?"

Maggie glanced over. Not surprised, because why else would someone stand right there if not to talk. "They're making a lot of money. Jerry's happy."

"And if Mr. Morgenstern's happy, you're happy?"

Maggie narrowed her eyes a little, but her tone was pleasant. "I'm here for him, yes."

Charlie was listening to that tone. That voice. It was soft and light, but throaty. A sexy voice. It was no wonder a rich producer would keep this woman around all these years, though – at close range – she was older than Charlie thought. *All those years, you idiot*, she realized. Even if Maggie had been only twenty-one when she and Jerry first got together, she'd be Charlie's age by now. Her skin had a tawny natural tan, not too dark, which might account for the slight crow's feet, and the faint freckles across the top of her chest. The copper-colored dress was in her signature style, cut to frame the collarbones in front and draped low in back, sleeveless to show off slender arms. *Yoga arms*, Charlie guessed, from the muscle definition. "That's a beautiful necklace." There was a tiny scar near it.

"Thanks." Maggie touched the choker, black pearls between X-shaped links of rose gold set with diamonds. Her hands, faint freckles there too. Nails not too long, though certainly not natural; the manicure was too perfect. Lacquer exactly the color of the gold. An opulent ring that matched the necklace, and a Bulgari watch. The black and rose-gold Serpenti watch. It looked great with the dress. "You're the photographer."

"Yeah. I got lucky, a friend of a friend of a friend threw me this gig. I've never done a party like this before. It's really fun."

"Well, I hope you're getting lots of great pictures. All these people love to see themselves looking their best."

"Don't we all?" Charlie noticed Jerry then, at the back of the room, looking around. "I think Mr. Morgenstern's looking for you."

Maggie turned instantly. "Yes. Thanks."

Before she could go, Charlie said, "Do you ever do any modeling?"

Maggie looked directly at her, eyebrows up. "Not generally, no."

"Could I give you my card anyway? If you're ever, you know, bored." Charlie dug for one and held it out.

Maggie looked at it for a moment, then took it. "Charlie Montgomery?"

She'd changed her cards very recently after one too many 'Charlotte's Web' jokes. "Short for Charlotte. You'd be amazed how much easier it is to get gigs when people think you're a guy."

Maggie smiled slightly, as if at some private amusement. She tucked the card into an invisible pocket on the hip of her dress. Held out a hand. "Nice to meet you, Charlie." A light handshake, and then she walked away. The heels of her black sandals were covered with rose-gold rhinestones. Her lithe back was almost bare under the shoulder-length tumble of blonde waves. A cascade of tiny, unconscious observations and impressions crystallized in Charlie's mind. *Oh my God she is a he*, she thought, and closed her mouth.

Three months later, Charlie was doing another charity gig and had a moment of vertigo. At first she thought it was only because she'd skipped lunch in her haste to get out of town before rush hour. This one was in Irvine, not Santa Monica, and it was for a new medical facility. The big honcho this time was Mrs. Rose Novotny, who'd apparently run out of new facilities to endow in Los Angeles. It was a long way to come for a gig, but then half the people here were also from L.A., so Charlie couldn't really complain. She located a server with a tray full of hors d'oeuvres, loaded up a napkin, scarfed them down and then found some water. It wasn't enough, but it would keep her going. After washing her hands she looked around again, spotted Mrs. Novotny again, and had that moment of vertigo again. *Who is that guy.* She knew she didn't know him. But that body language. He was standing beside Mrs. Novotny's wheelchair, wearing a tuxedo, with a glass of champagne in one hand. The other rested not on the philanthropist's shoulder but on the handle of her wheelchair. It was the shape of the face, the angle of his body, the grace of the hand on that long-stemmed glass. Then he turned his head for a moment, and she saw his profile. *Holy actual fucking hell.* Charlie couldn't believe it. It had to be the same person. Was he some kind of really gifted, really professional, really discreet escort? Was she the only person who'd noticed? Did people really not *look* when there was someone that beautiful in the room?

Charlie was used to not being looked at. There was nothing special about her. She wasn't ugly, she wasn't gorgeous, she was just a normal decent-looking human being who could dress well enough for most situations. Average height, with average hair and an average body. To the extent that she was remarkable, it was in her ability to put people at ease when they were vulnerable. She was great at photographing athletes. Every athlete was photogenic when they were doing their thing. Charlie's genius was in making athletes feel like they were doing their thing even when they were doing the exact opposite, namely sitting or standing still. She really loved to work with dancers and yogis. The guy with Mrs. Novotny looked a bit like a dancer. As Maggie Eisenstein - Charlie was certain of it – he had walked like a dancer. Even in high heels. Before she knew what she was doing, Charlie was halfway across the room. She fetched up beside the wheelchair. "Mrs. Novotny, hi. This is a great event. I wanted to ask if there are any particular shots you'd like me to try and get."

"Hello dear. Charlie, isn't it? Call me Rose." Rose didn't offer a hand. She hated shaking hands. Louise had cautioned Charlie about that; the old woman's hands were too delicate, she was too easily hurt. "The fun won't really start until the dancers perform." Charlie was looking forward to that. "Will your camera take video?"

"Oh, of course. Would you like me to get the performance on video? I could extract some stills for the website."

"That would be excellent, dear. You should make sure you get something to eat. Sacha, would you mind taking Charlie to the buffet?"

He'd been watching this exchange, composed as a cat. "Of course. Can I get anything for you first?"

"No, dear, I'm fine. Come find me later."

"I will." Sacha touched Rose's shoulder lightly, then turned to Charlie. "Shall we?"

"Uh, sure." They walked away. Charlie had not intended this. She had no idea what to say. What she wanted to say was so impossible, she figured she was better off keeping her mouth shut.

"I'm a certified massage therapist," Sacha said. His voice was barely loud enough for Charlie to hear. She wondered why he was telling her this. "I specialize in geriatrics. Rose was referred to me a year ago. She's a lovely person."

"She's wonderful," Charlie agreed. "I read up on her for this event. She does a lot of good." She couldn't tell if Sacha could tell she had recognized him. This was so mind-blowingly awkward. "I'm not sure why I went over there just now, but I'm glad I did. No-one mentioned taking video of the dancers before. Do you know who's performing?"

"A couple from L.A. Ricky Castillo and Anya Ivanova, they're doing three numbers." They had reached the buffet tables. Sacha escorted Charlie down the line. "I thought you might be curious why I was here with Rose."

Why did you think that. "I was."

"She asked me to come. She didn't want a nurse but her doctors don't want her to go to events without someone. Someone other than a driver, someone who knows what she needs to be safe. At home, she has a houseful of people. She says they all need a break from each other sometimes. And she said, I'd like to go someplace with a good-looking man again. How was I supposed to say no?" Now he escorted her to one of the bar-height tables, waiting for her to get on the outside of some food, watching the room. Alert and self-possessed.

Charlie didn't know what else to do, so she ate. The food was good. A bottle of water was welcome. "I hate bottled water," she said, "but thanks. I always feel like half of these bottles probably don't make it into a recycling bin, and I'm responsible for choking a whale somewhere."

Sacha smiled. It was definitely Maggie's smile. Maybe he saw that certainty. He dug in a pocket and handed a business card across the table. "There. Now you know who I am. You're very observant, aren't you?" His voice was quite a bit lower than Maggie's, still soft and throaty. Still sexy.

I am a mess, Charlie thought. *What IS it about this guy.* She glanced at the card, tucked it away. "I'm sorry. I'm not here to fuck you up."

"Thanks. Rose doesn't know Jerry. I don't think it would bother her, she might think it's funny, but all the same."

"I won't say anything. It's none of my business. Why are you even talking to me?"

He glanced away. Again Charlie thought, *don't people LOOK,* because to her the face was so distinctive. Isabella Rossellini's nose and Rudolf Nureyev's eyebrows, cheekbones that worked

27

perfectly with both. There were a lot of people here who'd been at the fundraiser in February. Maybe people really did see what they expected to see. And, okay, it wasn't the conventional leading-man kind of good looks. He didn't have the jawline that said 'stud.' He wasn't very tall. He was just … an incredibly interesting man who was also Maggie Eisenstein. She knew she was staring. She was dying to take his picture.

Without makeup, there were traces of minimal blond beard, and the promise of laugh lines around his mouth. His close-cropped hair was receding a bit at the temples, sandy, not the rich blended gold of Maggie's. Without false eyelashes, without the brilliant blue contact lenses, his eyes were only gorgeous, not stunning. He must have looked like a little Disney critter when he was a child. Then he looked back at her, and those eyes were desolate. "Jerry is dying. Nobody knows. He's been my best friend for a long time. I'm going to need a friend when he's gone."

"I'm so sorry," she said. "Are you sure you don't need a friend right now?"

He inhaled audibly and his eyes glistened. "I do."

"Call me anytime. I mean it." His hand - slim, tanned, the nails very short and very clean - was on the table. Charlie touched it briefly. "And thank you for trusting me. I have no idea why you would."

"Neither do I." He managed a tiny smile. "Maybe I like your eyes."

"I like yours too." It might have sounded flirty if she weren't ninety-nine percent positive he was gay. But he shifted closer, ever so slightly closer, and his gaze dropped to her mouth. Charlie thought *WHAT* and might have made some kind of accompanying

Scooby Doo what-the-fuck sound. "Jesus. I am so confused right now."

All the sadness was gone; he was laughing; it was the most beautiful thing she'd ever seen. Sacha said, "I don't blame you. Can I call you, really?"

"Yes, you can call me, really. But now I had better get to work."

"And I'll go see to Rose. Nice to meet you again, Charlie Montgomery." He offered a hand.

She shook it. "Nice to meet you, Sacha Lebedev."

The performance was terrific. Charlie reviewed the video as soon as the dancers finished, tracked them down for some posed shots afterward, and spent the next hour putting big-money, big-name people in flattering positions for their photographs. Most of them wouldn't remember ever seeing her, much less talking to her. Maybe one out of a hundred would, and if that one was planning an event, maybe he or she would call Charlie to document it. She handed out every business card she'd brought with her, anyway.

There was a silent auction at this one. Rose Novotny said a few words after the winners were announced. Charlie took the best pictures she could, wishing it was possible for Rose to stand next to her handsome escort. If she were an old lady, she'd want to stand, just once, with a man like that. Then Sacha bent to murmur in Rose's ear; Rose laughed; he stood in front of her and did something, and a moment later she was standing. He got his right arm around her waist, and braced his left arm under hers. He said something to someone, and another person pulled the wheelchair back. Rose laughed again, looking delighted. Charlie was certain it was no accident that they were in front of the big banner with the name of the foundation, the name of the new facility, and a huge bouquet of tropical flowers. She took pictures until Sacha turned his head and lifted his chin as if to say 'now please.' The wheelchair was back in place a moment later. He carefully lowered Rose back into the seat. She put one hand on his face, patted his cheek. Charlie blinked away tears.

"I wonder how much he's charging her for this," someone said behind her, in a snide tone of voice.

"He's not," someone else said. This voice was cool. "I asked Rose."

"Seriously?" Incredulity. "My massage person sure wouldn't give me a whole evening for free."

Maybe because you're a bitch, Charlie thought.

The other person said, "Well, Melissa, that's because you're a bitch." They both laughed, in that 'oh ha ha, we're all friends here, die in a fire' way. Charlie bit her lip and walked away fast, so they wouldn't hear her laughing too.

She was there till the end of the event, but didn't see when Rose and Sacha left. She didn't even see Louise – again the event planner – until she was packing up to go. "Oy," Louise said, flopping into a chair beside Charlie. "These things are exhausting. How'd you like those dancers?"

"They're great. I got video of the whole performance, and then did some staged shots after. They're based up my way, I might try to get them for some other modeling. That guy, wow."

"Oh, I know. Too bad he's gay." Louise shrugged. "So, worth the drive?"

Charlie was surprised. Louise knew exactly how much she was getting paid for this. It was plenty.

"Yeah, of course. I don't know if I'd want to try getting any further south, but this was fine."

"Thanks for talking to Rose's walker. Half of these rich assholes were pretending he was invisible." Louise sounded cranky. "I don't know why people can't believe someone is simply fucking *kind*."

"I don't know why people can't understand that a person might not want to be reminded that they're disabled every damn second of every damn day," Charlie said. "She was so happy to not be in that chair, even for a minute."

"Exactly! And you know she's out of it for therapy or whatever, but that's not the same goddamned thing. Jesus, I hope when I'm old and broken that someone will give me a moment like that."

"That's exactly what I thought." Louise held out her fist; Charlie gave it a bump. "He said he specializes in geriatrics. That takes a certain kind of personality."

Louise made an 'I suppose' face. "There's plenty of rich old people in Los Angeles. It's probably a good specialty. Did you get pictures, when he had her on her feet?"

"Oh yeah. That was a great moment." She was sure it would be one of those, of Rose standing with Sacha in front of the banner, that would go on the foundation's home page eventually.

Sacha was tired when he got home. It was always a strain to attend an event like that. He hadn't expected it to be even more of a strain to attend as himself. Maybe he'd been afraid of being recognized. In all these years, no-one had ever made the connection, except the photographer. Most people saw Jerry's blonde companion, made one or another assumption, and barely looked at him again. Unless they were making a pass, of course, but that stopped happening after Jerry was in the wheelchair. It was as if even the guys who would ordinarily be crass enough to try to pick up somebody else's date weren't crass enough for that.

Then, of course, there had been the conversation with Charlie. Telling her about Jerry, even that little bit. Saying that Jerry was his best friend didn't quite cover it. He wondered what Charlie would think if she knew the whole of it. She obviously had thought he was gay, which meant she assumed that Jerry was, but only after realizing that Maggie was Sacha and therefore a man. And then he hadn't been able to resist that glance at her mouth, and she'd looked so astonished. Sacha had lived like a monk for years. He'd barely missed sex. Or at least he'd thought so until he got his second look at Charlie.

He wasn't sure why. If you put her in a lineup with a dozen other women from any of these events, most people wouldn't look at her twice. They'd look at all the painted, gowned, glossy perfection and not even notice those all-seeing compassionate eyes, and that mouth made to smile. A mouth made to kiss. He'd wanted to touch her hair. He'd wanted to get close, to see if that whiff of spice and honey was a fragrance or simply a memory of comfort, something his mind supplied when she offered friendship.

Sacha got out of the tuxedo, and into warm-up pants and a tee shirt. Reviewed his calendar, sent reminder texts to his clients for the next day. Checked to see if he needed to stop at the supermarket. Then got down on the floor to stretch.

At bedtime, he texted Jesús: *How was Jerry today?*

Jesús still lived in the big house with Jerry, now also with his wife and child. His wife Carla was a home health aide. The answer came fast, as it always did: *Not too bad, he got out in the sun for a while. Said he hoped that event made a shitload of money*

I think it did. Mrs. Novotny was happy

You get a picture in that tux? You know he wants to see how you looked

The photographer got at least one picture of me and Rose standing up. I have her card, I'll see if she can send a copy. I'll stop by tomorrow around six OK?

OK I'll tell him

Gracias amigo, good night

Good night

Sacha put the phone on its charger and got in bed, wondering if he should move back to the guest house. He'd moved out ten years ago, mostly because it was easier to keep up his cover that way. His place now – another guest house - wasn't far from Jerry's. He could take care of his clients, take care of business, and still get over there quickly and discreetly. He liked not having neighbors, not sharing walls or a ceiling. His rent was high, but since Jerry insisted on paying it, that didn't matter. Except now, when it looked like time was running out. They'd gone out once in April, and on the way home Jerry said, "It was good to see everybody tonight. That's it though. No more. Can't take it." He let Sacha hold his hand in the car, because Sacha was still Maggie.

He almost never texted Jerry directly. Their whole relationship had been so undercover. Jesús and

33

Martin had never asked exactly what went on between them. Cecilia, the housekeeper, had joined the household five years back; she treated Sacha like some sort of pet. It seemed none of them cared what his role was, as long as Jerry was happy. And he'd been happy, or at least happier. He and Sacha both got a kick out of fooling everybody. They'd had such fun coming up with the Maggie Eisenstein character. Because of course, they needed to have a whole back story ready. People would ask. They started asking the very first time Maggie appeared with Jerry. The interest level was intense for a few years. Sometimes they had to think fast. It was like a game. *I'm going to miss him so much*, Sacha thought.

The five of them – Jesús, Carla, Martin, Cecilia, and Sacha – were the only people aside from Jerry's doctors who knew about the cancer. They all had their reasons for keeping Jerry's secrets, for trying to give him exactly and only what he wanted. Sacha decided he'd ask, tomorrow, if he should move back. So they could have more time together before the end.

Charlie saw the text and thought *eh*? Unknown numbers came in all the time. Her cell number was on her website, after all. About half the new calls she got were spam. Thirty percent were legitimate inquiries, and the other twenty were people with great suggestions for ways she could get more exposure by giving them artwork for free. This message read *casino night inquiry,* and it had been sufficiently long that she didn't immediately make the connection. She'd stopped thinking of that first charity event as 'casino night' and begun thinking of it as 'met Maggie night.' Only when she processed that did she say, out loud, "Oh!" and pull out the card Sacha had given her.

The numbers matched. She wrote back: *very cryptic Mr. Lebedev. Blackjack or roulette?*

I don't gamble. With a smiley face.

The hell you don't. Also with a smiley face, because Charlie didn't want him to think she didn't get the joke. *What's up?*

My friend wondered if you might have a picture of me with Rose that you could share

Yes I do. Already sent off a ton of material for them, but there's a few good ones I was keeping for myself. The ones that she'd used the zoom for, tightly framing Sacha, who was concentrating on Rose, while Rose laughed out at the room. *What resolution?*

Oh a phone pic is fine, we don't need to print it

Cool I'll do the conversion and send ASAP

Thanks

No problem. Charlie almost signed off. But he'd said Jerry was dying, and he'd said Jerry was his best friend, and if so maybe Jerry would like to see a photo only of Sacha. And of course, Charlie had taken some, because she was there for hours and for most of those hours she had been as aware of him in the room as if they'd been connected by an electric wire. So she wrote *I have some pictures of just you. Want to see?*

The next thing wasn't a text. It was the voice line ringing. Charlie picked up and said, "Hi Sacha."

"Why were you taking pictures of just me?"

"Why do you think? You were the most beautiful person there." It was goofy, it was adolescent, it was too much. Charlie squeezed her eyes shut, hoping he wouldn't laugh.

He didn't laugh. "Did you think I was beautiful when I was Maggie?" His voice was so soft.

"Yes, and I was so confused because I've never been attracted to a woman before." There was a questioning note in her voice, because she still wasn't clear on his gender. Gay, straight, bi, whatever. It didn't really matter, unless of course the answer gave her a chance of being more to him than a friend, and why did she even wonder when she didn't know him at all, except that he was someone who was loving with an old man who was dying, and sweet to an old woman who needed a moment of sweetness.

Sacha interrupted the churning thought blender by saying, "Or to a man you thought was gay?"

"Aren't you?" Holding her breath.

"No. It's a kind of game we played. I'll tell you all about it someday. It's complicated."

"I'll bet. Okay. I'll send you some pictures."

"Thank you Charlie. I was wondering."

She waited for the rest of the sentence. "Wondering what?"

"If I could take you to dinner sometime."

"A friendly dinner?"

"We could start with that." The soft voice was warm.

"Yeah. Okay. Yes." Charlie knew her voice had brightened. *Obvious girl is obvious.* Well, she'd already admitted she was attracted to him. "I'll send you those pictures. Gotta go now."

"Okay. Talk to you soon."

She disconnected, went to her computer to process the photos, and sent them to the cloud. Then she sent a link to Sacha, whose contact information was now in her phone. She took a few minutes to study the pictures again. *Am I seriously the only one who knows?* She opened the casino-night folder and looked at a few of those. The illusion was so complete. And at both events, everyone else was really looking at the honcho, not at the companion. She could see that people noticed Maggie in a way they didn't notice Sacha. But they weren't seeing her as a person. It might be a game, but it had to be the loneliest game in the world. Except there was Jerry, and she knew that 'best friend' couldn't possibly be the whole description.

After a while she shut it all down. Washed up, and stretched out on her bed, mind racing, wishing very sincerely that there was someone on earth she could tell about this. But there wasn't. 'This' was full of secrets that weren't hers to tell.

Sacha knew it had been a bad day as soon as he got to Jerry's house. Jesús met him at the door with a serious expression. "Damn," Sacha said quietly, and Jesús nodded. "Should I go away again?"

Jesús shook his head. "He's been living to see you."

Tears stung Sacha's eyes. It was like this about one visit out of five. Two months ago it had been one out of ten. The doctor said Jerry might, possibly, live to see Christmas. Jerry said he wasn't sure he wanted to. "Okay. The photographer sent me some pictures."

"Good. That's good. Come on."

Sacha braced himself as they went down the hall. Jerry could still tolerate the wheelchair, but only for long enough to get from room to room. He spent the rest of his life lying down, constantly trying to change position, trying to get away from the pain. The cancer had settled in his bones like some kind of curse. It was everywhere, relentless. The doctor had offered chemotherapy, radiation, every possible therapy. Jerry had looked at the statistics and said No. Even if they could hold it back, he'd never walk again. This time that was certain. The cancer had eaten into his spine and only a device he called his turtle shell kept him upright in the wheelchair, or on the toilet.

The worst of it was that Jerry's friends in the industry simply didn't know what to do after he officially retired, and then after he was in the wheelchair. He said 'maybe soon' to dinner invitations, then lunch invitations, then all invitations. Gave them permission to stop visiting, and they had, because they were all still working. He would die alone, except for Jesús and Sacha. It was only a matter of when. As he entered the den, Sacha wondered if 'when' was 'now.' His heart lurched. Jerry's eyes were closed and his face was grey. "Jerry?"

An eye opened. "Oh hey Sacha. Good to see you." The voice was faint, the attempt at a smile weak. "It's been a shitty day."

Sacha knelt by the couch and kissed his cheek. "I wish there was more I could do."

"Don't we all. So how was that party?"

"It was a good party. I would have had more fun with you."

"Yeah I'll bet. In between things today I read this shitty script. You would laugh."

"What's it about?" Sacha sat on the floor, folding his legs, Jerry's hand between his. One of Jerry's friends, a writers' agent, still sent him scripts. Everyone knew he'd never produce anything again, so these were always simply things the friend thought Jerry would find entertaining. For that reason he was Sacha's favorite of Jerry's friends, even though they'd never met in real life and probably never would.

"Bank robbery. They thought they were writing 'Dog Day Afternoon' meets 'The Italian Job.'" Jerry had to stop and breathe. Sacha waited. "It's more like 'The Town' meets 'Harold and Kumar.'" Sacha smiled. Jerry took a few more breaths, shifted his shoulders, winced. "I blame Quentin Tarantino. Everybody wants to write the funny criminal now."

Sacha understood because they'd watched so many dozens, hundreds, of movies together. "What can I do for you tonight?"

"Nothing, honey. Just hang out for a while, if you can." Jerry didn't seem to notice the endearment. He almost never said things like that to Sacha. He'd said them to Maggie.

Sacha noticed, and stored it away with the others. Maybe it was good they were rare; he could remember every one. "I can stay all night if you want. In fact, I wanted to ask. Would you like it if I moved back to the guest house? So I can be here more?"

Jerry turned his head. They stared at each other for a minute. Neither of them needed to say 'until it's over.' "Yeah," he said finally. "I'd like that."

"Then I'll move back on Friday." Sacha leaned in for a kiss. They never had kissed much, and always with closed mouths. It was never about desire. It was something that Jerry had never learned to do with a man, and Sacha had avoided during his brief career as a prostitute. For him, it was something one did with a loved elder, like his father or uncle or grandfathers, those two boisterous old men from the old country, who had routinely kissed everyone they could get their hands on. He'd told Jerry about that, about his family, after the Emmy awards that first time. When they were back at home, another statuette on the table, drunk half with champagne and half with delight at pulling off their big deception. Maybe for those reasons, it meant a lot to both of them.

"I love you," Jerry said. He hadn't said it until the oncologist gave him the news, and they knew he was going to die. It was as if only then could he risk it.

"I love you, too." Sacha laid his head against Jerry's shoulder and thought *how will I live without you*. They were quiet for a while. But Jerry wasn't sleeping, and Sacha knew he wouldn't, not until the pain got unbearable and he let Carla give him the heavy dose. So he said, "I have pictures. Do you want to see?"

"Yeah. From the thing in Irvine?"

"The photographer sent me some. She was nice." He debated for a second as he got his phone ready. "It was the same woman from the casino night. She recognized me. I told her about you, that you're my best friend. Maybe I shouldn't have." He felt Jerry's breath in his hair, such a rare almost-touch that he nearly cried.

"You're going to need a friend." Jerry's voice was a little scratchy.

Sacha swallowed hard. *Do not cry*. Took a deep, controlled breath and let it out slowly. "That's what I told her. She said I could call her."

"You should call her. Let's see these pictures."

CHAPTER 3

"It's beyond explaining," Sacha told Charlie a week later, after dinner, when they were both in the guest house behind Jerry's. "I expected certain things, you know. Expected to have to give him certain things. Was willing, because I owed him so much. I never wanted to do some of those things. Only ever did them because, well." He didn't want to say that again. Saying it once, saying 'I sold myself' had felt like swallowing broken glass. Charlie was the first person he'd ever told, since his shrink. The psychologist recommended by Jerry, who said 'she couldn't help me but give it a try' after Sacha confessed to having anxiety, nightmares, flashbacks.

Charlie had been listening for an hour. Every time she thought he was done with this incredible story, there was more of it. She couldn't believe he was even telling her all this. Couldn't come up with a single question. It was as if her silence impelled him to keep talking. *Maybe he's never told anyone else*, she realized, and wondered why he was telling her. Maybe because it was coming to an end. Maybe he needed to exorcise it. But he didn't seem traumatized by it. If anything, the deeply strange relationship he'd had with Jerry seemed to have been therapeutic. She wondered about his family, wanted to ask why he'd been so alone, and didn't quite dare. She was silent until Sacha asked her if she wanted a cup of coffee. "Yeah, sure." She watched him go to the kitchen. The third time she'd seen him, the third look. First Maggie, then black tie; tonight he was wearing jeans and a silk shirt. Open at the neck, no jewelry. He'd told her he slept with studs in his pierced ears, to keep the holes open between Maggie's appearances. "What do you wear to see clients?"

"Scrubs, usually," he said. "How about you?"

"Depends on the gig. Nobody really cares how I look. If it's not private, the Irvine thing is about normal." That had been black chinos with a white button-down shirt. "It's always a toss-up whether people assume I'm part of the catering staff." She waited until he brought the coffee and sat in the other rattan chair. "So can I ask."

"Ask anything."

"Never sex?" He'd said so, but she just couldn't get her head around it. It was twelve *years*.

Sacha had already said this, but if she wanted to hear it again, he'd say it again. This had never, for whatever reason, troubled him. "He wanted my hand on him sometimes. Sometimes he wanted to watch me masturbate. That was all." And always, only, in the guest house. They had never spent a night together. There were times when they'd stayed up very late together. Always in the den, on the couch. Always clothed. An early, tentative suggestion that they might sleep together – only sleep - had made Jerry uncomfortable to the point of panic, so it was never mentioned again.

"And you never saw anyone else?" He shook his head. "Why?"

"I dated a little. Never got serious. As time went by it seemed less important. I always had this idea that eventually I would meet someone, but obviously it took a long time." He sipped coffee, smiling at her over the mug. Then he set it down, smile fading. "Maybe I thought it wouldn't be fair. There would have been so much I couldn't tell someone, so many

42

lies. And it would have been so much more difficult to keep Jerry's secret." Charlie nodded. "I've been thinking about this a lot since I met you. In February. I didn't think you had me pegged then. Did you?"

"Obviously I didn't know who you really were, but yeah. When you walked away all these little things clicked together and I thought, holy shit, that's a guy, whoa." He laughed. "Such little things. The outside of your wrist. You've got really fine bones but that joint was the tiniest bit bulky, for a woman. The way you held your head. That angle to your body, suggesting more of a hip than you actually have. You liked being a woman? Or acting the part of a woman, I guess," she added, because she saw a flash of disagreement.

The amendment got a nod. "I really did. It was such a challenge, there were so many skills involved. It was so satisfying to meet people and to know, just *know*, they had no idea. I liked looking that way. I'm not that eye-catching as a man." Charlie made a sound of disagreement. Sacha smiled again. "And Jerry loved it. He loved being out with someone that people admired, and the fact that he could actually have a normal relationship. That we could go out over and over again, and do things as a couple. It was as good as being married, for him, except even better because he didn't have to hide."

Charlie let that bit about a 'normal' relationship go. She guessed for Jerry, it was close enough to the truth. And for his friends, it clearly had been. "But you were hiding."

Sacha shook his head. "Nobody knew who I was. So I could be whoever I wanted. Sacha Lebedev is a different person, with a public life. I know a lot of people as Sacha. As Maggie, I was a mystery." And Maggie would never be seen again, unless Jerry asked her to appear at his funeral. Sacha still needed to find out. They'd discussed it once, so far.

"Where did the name come from?"

"Maggie from 'A Chorus Line.' And Eisenstein from the filmmaker. He was a pioneer of the montage, where a series of short shots are cut together to make a scene. Jerry thought my whole presentation as Maggie was like a montage, every little piece was an essential part. You should have seen his face the first time I put her on for him." Sacha was smiling again, remembering the disbelief, and then the delight. "After that first time, when we knew it could work, he really threw himself into it. He bought the jewelry, he had the dresses made, the best-quality wigs. I practiced doing the makeup and the nails so they'd be perfect. That first time we didn't try the red carpet. But every year after, until last year." Until Jerry couldn't walk anymore.

"You had some great dresses. You looked amazing. And he did look happy." Charlie sipped coffee. "What happens when he's gone?"

Sacha sighed. "I don't know. I guess my life won't change much, from how it's been the past few months. I'll move somewhere cheaper. I won't need to be so close. Maggie will go back in her box forever."

"Does he have any family? Any other family," Charlie added, because clearly Sacha was that.

"His parents are long gone. No siblings. No children. His first wife lives in the south of France now, and his second, may she rot in hell, in Florida. I don't suppose either of them will come to his funeral."

"Does he want a big thing?"

"A memorial service, I think, rather than a funeral. We need to talk about that. Jesús handles

44

almost all Jerry's personal business. I've never had any official position."

"But you've been with him so long. You must know a lot about his stuff."

"I never tried to learn. It was none of my business. The first couple of years, while I was living here, I was sort of a personal assistant. But after I moved out, I was working full-time."

Charlie finished her coffee. She looked around the room. The guest house was like a really well-appointed studio apartment, a single big room with all the necessities and quite a few comforts. The closet and bathroom were on the wall opposite the galley kitchen. If what she'd seen was the entirety of Sacha's possessions, he gave new meaning to the term 'traveling light.' "You never think, I've given him twelve years, I deserve something?"

"Charlie. He saved my *life*." He saw her react to that. This time he thought she understood it. "He's like another father to me, and yeah that's a little strange because of the Maggie stuff and the almost-sex stuff. I won't lie, I was scared that first time. I had nothing. I was totally dependent on him and his goodwill. But you have to understand, he never abused it. Anything I gave him, I offered. And I did it because by the time he admitted he needed something, I already loved him. He is a good man." He blinked away tears. Tried to, anyway, but they were coming too fast. He turned his head, one hand over his eyes.

Charlie was there then, leaning over the back of his chair with her arm across his chest and her head next to his, saying nothing. Sacha wrapped a hand around her wrist and let himself cry.

45

Jerry didn't make it to Christmas. And he didn't want Maggie at the memorial. He said that was then, this is now, be yourself. Since Sacha had moved back, they'd gone to an open professional relationship. Sacha was officially Jerry's massage therapist. He still saw other clients. He went out on dates, occasionally, with Charlie. Dates that never went beyond dinner and a movie and a hug. Never even a goodnight kiss. Charlie didn't wonder about it. She knew that Sacha was, in a way, being faithful to Jerry. It was strange, but somehow honorable.

Aside from those dates, Sacha had dinner with Jesús and Carla and their little girl almost every night. Martin was never there anymore. He'd stayed available to drive Jerry as long as he was needed, but those days were past. He worked for a different family now. Cecilia went home, most days, before Sacha got home from seeing clients. His life gradually got smaller. He didn't go out, except with Charlie, who felt like a lifeline. He didn't want to depend too much on her, even though she seemed to understand what he was going through. He planned his days around the increasingly small windows of time when Jerry was both alert and wanting company. All they had was palliative care. Heavy doses of painkillers, and finally a morphine IV.

The end finally came two days before the Emmys broadcast. Sacha went over to the house early in the morning, as he always did since moving home. He met Jesús coming down the hall, looking devastated. "He's gone," Jesús said, and broke down crying. Sacha hugged him, aware that he would break down soon himself, but not right then. After a while, sniffing, Jesús said, "Thank God, his suffering is over." Sacha murmured agreement. Jesús went to the office to call the people who must be called. Sacha went down to the bedroom and sat by Jerry's bed, holding his hand, until they arrived. He didn't know if he wished he'd been with Jerry when it happened. Maybe it was easy, maybe he had slipped away in sleep. Sacha hoped so. He would believe so.

He cancelled his clients that day, telling them only that another client he was very close to had died, and that he would be in touch to reschedule. Then he sent a text to Charlie: *It's over*

As usual, she responded quickly: *Oh Sacha I'm so sorry. Is there anything I can do?*

I don't think so, but thank you. Jesús is handling everything

Let me know if you want company. Call if you want to talk. Text if you want to text. I'm here for you

I know. Thank you. I'll be in touch

Take care of yourself. Charlie waited, but there wasn't another text. There wasn't a call. She tried to put herself in Sacha's position, tried to imagine how he must feel, tried to remember how she'd felt when a friend died. She watched the Emmy Awards, which she didn't usually bother to do. There was a tribute. There were pictures of Jerry with Maggie, who wasn't mentioned by name. *Some game*, Charlie thought bitterly.

She saw a short article about Jerry's memorial, with a list of the prominent industry people expected to attend. There was no mention of Jerry's longtime companion Maggie Eisenstein, and no reference to Sacha Lebedev.

It was awful, awful, awful. Seeing the mortuary van come, knowing that Jerry was truly gone.

47

Watching it go, alone in the guest house, because he wasn't supposed to be more than the massage therapist, the renter. Jesús and Cecilia were distractedly kind. Cecilia was grieving too. Jesús was up to his neck in the business of death. Their advance knowledge that this was coming didn't help any of them.

Sacha watched the Emmys alone, knowing they would have thrown together some kind of tribute. It was exactly what he would have expected, a survey of Jerry's greatest hits with brief comments from colleagues, and a few words about his philanthropy. There were photos of Jerry with Maggie. Sacha wondered if he would ever run out of tears.

He went through his days like an automaton, seeing clients, not responding to Charlie's last message. In the days before the memorial he barely spoke. He could produce words when absolutely necessary, for a client or one of their caregivers, but there were too many words in his head that he absolutely couldn't say. A wall of those unspoken words, more impermeable by the day, between him and the world.

At the memorial, Sacha listened to people talk about Jerry. Telling stories about disasters on set, or ridiculous negotiations, or some of his many notable successes. They were at the Paley Center for Media, which seemed like an appropriate place for his memorial. He wasn't religious. There was no family to put up front in the pews. This was for his business colleagues from the past forty years, people who had worked with him or for him, to give them closure. Nobody there recognized Sacha, though dozens of them had met him – as Maggie – over the years. He was too exhausted to do anything more than listen, and too numb to cry. Jesús had said, you have to come to the lawyer's office tomorrow. He didn't know why, and Sacha could only wonder. He couldn't quite manage to care.

Two days after the memorial there was a news explosion about Jerry Morgenstern's estate. "Oh my God," Charlie said out loud, reading the story online. The first one was fairly uninflected, a brief recitation of the terms of the will. Over the next week, as the story proliferated, the content – mostly speculation; no one on the inside was talking - got nastier and nastier. She texted Sacha again and again, variations on *OMG this is horrible are you all right can I help*.

Jerry had left a million dollars to Martin, three million to Jesús, and the remainder of his estate – estimates ranged from twelve to twenty million - to Sacha.

She kept trying, for a while, but not for too long. She had to let it go. It was tough to keep her face blank at the next charity gig she did – oh, how Hollywood loved its charity events – when everyone, but everyone, was talking about the Morgenstern story. Everyone seemed eager to believe the worst of Sacha, that he'd been some kind of conniving gold-digger, that he'd somehow taken advantage of Jerry. It was all Charlie could do not to say something. Anything she said would only make it worse.

Except to Louise, who organized a gig in November. The gossip wasn't quite as toxic, people were losing interest. Louise remembered the event in Irvine, remembered that Charlie had talked to Sacha. "Did you have any clue about this? Did he even mention it?"

Charlie studied her for a few seconds. She knew Louise was motivated more by curiosity than by concern. On the other hand, everyone knew Louise and she was a trusted source. If anyone asked her, and she had something good to say about Sacha, that could only help. So Charlie said, "He told me that Jerry was dying and they were all trying to keep it quiet because Jerry didn't want anyone to know. He didn't want a lot of phony sympathy, which as we can see is exactly what he would have gotten, plus a lot of vultures."

Louise blinked. "Okay. Look, I thought he was sweet to Rose, and Rose has not had a bad word to say about him. If he was like that with Jerry, well, everybody needs a friend."

God, does he need a friend. "Sacha told me that Jerry had been his best friend for a long time, and that when Jerry was gone, he was going to need a friend. Nobody's really stepped up there, have they?" *Not even me.* At least she'd tried. She wanted to believe that Sacha was only waiting until the smoke cleared, so that she wouldn't get dragged into this too. It hurt, though, after all the things he'd told her. After trusting her that much, that he wouldn't trust her to hang in there with him. Or maybe he'd hit his limit on coping, and couldn't summon the energy to deal with another person. Charlie remembered a time she'd felt that way, told herself that was probably it, sent another text, and kept on working.

At the next gig, in December, things were better. Jerry's longtime assistant and the lawyers made statements. Still not much detail: only that Jerry Morgenstern and Sacha Lebedev had met in 2003, and had been in a relationship ever since, and that the executor and the attorneys were satisfied that the will was properly drawn. The court was refusing to hear the challenge made by the second ex-wife. And of course, after that, it was a non-story. There were no new facts. Sacha was nowhere to be seen. The gossipmongers went looking for a new scandal.

Charlie sent one more text, got no reply, kept on working. For the first time in a long time she thought *I need a friend.* All these years of scrambling, pinching pennies, working sixteen- and eighteen-hour days: there hadn't been time to miss having someone. And there still wasn't time to go looking for that someone to talk to. She had so hoped Sacha would be that someone, for more than the few months they'd had before it all blew up.

February 2016

Sacha pushed back from the conference table, nodded to the last remaining lawyer, and stood up. He held out a hand to Jesús, who shook it. "You're really going back to Mexico?"

"It's a lot of money, in Mazatlán. Carla and me and Olivia, we'll have a good life. We can help people there."

"Thank you for everything you did for me."

Jesús studied him. "Thank you for being there for Mr. Morgenstern." Then it was another handshake, one that turned into a hug, and Jesús was gone. Sacha slowly followed him out, speaking briefly to the lawyer's assistant, and to the receptionist. He went down to the parking valet, they brought his car, and he went back home. 'Home' that was now the whole property, but it still felt unreal. Home to sit in the guest house, staring at the pool, wondering what to do next.

Jesús had been named as Jerry's executor. He told the lawyers yes, Mr. Morgenstern met Mr. Lebedev in 2003. We were out for a drive, he always liked to

51

drive in the city at night. Mr. Lebedev was getting mugged, we stopped it. And of course all of that was true.

He persuaded Martin to talk to the lawyers, too, and say yes, this is what happened. Only the bare facts. He tracked down that therapist, now retired, who confirmed that Sacha had been there in 2003. He admitted that he didn't really think Sacha was Jerry's godson, but also that he thought they were good together, and that he wasn't surprised the relationship had lasted. He refused to speculate about Mr. Morgenstern's public companion, Maggie Eisenstein, who he'd never met. He pointed to the non-disclosure agreement he'd signed, which was not precisely standard operating procedure but also not so uncommon that he'd balked. Mr. Morgenstern, he said, handled sensitive and confidential deals all the time. And he respected his client's privacy. As, he was sure, did Mr. Lebedev. He shook Sacha's hand, and wished him well.

Jesús brought Cecilia in to say yes, he's Jerry's friend, he was the only person Jerry wanted to see some days and he would drop everything to come if Jerry needed him. He turned the first ex-wife's email – sent to Sacha through Jerry's account, with condolences that seemed sincere – over to the attorneys without comment. He wrote, in response to the second ex-wife's much less pleasant email, "Go to hell." Eventually, he gave a statement to the press. Because he'd worked for Jerry for twenty years, and because no-one anywhere, no matter how hard they tried, had come up with a way to discredit him, all the vicious gossip finally grumbled away into silence. Now he, like Martin, would be gone. Sacha was dreading it.

Over those dozen years he'd gotten used to the household. He'd liked it. It wasn't much like the family he grew up in, but it was a family nonetheless. He was glad that Cecilia was staying on. He told her, "I have no idea what I'm doing." She said never mind, he'd figure it out.

All he'd been doing since September was react. React to losing Jerry, then to that first disorienting meeting with the lawyers. To the paparazzi, the tabloids, the threats and the feeling of being completely under attack. Dodging the media when he was Maggie, with Jerry right there to protect him, had been part of the game. Now he didn't even have work to distract him.

Because of course, Sacha's clients had vanished more or less instantly. He still hadn't cleared things up with his family, who were caught between shock, outrage, and deep confusion – a sort of covetous revulsion - over the legacy. They were simultaneously hurt and insulted that he'd never told them about Jerry. They didn't understand at all, and Sacha didn't dare tell them the whole truth. Some of them thought he was a disgrace based on the little they did know. But it didn't really matter. One person knew everything. Now that this was finally over, Sacha wanted to try to bring that one person back into his life. He didn't know if she'd be willing.

Charlie read the news story. It was short, blunt, and nowhere near the front page. She wondered if Sacha would try to get in touch now. She'd gotten over feeling hurt, accepted that none of this was about her, and chosen to appreciate the way he'd trusted her before. He must have been desperate for someone to talk to. She didn't really blame him for going silent; in that kind of shitstorm, he was probably doing her a favor. In fact, he was *certainly* doing her a favor. Her business would have evaporated if people thought they were connected. He would have looked even more like a gold-digger, but the estate still would have come to him. A prominent estate attorney had written about the situation. The divorce settlements had been years old before the will was even drawn, and never contested. The estate plan was watertight. No-one else had a claim. Only Sacha and Jesús had been there at the end.

It had to have been awful. And now Charlie wasn't sure if contacting him was the right thing to do. If he might think she was only reaching out because she wanted some of that money. If the number was even going to work. But he had said, when Jerry is gone I'm going to need a friend. She couldn't stop hearing him say that. If that was true last May, it was surely even more true now. So Charlie picked up her phone and wrote: *Hi Sacha. Saw a story, seems like the worst of the shit may have stopped hitting the fan. If you still need a friend, I'm here.* She sent it. There was no out-of-service message.

Instead, half an hour later, there was a reply: *Oh thank God thank you Charlie I'm so sorry. This has been a nightmare. Can I call you?*

She didn't wait. She dialed, pressed send, heard half a ring. She heard the soft voice saying her name, and then breaking. He made almost no sound but she knew he was crying. She waited, tears streaming down her own face. When he finally managed another actual word, she said, "Don't be sorry. Where are you?"

"I'm at Jerry's house."

"Do you want me to come over?"

"Oh God, could you?"

"Yes, of course. I'll see you in about half an hour."

"Thank you. Thank you, Charlie."

She had an idea that he probably wasn't taking such good care of himself. She could get up to the house in fifteen minutes. She used the rest of her time to stop for food, crossing her fingers that Jerry had been a drinker because she personally could use a lot of drinks right now. She pulled up to the gate almost exactly half an hour after the call, and pressed the buzzer. The intercom responded. "Yes?"

"It's me."

"Come in." The gate opened. She drove in and parked. *This is so weird.* She'd only been there once before, the night Sacha told her about Jerry. It wasn't a mansion, it wasn't one of those monstrosity houses, but it was – had always been – clearly a rich man's house. Charlie had read a lot about Jerry since last summer. She knew about the TV shows and movies he'd been involved with. She knew about investments he'd made that had paid off. She wondered what Sacha knew about handling that kind of money.

"Nothing," he said exhaustedly, much later. He'd hugged her, without tears this time. He'd produced a bottle of wine that even Charlie – whose regular was from the second-to-the-bottom shelf at the supermarket - knew was exceptional. They drank it all, while eating the excellent Italian food from Pace, talking about the situation.

"So the first thing you need to do is find a financial manager, huh." He nodded. "I suppose all your rich clients bailed." A ghost of a smile. "Were there any of Jerry's friends that you knew?"

"I know a few names. There was one guy who kept sending him scripts even after he said don't visit any more. He'd send these really bad ones because he knew they would make Jerry laugh, and he'd put a letter with it, always something funny. I think he would have kept visiting. He seemed to really care."

"Then maybe he's someone who would talk to you. You never met?"

"I probably met him when Jerry and I were out sometime. When I was Maggie." That hadn't come out. Jesús and the others had said what was necessary and not a syllable more. Still protecting Jerry, but the umbrella covered Sacha too. The second ex-wife had suggested that maybe the lawyers should find Maggie, maybe she deserved some of the estate. It was so transparently a ploy to get someone who would favor her own claim that nobody had taken it seriously.

Charlie dragged his thoughts back on track. "Would he recognize you?" Sacha shrugged. It was possible. If the man had an open mind, if he put two and two together. "Would you mind if he did?"

It was a good question. There was nothing remotely fraudulent about Maggie Eisenstein. She was a figment, to everyone except Jerry and Sacha. "I wonder," Sacha said slowly. Charlie tilted her head like an owl; it made him smile. "I am Iron Man?" She laughed. "Oh my God, what if I did that. Should I do that?"

"Well, it would certainly prove that you and Jerry had a real relationship, even if everybody still can't figure out exactly what the fuck kind of relationship it was." She studied him. "Do you still have the stuff?"

"She's all here. The jewelry was always here, and the dresses, except whatever was newest." Because of course Jerry's glamorous date couldn't wear the same thing twice. "I brought the rest with me when I moved back." While he lived away, when he had a date with Jerry, he had carefully assembled Maggie at his own residence, which had a convenient back door to the alley where he parked. As far as he knew, and judging by the lack of any news breaking, no-one had ever spotted her coming or going. That lease agreement, of course, had been another piece of evidence for the lawyers.

"Well, you could sleep on it, but if you feel like maybe this one guy might not be one of the toxic avengers, you could get in touch and ask to meet. As Sacha. And then show up as Maggie, and see if he gets it. I mean, he has a sense of humor, right?" She stood up. It was late, time to clean up from dinner and get going.

"Can you stay?" Sacha was standing too. He didn't know exactly what he wanted from Charlie, aside from her company. But he desperately wanted that. "This house has four bedrooms and they're all made up." He didn't even know why. Cecilia simply did that without asking. Maybe she thought he needed some company.

Charlie gave him a sideways look. She wondered if he knew that she would have offered. "Which way to the kitchen?"

"This way." They transferred all the containers, the dishes, the glasses, the empty wine bottle. Sacha went back to wipe the table, then joined Charlie in the kitchen again. She rinsed the dishes and put them in the dishwasher. She still hadn't answered him. Sacha had to assume that meant 'no.' "Charlie. Thanks for coming tonight."

"I have to be out of here before nine," she said. "I have a shoot over at the Huntington in the afternoon and I have to get home for all my shit. Does the gate open by magic when you pull up or what?"

"Yes," he said, flooded with relief. "But I'll be awake."

"You don't have to be. You look like you haven't slept since August." Only a slight exaggeration. "Anyway, I will not wake you up, but if you do wake up, I'll see you in the morning. Point me at a bedroom."

"Down that hall, there's a bathroom on the right and then two bedrooms." He stood there not knowing what to do. Charlie stepped close and put her arms around him. Leaned in. She was soft, female, but most of all his friend. Sacha held her tight for a minute, then kissed her forehead. "Good night."

"Good night, Sacha. It's going to be all right."

"Yeah." He held her a little longer, with his face against her hair, eyes closed. "I wasn't sure this was real. Honey and spice."

"Burt's Bees and clove essential oil," she said, charmed. "Did you think you were imagining things?" She stood back, patted his chest. "Get some sleep."

She was gone when he woke up. He didn't even go looking, because he didn't wake up until almost eleven. There was a note on the kitchen table: GLAD YOU SLEPT. An almost-full pot of coffee. Another note on the refrigerator: EAT SOMETHING. Sacha laughed under his breath and opened the fridge. He was hungry.

After breakfast, he went to Jerry's office. He hadn't spent much time in there; Jesús used the room to work, and while he had handled incoming business promptly and efficiently, once something was done his filing system wasn't the best. Was, more accurately, nonexistent. He always said, the lawyers and the accountants have files, this is just trash, I'll shred it someday. Sacha didn't know where to start. There were stacks and drifts of paper all over the desk, all over the floor. Envelopes and bound scripts and God-knew-what jammed into the bookcases. The file cabinets looked like they were about to explode.

Eventually Sacha found that stack of scripts, each one with a letter. Printed on a plain sheet of paper, with a scrawled signature. The last one still had its envelope, with the return address. *You did care*, he thought. There was also a stack of cards in the in-tray, under a pile of junk mail and trade magazines. All opened, all with the date of receipt penciled in the corner. Jesús had done that. Sacha knew that he hadn't sent replies. After the memorial, when cards were still coming in, was when the news about the estate had broken. Sacha didn't know if he should send thanks. It couldn't hurt. There was one from Brooke, the first ex-wife, who he hadn't responded to before. The lawyer had said, "Not yet," but that was months ago. He set that one aside; he wanted to write back. As he flipped through the stack he found a card from the agency address. This one had the name of the agent, Gary Fisher. Now that he saw the name, he did remember the man, and meeting him several times, when he was Maggie. There had been the same joke each time, about Jerry and Gary and how to tell them apart. That was never a question, of course, because Jerry was six foot one and gray-haired, and Gary was five foot eight and bald.

And the other joke, about whether Maggie had a friend short enough for Gary. Sacha sat down at the desk, somewhat gingerly. He had never sat there before. But it was his now, all of it was his, and he needed help. He barely knew how to talk to the lawyer, his lawyer now. He hadn't signed anything yet, except for the only papers he understood, the ones giving him access to the trust checking account and a linked credit card. He needed his own accountant, and another lawyer. One to go through any papers the first one gave him, to make sure they said what Sacha thought they said, make sure he didn't do anything foolish out of ignorance. So he had to write this letter. He had to make it good. He had to pray that Gary Fisher cared enough about Jerry Morgenstern to offer a hand to the person Jerry had loved.

CHAPTER 4

March 2016

Gary Fisher looked at the envelope marked PERSONAL & CONFIDENTIAL and thought *eh*. He'd been scammed like that before, but usually if it was a ploy it was a bigger, thicker envelope. Somebody trying to avoid the slush pile, sending in an unsolicited script as if it were personal correspondence. Then he looked at the return address and said, "What the fuck." He stood up, went to the door, and said to his assistant, "Was this hand-delivered?" She nodded. "I'm on do not disturb for a few minutes." She nodded again. Gary closed the door, sat down, and opened the envelope.

What the fuck, he thought again about a dozen times while reading, and then about a dozen times after the letter was lying on his desk. He stared at the big photo print on his wall. It was a rainy-day view of a deserted beach in Oregon, and usually calmed him down. Then he stood up to stare out the window, watching the predictable traffic stupidity at the intersection of Wilshire and Santa Monica Boulevard.

All it came down to was a request to meet, at his office or for lunch, and a request for guidance in choosing advisors. It was the personal note that was killing him. The part about 'it meant so much to Jerry that you kept writing, that you sent him those scripts. Every time he got one it made his day better. His whole week, actually. He kept all of them.' Gary tipped his head back and pinched the bridge of his nose. *There's no crying in Hollywood*. He had known Jerry for thirty-five years.

There was an email address at the end of the letter. Gary didn't really want to get involved with this guy, but he felt some responsibility. *I should have known*. After a minute more to think, he sat down and composed a message.

Mr. Lebedev,

It was a surprise to hear from you as you can imagine. Thanks though. When I heard how long Jerry was sick I thought I must have been a bad friend. I'm glad I could do something for him.

You are obviously feeling like a truckload of shit has landed on you. As someone who has not just inherited eight figures I cannot precisely say I sympathize. However I have worked with people in similar situations and I know good news is often wrapped around a lot of bad news.

I know some people who might be able to help you straighten things out. I suggest lunch to get acquainted. There's a private room at this place down the street from my office. You can reply to this email address or text me.

Gary Fisher

He didn't put 'sincerely' or 'best regards' or any other phony sign-off because whatever he did for this guy, he'd really be doing for Jerry. When a text came in proposing a date and time, he made the reservation, cleared his schedule, and sent back a 'yes.'

They met three days later. Gary knew what Lebedev looked like – he'd been front-page news in the tabloids for weeks – and thought he knew what to expect. Someone had come up with a photo from the memorial. Gary had been there, and never even noticed the guy. He'd done a little bit of research. Or, more accurately, he'd had his assistant do a little bit of research. Contacting some of the guy's past massage clients who'd given him testimonials, including Rose Novotny, who had not pulled down the photo from last spring's benefit in which she was standing with Lebedev in front of the foundation's banner. Rose had said 'I would see him again in a heartbeat, it's my kids who keep saying no.' She also confirmed that Lebedev hadn't charged her for that time – seven hours altogether – and had sent, after his services were terminated, not a final invoice but a personal note saying he hoped she would continue to be well.

Gary got to Ocean Prime five minutes ahead of the rendezvous and was taken to the private room immediately. He paced restlessly. He wasn't usually a restless guy, but the whole situation was freaking him out. He wasn't sure why. Maybe because he had never remotely suspected that Jerry was gay, which again made him feel like a bad friend.

Then someone tapped on the door, a server opened it, and Maggie Eisenstein walked in. Gary was speechless for a second. It didn't even occur to him to wonder why she was there. The server stepped out, closing the door. "Hi Gary," Maggie said. "It's been a long time."

He moved toward her impulsively. "Maggie! What the *fuck*. Yeah, it's been a long time! How've you been? I haven't seen you since the casino thing! I thought about you when Jerry, you know. Thought I'd see you at the memorial. I wanted to tell you how sorry I was, where were you?"

"I was there." She stood still, about two feet away. Meeting his gaze steadily. Tall, blonde, gorgeous. Perfectly dressed in tailored black jersey, wearing those black pearls that Jerry had bragged about, and the Bulgari watch he'd been so thrilled with, and the black sandals with the rhinestones that Gary remembered because those sparkly heels had gone straight to his groin.

All of a sudden he realized what – who – he was looking at. His mouth dropped open. Maggie smiled, the tiniest smile. "I will be *damned*," Gary said slowly. He groped for the back of a chair, pulled it out, and sat down with a little bit of a thump.

"Can I sit?"

"Jesus Christ. Yeah, of course. Holy shit." So much was clear now. Any doubt about the legitimacy of the relationship, completely canceled. He couldn't think of a single thing to say for about three minutes. He was too busy remembering Jerry and the way he'd been, with Maggie, for all those years. Whatever it was, it had been real. It was no wonder nobody knew he was gay. Maggie – *Lebedev*, holy shit – sat silently, waiting. The only sign of stress was in her – *his*, mother fuck – perfectly manicured, tightly clasped hands. Eventually Gary took a breath and said, "Were you Maggie when you were alone?"

"No. Maggie was for the world. Jerry didn't like being gay."

"Are you gay?"

"No."

"Okay. What. No, I don't want to know, it's none of my business, it doesn't matter. Holy fucking wow." Gary sat back. There was a tap at the door. "Come in."

"Hi Mr. Fisher, would you like us to begin service?"

"Yeah. Yeah, sure. Wait." The server turned back, with inquiring eyebrows. "Do you have any other reservations for this room today?"

"No, sir."

"Can we have it, then? The rest of the day. Same rates, double rates, whatever. I need to get a few more people in here." Gary had gone straight from grudging assistance to white knight. The impulse was foreign but he didn't question it. All he knew was, this person had been important to Jerry, this person had asked for help, and Jerry would have wanted him to give it.

"Yes, sir, I'll inform the manager. We'll be in to take your drink order and tell you about the specials in a moment."

They didn't really speak until all that was taken care of. Wine ordered and poured; food ordered; salads and bread delivered. Maggie – *Lebedev*, goddammit – ate neatly and with good appetite, though she – *he* – looked thin.

"I can't figure out what pronoun to use in my internal monologue," Gary complained after about ten awkward minutes.

Maggie set down her glass. "Don't worry about it. If I seem like a woman to you, I'm doing it right. It was important to Jerry that I get it right." The voice was still soft and light, but – now that Gary was paying attention – no longer obviously a female voice.

"Are you going to keep up this persona?"

"I wasn't planning to ever use her again. But I need help, and my one friend said maybe this guy will help, because he cared enough to keep writing. And then we thought, what if I could make you understand, just by being Maggie."

Gary was silent for a minute. "I am sorry."

"Why?"

"A year goes by so quickly. I kept thinking, next time I see Jerry I'll give him some shit about dropping out."

"He knew you cared." The tiniest tremor in the voice.

Not as much as you. Gary took a quick breath, and grabbed for a lifeline. "Are your eyes really that color?" Gary hadn't noticed, in the pictures he'd seen online. At the time he was looking for reasons not to be impressed by Lebedev, and had thought 'why this, Jerry' because the guy seemed so nondescript. Thin, colorless, and barely taller than Gary himself. The best of those pictures had been the one with Rose Novotny, and Lebedev had been looking at her, not at the camera. *Of course,* Gary realized. He hadn't been caught, not once, looking directly at a camera. Always with his face turned slightly away, always with his eyes cast down. He wondered what color they actually were. "They aren't, huh."

"No." Another, more relaxed smile. Something else that had never appeared in a photo of Lebedev. "My hair isn't, either."

"I've gotta tell you, what I'm seeing right now is either an Academy Award-winning performance or an Academy Award-winning documentary. I'm trying to get my head around it. You have to have been an actor, something, it's just too good."

"I trained." Maggie shrugged, one shoulder, head tilted. Very feminine. "It doesn't matter. I literally crashed and almost burned, here in L.A. I would have been dead if not for Jerry. He saved my life, and so when he needed something I gave it to him. By the time he asked, I would have given him anything, because I loved him. It was a stranger relationship than I ever imagined, but it worked."

"It worked for a long time. If he hadn't gotten sick, would it have kept working?"

She answered the unspoken question. "I would have stayed forever."

66

"Even though you're not gay. And you were so isolated that even now you have one goddamned friend." Gary's heart was breaking a little. He could scarcely conceive of a love like that. From the moment Jerry made the approach, he was completely in this guy's power, and never, not once, not for a second, not by a fucking *blink* had Lebedev betrayed him.

Maggie shook her head, once. "I had a life, as Sacha."

"So what are you going to do now?"

"Try not to destroy everything he gave me. I'm dyslexic, it takes me forever to balance my checkbook, and I have no clue about all this legal stuff."

"What's still operating?"

"The lawyer made sure the bills got paid. Jesús was the executor. We were friendly, and he knew everything about Jerry's business, so he kept things running. But he's gone back to Mexico now with his family. Retired." She took a breath, and Gary thought *left you alone*. "The housekeeper, gardener, and security were kept on. They all knew me. We increased the security level because I was getting death threats." Another shrug, this one resigned. "But there's property, there's so much. I never made more than about sixty-five thousand a year. That's not the kind of money that takes a lot of managing."

"Yeah, I know." Gary got his phone out. "Hang on," he told Maggie while he selected a number. It rang twice. Gary heard the pleased, brisk voice at the other end and said, "Hi Patrick. What are the odds I can get you out of your office for the rest of the afternoon? I've got a situation. Yes I know it's tax season. Patrick, it's always fucking tax season. You know all those rich fuckers are taking extensions anyway. Ocean Prime, anything from the bar, anything you want. And bring one of your CFPs. Yes, it's a mess, no it's not my mess, do I have that kind of money? And an estate attorney, who can you recommend? Do you have his card? Could we get him here today? Yeah okay you don't know, fair enough, could you please call him before you head over. Tell him it's about the Jerry Morgenstern estate so he can do a conflicts check. If he can come, he will be lavishly compensated as will you and whoever else you bring. No, not by me, are you crazy? We have the room till we don't need the room. I already told you it's a mess. It is not your future client's fault. Stop speculating, shut up, you'll know when you get here. Yes. Thanks Patrick. See you soon." He disconnected and sighed. "Best tax and real-estate accountant in Los Angeles. He's bringing a certified financial planner from his office. If the lawyer guy can make it, we'll have the beginning of a team for you."

Maggie's eyes were wet. She sniffed, swallowed, and said, "Thank you."

"Could your one friend come? I'm assuming this person already has a career, but you're going to need a personal assistant. Maybe this person could fill in for a minute till we find someone else?" Gary didn't even know why he said 'we' again. He only heard it after it was out of his mouth. He didn't call it back.

"I don't know. I'll see." Maggie slid her fingers into her little black bag, pulled out her phone, and sent a text. Then she set the phone on the table and closed her eyes, taking a deep breath. Gary watched, still knocked off balance but full of admiration. Then the servers were back for the next phase of the meal, and for a while Gary and Maggie pretended that was all they were there for.

People trickled in over the next hour. First the accountant Patrick Sarkisian and his colleague Marisa Keller, then Charlotte Montgomery. She shook hands with everybody, said "Call me Charlie," kissed Maggie's cheek, and sat down, big-eyed and silent.

Finally the lawyer came in, a guy almost Gary's age. "Frank Cavatini," he said, shaking hands all around. "I understand we have a complex legacy situation here."

"You can call it that," Gary said. He waited for Frank to sit, filled a wineglass from the fresh bottle left by the server, and handed it to him. Then he sat down, gathered everyone's attention, and said, "I'd like to introduce you to Sacha Lebedev."

Hours later, everyone had gone except Gary, Sacha, and Charlie. "You've given up your whole day," Sacha said, still not believing it. "Thank you so much."

"Do not sell your movie rights to anyone until you talk to me," Gary said. "Not even kidding. Oh my God, Frank's face." He laughed all over again. "Patrick's face!" Charlie laughed this time; that face had been an epic 'what the fuck' face. "I'm sure that was exactly my face, too."

"Pretty much," Sacha agreed. "I really cannot thank you enough."

"Well," Gary said, "a bottle of wine now and then will do. I like real women. No offense."

"None taken." Sacha was holding Charlie's hand. "I won't be sorry to retire Maggie."

"And that said, if you know any real women who are looking for a sixty-eight-year-old short bald guy, send them my way." Gary sighed. "Holy shit, what a day. Keep me posted, okay?"

"We will," said Charlie, who felt a lot better about things now. "And feel free to keep sending shitty scripts. Now let's get out of here."

"Yeah." Gary stood up, offering a hand. Sacha shook it. "Incredible, just incredible." He did a 'mind blown' thing with his hands. Shaking his head all over again, Gary went out.

Sacha and Charlie looked at each other. "I can't even imagine what the bill is going to be like," Charlie said. "But I guess it doesn't matter, does it?"

"It doesn't. It's so weird." Then the server – not the same one they'd started with; the shift had changed long ago – came in with the folder. Sacha opened it, blinked, and showed it to Charlie. She choked a little. Sacha got the credit card out, the one linked to the trust account, and slid it into the folder. The server was waiting. By this time, Sacha figured everyone who worked there had to be wondering what the hell was going on. The reservation had been made in Gary's name. The card was in Sacha's. He would probably be in the news again tomorrow. And that was weird, but that was his new life. He'd simply have to get used to it.

It started sooner than he expected. There were paparazzi outside when they left. Sacha avoided making eye contact, glad they weren't looking for Maggie, grateful for the closed elevator bay. By tomorrow they would be looking for Maggie. Someone in the restaurant would talk, would mention that the woman with top agent Gary Fisher had signed Sacha Lebedev's credit card receipt. He escorted Charlie down to the garage, made sure she had cash to pay for the parking, and asked if she could come over again the next day. She said she could, and then she said, "We need to talk."

Sacha nodded. They needed to talk about a lot of things. He wanted to kiss her, but he was Maggie, so he didn't. Instead he waited for her to collect her car, and then collected his own, and drove back to the Hills alone.

Charlie got to Sacha's house by six the next day. He'd given her the code for the gate. She parked, walked up to the house, started to ring the doorbell. Sacha opened the door. "Hi Charlie. You wouldn't believe how many phone calls I was on today." She followed him in. "And how many phone calls I didn't answer."

"Did someone at the restaurant talk?"

"I'm assuming so. There were paparazzi outside again all day. It's definitely time to change my numbers." His cell phone, the main line for the house, the line for the guest house, the line for the office, the fax line. He would do that himself. It would make him feel a little less overwhelmed.

They were walking through the house. Charlie wasn't noticing much; she was grateful the gossip hounds were gone now. "So the calls you did take. Good news, bad news, medium news?"

"Mostly good. The best part is with all these experts looking at things for me, I feel like I'm not going to burn anything down. The worst part is I know it's never going to be simple again. Are you hungry?"

"Not yet. Did you cook?"

Sacha looked amused. "No. But Cecilia left something, or we can order in. How about a drink by the pool?"

"Perfect. I have questions, so a drink would be great."

He wasn't sure what questions might possibly remain; he felt like he'd been turned inside out the day before. But he nodded, and they went outside. There was an outdoor kitchen and wet bar on the patio behind the house, under a pergola. Sacha opened the cabinets and said, "What would you like?"

Charlie looked at the array of bottles. "Was all that Jerry's?"

"Yeah. He used to have parties. It's always in the shade here, I've tried a few things and they're all still good."

"I don't even know what half of those are. Wait, that's marshmallow vodka? Grown-ups drink marshmallow vodka?" Sacha was grinning. "Gimme that. Please." He took a glass out of another cabinet, filled it with ice (of course there was an icemaker), poured until she said "Stop! Jesus!"

He laughed. "Do you want soda?"

"Oh sure, why not." He added some from the (of course) siphon, and handed it over. Charlie tasted it, thinking about that laugh. "Oh yummy. You should try this." She offered him the glass; he took it back, sipped, made a face. "Fine, more for me." She retrieved the glass and went over to a lounger. The sun was off the pool area now, and before long it would be too cool for comfort. But, she noticed, there was a propane heat lamp beside each lounger. *Rich people do know how to live*, she thought, and stretched out.

Sacha joined her a few minutes later, with something in his hand that surely wasn't as delicious as marshmallow vodka. They sipped in silence for a little while. They could hear a siren somewhere, maybe down on the boulevard. Otherwise the only sounds were a distant TV and a tree full of chirping sparrows. "You have questions," Sacha said at last.

She'd almost forgotten, it was so peaceful back here. Her apartment didn't have any outdoor space at all, much less private space. She organized her thoughts. "Not about you, if you can believe it. First of all let me say it's so good to see you laugh. I was worried." She didn't check his reaction, simply continued. "Over the winter while you were in estate hell I was working on a series of portraits of public school teachers. I wanted to put together a book. It's almost done, anyway I met a lot of great people who should get paid a fuck of a lot more. So yesterday when Gary was talking about a personal assistant, I thought about this one lady I met. She is sixty-two. Her husband died two years ago after having cancer forever. They went broke treating him. Her house got foreclosed. She is now living in a garage apartment with her cat, about a mile from here. She is hella smart and tough and funny, in spite of everything." She stopped talking.

"I want to see your book. When could I meet her?"

"Probably immediately," Charlie said, relieved. "Want me to call her?"

"Yeah, please. I need help immediately. Do you think she would live in the guest house? Would it be weird to offer that?" Charlie gave him an incredulous look. Sacha laughed. "Okay, maybe weird but I'll offer it anyway."

"Okay." Charlie dug her phone out of her pocket, sent Sacha an are-you-sure look, collected a nod of agreement, and sent a text. There was another thing she wanted to ask Sacha, but it was more personal, so she chickened out. *Later for that.* They sipped in

73

silence for a few more minutes. Charlie's phone rang; she connected. "Hi Natalie. I have a proposition for you. Well actually a friend has a proposition for you. It involves a free place to live and working as a personal assistant. About a mile from where you are now. Yes, you could have your kitty." Charlie glanced at Sacha and saw no disagreement. "Are you free for dinner? I'm with him right now. You guys could talk about how many hours and all that jazz. About an hour. Okay. I'll text you the address. Thanks Natalie." She disconnected, sent a follow-up text, and looked back at Sacha. "How many hours, do you think? Could she still teach?"

"I feel kind of buried right now but that's probably because it's backlogged from last fall. All the real business stuff is getting handled. She might be better able to tell us, after she gets a look at the office. What should we get for dinner?"

"Let's order from Pace again."

Sacha sipped his drink, watching Charlie, wondering if this was what it was like to be married. Solving problems together, relaxing together. He wondered if that ever crossed her mind. They hadn't had a personal conversation, hadn't talked about Sacha-and-Charlie, for a long time. "You had more than one question," he said, not positive that was true.

Charlie turned her head and gazed at him. The vodka was starting to hit. She wondered what it was about his face, out of all the gorgeous faces in Los Angeles, that made it perfect in her eyes. "Would you consider putting on Maggie one more time, and letting me film you? And then let me film you taking her off? It's such an amazing transformation. It should be recorded for posters. I mean posterity. Holy crap." She set down the glass, noticing that it was almost empty.

74

Sacha was smiling at her, not laughing. "Gary said something about a documentary."

"You should totally make one! Oh my God, can you imagine? Somewhere there is another guy like Jerry who is miserable, and all he needs is someone like you, not that there is anybody else in the fucking world like you. Fuck. Is there potable water at that bar?"

"There is." He stood up, touched her shoulder, went over to the bar. She heard a cabinet door, ice going into a glass, water running. The water shut off and he was back a moment later. He handed her the glass and sat beside her on the lounger. "Charlie."

"Sacha." She swallowed some water. It was fresh and clear and cold. "I had one more question." He hadn't answered the last one, really. She couldn't wait. He was so close, and his eyes looked like the ocean, and he was everything she wanted. "Are you ever going to kiss me?"

"Right this second," he said, and kissed her. Her mouth was everything he'd imagined. His eyes closed, his mouth opened, and she was right there with him. He had his hands on the armrests of the lounger, bracketing her body. He wanted to put one, or both, his hands on her. But the kiss was so perfect he didn't want to change a thing.

"Eeek! Oh for, goddammit." Charlie was laughing. "Water."

"Sorry." Sacha sat back a little, enough for Charlie to brush some water off her leg. She handed him the glass. Then she lifted a hand and touched his face. He turned his head, kissed the palm of her hand. "Charlie, I -"

She put her hand over his mouth. "Don't say anything yet. We will talk more later. We'd probably better order dinner though. I want to kiss you more after dinner."

"You're right. I want that too." He stood up, collected his glass, and waited for her. She drank the rest of her vodka on the way to the house.

The restaurant's phone handler heard who was calling and got the manager on the line. She offered to set up a monthly billing arrangement. Sacha haggled for a minute over whether the standard gratuity and delivery charges should be twenty percent (the manager's suggestion) or thirty (Sacha's). Sacha won, of course. Then he basically ordered the menu. He had no idea what might happen during dinner, after dinner, the next day, or for the rest of his life. He had no idea if Charlie could stay tonight, or – if she did – if he could let her go in the morning without making some kind of desperate scene. Getting the question of what to eat out of the way for at least twenty-four hours seemed like a good strategy.

They were waiting for the delivery, looking at the wall of wine bottles in the butler's pantry, when the entry gate buzzer went off. Sacha stepped over to the kitchen wall and pressed the intercom button. "Yes?"

"Natalie Sanders."

"Come in." He glanced at Charlie. "I'll go get the door. If the restaurant gets here, can you buzz them in?"

"Sure." Charlie watched him go. She wondered if he was as nervous as she was. That kiss had been everything she was hoping for, except now she was hoping for a lot more. Except if there was ever a rebound situation, this was it, and it was extra exceptional because of the fact that there had been no goddamned sex for all those years. At least they had met before Jerry died, before the will was read, before everything. At least he knew she wasn't here for that. But she wasn't sure she knew why he wanted her here. It had to be enough, for now, that he clearly did. Maybe it was because of that, because he knew she had liked him before. He'd never be able to be sure of that with anyone else. *Ugh.* Charlie turned back to the wall of wine, chose two bottles more or less at random, and took them into the kitchen. It seemed like she'd been dithering forever, but she hadn't even found a bottle opener before Sacha came in with Natalie. "Hi! Any trouble finding the place?"

"No, thanks. I've never had a job interview like this before."

Sacha took over the wine opening duties. "I've never interviewed anybody before. You can tell me if I'm doing it right."

Natalie laughed under her breath. "I think offering dinner is a great way to do an interview, personally. My menu tonight was going to be box mac 'n' cheese and an apple."

"I'm so sorry about your husband," Sacha said. He got her a glass of water. "We need to let that breathe for a minute. I'm so sorry about your house. How long had you lived there?"

"Twenty years." Natalie shrugged. "It is what it is. It sucks," she added, "but if the choice was one more try at kicking cancer and a mortgage payment or six, well. There's always a place to live, even if it's a garage apartment. There was only one Leo."

"I'm sorry," Sacha said again. "I'm living here because someone who loved me died. Someone I loved. I would happily live in a garage apartment if he could have been healthy again."

"Were you married?"

"No. It's a long story. And you should hear it so you know what you're getting into." The buzzer went off. Charlie spoke into the intercom. "That'll be our dinner. And tomorrow's dinner. I'm trying to stop doing things one day at a time."

Natalie smiled. "It takes a while." She helped them bring in the vast quantity of containers, helped decide what they'd eat that night, helped set up the dining room. Charlie was nearly silent through dinner, watching and listening. She didn't want to get between Sacha and Natalie. It seemed like they had good chemistry right from the start. And both of them were motivated to make it work. They talked a lot, mostly about Natalie and about the past year of Sacha's life. After a while, Natalie said, "Have you noticed Charlie lately?"

"I notice Charlie all the time," Sacha said. "She's my best friend. She listens."

"My God, does she listen. I was talking to this other teacher at the school, after Charlie came in to do those photographs. He was like, I told her things I never tell anybody. I was like, me too!" Charlie laughed silently. Natalie was smiling. "See, there she goes. So. How did you and Mr. Morgenstern start?"

Sacha gave Charlie a sideways glance. They hadn't discussed how much he should tell Natalie. He didn't want to be like Jerry, a guy who couldn't speak of private things, who hid his true nature and who rarely spoke of his personal history. If Sacha told her everything she would have power over him. Somehow he didn't think she would abuse it. He checked in with both women, refilled the wine glasses. At this point, he knew, Natalie was assuming that he was gay. He wasn't tall, he was slim, he still had that almost-

78

feminine face, and he'd been left an enormous legacy by an older man. Who wouldn't make that assumption? "This is where it gets difficult," he said after a moment. "I want you to know I am not a person who deliberately hurts other people. I go to some lengths to avoid putting other people in a position where they could be hurt." He studied Natalie for a moment, registering comprehension. "But I have done some dangerous and self-destructive things. I came to Los Angeles to be a star. Within a year I was dancing in a bar for tips and turning tricks to make the rent. And for drug money." Drugs to help him sell himself, drugs he could only pay for by selling himself. A classic, vicious cycle. He looked steadily at Natalie. If she could stomach that, he could go on.

The question she asked wasn't the one he expected, which would have been 'did Jerry hire you.' She asked, "How old are you?"

"I'll be thirty-six this year."

He could tell she was doing some mental math, based on what he'd already told her. "So you were twenty-three when your relationship started, which means you were what, twenty-one and change when you came to L.A. You're the same age as my son. Ain't that a kick in the head?" Sacha nodded, smiling. "Look, I've been a teacher for going on forty years. I have seen some really good kids go down really bad roads, and I haven't been able to save them. If Mr. Morgenstern was able to save you, that makes him a good guy in my book."

"In mine, too."

"I'll bet. And frankly, if I thought I could have saved our house by selling my ass, I might have given it a try." Natalie swallowed some more wine.

Charlie laughed, she couldn't help it. "I've had the same thought." Natalie nodded, eyebrows up. "There was a minute after college when I might have been marketable."

Sacha was shaking his head, smiling. "You're beautiful. And you know what's possible with a little makeup."

"Uh, right." Now Charlie cherished the compliment at the same time she realized he was going to tell Natalie about Maggie. She suggested they take a short break, pointed Natalie at one of the bathrooms, and cleared some of the dishes. Then she went to the bathroom herself. *I am not super sober*, she thought, *and if she can't take the next part I may cry*. But so far, Natalie was coming up aces.

They reconvened in the kitchen, where Sacha made coffee. He said, "I'd like to show you the home office. That's where you would be working. But there's something I got ready on the computer this morning. It'll help us get into the next part of why it's going to be strange working for me."

"Sacha," Natalie said with mock reproach, "I work for the Los Angeles Unified School District. Nothing you can throw at me is going to seem strange."

"Hold that thought." They all went down to the office. It was a mess. Sacha didn't apologize for it. He sat behind the desk, asking the women to stand beside him so they could see. He woke up the computer and opened an image file, full-screen. It was a pair of photos. One of him in the tuxedo with Rose Novotny, and one of him at the casino-night fundraiser with Jerry.

Natalie only needed a few seconds. "That's you. Those are both you. I will be damned." She studied Sacha. "You make a beautiful woman."

"Thank you."

"The whole time?" He nodded. Natalie looked back at the pictures. "Okay. So I will confess I spent part of the time before coming over here Googling the address and finding out who lived here, and I saw pictures of Mr. Morgenstern with, well, you." She indicated the picture of Maggie. "And then I saw pictures of you in the past year, when the world was throwing bricks at you. I didn't make the connection. It's no wonder you pulled it off for so long. Why?"

"Let's go to the den, it's more comfortable." Sacha hadn't made that room his own yet, either, but he always felt close to Jerry there. They took their coffee with them, chose seats, sipped in thoughtful silence for a minute. "The tabloids got one thing right. Jerry was gay. He was in the deepest, darkest closet. He was attracted to me. I'm straight, but I loved him. I offered things. Anything and everything. I'd done everything for money, why wouldn't I do it for someone I cared for."

Charlie listened; his tone of voice was matter-of-fact. She watched; his body language was relaxed. She knew that Sacha believed he'd done the right thing. That what he'd offered had been justified, even deserved. That failing to offer the little Jerry could accept would have been cruel to both of them. How could you not help someone you love? She checked in with Natalie, who wasn't reacting. She simply looked thoughtful.

Sacha took a moment, waiting to see if Natalie got that. Apparently she did. He'd already told her enough for her to know that his morals – if not his ethics – were flexible. Helping Jerry had been expedient. It had also been what he wanted to do, and if the help he could offer wasn't something he would ever have chosen to do for someone else, it still had been his choice. He wouldn't tell her that Jerry had been impotent. It wasn't really relevant. "He would only accept certain things. Mostly things that a lot of people don't even consider sex. He never touched me beyond a hug, unless I was Maggie, which was always in public. He let me touch him."

"I noticed that," Natalie said. "There were a lot of photos of the two of you out on the town. He might have his hand on your back, or his arm around you, or even be holding your hand. Never at home?"

"Never."

"Didn't that hurt?"

Oh my God, she really understands. "At first, when I was younger. And then after we knew each other better, and he could tell me a little more, I understood that he was basically a solitary guy. He was very strong-willed, and he played the part of a tough good-humored straight guy really well. His wives did not know. He kept himself apart from everybody, it wasn't only me. But that public life was so important, in his profession. What he truly needed me for was the public relationship. And because he didn't want to be gay, much less to be seen as gay, the fact that I could be Maggie for him was like a miracle. On the red carpet, at charity things, at private dinners. We fooled everybody. He got such a kick out of it. And he loved, really loved, that it was a real relationship. That I was not a hired escort putting on an act, I was there because I cared. He allowed himself to love me, eventually." Sacha took a moment. "His friends were happy for him, they always invited Maggie to whatever. I went whenever we both thought it would be safe." Almost never

82

anything during the day, except the red carpet events. They were never the center of attention there.

"Because you loved him. What about your personal life?"

"I didn't really have one. I have to learn how to have one again. I am not solitary by nature, that's one of a zillion reasons when someone suggested massage, for my job training, I thought yes. I like to be touched. So even though I was the one touching, with massage, at least it was contact. And there was some, with Jerry. It was enough."

Natalie set down her empty coffee cup. "And all that time, you never spoke to the press. You never slipped with his friends. You kept his secret so perfectly that even after this shit broke, and there were pictures of you everywhere, nobody figured it out. Are you going public now?"

"Well." Sacha glanced at Charlie. "My silent partner here figured it out. Charlie suggested I ask one of Jerry's friends for help. We met yesterday. He was expecting Sacha. I was Maggie. He'd met me before, as Maggie. He got it, immediately."

"So if there's anybody out there still inclined to call you a gold-digger, that would pretty much shut them up, huh."

Sacha smiled. "There's that. But Charlie wants to make a film." She made an involuntary movement. "Gary said something about it too. And last night I was thinking, what if we did. What do you think? Would that be fair to Jerry?"

Natalie's eyebrows shot up. "You're seriously asking me for my opinion?"

"Natalie, I've laid this incredible story on you and you haven't even flinched."

"Well, I'm full of really good food and a lot of wine," she pointed out. "Maybe in the morning I'll freak out. I doubt it. I'm not seeing any malfeasance here. Any malice. Any harm to anybody. Just a lot of trust, and loyalty, and love. From both of you. If you want my opinion, that's a story worth telling."

Sacha nodded, swallowing, blinking away tears. "Would you like to see the guest house?"

"Yes. Yes I would."

CHAPTER 5

It was late when Natalie left. There were still some details to iron out, but they could do that the next time she came, or when she moved in. It wasn't urgent. Sacha closed the door behind her, locked it, leaned against it with a sigh. "God, I'm exhausted."

"Me too." Charlie was leaning on the wall. "And all I did was listen."

He huffed out a laugh. "Thanks for calling her. She's perfect."

"We should introduce her to Gary."

Sacha laughed out loud. "We should! We'll invite him over for dinner once she's moved in." Then they both seemed to hear all those 'we' words. "Charlie. Are we a we?"

"I hope so. Even if I'm only your best friend, or your silent partner."

"There's no 'only' there. But you're more than that."

"Let's not try to figure it out yet. We're both worn out." Charlie reached out a hand; he took it; they went through the house to the kitchen. "I was going to make out with you some more tonight, but I'm too tired. Could we do that tomorrow?"

He could tell she wanted to go down the hall to bed. He tugged her close anyway, and hugged her. "You're tired, so I won't kiss you. Tomorrow I'll kiss you. All right?"

"All right."

May 2016

Charlie was pretty sure that if Sacha didn't make the next move very soon, she was going to scream. She was spending four nights out of seven at his house, always in her own room. They had dinner together, they had drinks by the pool, they talked for hours. She showed him the proof copy of her book and that turned into a week of conversations about what she'd learned from the teachers. She saw his body, in the pool, in swim trunks. He saw hers, in a bikini, getting a tan for the first time since college thanks to cautious half-hours before ten or after three. She swam too, learning how to do it properly for the first time thanks to Sacha. She did yoga with him.

They touched a lot. They kissed a lot. The nakedest they'd been when kissing was in the pool, and that particular half-hour had taught Charlie a lot about Sacha's inhuman self-control. She would have had his trunks off, her hand on him, anything, everything. He gave her sex without sex, holding her close and letting her move until she came, gasping against his neck. Still holding her when she said, "Goddammit." Laughing, holding her, until they both relaxed. She wanted to ask why, she wanted to make demands. Maybe it was all part of recovering from Jerry. Maybe it was him getting used to being fully a man – a straight man - again.

She set up three GoPros, put her DSLR on a tripod, and recorded the entire process of creating Maggie, and then the process of taking her apart. It was mind-blowing to see. She'd had some inkling of how much was involved, thanks to having worked on various sets and observed various degrees of makeup and costume art. The fact that he'd been willing to do this, over and over, for *years*, still knocked her out.

Sacha narrated the process, at her request. He said he'd learned to do makeup, for the stage and for film, in college. Student productions couldn't really afford professionals. The facial makeup alone was more than she'd ever learned to do: the primer, the foundation that he blended himself, the shading and bronzer and blush, the powder. The eyes, and the subtle but amazingly effective lips. Maggie hadn't worn bright reds or pinks. She had worn plummy, coppery colors, emphasizing the shape of her mouth without drawing attention away from her eyes. Charlie had never tried colored contact lenses. She asked why Sacha chose the brilliant blue. He said, "Jerry did. Green or purple would have been too obviously artificial. He said, this kind of blue looks like Paul Newman. And then he shrugged and said, or Kurt Cobain, and we both cracked up."

They didn't talk about what to do next with the film. Charlie wasn't an experienced editor. She thought maybe Gary could hook them up with someone. There would be clips from all those awards shows, and other events, that Jerry had attended with Maggie. She had no idea how to get permission to use that material. Sacha didn't seem to be in a hurry.

Natalie moved in halfway through April and started excavating the office. Sacha got her a laptop, two different scanners, a wireless mouse, a second monitor. He said, "Anything you need," but she'd barely thought of something – much less asked for it – before it appeared. He wrote notes, a few at a time, to the dozens of people who'd sent cards after Jerry died, and after the memorial. Natalie sent them out, providing Sacha's new email address. The few people who wrote back were added to his address book. One person who did was Jerry's first wife Brooke. All the people who didn't were simply listed in 'past contacts.' They discussed, briefly, having some kind of meet-and-greet event, somewhere, sometime. The stacks of paper were slowly whittled away.

Charlie asked her once, because she had to be sure Sacha was safe with Natalie, "Are you really okay with this?"

They'd met in the kitchen, where they had both gone to get some coffee. It was an hour before the time they usually ate, and even that was kind of mind-blowing for Charlie: that there was a 'usual' to any part of this. Natalie had taken it in stride, at least after Sacha said 'I don't like eating alone.' Now she regarded Charlie for a moment before saying, "My son was deployed to Afghanistan twice. When he finally came home safe, he could have told me he was Osama bin Laden's love slave and I would not have given a flying fuck. It enrages me on a daily basis that Sacha's parents are shutting him out. He has nothing to fear from me."

"Oh," Charlie said, blinking. "Thank you for knowing what I was really asking."

"I know you love him. He's going to be okay." Natalie patted her shoulder and went out, leaving her speechless.

Natalie's big gray cat Moses learned how to work the lever handles on the guest-house doors, and started taking himself outside. He never left the yard. Charlie took dozens of pictures of him, of Natalie, of the roses. She took video of Sacha lying on the grass and singing 'Moses Supposes' to the cat, playing with his paws, when he was lounging under a rosebush. She was one hundred percent in love.

They still hadn't been to bed when Gary came to dinner. It was almost a month since Natalie had moved in; she had the desk cleared, and most of the office floor, and was starting to look at the shelves with intention rather than with horror. She was still teaching – she didn't want to give that up – but devoted almost every spare minute to building a new life for Sacha out of the scraps of Jerry's old one. She had also mentioned, tentatively, that there might be a book to be written. She was organizing things, in the third bedroom. Letters, notes, marked-up scripts. She said, this is the kind of career that should be documented. Sacha agreed. He would look at all of it later.

Cecilia, the housekeeper, seemed to approve of Natalie and of Charlie. As far as Sacha could tell, she approved of him too. On the day they were expecting Gary, he tracked her down in the kitchen to see if she needed anything. She frowned at him a little, drying her hands. "Four people," she said. "Mr. Swan, if I ever can't fix dinner for four people, fire me." She always called him that, after he told her the Russian root of his name. She liked it because her own name was Cisneros.

"Okay," he said, smiling.

"When you going to ask her to marry you?"

His eyebrows shot up. "¿Que?"

She snorted. "Oh stop it. You so in love, she so in love."

"We haven't even been to bed yet." He had no idea why he said that. He was pretty sure most people did not talk to their household staff about their sex lives. Although, now that he thought about it, maybe they did.

"I know!" Cecilia looked exasperated. "You're not getting any younger."

Sacha couldn't decide if he wanted to laugh or run away. *How the hell does she know, oh my God, don't even think about it.* He couldn't exactly say 'fine, I'll take her to bed tonight,' so he said, "I'm working on it."

"Work faster already. Now go, I gotta finish up here." She shooed him out of the kitchen. Completely at a loss, Sacha went out to the patio and fixed himself a drink. Natalie was at work, Charlie was coming later, he had some time to think this through. He knew he loved Charlie. He thought she loved him. It was reassuring that Cecilia thought so too. The big question was, would Charlie really want to take on everything that would go with being his wife. The tabloids, the gossip, the paparazzi. And on top of that would come the assumption that her career was only a hobby. He wasn't sure he could stand for that.

So far he wasn't going out much, and when he did he was intentionally nondescript. He drove a boring car. He dressed well, but not to attract attention. He was simply an average man of average height with average hair. But if he and Charlie went out together, they would be noticed. He wouldn't hide then. He would dress to be seen, he would dress her to impress. If she would let him. It was another big question.

It was time, he realized, to start answering those questions. Because he did want to take her to bed, very soon. Immediately, in fact. And if that went as well as he expected, he was going to ask her to marry him.

Gary hadn't been to the Morgenstern house for a long time, and didn't remember much about it. There was nothing particularly special about the architecture or the landscaping. When he'd been there last, about three years ago, it was for a cocktail party. Maggie hadn't been there. Jerry's housekeeper Cecilia had been the hostess, efficient and unobtrusive.

She was different now, laughing, in charge. Sacha's friend Charlie was there, and she was also different. Not the quiet (if occasionally snarky) observer she'd been at Ocean Prime. Gary immediately thought *they are in love* and the thought was pleasing. He didn't think Sacha had anything left to prove about loyalty. There was a fourth person, too, the personal assistant Sacha told him about. She wasn't young, as he'd halfway expected from 'teacher.' She had gray hair done in a shoulder-length French braid, and was wearing jeans with a sleeveless top that looked knitted, or maybe crocheted, Gary didn't know. Only that it was made of something that looked touchable, and that there was the slightest hint of something silky underneath. *Whoa*, he thought, smiling into her friendly brown eyes as he said hello.

Then there was Sacha. Not Maggie, and not the Sacha who'd been photographed countless times during the whole estate fracas. This Sacha seemed taller, stronger, more physical. Charismatic. Looking straight at Gary with those extraordinary eyes - blue-gray, he noticed - and smiling. This Sacha wouldn't have surprised anybody as a rich man's lover. Even his hair seemed brighter. "How the hell do you do that?" Gary asked at some point.

Charlie answered. "This is the real guy. That drab thing he does, that's so people don't pay attention. That's Verbal Kint."

Sacha was smiling, shaking his head. Gary laughed until he choked. "Why weren't you this way at the memorial, and all that shit after?"

"The only reason I even went to the memorial was to hear what people said about Jerry. Stories I hadn't heard. I knew there would be some. And after, because it would have made things worse," Sacha said. "All those people, a lot of them anyway, they knew Maggie. They might have made the connection, and they would have felt deceived. They *were* deceived. They didn't know I existed. If I seemed like somebody they should have noticed, they would have been even angrier. At Jerry," he added. "Everybody hated me already because of the money. I didn't want them to hate Jerry too."

Incredible, Gary thought for approximately the millionth time, this time because the guy's social intelligence was so acute. It really was no wonder they'd pulled it off for so long. "Okay, yeah. Sit on that until you can control the conversation. So is Maggie going public, like, ever?"

Sacha glanced at Charlie. "Well, you remember what you said about a documentary?"

Charlie wasn't surprised that Gary was thrown by Sacha's transformation. She might have been herself if she hadn't been there for the whole thing, watching as he gradually came to grips with his massive life change. Not simply with the legacy, but with what it represented: Jerry's totally unexpected proof of love.

She couldn't help noticing that something else was different about Sacha at dinner that night. Part of it was doubtless because Gary was there, being charming to Natalie and demanding updates. There wasn't really much to report, aside from Charlie's film. Gary wanted to see it. She said, making an 'eek' face, "It's not edited. It's literally just rough footage from three separate cameras. It's a mess, I have no idea what I'm doing. The only reason I even thought of making a film was because of Sacha and Maggie. Do you know any editor or filmmaker or whatever people?"

"Charlie," he said, with a look of sorrow, "I have been working in Hollywood for longer than you've been alive. What do you think?"

"You don't seem that old," she said, mostly because she knew he would laugh. So did Natalie.

"That old! That old, she says." Gary drank half of his wine, then set down the glass and stared at it. "What the hell is that?"

"Something from the pantry," Sacha said. He reached over to the sideboard for the bottle, set it on the table, turned the label toward Gary.

"Fuck me! I just guzzled that like it was Gnarly Head." Gary picked up the bottle, showing it some respect. Natalie was laughing again. "Do you have any more of this?"

"There's most of a case." Charlie wasn't sure how to get the conversation back to her film of Sacha. On the other hand, apparently Gary was open to being bribed with wine. "I'll bet Sacha would let me give you a bottle if you hook me up with a filmmaker."

"Mi casa es tu casa. Give him whatever it takes." Sacha was leaning back, smiling at her. It wasn't the first time he'd said that, about his house being her house. She knew he would be happy if she stayed over more often. She was starting to think he might ask her to move in. But they still hadn't been to bed. She wondered if her face said 'I'd like to give you whatever it takes.' His changed, and not in a bad way. The smile was still there, but it was the one that said 'I really want to kiss you.' Charlie inhaled on a sudden certainty that tonight was the night.

She couldn't have said, afterward, what else they talked about. She knew Gary promised her some leads. She was aware that he and Natalie talked, a lot, in the den over coffee while she sat and sort-of watched and almost listened. While Sacha watched all of them, especially her, with the cat on his lap.

"How did Moses get in?" Charlie asked, possibly out of nowhere.

"Cecilia saw him in the garden and asked him if he wanted some chicken mole, and because he is a world-class moocher he said sure! Be right there!" Natalie was shaking her head. "And then Sacha didn't throw him out."

"He's always welcome. I haven't had a pet since I lived with my parents."

"Yeah. How's that going?" Gary knew there was weirdness. Charlie had told him a little bit about it, one time on the phone when she'd picked up instead of Sacha because Sacha had gotten a hateful email from a cousin and didn't want to talk to anybody.

"They're still mostly shitheads," Charlie said. "Maybe if we get this film put together, and get it released, and if they actually watch it instead of getting all their news from the tabloids, they might stop being such shitheads."

"Ugh." Gary picked up his coffee cup, noticed it was empty, and sighed. "I should get going. This has been really nice, thanks for the invitation. Any time you want to open another bottle of that stuff, let me know, I can get here in twenty minutes. Or less."

Sacha said, "How about two weeks from tonight? Dinner again. We might have more to report by then."

Gary stopped halfway into standing up, looking surprised, as if he hadn't really expected to be asked back. He glanced at Natalie, at Charlie, then back at Sacha. "I'd be delighted. No no, don't get up, you have Moses the Moocher." He shook hands with Sacha, then with Charlie. Natalie was standing up. "You'll walk me out? Thanks."

Charlie waited until they were well down the hall before saying, "That was subtle."

"Wasn't it? Both of them." He smiled at Charlie. Moses woke up, stretched, and hopped down. Sacha stood up and went to the door. "I'm going to organize things for Cecilia. Can we talk after Natalie goes home?"

Oh yes. "Can we talk in your room?" Charlie said softly.

"Can you stay?" He always asked.

Forever. "Yeah, I can stay."

"Then I'll meet you in my room." For a moment she thought he was going to abandon the dining room, the kitchen, whatever. He could have. Cecilia was as apt to scold him as thank him for doing any housework. But she knew he wouldn't leave it. That was one of the reasons she loved him. She watched him go. A minute later she went out, down to 'her' bathroom, which now had duplicates of her stuff in it because that was easier than schlepping things back and forth. *Who am I kidding*, she thought. If he started to say 'would you move' she would say yes before he ever got to 'in with me.' Even though it was still awfully early, and still awfully risky, and if it didn't work out she was going to be awfully screwed because her apartment was rent-controlled and she'd never find another one that affordable in that neighborhood. She took a breath, finished washing up, took another breath. Studied herself. He knew so much about her by now. Everything important, except what he was about to learn. *Is this the face of a millionaire's girlfriend, lover ... wife?*

Maybe it was. Charlie put on her silk nightgown, a garment she had not owned until she started staying over here. Sacha hadn't seen it. Every time she'd spent the night she'd chickened out and gone with a long tee shirt. Every time, she'd put on yoga pants before going out to the kitchen. Now she put the matching velvet robe on, because the gown was kind of bare and she didn't want to be too obvious and she was kind of shivering. Finally, because she wasn't sure he would have thought of this, or maybe planned for it, she put a strip of condoms in the pocket of the robe, and went down the hall. The house was silent. Natalie must have gone home. Charlie looked out the window and confirmed. She could see the older woman moving in the guest house, a silhouette behind the French doors. There was a light in Sacha's room, at the end of the hall.

Sacha didn't want to be too obvious. He didn't want to be creepy. So even though he was hoping to be naked very soon, he wasn't naked when Charlie came in. He was sitting cross-legged in the middle of the bed, wearing a tank top and lightweight yoga pants that she'd seen many times before. He'd never seen the nightgown. "You look beautiful," he said softly. "What did I want to talk about?"

She smiled. "I don't know. Was it maybe that mi casa stuff?"

He patted the bed. She hiked up her skirt and joined him, sitting cross-legged in front of him. He reached forward so he could rest his fingertips on her knees. "Mi casa that I wish you would stay in forever. The only reason I haven't asked you is because we haven't done this before." 'This' was obviously 'being in bed,' and everything that might be expected to follow. "And the only reason we haven't done this before is because I don't know what I'm doing. About any of this."

"That's basically why I haven't thrown myself at you," Charlie admitted. "I mean, aside from that business in the pool." He smiled. "It's been such a huge change, and following such a major trauma, and following all those years when you weren't being fully yourself. I want you to want me for me, not for being familiar and safe."

"I wanted you a year ago. But all those reasons not to get involved with someone before, they still existed."

"I know." Charlie wriggled closer and put her hands on his. "And it's been, what, fourteen years since you were with a woman?"

Sacha closed his eyes and exhaled. He turned his hands under hers, his fingers contacting her palms. "Yes."

"I know you like kissing me."

"I love kissing you." Eyes open now, gazing into hers. "I love your body. I love your face. I love you." He had to say it. Couldn't not say it. He'd been wanting to say it for so long. But he was terrified, because he didn't want her to think he meant it the same way he meant it when he said he loved Jerry.

Charlie was smiling. "What else do you love about me? Because I could listen to that all night."

All right then. "I love your talent, and your sense of humor. Your compassion, and your loyalty. Your willingness to drink marshmallow vodka. Your ability to listen, and the way when you talk it's always about something. I love how you don't judge people. I love the way you challenge yourself. I love that you'll bribe a Hollywood agent with a bottle of wine or make a joke with a fancy lawyer in a terrifying situation. I love that you saw me," he said intensely.

Charlie leaned in to kiss him and the next thing he knew they were sprawled across the bed, hands all over each other, gasping into each other's mouths and making hungry little noises. They both lost track of time. She was on top of him for a minute, so Sacha stroked his hands over her shoulders, skimming the robe off. Then she was propped on her elbows, mouth against his throat. She moved against him and they both said "*Jesus*."

"Oh God Sacha. I love you." She slid off to one side and put her hand on him. "This, my God."

He turned to his side, got a handful of silk and tugged up the nightgown. She still had her hand on him, stroking through the yoga pants. He was losing his mind. His hand was on her now, between her legs, where she was hot and wet. "I'm not going to make it," he said tightly. "I need to take the edge off."

"Take it off. Take anything off."

"You too." He sat up, stripped off the tank top, then the pants. Collapsed on his back with his cock in his hand.

"Not by yourself," she said. "Not now." She was naked too. "Not anymore." She had her mouth on his chest, her leg between his, and her hand under his, cupping his balls. He knew she was watching. "Sacha. Hurry."

His body jerked. The surging release, the gasp at her teeth on his nipple. "Jesus *Christ*."

"God Almighty, no wonder Jerry wanted to see that. Kiss me." Her mouth was right there, so he did, turning to her and wrapping her in his arms for a long minute as his breath settled. She was urgent against him.

He moved down her body, kissing everything he could, everything he'd been craving. "Beautiful." Mouth on her breasts, listening to her reaction, learning what she liked. More areola, less nipple, a whimper. Then moving down again. Teeth on the bottom edge of her rib cage, that made her gasp and squirm. Tongue in her navel, she grabbed his hair. And then his mouth on her, the taste of her, she was drenched with wanting him. He licked through that wetness. Pressed her thigh back with one hand, the other thumb stroking lightly above the clitoris, something he hazily remembered from long ago and three thousand miles away. She was panting, exhalations sharp and vocal. Then he closed his mouth on her and she screamed. He felt her contraction, felt her pulse, and closed his eyes. Didn't move, didn't change anything, until the pulse faded. He was hard again.

"Kiss me," she said faintly.

"If I move to your mouth I'll be in you."

"Condom. By the pillow. Now."

"Will you come again?"

"Like I know? Sacha, *kiss me*." She flailed, found the strip of condoms. Sort of threw them at him. He caught them. Ripped open a wrapper, rolled on the condom, and moved up between her legs. Mouth still wet from her. She pulled him down, made a small moaning sound at the taste of herself. Then he sank in and she said "Oh God" into his mouth.

He felt her grip him, felt every inch of himself and every breath of her. Mindless, reduced to nothing but sensation. Kissing hard, deep, slow as he moved, able now to savor it, starting to concentrate again when her breath hitched and her foot hooked over his thigh. *Yes you will*, he thought, the first conscious thought for a while, and kept doing what he was doing because it was going to work for her and when it did he would go too. *Yes.* "Yes. Charlie." That whimper, she was panting again. Then she clutched at him and cried out and he came again, inside her, part of her.

Collapsing to the side. Breathing hard. Relaxing, reaching for the tank top to get rid of the condom because he hadn't thought of a towel. *It's all just laundry*, he thought, and almost laughed because unless he wanted to know that Cecilia knew, he needed to do the laundry himself.

"What's so funny." Charlie sounded stoned.

"Cecilia. Today. She told me to quit wasting time." Charlie laughed. "She said, you're not getting any younger." He was laughing too. "Will you marry me?"

"Yes." She patted him randomly.

"Even though you're going to have to deal with paparazzi, and all the lawyers in the world, and my family?"

"Honey, I have news for you."

"What."

"My family's worse than yours." Charlie rolled to her side so she could see his face. "My dad is an administrator for a community college. My mother is a bookkeeper for a church. I have three siblings, and they are all religious nutjobs. They live in Indiana. All of which is one reason I live in Los Angeles."

He turned to his side and they stared at each other. After a moment he said, "That sounds like more than one reason." She laughed again. Sacha smiled. "My God, I feel like a new person."

"I know! Me too." Her smile faded. "Do you want me to sign a pre-nup? I probably should."

"No, of course not." He hoped he didn't sound insulted. Then he got worried. "Unless you really think this might not work out."

"I don't. I mean, I don't really think that. But I don't even know, like, *anything*." That word encompassed so much. The properties, the other investments, the income. They simply hadn't talked about it. Sacha knew she was right. He barely understood all of it himself.

"Okay," he said slowly. "Okay. Let's take some time and bring you up to speed. Make sure we both know what's really going on, what 'normal' really is in this situation. Make sure we're on the same page with things. And one thing I'll do for you right away is a trust. So that if something happens to me before we get married, or you decide this is too much, or you just don't want to do it anymore, you can afford to live. I'm doing one for my family anyway," he said, foreseeing a protest. "I'll ask Frank to start one for you. Because I love you."

"I love you too." She didn't argue about the trust. They both knew as soon as the world found out about them – and it would, it was kind of surprising that it hadn't already – her commercial business would dry up. She would get calls only from people who wanted to be celebrity-adjacent.

Sacha kissed her again. "As soon as it's done, you'll move in with me? Because I'm greedy now. I want you here."

"I want to be here. I can do that deal." Charlie pressed close. "That was some really high-quality sex.

You must have been thinking about it for a while." Sacha laughed and kissed her forehead. Then he groped around for that velvet robe and pulled it over both of them.

They talked again in the morning, briefly. Charlie asked, "Are you going to tell your parents?"

"Of course." Sacha was a little surprised, then realized she didn't know what he'd told them so far. "Do you have time for coffee?"

"And breakfast," she said. So they went to the kitchen, where Cecilia already had coffee made. She offered to cook them something. "You're busy with our mess from last night. We can handle it." Charlie had one of those moments, realizing this was how it was going to be. If she never wanted to cook her own breakfast again, she probably didn't have to. She made big 'this is weird' eyes at Sacha and he laughed under his breath. Then he told her to go sit down, brought her some coffee, and assembled some breakfast.

"My parents know about you already," he said after a while. "They know we've been friends since last year. Once we got back in touch I told them I was seeing you. My mother, I think, is pretending that Jerry was like an uncle, or a godfather. My brother hasn't had much to say and my father, well." Not quite a shrug.

"Is he talking to you at all yet?"

"Not really. Mom says, your father says hello. That kind of thing. Anyway, she said she was glad to hear I was seeing someone, she didn't like to think of me out here all by myself."

"Sacha." Charlie wasn't sure she should ask this question. *He loves me*, she reminded herself. If they

102

were going to get married, they needed to be able to talk about everything. "Why did they let things get so bad? Why couldn't you go home?"

Sacha wasn't ready to tell her the whole truth, so he told her a version of what he'd told Jesús all those years ago. "They didn't know how bad it was. I never told them. I was too proud to ask for help until I was such a mess I basically couldn't. Neither of them wanted me to come out here. I couldn't think of a way to go back," he finished in a rush.

Charlie could tell he hadn't meant to say that, didn't really want to say that. He wasn't talking about the logistics. She put her hand on his. "Okay. It's okay. When you tell them we're engaged, tell them I said hello and I hope to meet them soon."

He studied her for a moment. "Maybe by the end of the year they'll be over all this."

"Maybe by the end of the year I won't want to smack your dad and say, you know your son didn't do anything wrong, right?" Charlie shook her head. "We'll be okay."

"Yeah. We'll be okay."

Natalie wasn't the least bit surprised when Sacha told her Charlie would be moving in soon. She was a little bit surprised when he asked her about Gary. "What about him?" she said, stalling.

"Well, it seemed as though he liked you a lot. I like him, and he seems to like me too, so he'll probably be part of my life. I wanted to be sure you'll be comfortable if he's around."

Oh, she thought, charmed. "He definitely likes you too. I think he's a little surprised by how much he likes you, but he's rolling with it." She watched Sacha try not to laugh. He was sitting on the edge of his desk, a thing it was now possible to do without precipitating a paper avalanche. "You're a little younger than his son. They have kind of a scratchy relationship. He might feel as though he's getting a second chance with you."

That was unexpected. "Really? We haven't talked about his family."

Natalie answered the silent question. "We haven't either, really, it was this quick info dump when I walked him out. How old he is, how long he's been divorced, the basics on his kids. I gave him the same kind of thing. I like him a lot. I've never met anyone like him."

Sacha didn't ask what she meant by that, or what it meant that they'd shared their personal histories. He didn't want to get pushy, and the important question was settled. So he said, "I haven't either," which was true, and changed the subject.

Frank and his team were good, but Sacha wasn't their only client, so the paperwork took longer than he would have liked. They haggled a little bit over funding the trusts. Frank suggested one number beginning with 'm,' the same for the Lebedev family and for Charlie. Sacha said, "Two for my family. Four for Charlie."

Frank said, "Are you sure? You aren't even married."

"That's why," Sacha said. "The estate plan isn't done. If something happens to me, this has to be *enough*." They both knew it was going to take about six months to get the estate plan finished, because a full audit wasn't even finished yet. There were cost and cash-flow and tax projections to generate. There were tenants to be considered and contracts to be reviewed. There were insurance policies to choose. There was Cecilia, and now Natalie, to be accounted for, and an executor to choose. Sacha knew all too well how important that was.

Frank promised to wrap things up as soon as possible, saying, "I agree with you. It's my job to make you think twice."

"I know, Frank, thanks." They were all making him think twice, or three times, about almost everything. Nothing made him think Charlie wasn't the right choice.

CHAPTER 6

Charlie was at the house with Sacha almost every night now. Always bringing something with her, because why wait. She told him how empty her apartment was getting. "How does it look?" he asked.

"Horrible. I remember now how ugly I thought it was when I first moved in. I was all, how many posters will it take to hide all this hideous beige. I like this new lounger."

"I like it too." A double, one that they could lie on together. Sacha supposed it was possible they could be seen from some angles. He didn't care, and apparently neither did Charlie. The first time they made love outside he thought he saw a shooting star. On this particular evening he had the back set at a nice angle for holding Charlie in one of his arms, reclining against his chest. She had a glass of that unspeakable marshmallow vodka with soda, and he had a gin and tonic. "I never asked what brought you to Los Angeles. I mean, I know why you left Indiana, but that's not the same thing."

She laughed under her breath. "No, not quite. I had a friend." She swallowed some vodka, put the glass aside, and patted Sacha's hand. "He was the one out gay kid in my high school. He didn't go to college, and we kind of lost touch. When I came home after graduation I ran into him at a bar. I met up with some other friends from high school and he was there serving. He looked terrible. I got him alone and asked how he was. He said he was HIV positive. He was pretty sure he'd gotten it from some guy who picked him up at a truck stop. He was uninsured. His parents weren't helping him at all. He wasn't getting any of the drugs that could have helped keep him healthy. He said, the minute anybody knows, I'm going to lose this job. He shrugged. He said it didn't matter. That he didn't have anything to live for anyway. Sacha, I felt like the worst person in the world. For forgetting about him when I went away. I mean we weren't super close, but we were friends. He was so cute and funny and, you know, harmless. Basically the opposite of most of those redneck sports nuts." She picked up her glass again and drained it. Sacha was petting her arm, saying nothing. Charlie thought back over the years to that conversation. She thought about the joke Gary had made, about his white knight moment when he realized Maggie was Sacha. She turned her head and Sacha kissed her. She smiled. "I did a Gary." His eyebrows went up. "I was like, how can I help you. Where do you want to go. Let's get out of here, let's find you something to live for."

"What did he say?"

"He said, are you out of your mind? I said yes and, like, ditched my other friends. Didn't even say goodbye. I grabbed his hand and said, fuck this place, let's go. He let me drag him out of there. He was untying his server apron and he handed it to the hostess on our way out, and there were tears pouring down his face but he was laughing. Laughing!" Charlie wiped her eyes. "His name was Steve. Steve Candler. I said you know what Steve, there was no chance in hell I was going to stay in this town. We went back to my house, and I told my parents I was moving out. Packed up my car. They were like, what the what." Sacha laughed. "They still don't know what happened. I had a little money from my college job and I had a credit card. We got in the car and I said, okay, where. He looked at me and said, let's go to Hollywood. I said okay." The rest of the getting-out-of-town story was unimportant.

"What happened to him?" Sacha assumed Steve was dead now. Otherwise, he knew, they would have met. Charlie wouldn't have let this story go untold if the person involved were still her living friend.

"He had six years," she said. "We found a cheap apartment. I got a job right away. We hooked him up with AIDS Project Los Angeles, they found him a part-time job and some healthcare. Once we'd been here for a while he was able to get more. But the virus had its hooks in him. He died six years ago of pneumonia."

"Were you still roommates then?"

"No, he had a boyfriend he was living with. It wasn't a forever of torture like poor Jerry. He went fast." She wiped her face again. "The boyfriend was sweet, but we didn't stay in touch. He wasn't HIV positive, can you believe it? They were careful. I learned a lot from Steve. He heard about some of my college stupidity and said, you need to get tested. So I got tested every year for five years and then the clinic said you know what, if there's no trace of it now I think we can call it."

"That's what they told me too. I wasn't always careful, or rather the people who picked me up weren't always careful. I had other things, but none of the viruses. I was lucky."

"I didn't want to ask." Charlie turned her head again so they could see each other's eyes. "I should have asked, but I love you and ultimately I didn't care, I was going to be with you anyway. I had a cold sore once and freaked out. Went to the clinic, they tested it, they said it's not that kind of herpes, take Vitamin C and manage your stress better and there's a good chance it won't recur. So I did, and it didn't." Sacha kissed her again. "The things we talk about, I swear."

"We need to. We need to talk about everything. What did you think of that report Marisa gave me?" He'd finally gotten one that made complete sense.

"That was so great! Writing out all the numbers like that!" Instead of a table of figures, it was short paragraphs of text. Eight thousand instead of 8000, which Charlie knew Sacha was apt to read as 800 or 3000 or anything but what it actually was. "I never knew that could work."

"Neither did I. I guess dyslexia is different for everybody. I feel smarter now." He was smiling against her hair.

"You're plenty smart."

"I guess. I barely got into college. My major didn't call for much math. Every job I tried to get out here, I felt like a moron. Everything required math, such simple math a six-year-old could do it. I basically made change by knowing the size of each coin and the face of each president on the bills. It's like, I knew this many George Washingtons would make change for an Abraham Lincoln. Even using a calculator didn't help because it was the damn numbers again."

"I wonder if there's a calculator that you can punch in one zero zero and it spells out one hundred."

"Who knows." They were quiet for a minute. "So I think the papers will be signed next week." Charlie nestled closer, turning so she could wrap an arm around him. Sacha kissed her hair.

"I am not bringing any furniture," she said. "Mine is all garbage. I'm going to need some help hauling books and my image files, though."

"I'll call Royal for you."

"If you do that, we're going to be in the tabloids."

"I don't care. I'm so glad you're going to live with me." He tipped her face up and kissed her again.

Natalie ended up handling the face-to-face parts of Charlie's move. She was at the apartment to direct traffic on moving day, and went back the next day to meet 1-800-Got-Junk. Charlie fidgeted in the Hollywood Hills until the Royal truck arrived, and then Cecilia wouldn't let her do anything until the movers were gone. "This is weird," she said to Sacha, tracking him down in the den. "I have never even hired movers before."

"There's a lot that's not great about this situation," he said, patting the couch. She sat down next to him, thinking about the continuing shitheadedness of his family and the periodic gossip attacks online, and saying nothing about those things. Sacha picked up her hand and kissed it. "But being able to hire things done, things that are no fun, is great."

"Yes it is. It's just weird."

"I was going to ask you to help me redecorate. Is that weird?"

Charlie stared at him. He kept surprising her. She knew that the house held a lot of memories, mostly good. "What did you have in mind?"

"Nothing in this room yet. I'm not ready for that. But we never use the main living room. It has a wet bar, and those doors close it off from the dining room. That could be your office. What do you think?"

The living room overlooked the front yard, which wasn't very inspiring. Though who knew, maybe

Sacha had plans for that too. The room had wall to wall carpet, which Charlie hated. Otherwise, it was great. The wood-framed glass pocket doors let in a ton of light from the dining room, which was in a corner of the house and had two walls of windows. The wet bar had built-in cabinets, enough counter space for a coffeemaker, and a mini refrigerator. Floor to ceiling bookcases surrounded the big picture window, making a window seat long enough to nap on. The whole interior wall could be workstation, storage, a layout table. There would be enough open floor space to work with models. Charlie felt her horizons expand. "Can I rip out the carpet?"

"God, yes, I hate it." He smiled, watching her laugh. "Those drapes too, please."

"Jesus, yes. What else do you want to rip out?"

"We'll re-do the master, don't you think?" It had been Jerry's room, but his personality didn't live there. Sacha wanted to make it *their* room. "But first we need to go through all the books. You might want to keep some of those. I've already read most of them. I didn't have much else to do for a while."

Charlie grimaced at that. She knew all about those lonely, dazed months after Jerry's memorial, before the estate was settled. "All those celebrity memoirs. Did Jerry read them?"

Sacha made a face. "Kind of. Enough that if he met one of those people, he'd be able to say he read it." Charlie laughed.

She sat and thought for a few minutes. Her own apartments had been furnished from thrift shops and IKEA. "I'm not sure I know how to shop for an actual house."

"Only one way to find out." They smiled at each other. "You could watch a ton of HGTV and see if that gives you any ideas."

"Oh my God I forgot, you get all the channels. Oh honey you're never going to get me out of this room." He was laughing. "What are *you* planning to do with yourself?"

"I'm in how-to-be-a-millionaire school. I'm not bored with that yet. Plus I'm busy being in love with you." Charlie leaned over for a kiss. "I'm thinking. There are things I used to love that I haven't done for a long time. There are things that always sounded like fun that I never thought I could afford. Once you're settled in, we'll see if any of those are things you want to take time away from your work for."

"You know," she said, "a lot of my work was only to make money. I would happily never shoot another charity gig again, or another wedding, or another portfolio, even if I could, which I kind of can't, which is fine." She let herself think out loud, because she knew Sacha wouldn't mind, and might enjoy it, and would be there for whatever she wanted to do. "I really loved doing the teachers book. I might want to do a show about that. I've never done a show. And I've never been able to travel. Is that something you want to do?"

"As a matter of fact it is." He gazed at her, smiling. "Guess I should get a passport."

"Jesus, me too!"

The next time they saw Gary, they had a lot of news, starting with Charlie moving in and then about the film. "So thanks for the tip about Patrick," Charlie said, while they were hanging around in the kitchen getting in Cecilia's way. "I called him. He does have connections. The woman who manages his husband's dance studio is married to this guy Tony, who makes a series for Ovation. And Tony is making his own documentary about dancers associated with the studio. But he said it's not super hot right now, something about competition partners not being ironed out. He's only following one couple, which happens to be his wife and her partner. Anyway, he said he could look at one of the tapes and let me know if he thought it might be pitchable. And if it is, then he'll help me put together a pitch. So that's where we're at on that. I'm taking the tape over on Sunday."

Gary listened to all this with a smile. "Are you going to get to see any of his work?"

"Well I've been mainlining the Ovation thing ever since we talked. It's called 'Live Work Dance.' I get the idea he doesn't do a hundred percent of the actual taping, and he doesn't do the voice-over, though I do not know why because oh my God that accent." The filmmaker was Italian. "But he does the rough cut of every episode. I'm hoping he'll let me sneak a peek at some of his footage because then we'd be able to tell if his approach is what I had in mind, you know, for talking to Sacha."

"You're not going to do that yourself? You're such a good interviewer." Natalie sounded disapproving. "And it's not like you're not comfortable with your subject." Sacha snorted. She glanced at him. "Are you going to this meeting?" He nodded. "Well, let me know if you need me to do anything. I'm about to start on the file cabinets otherwise."

"I have a job for you actually," Sacha said. "Marisa says I need to give some money away. I don't want to give it to the things Jerry gave it to."

"Why's that." Gary picked up the wine glass that had appeared by his hand. "Is this the good stuff or can I guzzle it?"

"This is the good stuff," Charlie said. "We'll put a guzzle bottle on the table for dinner."

"Well," Sacha said, answering Gary's first question, "Jerry's charities were all the big healthcare ones, you know, they do the big events and all the rich people get dressed up and have fun and throw money. Fine, whatever. I went to a lot of those. But nobody, *nobody* associated with those was there for him. He gave a lot of money, they knew who he was, but he was only a wallet to them. They've been coming at me the same way. So screw them. I want to give money to people who will appreciate it. Or who really need it." He glanced at Charlie. "AIDS Project Los Angeles, for sure. Then I thought you might help me find other people," he said to Natalie. "Isn't there something for teachers?"

"Donors Choose," she said. "Teachers post their projects and how much they need. It's crowd-funding, like Kickstarter, only for classrooms."

"That sounds perfect."

"Kickstarter's a good way to get rid of money, too," said Gary. "There's a lot of bullshit projects but also some cool ones. I know Jerry did a few of those. We both helped fund one back in 2012, a play here in town."

"I remember." A ghost of a smile from Sacha. "I went to the wrap party."

"Oh my God that's right you did." Gary laughed into his glass. "Where did all those dresses go?"

"I still have them. The fourth bedroom is like a Maggie museum right now."

"I told him to keep all her stuff," Charlie said. "In case this film project goes anywhere, it could come in handy."

"Go to the dining room," Cecilia said impatiently. "Some of us work here." They moved out on a chorus of 'oops' and 'sorry' and 'jeez okay.' Sacha was laughing again.

"So what's new with you, Gary." Natalie made sure he had water, topped up his glass with the good stuff, then emptied the bottle into the other glasses. "Jeez, I'm getting spoiled really fast around here."

"Good," he said. "Me too. Uh, let's see, what's new, well actually I decided to retire." He sat back and listened to the chorus of astonishment. "Well, I'm sixty-eight, and while it is still possible to be entertained by the dreck and drivel that comes over the threshold on a daily basis, I am getting tired of trying to sell it. There's a lot of interesting stuff going on and I've been on the wrong side of it. Somebody offered me a gig on the other side." He told them about a streaming platform that was building its development and acquisitions teams. "I'll be choosing things. Who knows, maybe I'll want to pick up a documentary about the most confusing love affair in the history of cross-dressing. But you have to get it finished within a reasonable amount of time, because at seventy-two I'm retiring for real."

Natalie said, "Why seventy-two?"

"Because that's how old my father was when he died. I figure if I make it that long, I've got a good chance of another ten years, and I'd like to be a lazy son of a bitch for ten years. Hang out at the country club and gripe about how my kids never come to see me. Call up the ex-wife and give her shit about her latest plastic surgery. Maybe chase some hot young schoolteacher around." He was smiling at Natalie. She was blushing.

Charlie glanced at Sacha. "Those sound like great plans, Gary. If Tony and I hit it off, I think we can find a sucker to help us make this documentary."

"I'm sure you can. Speaking of which, when are you two getting married?"

Charlie nearly did a spit take. Sacha was bent over the table laughing. He didn't even try to answer for a minute. Finally he sat back and wiped his eyes. "Why is everyone asking me that lately? Oh my God." He was saved by Cecilia, bringing in dinner. They didn't return to that subject till dessert and coffee were on the table. "Thanks, Cecilia. I'll clean up."

"I know. Good night, hasta mañana." She went out, patting Natalie on the way.

"So who is everyone?" Gary never lost track of a conversation. Charlie rolled her eyes. Natalie shook her head and drank some coffee.

Sacha looked around the table and thought, *family.* "You. Natalie. Cecilia. Marisa. Patrick. Frank. Rose Novotny, who I saw last week."

"How does she even know who the hell I am?" Charlie said, amazed.

"She remembers you from the event in Irvine. She remembered that I laughed, when we were talking."

"Did you not laugh very much?"

"No, not last year."

"Yeah," she said, hand on his. "I guess not. Anyway, Gary, the question has been asked and answered but we have a lot of shit to figure out first. We will keep you posted."

"I promise, Gary," Sacha said. "You'll be the first to know."

They were meeting filmmaker Tony Benedetti at his home, an apartment in West Hollywood. He told them he worked at home, he had a big screen to view Charlie's footage, and after their meeting they could go down the street to an Italian restaurant he could recommend. Charlie was certain that after a couple of hours listening to him talk, Italian would be the only possible choice. Sacha said, "Do I need to learn Italian?"

She pretended to consider it. Then she realized that was actually a great idea. "We both should. I'd love to go to Italy. We need to see Venice. And Rome. We could go winetasting. Oh my God, I could stalk George Clooney at Lake Como." Now she was pretending to put that on her to-do list, and pretending not to notice Sacha laughing.

They followed Tony's advice and parked behind the Shall We Dance studio owned by Patrick's husband, then walked down the street to the apartment building. Charlie texted to let Tony know they were almost there; he met them downstairs. "Charlie? And Sacha." They all shook hands. "Come up, I'm looking forward to seeing your tape."

"That is literally all it is," Charlie said. "I hope you can tell me there's a way to turn it into a proper film."

"Why did you take it?" Tony asked, then interrupted himself. "But first, would you like coffee? Yes? Cream or sugar? Bene. Make yourselves at home." He turned to the tiny kitchen. The apartment was like many one-bedrooms in Los Angeles, with a single room for cooking, eating, and lounging, attached to the bedroom and bathroom. Tony's home office occupied about half the available space. His big work screen could be seen from any angle; three smaller ones stood in a row beneath it.

Charlie answered the first question while they let Tony play host. "I took the video because I wasn't sure Sacha would want to do it later. He was in a pliable kind of mood at the time." Sacha was laughing under his breath. "Of course, since then, I have discovered he is very easy to work with almost all the time." Tony laughed from the kitchen. "So if this tape is useless, maybe I have time to educate myself for a do-over."

"It's not going to be useless," Sacha said. "I think the real question is, will anybody be interested in the subject matter."

"You know they will be. Gary and Natalie both said so. Thanks, Tony. Wow, that smells good." Charlie sipped the coffee. "Oh yum. Tony, those people I just mentioned, that's Sacha's assistant Natalie who is super-smart, and Gary Fisher who used to be a big shot writers' agent and is commencing to be a big shot acquisitions director." She could tell Tony perked up at that. She told him what streaming platform it was, and he got even more interested. "Anyway. This is a long-ass recording," she warned. "And I made poor Sacha talk all the way through it, so you might want to skip through, and then if there's any background you need in order to tell me whether it's useless, we could cover that later?"

"Good. All I know is who you are," he said, looking at Sacha. "And the little Charlie told me on the phone. There is only one question before we begin. Did you consider this a performance, or was this a lifestyle?"

"Performance. But it was a very important part of Mr. Morgenstern's life. And only a few people know about it, the truth of it."

Tony nodded, and held out his hand for the data card. Charlie gave it to him, feeling more nervous than she expected. She glanced at Sacha, who also looked nervous. He patted her leg. They sat back and tried to act as though nothing big was happening.

Two hours later, Tony said, "A break. The bathroom, there. More coffee, or water?" Charlie and Sacha both asked for water. They all took turns in the bathroom, Tony last.

Charlie and Sacha stared at each other for a moment while they waited for him. "I can't believe he watched the whole thing," Sacha said.

Charlie grinned. "I *told* you it was fascinating." She hadn't brought the entire recording. This one went from Sacha shaving his face and netting his hair to the full Maggie experience, gowned and jeweled. Talking all the way through, in response to Charlie's questions or on his own initiative, about the how and the why. "The only thing we didn't get is you doing your legs and stuff, and the pedicure." She had to draw the line somewhere. If Tony thought they needed that, she could always get it later. And if he wanted to see the disassembly, she had that too.

He re-joined them, looking thoughtful. "You said you used three cameras?"

"Actually four. I had three GoPros and my DSLR for stills. The second GoPro was on the other side of the vanity and took him at a forty-five degree angle. The third one was behind Sacha, angled to catch him in the mirror. I was behind this profile camera, barely out of frame for camera three, we had to adjust it about six times."

Tony made a not-bad face and gave a little nod. "How much footage altogether?"

"Over ten hours, which is one reason I thought I cannot do this by myself."

Another nod. "I tell the truth, editing in the different angles will be easy. It's a shame to break it up, but for a marketable film you will need more interviews. Words from people who knew Mr. Morgenstern, and who knew Sacha."

"Maggie," Sacha said. "This was Maggie. Nobody in that world knew Sacha." It never stopped being strange to talk about himself in third person. He realized he had always thought of Maggie as a different person.

Charlie said, "I was thinking if we could get some clips of Jerry's appearances with Maggie, that would show why he needed her. And how well it worked."

"Yes, of course. The performance. The role as it was played." Tony sat back in his task chair, staring into space. After a minute he made eye contact with Charlie. "I am understanding that this is self-produced, yes?"

"We're producing it," Sacha answered. "We want to keep creative control. If you think it's worth proceeding, I'll have my attorneys set up an LLC."

"Perfetto. Yes. Once this is done, I can send you my proposal. You can choose to retain me as your editor, or not. If you do, I can work with the news agencies to license the clips you need."

"What about more interviews?" Charlie said. "I was assuming you wouldn't have a lot of time for that with your other stuff going on. I could do some of that." *Definitely Gary*, she was thinking. And, she realized, she wanted to do an interview with Sacha that was about the relationship itself, and not only about creating Maggie. She didn't know if he was going to be willing to do that, though. All she could do was ask.

Tony was thinking again. "Eh. Interviews, they don't take long. I would need to see clips before I know who we should speak to, before we can contact them. This may take a while," he warned. "Do you have a target date?"

Sacha shook his head. "Would you say it's most likely to find an audience in streaming?" Tony made an 'oh yes' gesture. "Then maybe next spring. So it has plenty of time to play before promotion begins for the Emmy nominations."

"Excellent. Yes." He ejected the card and handed it back to Charlie, who slid it into its tiny case and that, in turn, into her shirt pocket. "Now, will you care to see one of my interviews?"

"Yes please," said Sacha.

Tony's wife Elena joined them at the restaurant, where they ate well while getting better-acquainted and laughing a lot. Elena was in what she called maintenance mode: rehearsing routines with her partner Mateo, in between travel to ballroom competitions. They were aiming for a big event in November and had others on their schedule every month except August. In between, Elena managed the studio and did a little teaching. Mateo was in rehearsals for a big dance concert in Hollywood. "It's at this nightclub called Chrome," Elena said. "Have you ever been there?" Neither of them had. "They have a regular schedule of dance things. The one this August is based on martial arts. It's going to be super cool, they're doing some wire fu. A ton of people from the studio are involved."

"I'd like to see it," said Sacha. "I've been thinking, lately, of getting dance in my life again. It's been a long time." Elena got excited and asked about his background, and that took them through coffee and dessert. By the time they said goodnight, Charlie and Sacha felt thoroughly comfortable with Tony and willing to put the documentary in his hands, as soon as the lawyers said 'go.'

On their way home, they were both quiet. Charlie's brain was buzzing along at top speed, thinking about what she'd learned – from that half hour of watching Tony's work – about how to structure an interview. Sacha was wondering if this whole idea was going to toss them both into another tornado of tabloid press. The more he thought about it, the more he wanted the story told. He couldn't help wishing there was a different way to do it. But there wasn't, not to tell the whole story. The true story.

July 2016

Not long after their meeting with Tony, with the film project at least temporarily out of her hands, Charlie got started on her home office. She began by sitting in the living room staring at it, making notes and sketches, and contemplating her mixed feelings. It was great to be given a free hand. It was amazing to think she could spend whatever it took to get the room perfect. It was also setting off her ethical flares because it wasn't her money, and it wasn't her house, and what if what if what if. The trust account alone gave her agita. She knew it represented love, appreciated it more than she could even say because yes, if anything went wrong now, she would never end up in a garage apartment eating box mac 'n' cheese. She could make that money last forever. And she knew, now that they'd both seen legible reports, that the money Sacha had given her and his family didn't even make a dent in his income. Most of that was from real estate. He would never end up in a garage apartment either, and he'd never need to work again. Everything was still so new, though, and he was still on sort of a high wire.

And what would he do with his life? He couldn't work as a massage therapist anymore. Though he was seeing Rose again, he told her it was a 'friends with benefits' arrangement. Rose laughed, and didn't try to pay him. He already worked out every day. He spent at least an hour a day reviewing the papers Natalie had begun organizing, the history of Jerry's career. An hour a day, on average, went to reviewing material from the lawyers or the accountants, or to reading books or articles they recommended. That left a lot of time. Too much time. He was restless.

Charlie put that away. They'd have to keep talking about it. She did a fast sweep of the books in the living room, pulling out a short stack of things she wanted to read, but not keep forever. Jerry had a lot of large-format books about cinema arts, ranging from animation to costume, that she did want to keep. After clearing off a couple of shelves of mostly junk, Charlie reorganized what was left, putting all the good stuff together. Then she told Sacha to come in and take a second look. "I found this company that will come and haul away the other stuff for recycling," she said. "But first make sure there's nothing you want to keep, aside from this stuff down by the bar."

He looked at those shelves first, nodding approval, then took his time looking at each title of each book on each shelf. "So many books," he said finally. "And mostly mulch, huh." Charlie laughed. "I always liked reading because words didn't make me feel like an idiot. In high school, I was turning into a book hoarder. Mama finally had a fit and said, go to the library, this is ridiculous."

"Did she throw out all your books?"

"Gave them away." Sacha shrugged. "All but a few. But when I moved out here, I didn't bring them with me." A day after accepting Jerry's terms, he returned to his apartment with Jesús and Martin. It only took four cartons to pack up everything he'd owned. Seeing it through their eyes would have been humbling, if he'd had any pride left at that point.

He walked back down the shelves. There wasn't anything calling to him. He'd already read anything that looked interesting, and flipped through everything else. This room had been for show, for occasional cocktail parties, not for Jerry to live or work in. There were no letters or notes hidden here, the way he knew there were in the office. Natalie would find anything important in there. "I think you're good to go here." He kissed Charlie. "Thanks for taking the time to do that."

"Well, these down here are books I mostly saw in the store and thought, gaahh, I want that, but couldn't afford or couldn't justify as a business expense. So I'm like a kid in a candy shop. And speaking of which, I'm hungry. But anyway I'll call the recycling guys. Once this junk is out, I'll call the people to pick up this furniture. And then I'll call the people to pull out this carpet. God, I hope there's wood under here."

"There is," Sacha said, smiling. "I asked Jerry once if it was the same floor as the dining room. He said it was. He said his first wife put in the carpet because she wanted to have kids and it would be quieter, and nicer for them to play on."

"But they didn't have kids. Is that why she left him?"

"Yeah." Sacha gave her a sideways glance as they headed for the kitchen. "He never told her he had a vasectomy."

Charlie pulled up short at that. "Oh my God. That was, huh."

"I know. He said he knew it wasn't fair. They never talked about it before they got married, and he was scrambling to get his career off the ground. Then he started to make money, and Brooke brought it up, and he never told her. He got it before they even met."

"Jesus, why?"

They were in the kitchen now, which was empty and quiet. Natalie was down at her school taking care of some administrative stuff. Cecilia was out getting groceries. It was nice being alone with Charlie. Sacha opened the refrigerator and found some prepared things, cold food for a hot day. After they had their plates assembled he poured them each a glass of Riesling. "I used to think wine with lunch was so self-indulgent. Now I'm all, you know, why not." Charlie laughed under her breath. They sat at the kitchen table and he finally answered the question. "Because he didn't trust her. He didn't trust himself. He said he had a hard time, before he was forty, being who he was. A lot of temptation, a lot of urges. He cheated, a couple of times, with other women. He was trying so hard to be straight. And he was smart, you know. Even in his thirties he was seeing colleagues going through these devastating divorces, losing everything. He had the vasectomy straight out of college because a friend got trapped, his word, into marriage. That's like a kind of fraud. Brooke could have destroyed him. So he never told her, and paid off a doctor to say he was infertile."

"Well, he was." Charlie drank half her wine. "Holy shitballs." Sacha laughed. "I know you loved him, but honey, that guy was a piece of work."

Sacha made a 'kind of' face, nodding. "I know."

"Did you tell her?"

"No. But now that she knows he was gay, I think she's figured it out. She told me, now I can get over it. I know none of it was my fault." After they'd eaten, he sat back and watched Charlie fidget with her wine glass. He thought he knew why. "We haven't talked about kids."

"No we have not."

"We should."

She sighed. "I guess so. You first."

"I want what you want." It was true. He knew she'd hear that in his voice. "That said, if you and I had never met, I could have gone through life happily without kids."

She blew out a breath of such obvious relief that he reached across the table for her hand. She gripped his and they stared at each other for a moment. "I don't want any. I would have had my tubes tied ages ago if I could have first found a doctor to do it and second been able to pay for it."

"Well. Do you still want to do that, or would you rather I do it? It's less of a procedure for me."

"Oh my God. You are truly unbelievable."

He was smiling. "You could stop taking the pill."

"I'll probably go nuts from the hormone withdrawal for a while."

"That's okay." He was sure Charlie's version of 'nuts' wouldn't bother him at all.

126

Charlie drank the rest of her wine and stood up, still holding his hand. He pushed his chair back a little so she could sit on his lap. He put his arm around her and she kissed him. "I love you."

"I love you, too." Another kiss. Then he lifted their joined hands. "There is something missing here."

"Huh?"

"We need to get you a ring. You did say you would marry me."

"I did say that." She was smiling. She kissed him again.

He held her for a minute, waiting. Another minute, starting to laugh silently. Finally, "Well?"

"Well what?"

"Do you want me to guess, or are you going to tell me what you want? New, old, big, small, gold, platinum, what?"

Charlie was laughing now. "Wasn't there something of Maggie's that would suit me? I mean, it doesn't really make any sense to buy new shit. Unless you're planning to wear that again."

"You never know." He regarded her for a moment, still smiling. "Okay. We'll go shop in the Maggie museum. But if there isn't something you really love, you have to let me take you shopping in an actual jewelry store."

"Not Tiffany, those rings are boring."

"Bulgari?" Her face lit up and he laughed again. "I like Bulgari, too. Let's go see what we have." He patted her hip. She stood up, they cleared the table,

127

and then they went down the hall. The Maggie room had a reach-in closet that stretched all the way across a wall, twelve feet long. Sacha opened one set of folding doors, pushed back the dresses, and opened the safe. He'd mastered the combination years ago.

"These dresses, oh my God, lucky for you they won't fit me." She'd seen them before, of course. There was no living in that house without snooping through Maggie.

"Those were all made for me. Complete with the built-in boobs, because I don't have nice ones like you." Charlie laughed, pretending not to watch as he took jewelry boxes out of the safe and set them on the bed. "Jerry told the designer they were for someone who'd had a double mastectomy without reconstruction. Sneaky, huh."

"He was *so* sneaky. How did you get them fitted?"

"The designer sent someone. I had one of those prosthetic bras. I did the hair and face and nails, wore this silk slip. Said I didn't like people to see the scars, so measure over the slip. I was such a liar."

"Both of you. If you hadn't told me ten thousand things you never needed to tell me, I would worry." She couldn't help noticing the rows of velvet boxes now. They covered the king-sized bed. "Oh my Jesus." He'd been opening the boxes as he set them down. "Oh my *lord*." It hadn't been new jewelry with every outfit, of course. The first year there had been four events, and the last year only three. But in each of the other ten years there had been an average of fifteen appearances together. In the first few years, Jerry had bought a lot of jewelry. Seeing it all together was dazzling. "Shit, Sacha. Maybe you should close everything but the ring boxes, the glare is blinding me." He laughed. "I can't believe he kept all that in the house!"

"It should probably be in a safe-deposit box. Another thing to put on the to-do list." Until and unless the world knew he was Maggie, nobody would suspect this hoard existed. But if and when the documentary came out, Sacha knew, there were people who would think of it. As soon as Charlie chose her ring, he'd take care of that.

"I honestly don't know where to start." She really didn't. So she started at one corner and simply looked at everything, row by row. It took a while. Some things, she realized, were easy to dismiss. Too big, too flashy, too much. She started closing boxes. Sacha sat on the vanity chair and watched, faintly smiling. Not pearls or opals, couldn't wear those all the time. Nothing black, and there was a good bit of black. Onyx, enamel, and sapphires, which she only knew came in black because of a gig photographing a collection for insurance. There were many big colorful pieces, the kinds of things that would be noticed and would make Sacha's hand look small and delicate. A statement ring always had a complementary bracelet, something to minimize the wrist. Necklaces were always short, to draw the eye to those narrow collarbones. The consistency and intelligence of the selection blew her away. "Did you tell him what to buy?"

"The style? Yes. I went as myself to some pawnshops on the south side, tried things on to see what made my hands look the best. Bought a couple of cheap things so he could see." Jerry had gone outside the guidelines only twice. The first time was with an Art Deco wristwatch, platinum and diamonds, for a Gatsby-themed gala. The second time was with the Serpenti watch.

"What did he give you that first time, for the Emmy awards?"

Sacha looked for it. He'd worn that set many times, because it was versatile. And because it had been the first. "These."

"Holy shit, Sacha." Charlie stared at him for a second, wondering if he'd ever thought this through. *This is not something a man buys for a game.* The choker was three strands of diamonds set in platinum, with a front clasp made from a carved piece of jade. There were earrings with jade drops garnished with diamonds, a matching ring, and a wide bracelet made of sixteen strands of jade beads run through four long spacer bars set with diamonds. It looked like a suite made for a royal wedding. It was the jewelry Sacha had worn for Charlie's recording of the Maggie assembly. *Did you even know why you chose that.* "Did you ever ask him where this came from?"

"No, I never did." Sacha realized he'd never given much thought to where Jerry found the jewelry. He'd never shopped for any himself. Now that he was looking at the whole collection, he realized that first set was probably the most valuable. "I wonder if he got that because it might be the only time we tried Maggie. If it didn't work. Maybe he wanted to go big. Bet it all on one throw."

"Maybe." Charlie was thinking she'd have to get him to talk more about this. But first they needed to get this job done, so all of this could go back in the safe. Even having it out on the bed was making her nervous.

There was nothing that looked like a traditional engagement ring. Of course there wouldn't be; if there ever had been, Jerry and Sacha would have had to deflect even more interest and speculation. Charlie looked, and coveted, and pondered. There were plenty of things she would love to wear, not many she knew she would want to wear daily. "Tell me this is all insured. Photographed. Something."

"I doubt it." In fact, he was sure of it. Something would have turned up in the audit, and nothing had. An oversight of his. He had a thought, opened a box, lifted out the jewelry and found a receipt under the box lining. "I never even looked." Checked one more box, same thing. At least they would know how to value the collection. "Before we put this away, could you take photos?"

"Sure, no problem."

Finally there were only three boxes open. "Try them on," said Sacha. "We'll have to re-size, of course, but see what you like best on your hand. And if you don't like any of them, we'll go shopping."

"You're enjoying this, aren't you?"

"I love the idea of taking you out, dressed to impress, wearing my ring," he said softly. "So yeah, I'm enjoying this. Don't look at the receipts."

She paused in the act of taking a ring out of a box, laughed under her breath, shook her head. She really didn't want to know if she was about to choose something for daily wear that cost more than her car. "You know I had this fantasy once."

"What kind of fantasy?"

"Walking down the red carpet with Maggie." Sacha laughed. "But then I thought, nobody would look at me, so screw that. I want them looking at me." She put the ring on, studied it, shook her head. Went to the next option and repeated the process. Only one left, the one that she had seen right from the start and thought *that's the one*, but when was she ever going to get this particular experience again, and when was that particular expression going to be on Sacha's beautiful face. "This one."

Sacha stood up and joined her, studying the effect. It was a vintage gold Bulgari ring, set with a star ruby flanked by diamonds. It was the right scale for Charlie's hand; it had looked a bit small on his. "A great choice. It suits you." He lifted the coordinating choker out of its box. It wasn't the same age or maker, and skirted the line between costume and fine jewelry. It was made of gold and ruby beads, with a fringe of smaller beads. "I wore these a few times. The first time was for an advance screening party on the lot." The necklace shimmered, rather than sparkled. He fastened it around Charlie's neck. Then it was the bracelet, a cuff of woven gold with a caterpillar of gold and ruby fringe down the middle. He walked her over to the vanity mirror, then went back for the matching earrings. Took out her plain gold studs, and fastened on the gold and ruby tassels. Set his hands on her shoulders, thumbs lightly brushing her neck. Her eyes met his in the mirror. "I want to make love to you, right now. Wearing that jewelry. You're so beautiful." He kissed the side of her face, her neck below an earring, her shoulder below the necklace. Charlie turned her head and he kissed her mouth.

"Oh God," she said, flooded with desire. She was right up against him, feeling his arousal. He had his mouth on her neck again, one arm wrapped around her. "We can't leave all this stuff out. The door's open. Cecilia must be back by now. Sacha," because he'd turned her into his arms and his hands were everywhere. She was clutching him, panting, already wet. His mouth on hers again, his hands under her shirt and then on the waistband of her jeans. He went to his knees, peeling those jeans down. Charlie thought *screw it* and pulled the tee shirt over her head. Unfastened her bra and threw it somewhere. Stepped out of the jeans and then her underwear. Sacha's mouth on her, her hands in his hair. She tried to say something and all that came out was a moan. He stood up and kissed her again, so hard against her she couldn't stand it and didn't know how he could. He walked her backward to the chaise. *Thank God that thing is there.* She sat down, or collapsed, and he went quickly over to the bedroom door. Closed and locked it. Stripped off his shirt as he crossed the room again, then his pants. "You're so fucking gorgeous," she said, lying back. "Get in me *now*."

He laughed breathlessly, mouth on her neck. Nudging her legs apart with his knee. Sliding against her, through her, and finally into her. "Oh Christ, Charlie, I love you."

She made some kind of sound, wrapping a leg over his, straining against him for the climax that was building, peaking, crashing over her in waves. He got a hand under her hip and pulled her tight against him, propped on his other hand, going so deep and hard she knew she'd feel it the next day. *Oh God let me feel that forever.* Then his head went back and his body arched. His teeth were sunk in his lip and his throat worked, and she felt him come. *This, this, this, forever.* He was flat against her now. They were both breathing fast. After a minute he lifted his head, and kissed her again. Disengaged, slid to the side, brushed back her hair. "I love you," she said. "How does the jewelry look?"

He huffed out a laugh. "Perfect." Another kiss, and then a few minutes of simply holding each other. "I'm

133

going to think of that every time you wear it. I'm going to see that fringe move and think, that's how it moved when I was inside you." He ran a fingertip under the beads at her neck. "God, just the thought of it."

"Me too," she said, fairly certain they'd be at it again soon, because his hand was tracing a path down and around her body, settling between her legs. Palm flat on her, barely moving, as he kissed her again. Now she had her hand on his neck, brushing down to his chest, to the nipples she knew were most definitely erogenous. He was reacting, vocalizing, moving a little. She smiled against his mouth. They had so much lovemaking to do, to correct that deficit of his. She pushed him onto his back and moved down to get him in her mouth. "Mmm," they said together. He was hard again. She couldn't decide if she wanted to get him off this way, or do something else. He was trying to get her hips over his face, she was laughing and resisting. She let go of him enough to say, "You won't be able to see my tassels when I come," and he jumped in her hand. She couldn't stand it. She turned around and settled onto him. "Jesus Christ." They said that together, too. Then he put his hands on her hips and she rode him over the edge.

When Sacha eventually left the Maggie room, it was to go get Charlie's camera and his phone. Charlie stayed in there, grateful that there was an adjoining jack-and-jill bathroom, because she looked like she'd been doing things with her fiancé. Some remediation was required. She was also deeply grateful there had been a washable quilt spread over the chaise. That velvet upholstery and their recent activities would not have been a good combination. When Sacha came back she said, "You know I have to see the receipts in order to photograph them."

He made a face. "Yeah, I know."

"Don't worry about it. This is much more economical than going out for something new. And besides. Tassels." She was smiling to herself, feeling the earrings swing. Sacha got on the phone to send a query text to Marisa, about the best place for a safe-deposit box. He kept Charlie company while she worked her way through the hoard, putting things back in the safe one by one. She didn't comment on that very first set, even though the number on the necklace receipt took her breath away. "This is bananas," she said when all that was left was the ruby set she was still wearing. "I stopped even trying to add it up."

"He really must have enjoyed this stuff." Sacha gave her the last boxes.

Yes, and. She pulled out the receipts, removed the jewelry (regretfully), and took those last few photos. Handed the earring and bracelet and necklace boxes to Sacha for the safe, set the ring box aside for them to take to a jeweler, put her plain studs back in. "He really loved you." Their eyes met in the mirror again. "Right from the start."

After a moment, Sacha nodded. He heard his own words, 'taking you out, dressed to impress, wearing my ring.' The conclusion was inescapable. He had always thought if they hadn't come up with a good story, Jerry would have abandoned the idea of taking Sacha to the Emmys, or anywhere else. But Jerry had wanted Sacha with him, at his side, in public. Maggie had been even more of a gift than he knew.

He was still thinking about it later – much later – when he and Charlie were in bed. The room was dark and quiet; she was asleep, breathing slowly and deeply. He was wondering if he had somehow missed something, if there had been other signals. Jerry was the best liar in the world, though, when he wanted to be. He had seemed completely thrilled, from the first, at the idea of fooling everybody. Completely satisfied with the success of the masquerade for his social life. All those dinners and cocktail parties, where so much business got done. If for whatever reason he thought it was better, or safer, or wiser to pretend Maggie was a game, he wouldn't have let it slip for a minute. Sacha was asking himself if there was something more he could have done, to let Jerry know it was all right. To let him know Sacha would have welcomed his love from the beginning. *Did I fail him after all.*

As usual, once Sacha decided to do something, it got done. All the jewelry except the ruby set went into a safe-deposit box. The ruby ring was promptly resized, and Charlie wore it to dinner with Gary, Natalie, Patrick, and his husband Dmitri. They met up at Ocean Prime, in the private room. Gary took one look at the ring and said, "Have you set a date yet?" He watched with something close to delight as they both giggled. "Before I die, please."

Charlie shut down the giggles with difficulty. "Gary! For God's sake. I've known Sacha for fourteen months and for half of that he was AWOL."

"I'm lucky she said yes at all." Sacha was smiling. "Besides, I want to figure out our honeymoon before we set a date."

"Okay, fine. What are the top contenders?" So then, in between hearing from the server, placing their order, getting some wine, and starting to eat, there was a long debate about the most romantic destinations in the world. Gary had traveled a little. Natalie, not at all. Patrick and Dmitri had been to Japan, to Argentina, to various destinations in Canada, and to Europe on several occasions.

Patrick finished his salad and said, "After Dmitri won the world championship the second time, we went to Vienna. And we went in December. It was cold as fuck. There was so much snow, you could hardly see the buildings. No lie, everything looked like a slightly melted wedding cake." Dmitri snorted.

"Sounds gorgeous," Natalie said.

"Yes, if you are staying indoors by a fire with an endless supply of coffee, brandy, and Sachertorte. Which is not what we were doing." Patrick gave his husband a sideways look. Dmitri looked amused.

"What were you doing?" Charlie was enjoying herself much more than she would have predicted. Dmitri and Patrick seemed to be close to Natalie's age. Three out of four of the older people were so sharp, so funny, and so kind. Dmitri probably was too, but he hadn't said much.

Then he did. He said, "We go to a ball. Viennese waltz for hours. Patrick is complaining."

"Yes, Patrick was complaining," said Patrick. "That ballroom was so crowded, and we were in these tailcoats. I felt like I was having a nonstop hot flash." Natalie laughed. "But I had the best dance partner in the room, so." He shrugged, giving Dmitri a little sideways smile.

"I don't know how to dance," Charlie said. "At all. Sacha has a degree in dance." Dmitri looked interested.

Sacha said, "It was one of those theater degrees, really, with a focus on dance. Ballet, jazz, tap. I was a

137

better actor than dancer, but my advisor talked me into doing the dance concentration. He said it would be easier to place me." He did that half-a-shrug thing. "I might go back to it. Now that I can afford it." That got a laugh from everybody.

"Will you learn?" Natalie asked Charlie.

"Uh, not ballet, jazz, or tap, no. How hard is Viennese waltz?"

Patrick and Dmitri simultaneously said "Hard" and "Not hard." Charlie laughed, along with Gary and Natalie.

"Who is she supposed to believe here?" Sacha took her hand.

Dmitri said, "Instructor, of course." Then the servers were back with entrees.

"If anyone can teach you, Dmitri can," Patrick said after a few minutes, picking up the thread. "He's taught me Argentine tango, Viennese waltz, foxtrot and rumba. And I have three left feet."

"You have disinclination." Dmitri again looked amused.

"Yes, sweetheart, I do. I swear," Patrick said to Gary, "I thought once disco was over the hardest I was ever going to have to work was doing my Cher thing at the drag club. Little did I know." He turned to Natalie. "What about you?" She made a startled sound. "Do you dance?"

"Um, not really. I'm a teacher, by the end of the day all I want to do is sit down." Then she glanced at Charlie and Sacha. "But I danced at my wedding. Forty years ago in September, can you believe it?"

"Oh, Natalie." Charlie was regretting this conversation now.

Natalie wasn't upset. "Leo and I had thirty-seven great years. Even with the cancer, it was great. He was great. I am grateful for what we had."

"My colleague Paul lost his husband going on three years ago," Patrick said. "They'd been together twenty-two years, Bob had cancer for five years, ugh. Paul met someone and he's remarried now. His husband is a yoga teacher, they do all this crazy partner stuff, it's like Cirque du Soleil."

"Wait a minute," Charlie said. "Paul who?"

"Paul Xiao. Why, do you know him?"

"Did he marry Kevin Park?"

"Yes! What the hell!"

"I was doing a photo shoot with Kevin, like two years ago? And he brought Paul, and there were partner things in the specs so he and Paul did them, and they were great. I never did get another assignment like that, though, and I never saw them again. That's so nice, that they got married. I have this awesome picture that I took when they weren't looking." She dug out her phone, woke it up, found the picture and passed it around. The photo showed Kevin applying eyeliner pencil to Paul; both of them were smiling. "Aren't they adorable?" Everybody seemed to agree. "Huh. I was thinking about yoga recently. I mean, Sacha makes me do yoga, which," she rolled her eyes and Patrick laughed. "But I was thinking about photographing yogis. I used to do a lot with athletes. I think I'll pester Kevin, see if he can talk Paul into doing something." Her phone came back around; she made herself a note and then put it to sleep again.

"Well," said Gary, who'd been quiet for a while, "what *are* you working on?" It might have been a hint about the documentary.

Charlie didn't want to talk about that tonight. They were still waiting for lawyers to do things. "I think I'm going to do a show of the photos I took of LAUSD teachers. That's how I met Natalie. I need to find someone who's done one, see if they can give me some tips."

"We know a guy who does a show at least once a year," Patrick said. "We've known him for what, nine years?" Dmitri nodded. "He's never happy unless he's too busy. He shot something recently. I'll bet he'd talk to you. Hand over that phone." Charlie obediently did. Patrick did a few things, then passed it back. She read the text he'd sent: *Hi Andy this is Patrick from the phone of Charlie Montgomery. She is a lovely young photographer looking to mount her first gallery show. If you have a minute to talk after you're done with the chorus boys, please reply to this text. Love & Kisses*

Charlie looked up. "Chorus boys?"

"Tango," said Dmitri. "Nine men. Andy." As if that said it all, which the eloquent expression he produced kind of did.

"Come on, Andy who?" Charlie was laughing now.

It was Gary who answered, which seemed to surprise everybody. "Andy Martin. He hung a show called 'Pacific' last year, I bought a print for my office. A friend of mine is his agent. He's an actor on 'L.A. Vice.' One of my former clients is a writer for the series."

"I've never watched it. Have you, honey?" Charlie looked at Sacha, who'd been even quieter than Gary.

"No." He was smiling. "Jerry didn't produce it." Then he changed the subject, and got Gary talking about his new job.

Gary obligingly made them all laugh by describing his first few weeks of reviewing scripts. "I kept catching myself thinking, how could I sell this. And usually the answer was nobody would want it, and then I would remember I was the one who didn't want it. When we finally got through the paper and started on the other media, it was such a relief. I never worked with stuff that was already made." He pointed at Charlie. "Keep me posted."

"No action yet," she said. "Lawyers." He performed a 'say no more' gesture.

Patrick said, "Wow, that was almost as good as one of Dmitri's." They had all noticed that Dmitri talked more with face and hands than he did with actual speech. He now created an 'I don't know what you mean' gesture that Gary immediately copied. Patrick inhaled some coffee, Natalie laughed into hers, and Sacha had another moment of thinking, *family*.

"Jeez, that was great," Charlie said on the way home. "I feel like that was all about me though. I hope you weren't bored, Natalie."

"Not in the least. I will have to go out to a lot more fancy dinners in posh restaurants before I start getting bored. And it's always nice to see Gary."

"Has he asked you out yet?" Sacha glanced at her in the rear-view mirror. She was laughing. "Hey, if people are going to pester us about a wedding date. Fair is fair."

"Fair is fair," she agreed. "Not yet. I do think it's a case of not yet, though, versus not going to happen."

"Duh," said Charlie. "I was surprised he didn't ask you out the first time he met you." She glanced over at Sacha; they both smiled, listening to Natalie giggle.

A couple of days later Charlie got a reply text from Andy Martin. She was so excited she immediately went to find Sacha. Then she forgot all about the text because she found him in the office, and something was wrong. He had his elbows on the desk and his face in his hands. There were a few sheets of paper on the desk in front of him. They had the look of having been folded twice, as if for a regular envelope, for quite a while. *Oh fuck what now*, she thought, and tapped on the open door. He didn't move, but he said, "Charlie?"

"Yes. What's the matter?"

"This letter. Oh God." He took his hands away, wiping his face. "Natalie found it in one of the file drawers."

Okay, Charlie thought. *That means something about Jerry.* "Is it horrible?"

"No, it's beautiful. You remember when you were choosing your ring."

"I'll never forget that."

"What you said. You were right." He pushed the sheets of paper toward her. Charlie approached, strangely hesitant. "You should read this."

"Am I going to cry too?"

"Maybe." He smiled a little. "If you don't want to read it right now, it'll be right here."

"No, I'll read it now. Then we can both have a drink out by the pool to settle ourselves down." She went to the guest chair in the corner, on the same side of the room as Sacha but not behind the desk. The room felt half again as big without all the paper in it.

Sacha handed her the letter, then leaned back in his chair. "And you can tell me why you were looking for me."

"I got a text," she said absently, "from that TV guy. Reading now." He didn't say anything else. Charlie quickly scanned the handwritten pages. She hadn't seen a lot of Jerry's handwriting, but he'd signed the letter. There was no date. She wondered how long ago this had been written, and then stuffed into the file cabinet. She wondered why he hid it. Then she remembered everything Sacha had ever told her about this brilliant, troubled man, and started reading.

Sacha,

I've been telling myself for years that I should do this, and for years I've been telling myself it won't matter in the end. But that's a lie. I know it will matter to you. So I am writing this, and I'm going to tear through it because if I try to make it good I will talk myself out of it. You've read worse speeches plenty of times, I know.

By the time you find this I'll be gone. You know what the doctor said, you've seen what's happening, there's no doubt I am fucked. Well, that's how it goes, and I've had a better life than most. I know you will find this because I know you. If you're reading this then you've finally dug through whatever mess Jesús left. Great guy, lousy record keeper, nobody's perfect. And if you've dug through the mess then the whole will thing is over. I'm sorry I didn't warn you. You probably saw the date on it and said what the fuck. The lawyers sure did, when I told them what I wanted it to say.

Anyway this is about why, which you basically know already, even though I was too much of a coward to say the words for so many years and even when I worked up the nerve I thought this isn't fair, because of how we were. Then of course you said it back, because of how you are, which is perfect and beautiful and the love of my life. And I knew you meant it, because we lied our asses off to everybody else but you never lied to me. I never understood why you would love me too, but I believed it, and it meant more to me than you could ever know.

I was so glad we got to go out a few more times after I finally said it. Did I tell you how beautiful you were? Did I tell you I loved you every time? I hope I did. I hope you knew even when I choked. Let me say that again, you are the love of my life. You were. From day one.

I wondered so many times what might have happened if I wasn't the way I am and if you weren't the way you are. But then, if I wasn't the way I am I wouldn't have been out cruising with the guys that night and we might never have met and you might not have survived, so whatever else happened between us and to us I am glad nothing was different. I would not want the world to go on without you in it.

When Jesús looked down that alley and said there's some trouble, I told Martin to stop the car and figured at best we would get some food into somebody and go home having given that somebody one more night to think about maybe not doing drugs. Maybe even not doing the other stuff. Sometimes it worked. Then I heard Jesús yell and I thought, shit, and I got the gun out. Did

144

you know I had one? Got rid of it after you came to the house. After that we never went out again. Did you know that? Not unless Jesús or Martin told you, huh, and I'll bet they never did.

Anyway that guy ran off and I put the gun away. Jesús helped you up, you looked down the alley at the car. Do you remember? You were pretty fucked up. I saw your face. I saw those eyes and I thought, even with the makeup I thought fucking Christ, I cannot leave that much beauty there to be destroyed. So when Jesús came down to tell me the situation I said, get him in the car. We brought you home.

The next day I was in a panic, like what have I done. Then Jesús came in and said, the kid is all right, and I said I wanted to talk to you. I know what you expected. Did you know I saw you all cleaned up and thought, my God, I could make him a star? But if I did that I would lose you. I was a selfish son of a bitch. I wanted you for myself, at least for a little while. I told myself it was just to make sure you were safe, to get you healthy, to get you ready for a decent job. It was really because I wanted you there, so I could look at you.

And then you were how you are. Honest and brave and I want to say pure. I think I was already in love with you at the end of that first conversation. Which makes me just as ridiculous as all those love at first sight goombahs in all those shitty scripts we ever looked at together. God I loved reading scripts with you. I loved watching movies with you. I loved being able to teach you something, and you were so smart and thoughtful and kind. I am not that nice a guy, you know that as well as anyone, but I tried to be

145

nicer for you because I never wanted to hurt you even by accident.

I knew you loved me. You kissed me that time and I said you didn't have to, and you said you wanted to. And then after the Emmys that first time you told me about your family, and I knew. I should have told you then. I should have told you every day. I was afraid that would be laying too much on you, because of how we were. But you wouldn't have minded, would you? No one in my life ever loved me like you.

I was glad I couldn't get it up anymore, you know that? I couldn't be tempted to do anything unforgivable to you. You would have let me do it because you loved me but that would have been so gross and unfair. Even letting you touch me was unfair but sometimes I needed it so much, and you were always there. Thoughtful and kind and willing and so goddamned beautiful I went back in the house and cried sometimes.

Thank you, by the way. Thank you for somehow knowing what I could take and what I couldn't, even though I could not utter a useful word half the time. I think I hurt you by not letting you touch me more. By not touching you. But it didn't make sense to me that you would want to do that, or want me to do that, so I'm sorry. As you know there is a lot wrong with me.

This is getting to be a book but now that I'm finally going I guess I can't stop till I say it all. I wish I was saying this to you, not just writing it down for you to find later. If I tried to say even part of this I would be a complete fucking mess so this will have to do. I hope it's not too bad for you at the end. I hope this doesn't drag on too long.

Thank you for Maggie. What a great time we had. I will never forget that first time. I was so fucking scared. I couldn't believe people wouldn't guess, or wouldn't see. But you were perfect. You were always perfect. There you were, as beautiful as day, and when I came back with that stupid trophy you were smiling as if you'd won it yourself. And you kissed me. Could you tell I almost cried?

When you were Maggie I could touch you. Everyone expected me to. What a fucking gift that was. The most beautiful woman in the room, and even more beautiful because she was you, and it was all your idea so it was okay. You chose that design with the bare back, and you never said so but I knew it was so I could touch your skin. Jesus Christ, the first time, I almost fainted.

You would give me that little smile, no matter where you were it was like you knew when I was looking at you. Everybody knew I had it bad. I still can't believe we pulled it off. I guess that was the best cover story ever written.

You were so brave. You had to be a little bit scared too. I never could tell. Best fucking actor in the fucking world. It's a goddamned shame you can't win any awards for that. Well, at least I can finally give you the money you wouldn't take before. If you want to give it all away I guess you will. But I hope you'll enjoy it. Enjoy the hell out of it. Marry that wonderful girl and have a wonderful life. I'm so glad you're still young. You have time.

I really loved you Sacha. I always will. You gave me the best almost-twelve years of my life. I love you.

Jerry

CHAPTER 8

Charlie held out the letter to Sacha. He took it from her. She pressed her hands to her face and breathed deep for a few minutes, sniffed, swallowed. "Jesus," she said after a while. "No wonder you looked like this when I came in. He must have written it close to the end." She wiped her face and tipped her head back, trying to relax her throat, which had been painfully tight almost from the first line of that letter. Took another deep breath and blew it out through her mouth. "What was the date on the will?"

"Eleven years ago. The month I moved out. It was his idea for me to move. I was building my practice and he said it would be better for me to have a separate address. He was always right about things like that. And then he couldn't ask, you know? If I would still come to see him, if I would still be Maggie. I told him, this is for both of us, so Maggie and Sacha won't get mixed up. I will always be here for you. He nodded and went in the house. I knew he almost cried, that time."

"Oh *fuck*." Charlie wiped away fresh tears. "He knew about me?"

"I told him about you right away. I said, I talked to the photographer, she wants me to model for her. He laughed and said are you gonna do it? I said probably not. I said that I liked you. He said, you've got a lot of living to do. We left it there till May. Then he was so much sicker, but I told him you'd figured it out. That you knew I was Maggie. He said, you're not worried about it, are you. I said no. He said, take her out and tell her everything."

"My God."

"I think I know when he wrote this. I think it was about two weeks after I moved home. He was in so much pain, so exhausted. After he went to bed I asked Jesús what happened that day. He said Jerry wanted his lap desk, he wouldn't let me help, I have no idea why."

Charlie sniffed again. "It must have made him so happy when you asked to come home."

"I think it did." Sacha slowly folded the letter, then opened the center drawer of the desk and set it inside. Sighed, closed the drawer, and said, "Time for that drink?"

"God, yes. Time for all the drinks."

"Tell me about the TV guy." He stood up, offered a hand. Charlie took it and let him pull her out of the chair. They went out to the patio together, got drinks, and settled themselves on the double lounger. Charlie told him about Andy's invitation to come over to his home studio and talk about the mechanics of a gallery show. Sacha told her he was looking forward to seeing those portraits up on a wall.

She was halfway down her drink – not marshmallow vodka this time, but something else sweet; she told Sacha she was doing him a favor by drinking the things he didn't like – when he sighed, kissed the side of her face, and said, "He left the door open. All the time. It was never an expectation. And he said that."

After a moment, because for once she had no idea where Sacha was going with this, Charlie said, "What?"

"Said he could make me a star. It was after the Emmys in two thousand four. We'd done the red carpet. Everyone saw us. Not just the people there, but everyone watching, everywhere. Everyone was like, oh he's brought Maggie again, who are you wearing. The same questions they ask every guy's date. He gave me that sideways look that was halfway to cracking up. I told him to knock it off and then he did laugh. The next morning I went for a swim and he came out and sat with his feet in the water. I went over and said, need me for something? He smiled and shook his head. He said if you ever get tired of this I could find the right project for you in about ten seconds. I could make you a star. I hung on the edge of the pool for a minute and tried to figure out what he was saying. Was it, it's never going to get better than that, let's quit while we're ahead, you know." Charlie nodded. "I said Jerry, there's no TV or movie project in the world that could be more fun than being Maggie for you. Seriously, you work your ass off three hundred and sixty-four days a year to get to the Emmys. All I have to do is get dressed. He laughed, but he shook his head again. He knew it was more than that."

"So then what?"

"Then he said, the offer is always open, and then he changed the subject. We talked about my business, I was just getting started really, but he steered some people my way and that helped so much. That was the only time we had that conversation. When he suggested I should get my own place I thought there was a moment he was going to say that again. But by then I really understood how important Maggie was. She was making a difference in his work life. And by then I knew how horribly lonely he would be if I took that away. So, you know. I'd had a few moments of thinking, I will never be able to seriously date, how long can I keep this going."

Another pause. Charlie wanted to hear the rest of it. She wanted him to say it. "Sacha, keep talking. I love you. I want to hear it. You never got to tell anyone these things. You can trust me." *I will never not love you.*

He squeezed her shoulders and took a breath. "Okay. So I did the hard math. He was sixty. I was twenty-five. If we kept it going for ten years, he'd be seventy. I would still only be thirty-five. I could build my own social life. I could have friends, even a girlfriend if I wanted to, though I never did meet anyone I thought I could trust with the truth, until I met you. He would never have anyone if I left him. Because we made such a splash, you know? People would ask, oh what happened with Maggie. They'd assume he screwed up, because of those divorces. They'd be like, he's struck out again, what's wrong with him. I couldn't stand for that. I loved him." He swallowed some of his drink, forcing it past the tightness in his throat. "So before he could say anything about maybe I wanted to stop, I said I didn't want to stop. To call me, or email me, or have Jesús call me, whatever. Whenever there was a thing he needed Maggie for. Even if he only wanted some company. If he got a particularly shitty script and wanted someone to help him laugh at it, I would be there."

"No wonder he almost cried," Charlie said, wiping her eyes. "He must have really been sure then. Sure that you loved him."

"I really wanted to say it." Sacha inhaled, blew it out through his mouth. "I didn't want to freak him out."

"Well, honey." Charlie patted his leg. "That guy knew all about subtext, didn't he?"

"Yeah. I guess he did."

Charlie gave herself a little research project after that. She went through the jewelry inventory they'd made from the photographs, and started calling the dealers. They weren't all in Los Angeles. Jerry had been, in this as in so many other things, secretive. He'd somehow found pieces in New York, in Miami, in Las Vegas. San Francisco and Paris and Hong Kong. The first one, that stupendous diamond and jade set, had come from London. When Charlie finally got through to someone there, she told them the truth: that they were writing a biography and wanted some detail on how Jerry had come to purchase these particular jewels. The dealer agreed to being recorded. He said, "Mr. Morgenstern was referred to us. He asked for something no one would ever forget. He said, I'm taking someone very special to the Emmys. I want her to look like a queen. Those pieces had been placed with us by an estate. We sent him photographs and he wired us the full price. He also paid to have the pieces hand-delivered by courier. We saw photographs later, of Mr. Morgenstern with his companion. We were," he paused, "gratified."

"Thank you very much," Charlie said, and after an exchange of courtesies ended the call. If they hadn't found Jerry's letter, if he had never even written it, this would have been enough. She sent the recording to Natalie, who typed up a transcript and put it with the others, so many others, all amounting to the same thing: Jerry, completely in love, and showing it in the only way he thought he could.

Sacha knew about that project. They all talked about it, briefly. It wasn't essential to the documentary, or even to the book. The accountants and insurers didn't need to know why Jerry had spent a fortune on jewelry. For Sacha, the letter was by far

152

the greater treasure. All the same, to know that Jerry's heart had been in the Maggie game every bit as much as Sacha's was like a warm drink on a cold day.

Natalie was nearly done with the file cabinets. Half the stuff in there was quickly determined to be shreddable. The machine in Jerry's office was nearly dead already, so Sacha told her to get what she needed. As soon as a new heavy-duty crosscut shredder came in, she got back to work.

About half of the remaining paper was copies of scripts. There were tons of those on the shelves, too. Natalie had found a journal – a real prize – with entries about every one of the movies or TV shows Jerry had worked on. There wasn't much detail for each one, but it gave her the best possible reference. Any script that wasn't something he worked on, she tossed into recycling. Unless he'd written notes on it, which he sometimes did. "Sometimes a thing was so good, or so bad, he'd do this," Sacha said. "Do you think there's any value to that for the book?" By now they were all pretty sure he wanted to write one. Who better, Natalie said, and while Sacha had very little confidence in his writing talent, what he produced couldn't be as bad as some of those ghostwritten memoirs Charlie had chucked out of the living room. And at least he cared about the subject.

"Well, I was wondering," she said. "The narrative should be about his life. But a lot of people buying that book are going to be interested in how he approached his work. So I think we might want to hang onto this kind of thing until we know how you could work that in."

"I might need to get someone in who knows more about the mechanics of it. We talked about the scripts a lot, but I never saw him on a set." Every time he thought about how to make the project good, it seemed more daunting.

Natalie may have seen that; she patted his arm. "Don't let it freak you out. I know you're thinking it would be great to have the book out at the same time as the documentary. But it's really not necessary. Let it take as long as it takes, and I guarantee you people who buy the book will go looking for the film."

He smiled at her. "Do you have any idea how lost I would be without you?"

"You're tougher than you look," she said, and went out. He was left in the office thinking about that. It was one of the words he always thought of when he thought of Jerry: tough. And he knew she was right, he was tough himself, or he wouldn't have survived. His life was so easy now, he tended to forget the times when it hadn't been. And it had never been as easy for Jerry, because the only times he'd really been himself were with Maggie. Sacha turned back to the computer, to add that thought to the document he hoped one day would turn into something that did justice to its subject.

Charlie was glad Sacha had that project. She was thoroughly occupied with her office renovation. Getting the old furniture out, and then the carpet and drapery, made an enormous difference. Then she had a custom workstation built. It was perfectly scaled to the room, looked good with the woodwork in the wet-bar area, and gave her more space than she'd ever dreamed of having. It took time, of course. She used some of that time helping Natalie move books out of the office and into the living room.

Everything that came out of the office probably had some kind of story. Some of the books were obviously connected to Jerry's productions. For those, they matched up the scripts and other notes, and shelved them with the books so that Natalie and Sacha could find them again easily. Others were complete conundrums. There was simply no way to know why he had kept a cheap paperback of 'Gone with the Wind,' unless it was some kind of private joke. Charlie took a photograph of it, made sure there were no notes inside, and put it in the box for recycling.

Once her workstation was complete, she had the room painted, blinds installed, and the floor refinished. Sacha closed the door behind the contractor and said, "Do you like it?"

"Oh my God, Sacha, I can't wait to work in there. It's three times as much space as I ever had before. Not to mention that printer I've been lusting after for years. Thanks for that." She tugged him close for a kiss. "Now I have to ping Kevin and see if I can get him and his husband to model for me again."

"You still want to do a book about yogis?"

"I think so, yeah. Same approach I took with the teachers. Kind of celebrating the profession, but showing how strong and beautiful these people are in their element."

"It'll be great."

"But first I need to talk to that guy about how to even do a show. I just can't wait to take some new pictures, in my nice big empty room." Charlie eyed him for a second. "Can I take your picture?"

Sacha laughed. She took his picture all the time. "What kind of picture?"

"I don't know," she said unconvincingly. "Maybe *that* kind of picture." He slid his arm around her waist.

She lifted her face for a kiss. "If you let me take that kind of picture, I'll let you do whatever you want with me."

"I think I'm already doing that," he said against her skin.

The estate plan still wasn't done, but the lawyers had the LLC operational. Sacha and Charlie signed a contract with Tony Benedetti, and he got straight to work on licensing news clips. He sent them a list of potential interview subjects and then asked if they wanted to join him and his wife for dinner. "I've had an idea for how to structure the film," he said on the phone. "We should discuss it."

"Counteroffer," Charlie said, glancing across the kitchen at Sacha. "Could the two of you come to our place? We'll get Pace to deliver, open a bottle. You should see this place anyway. If Sacha decides to give us an interview it'll be here."

Tony agreed with that plan, and they worked out a date. His wife and her partner had a break before their next competition, and (Tony said) needed a break from each other as well. "Which is good for me and Gio."

"Bring your little boy," Charlie suggested. "I mean, if you want to."

"Grazie." Tony sounded amused. "I will confess a night out with only adults will be pleasant." Charlie laughed, and agreed.

Because they were ordering in, Cecilia went home at her usual time. Natalie, who was half of Sacha's brain by now, joined them. Tony and Elena arrived in time for a drink by the pool before dinner. They talked more about ballroom dancing – Elena and

156

Mateo were rising fast – and then she asked Sacha if he'd done anything about his dancing yet.

"Not yet," he said. "We've been making some changes here and I didn't want to be halfway across town if a question came up."

"Also I have been a total pest now that Jerry's papers are starting to come together," Natalie said. "I heard 'movie producer' and thought oh, a guy who's on set all the time with a bullhorn and a clapper board, right, but no. The producer is in an office buried in paper. This one was, anyway."

"He was on set plenty of times," Sacha, amused. "But yeah, it was not all day every day. It was dropping in to hassle the director and sweet-talk the cast, or vice versa, and remind them whose money they were spending." Tony laughed. Sacha's phone buzzed. "That's the restaurant letting me know they're on their way. Let's go in and choose some wine."

"I'm the designated driver," Elena said. "One's my limit. So don't let me look." They all went inside. Sacha turned Tony loose in the butler's pantry; he found a bottle of Brunello somewhere and held it up with triumph. It was opened, sampled, approved, and poured. They took their glasses into the dining room and had just chosen seats when the delivery arrived.

Once they were set up, Charlie said, "One thing we've discovered is that Jerry was really hands-on with the scripts. He was always the budget and schedule and contracts guy, but we've found some kind of script involvement with almost every project. Is there usually a script for a documentary?"

"An outline, at least," Tony said. "You have to know there is a story to tell before you can film it." He told them about the first few months of working on his series, making the pitch, creating the first episodes. "I met Elena because of the series." He was smiling. "I was with my brother and his wife at the Emerald Ball here in Los Angeles. Elena was there, competing with her students. It was love at first sight, for me."

"Me too," Charlie said. "And boy was I confused. I was so confused, I didn't even know what had happened to me until like six months later."

"Right before the tornado." Sacha had his arm across the top of her chair, thumb lightly stroking her shoulder. "When I couldn't even text you back. I was afraid if I did, I wouldn't be able to resist meeting you, and then the tabloids would find you and wreck your life."

"I figured that was it. I still missed you." Then Charlie remembered they had guests, and turned the conversation back to Tony and Elena's whirlwind romance.

Tony waited until they were mostly done eating before bringing up the documentary. "Charlie, you said you had footage of Sacha taking Maggie apart again."

"Yes, that's right. Same camera setup. It's not two hours, obviously. You had an idea?"

"I thought to begin and end with the complete Maggie. So begin in full costume, then disassemble. Toward the middle of the film, it is Sacha. And then he creates her, so at the end we see her again and now people know why." Charlie and Sacha looked at each other. Tony said, somewhat anxiously, "If you prefer another way it's all right."

Sacha studied him for a moment. "You're the expert here. What do you think, Natalie?"

"I who am the least educated viewer at this table? I think it's a knockout idea." She did a half-a-shrug

158

thing that was so like Sacha, he laughed. "Look, I'm invested in this project, but I really do like the idea of beginning and ending with the full Maggie experience. She was beautiful. It's a great way to leave it."

"We realized something recently, Tony." Sacha glanced at Charlie. "The jewelry I used for that recording was the first jewelry Jerry gave me. We should try to find a clip from that event, the 2003 Emmys. The dress and the hair weren't as good then. The way I put her together for the recording was kind of best case scenario." Now he looked at Elena. "You haven't seen any of this yet, have you?"

"No, Tony was going to ask you for the media tonight."

"Sure." Charlie pushed her chair back. "I'll go get it now so I don't forget." She went out of the room.

Sacha said, "The jewelry was a declaration of love. I didn't realize it at the time. I felt that he cared, in his way, but he was so conflicted about it that I didn't get it."

"Sure you did," said Natalie. "Why else choose that stuff when Charlie wanted to film you?" He stared at her, startled. "Sweetie, do you honestly think you could have been like that with him if you hadn't *known*?" Sacha couldn't think of a thing to say. Fortunately, Natalie filled the gap by asking Tony about his personal project. They were talking about that when Charlie returned to the dining room a few minutes later.

"I never talked about Jerry with my shrink," Sacha told Charlie later, when they were in bed. "I guess it makes sense I would still be discovering things about the whole relationship. I only started talking about it last May, with you."

159

"You have a dozen years to unpack." She kissed him. "Don't keep thinking you must have done something wrong. He knew you loved him. He thought you were perfect. It's awfully nice that he finally told you."

"Yeah. It is."

"For the record, I also think you are perfect." He laughed. Charlie turned into his arms and settled against his shoulder. "I think Tony's going to do something great with that film. I would have been in way over my head."

"It's still your idea. Your project. You should invite yourself over to watch him work."

"You're right, I should. I could learn a lot from him."

"You can be the producer. Remind him whose money he's spending." Sacha held her close, listening to her laugh, and smiled.

Sacha was tired, in a mild amount of pain, and excited when he got back from his first ballet lesson in fourteen years. Doing a private lesson was a completely new experience. He'd found a teacher who had a studio not far from the house, but also a live-work space at the Brewery complex above downtown. She apologized for the distance from the Hollywood Hills. He said it was perfect. "I would draw attention at your studio, and not the kind you want." That was probably true, so she nodded, and they got on with it.

At the end of that first session Mandy claimed to be impressed with what he could still do. "Probably the yoga," she said. "Good for you, keeping up with that. How often do you want to come?"

"Often," he said. "How often can you fit me in?" She smiled and pulled up her calendar. They talked a little more, and he entered 'Mandy – 10:00' on his calendar, every Tuesday and Thursday for the next four months. Then they shook hands, and he headed out.

When he walked into the kitchen he heard Charlie talking. At first he thought she must be with Natalie, but the exasperated tone was something he'd never heard between them, so he stopped to listen for a moment. *Oh*, he thought.

Charlie was saying, "No, sorry, no plans to come to Indiana for the foreseeable future. We have a lot going on here. Mom, it hasn't been that long, I was there last summer. Well of course I didn't stay long, there's nothing to do and anyway all you guys ever want to do is go to church or watch TV. Yeah, I know, sorry. No, I'm not really working per se. Well, I moved in with Sacha. No, we haven't set a date yet. Mom, it is in fact socially acceptable to live with someone you are engaged to. And it is very convenient when you are also sleeping with that person." Sacha bit his lip, stifling a laugh. He went out of the kitchen and down the hall to the den. Charlie was lying on the couch, staring at the ceiling until she noticed him, which didn't take long. She crossed her eyes at him, clearly listening to something she'd rather not be listening to. Sacha perched on the arm of the couch. "Mom. Mom. Mom, please. I am thirty-four. I've been sleeping with people for eighteen years. Sorry about that." Sacha barely smothered a snort. Charlie grinned at him. "Yes, I'm pretty sure this is the last person I'll be sleeping with. Yay me." Sacha laughed as silently as he could. "Anyway as I was saying I'm working on putting together my first gallery show, which is a complicated thing. I'm also working with someone on making a documentary film, which is a very complicated thing. Yes as a matter of fact Sacha is helping me pay for these projects, because he loves me and he thinks they're interesting. Well, maybe you'll see them someday. The gallery show is for those teacher portraits I told you about. I have a book. Yes, I'll send you a copy of the book." A pause. Charlie frowned. "Well, no." A longer pause. "No, Mom. I'm sorry, but it's his money, not my money. He has his own family to take care of and they are a barrel of monkeys. If I ever make any money I will share, I promise. Mom! No, I'm not going to ask him. Do not start living on my expectations because I don't have any expectations. I am marrying this man because I love him, not because he has money." Another pause. Charlie sat up suddenly. "Are you kidding me? Are you even serious right now. Mom I'm hanging up before I say something we'll both regret. Bye." She disconnected, clearly furious. "Mendacious *bitch*."

Sacha gave her a second. "It's probably good you didn't say that on the phone."

"Jesus I'm glad I didn't tell her about the trust."

"Why didn't you? Or do I need to ask." Charlie's expression was eloquent. Sacha reached over for her hand. "Do they actually need money?"

"I don't think so. They own their house, they both still have their jobs which they like, and as far as I know none of my asinine siblings have run into trouble. I'll bet they want to shake some of your sin money out of you and give it to their stupid church."

"Do they think it's sin money?" Sacha knew, from previous conversations, that Charlie's parents were squarely in the 'gay people are going to Hell' camp. They wouldn't care that he wasn't gay; to them, his relationship with Jerry was wrong with a capital W.

162

"That's why I'm so mad, she actually pretty much said that. Like, it wasn't right for you to profit from such a degrading relationship. Like she fucking knows." She made a disgusted noise. Then she laughed. Sacha raised his eyebrows in inquiry. Charlie said, "Her head is going to fucking *explode* when that documentary comes out."

"So I guess we won't be going to Indiana for Christmas." Sacha watched her laugh again and knew she was all right. "Want to hear about my ballet lesson?"

"God, yes. Kiss me first. And then let's get some coffee. I'm going to put a gallon of Bailey's in mine."

Charlie sent a message to Kevin Park not long after the annoying conversation with her mother. She was feeling a little guilty about having so few obligations, didn't have an immediate project for the documentary, and had finished selecting the images to print for her teachers show. She wanted to fill up the time somehow. Kevin texted her back: *Hi Charlie nice to hear from you again. Did you get another assignment?*

Hi Kevin nope I am sort of unemployed right now but also sort of working on a personal project. I remembered how great you and Paul were to work with and wondered if you'd be interested in this new thing. It'll be a book and possibly a gallery show about L.A. yogis. Standard fees

We do partner yoga sessions now almost every Sunday morning at Tidal Flow. Is that the kind of thing you'd like to see?

Yes yes yes

LOL okay, this weekend? 0800

163

God you guys are hard core, okay see you at the crack of dawn on Sunday. Take care till then

You too.

"I am super excited about this," she told Sacha. He was out by the pool, drying off from a swim. "I always liked photographing athletes. Do you want to come?"

"At eight o'clock?"

She laughed. "I know, it's too early. Maybe you could join me for brunch or something after. Oh wow." She realized they hadn't been out, actually out, together for weeks. "We need to get out a little anyway, don't you think?"

"I suppose we should." Sacha realized he sounded slightly reluctant. "It's not that I don't want to go out with you. I think I'm always afraid it's going to be like last fall."

Charlie sat beside him on the lounger. "We have to get out there sometime, though, honey. Like an official couple. It'll be easier when we're together. Except I guess I need to actually plan to look a certain way, and not roll out in jeans and a tee shirt like I usually do."

"Me too." He studied her for a moment. "You've done some shopping."

"I have. What's a good look for an early Sunday photo session and brunch?" It was a rhetorical question. Sacha waited to hear how she answered herself. "Brunch in that neighborhood is always a wait in line proposition. So maybe jeans, and comfy shoes, but with that tank top that looks like the English flag only in orange and turquoise, and the linen jacket that has the denim trim?"

"Sounds perfect," he said, smiling. "I'll meet you at the yoga studio at nine?"

"And be Keyser Söze. If someone starts taking pictures I want you to be something they thought was a myth." Sacha was laughing. "Be the man Rose stood up for. Be the man I take pictures of. Be Jerry's beautiful perfect love." That one got away from her. Charlie stopped talking. He was staring at her.

After a minute Sacha said, "It really doesn't bother you, does it."

"No, sweetheart, it doesn't. I'll admit it took me some time to get used to the idea, but once I thought about it I realized every woman I know has at some point done something for a person she loves that she would not have done for anyone else. Every single woman. I'll bet nearly every man has too, if they thought about it. He loved you the best he could. You loved him the best you could, which was better than anyone else in his life ever did. It was less ideal for you than it was for him, but you were true to him all that time. How do you really think that makes me feel? When I know how much you love me? Could I ever, *ever* doubt you?" Sacha seemed to be speechless. He was on one of the single loungers, so she twisted around and inserted herself between the armrests, cuddling sideways onto his chest. His arms came around her. They lay there in silence for a while. "Your trunks are still wet."

"Yeah. I almost warned you, but I wanted you to cuddle." He kissed her forehead. "I love you so much."

"I love you too."

"I might have to buy you some jewelry." He felt her laugh. "Or should I shop in the vault?"

"Shop in the vault. Get me that necklace with the white enamel and the turquoise flower thingies. And something to wear to that dance thing Elena told us about."

165

"The martial arts thing."

"Right, that. I'll wear the red top that looks like a kimono, and that black pencil skirt you like. The one with the fan pleats."

"Sexy." He tipped her chin up so he could kiss her properly. "Only the necklace?"

"Yes please. I want to make sure people notice this ring." Her hand was wandering now, on his neck, his shoulder, his chest. His breath caught when she started drawing circles around his nipple with a fingernail. "You know, honey, I think I need to go inside and get out of these jeans. They got wet somehow. And they're getting wetter."

"God, Charlie." He kissed her again, his own hand wandering down her shoulder, fingers brushing her breast. "Let's go inside."

Sacha was amused to see that Charlie's 'comfy shoes' for the photo shoot were cork wedges with a one-inch platform and three-inch heel. The denim tops looked great with her outfit. "You're a good height for kissing," he said, after kissing her goodbye. "But then you're always a good height for kissing. I'll see you in a little while."

She got in her car and waved. He watched her go. It had been a good long while since they had any paparazzi hanging around. The whole neighborhood was quiet this morning. He stayed outside for a minute thinking about the front yard. The gardener had mentioned they were coming up to a good time of year to make changes. What they had was halfway to a blank slate: nothing but lawn inside the curve of the driveway, with an assortment of flowering plants and shrubbery up by the house, and a tree in one corner.

Sacha took a few pictures with his phone, in case they met up with someone who seemed to have ideas. Then he went back in, thinking about getting ready to be seen.

The first thing he noticed when he got to the yoga studio was the landscape painting behind the reception desk. The second thing was the laughter coming from the big room in front. Through the window he'd seen Charlie in there with three other people. If they were having that much fun, she was probably getting some great pictures.

He was a little bit early, so he took a seat on the wooden bench in the tiny lobby. Before long the front door opened again, and a few people came in. One went to the reception desk and started to look sleepily official. The others must have been students. All of them noticed Sacha, but none of them seemed to recognize him. All of them went about the business of signing in, then dispersed into either the front room or one behind it. After a few more minutes Charlie and her subjects came out of the vinyasa room. Two middle-aged Asian men and a slender woman close to Charlie's age, probably close to Charlie's height if not for those platform sandals. Charlie mentioned breakfast, they all seemed to concur, and then they went down the hall. Sacha assumed there was a changing room, maybe even a shower room back there. He didn't stand up, simply sat and watched Charlie smile after them, then turn to find him. She rested the feet of her folded tripod on the floor and tilted her head. "Hi honey," she said. "Did you see what those nutballs were doing?"

He smiled. "The stacked planks?"

"Among other things. Kevin said he and Paul were doing the partner yoga one time when Karen came in and

167

said Hey! I wanna do that! So they started practicing together. You look kind of amazing."

"Thank you. Did you get good pictures?"

"Did I ever." Her camera was still hanging around her neck. She took a picture of him, then propped the tripod against the wall by the bench and sat beside him. "They'll be out in a minute. Swingers for breakfast?"

"That's fine." He kissed her lightly. "I'll have to watch you work sometime." She was studying his face now, faintly smiling. "You said be prepared to be photographed."

"Somehow I didn't expect this. God, you're good at that, didn't even see it until I was really looking." She was talking about the subtle darkening of his brows and lashes, the ever-so-slight smudge of shadow pencil at the base of his eyelashes. A tiny enhancement that gave his face true star quality. "Kevin and Paul did that too. Kevin said, we all do it now when we're being photographed. Are those your new ones?" Now she was talking about his custom Vans loafers. He nodded. These were printed with multicolored stripes made up of words, the titles of some of Jerry's biggest projects. "When you told me you were doing that, I thought it was so cool."

Aside from the loafers, he was wearing oatmeal-colored jeans and a short-sleeved linen shirt in faded indigo with abalone buttons. Simple, mostly distinguished by the vintage gold Patek Philippe watch strapped around his wrist. Sacha saw her noticing that too. This was the first time he'd worn it. "It was Jerry's," he said. "He had it for a long time and the original strap wore out. I got him this sting-ray strap for the Emmys two years ago." Right after the oncologist gave them the terminal prognosis, when

Jerry wasn't sure he even wanted to go to the awards show. It was the first time Sacha had given him a tangible gift. And that night they'd finally spoken the words. "He wore it every time we went out after that, even with his tux."

"He loved you," she said quietly. "It's nice you're wearing that today."

"Someone will notice. Someone will post, or tweet, whatever. Whoever shows up to take pictures might not register the shoes or the watch, but someone sometime will look at the pictures and make the connection." Sacha wrapped his other hand around his wrist for a moment, covering the watch. "I had to put it on the last hole. Jerry's wrist was so much bigger than mine."

Charlie leaned over and kissed him again. "How do you like that painting?"

Sacha was grateful for the change of subject. "It's really beautiful. A wonderful thing to see when you come in."

"Yeah, exactly. Kevin painted that. He and Paul took a vacation up in Cambria, two weeks of wine-tasting and yoga and painting. Doesn't that sound amazing?"

"Yes it does." They were talking about places to go, all the dozens of places neither of them had ever been, when Kevin and Paul came back down the hall. Sacha stood up to greet them and introduce himself. He complimented the painting. Kevin told him where it was done. Karen joined them not long after, and they all walked out.

The line at Swingers wasn't terribly long. They stood outside waiting their turn for a booth, one big enough for five. Nobody in the queue said anything to them, and no-one was obvious about taking phone pictures, but Sacha knew a few people had heard him give his name – only his first name, but it was unusual – to the hostess. Over breakfast the conversation was all about yoga and art and wine. Karen cheerfully admitted to near-complete ignorance of two of those subjects. Charlie asked what she did with her spare time. She said, "I crochet, and I take ballet classes."

"Oh! So does Sacha! He just started back again, with a teacher over near downtown." So then Sacha and Karen were talking ballet, and Charlie took the opportunity to get some names from Kevin and Paul, people who might be open to modeling for her. "I have a space at home now, or I can go to studios, and I'd love to do some outdoor stuff like we did that time in Griffith Park. My schedule is very flexible these days." She made a face; it was still weird to realize that she had complete control over her time, for the first time ever in her life.

Chapter 9

And boy was it weird to step out of the restaurant and see three people with professional-looking cameras. "You might want to do a fade," Charlie said softly to Karen, with the barest glance, trying not to draw attention to the fact that they were together. "We kind of expected this but you don't have to deal with it."

"Thanks." Karen got hold of Kevin's hand, did a 'let's go' thing with her head. He connected with Paul and they managed to get away before anyone realized they'd been with Sacha and Charlie.

"Did you tell them why?" Sacha said, very low, close to Charlie's ear.

"Only a little," she murmured. "Only that you were in an under-the-radar relationship with a high-profile person and it went public when he died, that this was the first time we'd been out in a non-controlled environment, and apologies if it got weird."

He laughed under his breath. The photographers were taking pictures and spouting questions. Sacha looked directly at the cameras and said, "Let's step away from the door so people can get in and out, okay?" He moved down the sidewalk and started answering questions. "Yes, I'm Sacha Lebedev. This is Charlotte Montgomery, my fiancée. We just felt like going out for breakfast, it's a nice day. No, I've been spending a lot of time on paperwork, a lot of time with lawyers and accountants. I'll be thirty-six next month. We haven't set a date yet." He ignored the questions about how long he and Charlie had known each other, where and when they met. When someone finally asked her a question, it was about the ring.

Charlie checked in with Sacha. It seemed he didn't mind if she answered it. She thought *why did we not decide on a story?!* "It's vintage Bulgari. Yes, it was my choice." She didn't answer the follow-up about where they got it. Then all the attention focused on her and she started to freak out a little. "I'm thirty-four, but I'm not going to answer any more personal questions. And I think we're going to go now, right?" She glanced at Sacha, who gave a slight nod and started moving, arm around her waist. He didn't push, but people gave way. One of the photographers trailed them down the sidewalk for about half a block but eventually gave up. "God I'm glad we dumped my gear in the car first," she said when she was sure nobody was listening. "I might have whacked somebody with my tripod." Sacha laughed. "You were great."

"That wasn't so bad. Next time we go out it might be worse." He patted her hip. "Will probably be worse. I'll ask Natalie to find us a car service for when we go places together. It'll be safer." He thought it would still be all right to go and do their usual things. Hoped it would. "If you ever feel uneasy when you go out by yourself, tell me. Is that guy still following?" Charlie looked over her shoulder, couldn't spot him, shook her head. "They'll be looking into what we drive now. If you ever see people hanging around your car, go inside a business and call me. Okay?"

Charlie didn't say anything for a minute. She was realizing that this was what could have happened, what certainly *would* have happened, if her connection with Sacha had been known last year. As they got to the yoga studio's parking lot she said, "Thank you."

"For what?" Sacha was scanning the perimeter as she opened her car door.

"For not letting this happen last year. I told myself it was for my own good that you went silent, and after a while I believed it, but I didn't really *know* it till this minute."

He was looking at her now. He kissed her lightly. "I needed you so much. Too much. If I'd dragged you into it before I had a handle on everything, it would have been such a burden for you. I love you." He kissed her again, not so lightly, one hand cradling her head and the other holding her against him. Wondering if he could ever have looked in those eyes and not wanted her, trusted her, loved her. He wanted her now. "We'll talk when we're at home."

Charlie was hoping they'd do more than talk. She let go of him reluctantly. "Okay. Yeah. I love you too." All the way home she was thinking. About what she wanted to do with him, but also about the looming necessity of using a car service, giving up a little piece of independence in order to feel safer. About what other measures they might have to take, and how she'd never really thought about these things before. *Oh my God, Natalie*, she thought. How long would this go on? Would the gossip rags send people after her, trying to get the inside scoop on Sacha? Would she be able to keep her job at the school? Would she see a mob of paparazzi and say 'you know what, peace, I'm out'?

They all talked about it later. Sacha called Gary and asked him if he could come over for dinner. Then he asked if Gary could give them a little insight into how his clients dealt with this kind of thing.

"Well," Gary said, almost apologetically, "you have to understand that writers are not very high profile. Most people barely think about the fact that television shows and movies have writers. They look at the faces of the project, the actors. So I'm not sure my clients' experience is going to speak to your publicity issues. I can't think of a single one of my clients who even had a PR person. I mean, I did not have Quentin Tarantino."

"Thanks for nothing, Gary," said Natalie, but with a smile. They were all sitting by the pool, cocktails in hand, promised something good for dinner. Cecilia was working on it right that minute. "You have lots of other industry friends, though. People who handled actors?"

"Yeah, sure. My friend Raquel Schumann, one of her clients is Andy Martin. Patrick pinged him for you, right? Did you ever hook up to talk about your gallery thing?"

Charlie shook her head. "Not yet. Soon, though. I mean, we've been in touch and I'm going over there in a week or so."

"He and his boyfriend have a manager who handles all their personal PR. You might ask him for a referral."

"I'll do that," Charlie said. "If we get along. I don't want to be shaking him down for names if we're all, like, ew." Natalie laughed. "I'll shake *you* down. You'd call up Raquel, right? Say, who has people?"

"Sure." Gary reached for Natalie's hand. It looked like a total impulse. Charlie waited to see what was about to happen. "What about you, Ms. Sanders? Any paparazzi hassling you?"

"Not yet," she said, looking slightly surprised but not pulling away. "Do you think they will?"

"I was obsessing about that today." Charlie drank some of her Cape Cod. "I was like, oh em gee, what if they go after Natalie, are they going to fuck you up with your school, ugh."

They could all see from Natalie's expression that this hadn't occurred to her. After a minute she said, "They can't fuck me up in the sense of costing me my job. They could cost me some time and annoyance. I'm pretty good at not talking to people I don't want to talk to."

"I feel better now," said Gary. "You always talk to me."

"Gary, for God's sake." She squeezed his hand. "Okay, I have a confession."

"What's that." Sacha was hoping Natalie wasn't about to say 'I'm ready to get my own place again.' He glanced over at Charlie, who made an 'eek' face.

Natalie may have noticed that. "I was thinking maybe it's time to retire after all. I mean, I really like living here, I like the work I'm doing for you, and I should probably get my pension out of the system while it still exists. We could really get this book moving."

"Oh thank God." It was Gary, not Sacha or Charlie. "I've been wanting to ask you out but you're always so goddamned *busy*." Natalie laughed. Gary kissed her hand and Charlie nearly swooned. "Can I take you out to dinner? Without the kids?"

"Yes, Gary." Natalie was still smiling. "I'm sure the kids won't mind being left alone occasionally."

"No. Or yes." Gary was suddenly looking much younger than sixty-eight.

"Let's go check on Cecilia." Charlie stood up, tugged Sacha to his feet, and said, "You two stay out here." They went in the house, determinedly not looking back even though both of them were dying to know if Gary was kissing Natalie.

They went in the house, went through to the kitchen, and found Cecilia at the window. "Gary is kissing her," she told them. "It's about time."

August 2016

Charlie asked Sacha if he wanted to come along to her meeting with Andy Martin. He said, "I never thought I would say this, but I have too much to do." She laughed. "I'm thinking back to last winter, when I basically didn't leave the house, or even March when there were three people in my life. And now I have classes and meetings and a social life, and Natalie is flogging me through all this document review."

"Who wants to be a millionaire," she said, and kissed him. "A millionaire who is writing a book."

"I have no idea what I'm doing." He pulled her down onto his lap. She didn't resist, even though she needed to get going pretty soon. "But I couldn't not try, not after she found that letter."

"I was going to interview you again for the film." She regarded him for a minute. "I thought it would be good to put in more about the actual relationship. But now I wonder if Tony and I should concentrate on the outside. You're going to have the inside story in your book. Unless you want to say something?"

Sacha had been thinking about the same thing. He still wasn't sure which way to go. "I kind of want to, because otherwise there's this giant 'why,' you know. If I were seeing that story and didn't know why it all happened, and nobody told me, I think I'd be annoyed." Charlie snorted. "But also I kind of don't want to because it's still really fresh and that letter kind of tore it open again and then there's you. You are so important to me. Being engaged to you, planning to marry you. Being in love with you. Maggie's story is about Jerry. I want my story to be about you."

She kissed him again. "There is one way around that." He looked up, questioning. "Turn the page before we pitch the film. Get married first." Sacha smiled. "What do you think? January maybe?"

"We could go to New Zealand for our honeymoon," he said softly. "It'll be summer there." They held each other for another minute. "Oh my God."

"What?" It didn't sound like something bad.

"What if we used the letter in the film, too? What if someone read it, like voice-over?"

"Oh my God!" Charlie could almost hear it. She knew what Jerry's voice sounded like, from those TV clips. What if they could find someone with a similar voice, an actor, someone who could make all that painful love come across? "People would be *bawling*. And you wouldn't have to say a word. I'll ask Tony."

"Okay. Yeah, ask Tony." He patted her hip. "But you'd better go or you'll be late."

"I'll ping you when I'm about to start back. I love you."

"I love you too." He let her stand up, and watched her go, and stayed in the office for a minute because the more he thought about it, the more he thought using that letter was the perfect way to tie film and book together.

Charlie picked up her camera and a notebook, then went out to her car. Before starting out she sent a text to Tony: *Hi boss, we had a brainstorm. We found this letter from Jerry to Sacha, it's long and heartbreaking and we wondered if maybe voice-over? Need a voice like Jerry's which means we need an actor who is not Sacha. Anyway will send it to you soon, on my way to meet Andy Martin now, available tonight. Ciao!*

She was thinking about it all the way to Andy's house in Mid City. She and Sacha hadn't really discussed whether he would use the full letter in the book. They hadn't discussed whether he would go public with the state he'd been in when Jerry found him. Charlie kind of thought he shouldn't. It would be easy to redact a few words – it would only take a few – from the letter. It would be easy to say he'd had experience with men before, without saying he'd been paid for it. She would be astonished if any of the places he'd worked thirteen years ago were even still in business, or at least under the same management. There wouldn't be anyone to come up and say hey, I know that guy, he was a hooker. He used drugs. No-one had last year, when everybody was looking for someone to say shit like that.

Charlie knew Sacha was well-adjusted, under the circumstances. He'd had a lot of time to cope with his past. He'd had therapy. But when someone picks up a piece of your past and beats you with it, no amount of coping skills could make it not hurt. And in his position now, that would cascade for the rest of his life. She thought she'd suggest typing out the letter, and leaving out those few problematic words, before sending it to Tony.

She parked at the back of the faux-chateau-style duplex as instructed, and walked through the back gate. *Why don't they have a security guard*, she thought. She'd done a little reading about Andy and his boyfriend Victor Garcia. They'd been news for a year and a half, thanks to a controversial relationship arc on that cop show. The first gay couple to play a gay couple, the first major kiss in a primetime broadcast, and then this spring, a full-on love scene with partial nudity. The news stories she'd found were now closed to comments, but there had been hundreds, and many were frightening. *Men are insane*, she decided. Yeah, they had security cameras and 'armed response.' That wasn't going to do them a damned bit of good if someone truly crazy came to the house.

She pushed the buzzer next to the door set into the garage wall. Heard someone jogging down stairs inside. Then the door opened and she was looking up at him. "Hi Mr. Martin, I'm Charlie Montgomery. Wow, you are really good-looking."

He laughed, shook her hand, and stood back so she could go inside. "Thank you very much. Call me Andy. Right up these stairs. Any trouble finding the place?"

"No. Why don't you have a guard?"

"Eh." He was behind her, but there was a shrug in his voice. "You missed meeting Victor. He was called today for this movie. It's so stupid, but they're having fun making it. I've gone to the set a couple of times."

"What's it about?" They were in his studio now, a big empty room with three generous windows, a high ceiling, and a dance barre on one wall. The staircase end of the structure held a full bath and a kitchenette with a desk. There was a pretty blonde dog under the desk. "Hey, who is this?"

"That's Molly. Say hi to Charlie, Molly." The dog got to her feet, wagged her way over to Charlie, and they got acquainted. Andy offered coffee, which she accepted while petting Molly.

Then she turned to the desk. He had a big monitor next to an almost-as-big laptop; both had images on screen. She forgot all about Mr. Garcia's movie. "Oh, are those from your chorus boys thing?"

"They are! Oh my God that was fun. These gorgeous guys. Come and see." They sat down and he started to scroll through what she suspected was a fraction of the photos he'd taken. Everything she was looking at was great; they looked almost like movie stills, going from afternoon to dusk. And yes, the guys – including Victor - were gorgeous, which she made a point of telling him. He looked pleased.

"So you're doing a show with these?" she said after a while, and that led into what she'd come there for. Andy talked to her like they'd known each other for years. She was developing a celebrity crush.

He told her about his history with photography, and his very first gallery show. "I was roommates with Dana Richardson then. She's on that other cop show, plays the captain. Anyway, she'd just moved to West Hollywood and we knew each other from way back. She helped produce the whole thing. We hung it at a dance studio."

"Shall We Dance?"

"That's the one."

"We met Mr. Vasko really recently. His husband is Sacha's accountant. Sacha Lebedev, he's my fiancé." It still sounded strange.

Andy blinked, clearly assimilating the name into whatever idea he'd had about her. "That whole situation. Any issues?"

"It's been pretty calm lately. It was terrible for him last fall." She told Andy about how she'd come to know Sacha, and how they'd fallen in love, and how her life was changing as a consequence. She told him about the paparazzi issue, and he gave her his manager's name without hesitation. "Thank you so much. It might turn out to be no big deal, but we want to be prepared. Anyway that's how I have the time and money to look at hanging this show." She dug the proof of her teachers book out, and then it was another half hour of talk about that while he looked through it.

"Totally different from my style," he said with approval. "Great photographs. I can send you some contacts for galleries once you decide how many of these you want to print and hang. And I'll send you the link to the company I use for printing and mounting."

"What was your first show about?"

"It was about being an artist in L.A." He stood up, went to the shelf over the kitchen counter, and pulled down a book. It had a plain black cover, glossy canvas, with 'City of Angels, 2007' written on the spine with silver marker. He handed it to her without comment.

Charlie started paging through it. "Holy shit, Andy." The photos were of Los Angeles at night, dreamy, almost phantasmagorical. Many were completely devoid of humanity. Only a single human appeared in the others. "These are *fantastic*. Who was your model?"

"Dana's girlfriend Rory. There was a hotel rep who came to the show, they ended up taking prints for each of their guest rooms. I still get comments."

"Yeah, I'll bet. And now you're a TV star. What a trip."

He laughed. "It is a trip. I hate that fucking show. But it's good for Victor, and we're representing."

"You need a security guard."

"Eh," he said again.

"I should let you go. This has been great. Thank you so much."

"Let me show you one more thing before you take off. It'll make you laugh." Andy turned back to the computer and pulled up a video. "I took this on the set and they would kill me if they knew, even though this is not from the actual movie. They're just being goofballs." It was Victor, with a bigger, taller guy. They seemed to be doing a scene, which seemed to be about some kind of investigation, but they were in what looked like a craft services area and they were surrounded by crew-type people who were all cracking up. Every line they said was so inventively profane that Charlie started giggling too. They wound it up to a truly obscene punch line and she laughed out loud. "Who's that other guy?"

"That's the star, Jonathan Morris. It's his first above-the-title part. He told Victor he was shitting bricks, he was so glad they got along because having this thing riding on him was freaking him out. He's a nice guy. Used to be a professional wrestler."

"He's funny. And Victor is hilarious. He never broke."

"Yeah, he's good like that. He can look so serious and say the filthiest things. But this movie is fucking me up."

"Why, what's going on?"

"We're trying to record an album, and we will get it done, but with his shooting schedule it's been a little bit here and a little bit there, which has broken up my time in a way that I generally prefer to do by myself." He rolled his eyes. "Whatever. Did we get through everything you need?"

"You are spectacular," she said sincerely. "I feel so much more prepared to do this. If I could ask you one more thing?" He made a 'sure why not' face. Charlie smiled. "I'm kind of in adding contacts mode because we're working on a documentary. Who are you working with for the album? Our editor guy is going to need a sound and music person."

"Well, this person would be a good person. Her name is Valerie Benton. I can send you her website too."

"Thank you. You are fantastic. I'm so glad I got to meet you."

"It's been a pleasure. Let me walk you out." He switched off the screens and said, "Come on Molly," and they all left the studio.

Charlie took a moment in her car to check for messages. There was a text from Tony: *Will look forward to seeing the letter, it's a good idea*

She wrote back: *And I know who could do it if we could get him. Jonathan Morris, Mr. Martin had a video of him and he sounds JUST LIKE JERRY. Andy says he's a nice guy, the movie he's shooting is supposed to wrap by the end of this month. Also have a name for sound and music person, Valerie Benton. See you soon*

Thanks Charlie! Will be in touch

Charlie sent a quick text to Sacha to let him know she was on her way home, and rolled out. She was thinking about how busy they both were now, and how glad she was that they lived together. It was still so weird not to be working, but they'd never be able to get all this done if she were.

Back at home, Charlie went straight to Sacha with her thoughts about the letter. She found him in the office again, or still. "I don't want you to end up regretting this," she said. "It's already so much. There are things nobody needs to know." *Especially your family.*

"You know. Natalie knows. And since she knows, Gary will know eventually, if he doesn't already." He was giving her that steady look, the one that said 'prepared for anything.' Then he smiled and said, "But generally speaking I agree with you. It wouldn't take much, would it?"

"Only a few words," she said, relieved. "Do you want to do that, or should I do it? I'd get you to look at it before I send it to Tony."

"You can do it. Thanks." Sacha sat back, rolled his neck, thought *it's time to call it a day*, and stood up. "What did you think of Mr. Martin?"

Charlie picked up his cue, and followed him out of the office. "Oh my God he's such a sweetheart. He's so much like that bartender character he plays. They either wrote it for him, or told him to play it like himself, or something. He says, quote, I hate that fucking show." Sacha laughed. "I did not pursue it because I'd already been there almost two hours and I think originally we both thought it would be, like, a half hour. Can you believe those idiots don't have a guard?" They were heading for the patio, which suited her fine.

"No." He really couldn't. Sacha wasn't exactly fond of having an armed guard, but Jerry had told him about three separate break-in attempts in the two years before he took that measure. Sacha was not willing to risk anything like that, not with Cecilia and Natalie and Charlie to consider. And of course, he'd gotten enough threats himself to accept that expense as simply part of 'utilities.' He went over to the bar. "Your usual?"

184

"Have I not drunk all of that yet? You know not to replace that, right?" Charlie looked at the contents of the bar cabinets. They were never going to get through all of it without help. "We need to have a party."

The next time they met with Tony, it was to see the cut-together footage showing Maggie disassembled, and then re-created. "About this letter," Tony said after putting the big screen to sleep. "I think the voice-over idea is wonderful. But we will need some music. Most viewers have trouble accepting film, even documentary film, without music. Obviously not where we use a clip, or where we hear the voice-over. But in the moments where all we see is Sacha creating Maggie, or taking her apart. Even when he's speaking, some music under that, I think we need it."

"Well, we have this referral from Andy," Charlie said. "I think we should talk to this woman. Get a professional opinion. Because maybe it's quicker or cheaper or just plain better to write new music, but maybe it's better to license some."

"Original songs, or covers?" Sacha couldn't quite see doing it with originals. There was already so much going on. Charlie's footage, the clips, interviews, the voice-over. An original song might not be granted because of the documentary's subject matter. A cover version could at least be tweaked so that it didn't overwhelm the rest of the material.

"I think covers would be best. Only one, even," Tony added. "A single song that occurs several times. A leitmotif." Sacha knew what that was, thanks to Jerry. "But then it becomes very important, the viewer

185

hears it again and again, it must be exactly the right thing."

"Ugh." Charlie couldn't imagine what song would possibly work. And then what if they found the perfect one, and the rights owner wouldn't let them use it. "I wish Sacha could sing," she said before she could stop herself. "I mean, I wish you would sing for the film."

He was looking at her like she was crazy, which she might be. "Why?"

"I don't know. Wait. Yes I do. It's because we're not hearing your voice, you as you, in this thing yet. What you say in my footage is so, like, technical. It's about how you hit on the different elements of the character design and then implemented them. It's not about the relationship, it's not about Jerry, it's not about you. I'm sorry, I know we kind of talked about whether you wanted to do an interview and we both know you kind of don't. I'm afraid if we don't hear from you on this thing people still won't get it." Sacha didn't say anything. Charlie added, "For the record, Tony, Sacha can really sing."

After a moment Tony said, "I agree with Charlie. But if you sing, it's so much more personal. So," he searched for the word, "vulnerable. The song would have to be perfect. Would you consider it, if we can find the perfect song? If we can get the license?"

Sacha sat back on the couch, stared at the ceiling, sighed. "I want the film to work. I want people to see it and understand. If you think me singing would help with that, or me giving an interview would help with that, I'm not giving you a definitive no." He sat up and gazed at each of them. "Could you meet with this music person? Or talk to her, at least. See what she thinks. Maybe she'll have an idea."

They left it at that, and over the next week Tony contacted Valerie Benton to discuss the project. He sent Charlie a text after their conference: *Valerie says she has room in schedule in January, and is interested. Says we definitely need music, leitmotif best choice given anticipated complexity of sound design, with new music for titles and credits. A known song will help people connect to the subject matter - the simpler the arrangement, the better it will be. As to Sacha singing, she says she'd have to hear him first*

Charlie laughed under her breath. She didn't at all blame the music professional for being noncommittal on that point. There were a lot of people who wanted to be singers who really shouldn't. *Understood. Any word back from J Morris agent re voiceover?*

He is at liberty in three weeks and willing to meet. I will set something up. Till then, can you ask Sacha to prepare something for Valerie?

Eeek yes sometimes I feel like this is so rough on him

I know, apologies, the viewers like to see people bleed

Jesus Tony. Why did I have this idea. Will be in touch soon. Charlie disconnected, shivering a little, because the last thing she wanted to do was hurt Sacha. She didn't even know how to take this new request to him. This was never his idea, he was humoring her, it was a bad idea, she should pull the plug.

She was still sitting in the kitchen when he came in from the office. "Did Cecilia go out?"

"Yeah, she went to the market."

"Everything all right?" He set his hand on her shoulder, looking at the phone in her hand. "Bad news?"

"Not exactly." Charlie sighed, woke up the text exchange, and handed the phone to Sacha. He handed it back after a couple of minutes.

He leaned down, arm around her shoulders, face close to hers. "I sing all the time, you know that. I sing to Moses, I sing with Cecilia, I sing in the shower. I don't mind. And my feelings won't be hurt if Valerie says no."

"Are you sure?"

He kissed her cheek. "You found the perfect voice for the letter. I'm sure Tony will talk Jonathan into doing it. We can find the right song, the right singer. That's what producers do, remember? Watch what's happening, stop what isn't working, find a different solution."

Charlie sighed. She knew what she was doing barely qualified. This whole process was such an education. "Yeah. Okay." She turned her head and looked up. Sacha still had his hand on her shoulder. It seemed he was waiting to see if she was settled. "Why are you worried about me? I'm barely even doing any work on this. You're the one being put through a wringer." She stood up and hugged him.

"That's not what this is," he said after a moment. "This is more than that. I know why you feel it's important. I do too. This was twelve years of my life, a third of my life. My whole adulthood so far, really. We're both learning so much about Jerry, but also about me. These are things I didn't explore with my shrink."

"I know."

"I'm a public person now whether I like it or not. These giant questions of why, why Jerry left me so much, why we were together in the first place. If these questions aren't answered it's not fair to him or to me. So yes, sometimes it's rough. But it's necessary."

"I love you so much." She tipped her head back. He kissed her. "I love how brave you are. I loved you right from the start for being so sweet with Jerry, with Rose. And then for being so unselfish, because I saw in those pictures how nobody really noticed you. I didn't understand it, because to me you were so *everything*," she added, which made him smile. "Then when you told me so much, so much you never needed to tell me, when if I had been the wrong kind of person it could have really blown up in your face."

"But you weren't that person. You were the person who asked if I needed a friend. The one person."

"I hate people sometimes." That made him laugh, a little. Charlie rubbed her hands up and down his back. "When's the last time you had a massage?"

"God, I don't even remember."

"You should add that to the schedule. You must know people. But if you want to go lie down, I could give you my uneducated version of a back rub. Unless there's something you need to be doing."

"There's nothing that can't wait." Sacha stood away a little, so he could start moving toward their bedroom. Charlie kept one arm around his waist, her thumb stroking the bottom of his ribcage. It made him think of other things they could do lying down. After ten minutes of back rub, it seemed she was also thinking of other things. Her hands moved to his hips and thighs, and then he rolled over. She stretched out beside him. "Honey," he said against her mouth, "now there's something that can't wait."

A week later, Charlie got home from another session photographing yogis, registered with relief that once again there was no sign of press interest in their house, and went inside to find Sacha. "Whatever Cecilia made today smells amazing," she said as she stepped into the den. "What are you watching?"

"Wings of Desire," he said, pausing the movie. "I think I like it."

"Why are you watching it?"

"Jerry made a note on this script." He indicated the bound screenplay on the side table. "I have no idea why because this script has nothing to do with Germany or angels or love or sensation. It's a stupid horror movie set in New Orleans. All the note says is the movie title, and he must have jotted it down for some other reason."

"Which is good, because now you can chuck out one more stupid horror movie script, right?"

Sacha laughed under his breath. "Right."

"How much is left?"

"Only about fifteen minutes."

"I'll watch it with you." She sat down beside him, prepared to zone out a little, which was a thing she liked to do anyway after a photo session. Sacha put his arm over her shoulders and hit 'play.' When they got to the end she looked up at him and said, "Okay, I guess I'm going to have to watch the whole thing. But not right now, I'm hungry."

"Me too. I was going to watch this other thing next, it's an adaptation, or re-make." Sacha indicated 'City of Angels,' next in his queue.

"That was the title of Andy's first gallery show. Unbelievably good photographs, I hate him. Anyway sure, let's watch that after we eat, and then I'll watch the German one tomorrow when I can concentrate."

After dinner, and after watching the other movie, Charlie made a disgusted sound. "Fucking Americans." Sacha laughed. "Why would they turn that into this? Why? Why kill Meg Ryan? Why? What was the fucking point of that?"

"I think it's one of those things about how a man has to suffer in order to be fully actualized. Preferably by something awful happening to a woman." Sacha loved it when Charlie got pissed at a movie. It reminded him of all those times he and Jerry had sat in here bitching about some terrible writing, or acting, or whatever.

"I personally think that's a load of crap, and also a surgeon would never be that fucking dumb! Seriously!"

"But there was something." Sacha reversed the movie, slowing down, looking for a visual cue. He re-started the playback in time to see Nicolas Cage hitch-hiking. "This song."

Charlie listened. "I know that song."

"I do too." He fast-forwarded again, going for the credits. They read through to the end. "Hang on." He stood up, went to the office for one of the laptops, came back. Opened it up, did an internet search, and found the official music video. They listened to the song. "Charlie."

"Find the lyrics?" In a minute he had those in another tab. "Holy shit, Sacha. Email that to Tony."

"Why is the song called 'Iris'?"

"Why is the band called Goo Goo Dolls? Some questions have no answers, honey." Charlie watched him send the email. Then he did a print operation on the lyrics. They heard the printer wake up down the hall in the office. "Did you ever play guitar?"

"No." They stared at each other for a few seconds. "But I can learn." An email reply pinged softly. Sacha opened the message. "Tony says yes. I'll find a teacher tomorrow." They listened to the song one more time. "My God, it's everything. It's why Jerry needed Maggie, it's why we're making this thing, it's why I love you. You knew who I was." He set the laptop aside and reached for her. "I love you."

"I love you." Charlie felt all the complicated emotion in his kiss, all the passionate commitment in his touch. She lay back on the couch, pulling him with her.

CHAPTER 10

They hadn't seen Gary for almost a month; he was putting in long hours, including a lot of business dinners. Several tentative dates got cancelled at the last minute. He finally sent Sacha a text: *Culver City is eating me alive send help.*

Sacha decided to take this literally. He felt like going out anyway, so he rounded up Natalie and Charlie. "Let's pick up Gary for a birthday party."

"Cecilia made you tres leches," Natalie said. "She put it in the fridge before she left. You'd better eat some when we get home."

"We'll all have some when we get home. Right now it's time for a rescue operation." He showed her Gary's text. She made an 'oh poor baby' face. Charlie was already putting her shoes on. They were on their way a few minutes later, and arrived at four o'clock without even telling Gary they were en route. "Okay. Who wants to go in and get him?" Sacha pulled over on a yellow curb with his hazard lights on.

"I'll go," Natalie said, which didn't surprise the others. "Don't get a parking ticket." She got out of the car and went into the building.

Charlie said, "How long do you think it will take her?"

"I think unless he is actually in a meeting, he'll be out of there like he had an ejector seat." Charlie laughed. Sacha was grinning. "Did you decide where to give the money from your show?"

"There are so many education charities," she said. "It's exasperating. I decided to go with the Khan Foundation. They're going to send me some promotional stuff to have out. I'm putting the Donors Choose information on the cards and brochures, and it's in the book too."

"That's great. Natalie's come up with so many great projects through that. And most of them need such tiny bits of money, it's annoying."

"Exactly! It's like, why the hell are they having to ask the world for this pocket change for this potentially life-changing project. I'm so glad you're supporting that." She patted his leg. Then motion at the front of the building caught her eye. "Oh here they are. Must not have been in a meeting." Natalie was laughing; Gary was taking off his tie.

They were at the car a few seconds later. Gary opened the door for Natalie, then went around to the other side. He got in saying "Boy, when you ask this guy for help, he helps. Thanks, Sacha."

"I figured you were probably only half-serious, but half was enough. Is there really that much work?"

"There really is. I need to learn how to say no. I'm a fucking director, I can say no."

"Say exactly that, Gary," Charlie advised. "Next time someone says oh we need to discuss this over dinner, say that." Natalie was laughing again. Gary was stripping off his suit jacket. "Strap in so we can get out of here before they send a posse after you."

Sacha was already pulling away from the curb. "Where should we go?"

"The closest bar." Gary sat back, smiling at Natalie. "It sure was nice to see you walk in." The bar they went to wasn't the closest, but it wasn't far. They left the car with the valet and walked into City Tavern not much later. As soon as they were seated Gary wanted to know what everyone was up to. "I feel like

I haven't seen you for months, but that's probably because each day is about four days long."

Charlie said, "I'm rolling with the teachers gallery show, Tony's rolling with the documentary, Natalie is rolling on the life of Jerry, and Sacha is taking care of business."

"Also various classes," Sacha said. "So have you started acquiring things yet or are you still sorting through stuff?"

"Sorting. Turning the giant pile into three less-giant piles. Well, into one slightly less giant pile, which would be the stuff we never want to see again, and two smaller ones which are things we're going to make offers on, and things we're going to take options on." A first round of cocktails arrived. Gary took a sip, approved, and set down the glass. "I'm having to be very aware of this stuff. Everyone I'm working with is ten or twenty or forty years younger and they're all, one more round! And I'm all, you will kill me."

"They can't kill you," Natalie said. "They need you to give this operation some legitimacy. I've been reading the trades, I saw this really snarky thing about that platform."

Gary looked around as if to make sure nobody was listening. "Justified. Their first few projects were not the stuff of Emmy awards. But they've got some capital now. If we can get some of this stuff produced quickly there's hope. And yes. They need me. They brought me in because one of the other directors is a guy whose first script I sold, back in the day. He was like, this guy can spot quality." He rolled his eyes as everyone else laughed. "No, he's a good guy, he's talented. They started out with this kind of utopian United Artists idea, right. Like, writers and actors would put together the content and control the outcome. It's a sweet idea." He shrugged. "You can imagine what Jerry would say."

"He would say, I give it two years before they go broke." Sacha sipped his drink, smiling at Gary. "Are you steering them off Dream Street?"

"Trying to. There's a place for very personal independent dramas in which a bunch of guys sit around and talk earnestly, or a love affair slowly goes wrong. That place is the bottom two rows of your menu. Up at the top, you want buzzy stuff, lots of action, at least some violence, and either monsters or nudity." Gary gave Natalie a look; she was laughing again. "Sometimes both." Sacha was also laughing. That sounded exactly like something Jerry would say. "There's a place for high-quality documentaries, too. We've already got a couple in the pipeline."

Toward the end of the evening (which wasn't terribly late), Charlie said, "Okay, Gary. When we take you back there, you have to promise you'll go straight to your car."

"I promise."

"You also have to promise to come with us to this dance thing at Chrome." She told him the date. He got out his phone and put the information in his calendar. "And now I will go and get the valets to bring up the car, and Sacha will go take care of the bill, so you and Natalie can have a minute." She kissed his cheek and left the table.

"Actually," Gary said, "Sacha will not take care of the bill, because it's his birthday. Go with your fiancée. We'll be with you shortly."

"Okay." Sacha stood up, stepped around the table, and also kissed Gary's cheek before he walked away.

September 2016

"They've been at the event for two days already," Tony said. "They both have students competing." He was in the back seat of Sacha's car. Sacha was driving, Charlie was in the front passenger seat, and the rest of the back seat was full of camera gear.

Tony had arranged to do interviews with some of the top couples in the American Rhythm professional division; Elena and Mateo would be going up against them at competitions in October and November. Charlie had expressed an interest in seeing what ballroom competition was all about, and Sacha was more than willing to get out of Los Angeles for a minute, so they were going down to Irvine with Tony.

Charlie would have asked how Elena and Mateo's competition season was going, except she kind of already knew. She'd been in and out of the Benedetti apartment so much that any update was delivered without delay. "That was an awfully tight schedule for Mateo." The big dance concert in Hollywood had closed Sunday night, leaving him less than a week to rest, recover, and refresh all of his students before their competitions. "He was amazing in that show. Some of those numbers were brutal."

"He was back in the studio Monday morning. He isn't thirty yet." Charlie laughed. Tony smiled. "I only turned thirty two years ago."

"Yeah, but you have a baby. All Mateo has to contend with is cats. Are you going with them to their competition in Seattle?"

"Yes, I'll be there. Have you ever been there?"

"No, I haven't been out of California since I got here. And when I moved here, my friend and I only stopped twice, for long enough to sleep in the car. I don't consider I really saw anything on the way."

"We're going to travel someday, Tony," said Sacha. "Starting with our honeymoon." He already knew Tony and Elena had been married in Italy, with Tony's family; their honeymoon was a weekend in Capri. "We just got our passports."

Tony asked where they planned to go, and when they planned to get married. "We talk so much about the project, and about my own film, and not enough about you," he said to Charlie.

"All I'm really doing is the project right now. Once those prints come in I have quality-control to do, and then I have to print the histories that we're hanging with the portraits. Can't believe that's happening next month. But I think the idea is to get married in January and take off for New Zealand right after."

"That's the idea," Sacha agreed, smiling. "We should fill in the details though. The getting-married part." Charlie laughed. "I could put Natalie to work on that."

"Oh, she'd love that. God, can you even believe this traffic? I haven't been to Irvine since Rose's event last year."

"Neither have I." Sacha let the navigation system tell him how to get off the freeway and to the event hotel. He dealt with the parking valet while Charlie and Tony wrangled camera gear.

They could hear music as soon as they were through the main lobby. Tony led them down a long hallway, past some costume vendors' displays, and then around a corner where the music was suddenly much louder. "I'll be setting up back around the

198

corner," he said. "After we check in." There was no such thing as free entry to the ballroom. Sacha didn't mind paying admission. They wouldn't be there all afternoon or evening, but he was already enjoying the music and the energy. He waved goodbye to Tony, who made an 'I'll call you' gesture, as they went in.

Charlie could have done with a slightly lower noise level, but the ballgowns were knocking her out. She leaned close so Sacha could hear her say, "I'll bet ninety percent of why people do this is to wear dresses like that."

"Would you do it to wear a dress like that?"

"Duh, yeah." He laughed. Charlie started taking pictures.

Elena finished up with her students before seven o'clock. She suggested they go and get some dinner while they waited to hear from Tony about his status. "If he gets everybody during the break, he'll be happy," she said. "But that's basically the dinner hour. Oh, it's better out here." They'd turned the corner, heading back toward the main lobby. "Mateo's gone up to his room, Sam came down and they're going to have dinner together. So it's only the three of us."

Sacha was on his phone, talking to the hotel restaurant. "Twenty minutes," he said after disconnecting. "Elena, Charlie wants a ballgown."

Elena laughed. "The people who make mine also do wedding dresses. They're in West L.A. Matsumoto Costume and Couture. Have you set a date yet?"

"No." Sacha glanced at Charlie, who was snickering. "We were talking about that on the way. The necessity of actually making wedding plans." They ended up talking about it all through dinner.

Charlie confessed, "I kind of thought I was never going to get married. And then I met Sacha, and I was in love with him immediately, but there was all that mess to get through."

"We made it through," he said, smiling. "We don't want a big wedding, do we?"

"No." Charlie made an 'ick' face. "If you have a big wedding you have to invite a lot of people. I don't even know a lot of people."

"What about your families?"

"I will invite mine, because I have to." Charlie grimaced again. "But I don't expect them to come, and I don't especially want them to come. My mother has said disgusting things about Sacha and my siblings never go anywhere without their ten thousand brats."

Elena unsuccessfully attempted to stifle a laugh. "I'm so sorry." She noticed Sacha, who was smiling but looked a little sad. "Your family too?"

"Afraid so. We're in touch, but they feel like they don't know me anymore, and what they've heard has confused and upset them. One day I hope they'll come around. I know they'd love Charlie."

"I would have thought they'd had plenty of time to get over whatever." Elena was frowning now. "It's not like you did anything wrong. And, I mean, really. About yours?" She indicated Charlie's ring. "That is not the kind of son-in-law situation most people would object to."

"They think it's the wages of sin," Charlie said. "They can choke." Elena laughed out loud. "Anyway the more I think about it, the more I think let's throw open the bar cabinet and do it in the backyard by the pool. All we need is an officiant, right?"

"Well, once we have the license, yes." Sacha liked this idea. He was sure Natalie and Cecilia would like it. They could get a valet permit for parking, turn on the outdoor speakers, shut Moses in the house with some chicken mole so he didn't get scared. "I love this idea." He leaned over to kiss Charlie. Then went the other way and kissed Elena. She laughed again, pleased. "I don't suppose you know an officiant."

"Actually," she said, "I do. Rory Atwood, who is one of Dmitri's best friends, is ordained. I could introduce you."

"Jeez, by the time we get home we're going to have this whole thing figured out." Charlie put her elbows on the table and gazed at Elena. "Tell me more about this ballgown company."

The drive back from Irvine was only slightly less annoying than the trip down. They took Tony back to West Hollywood, thanked him for an entertaining afternoon and evening, and drove home. "I like her," Charlie said. "I mean, I like them both, but I really like her. I haven't met that many women close to my age that I could really relate to. She works so hard."

"She's like Natalie, isn't she?" Sacha said. "Creative. Smart. A problem-solver."

"Also, of course, fricking gorgeous. Which would in most situations make me self-conscious, but then you look at me like I'm the most interesting person in the world and I think oh, okay." He laughed. Charlie was smiling. "I'll go over to the dance studio sometime soon and see if I can arrange a meeting with this Rory. I've only been to Dmitri's once."

"When were you there?"

"It was after a session with Tony, watching him cut in some of those video clips. My eyeballs finally gave out and he was hungry, so he said he would walk me to my car and then go get dinner. And we walked through the studio for some reason. It was packed, so much going on, it was basically like the competition today only not quite so loud and nobody was in a ballgown. Dmitri was there but he was working, I kind of waved and went on through."

"I'm sure he'd love to teach you Viennese waltz." Sacha glanced over at her. "I'd love to dance it with you. I've only ever learned ballet waltz. It's not the same, I'd need lessons too."

Charlie regarded him for a moment, thinking about the couples they'd seen swirling around the floor at the competition. "I would do that."

"We could set up a dance floor in the backyard. And then a ballgown wedding dress would be perfect."

"It would, wouldn't it?"

A week later, Charlie was back at Gary's office, and actually inside it. This time he was going on camera. "I am not the most photogenic human in the world," he said. "Are you going to make me look good?"

"Gary, you look fine." Charlie was finishing up the very basic makeup that would help him look alive on camera. Sacha had given her some lessons. She stood back and let Tony have a look; he nodded approval. "Okay. Whenever you're ready." The cameras were set. Tony was there to help move things along in the unlikely event that Charlie needed him, and to operate the second camera. Gary'd had the list of points to cover for more than a week. It was only nominally an interview; he would talk, and if he stalled one of them would prompt him. They had a portable light for the cameras, with the window blinds up to add natural light. Since it was a Sunday, only a few other people were in the office suite. It was quiet, and they wouldn't be interrupted.

Gary was pacing again. Restless again, and for pretty much the same reason he'd been restless in March. This was when he told the world how oblivious he'd been. How someone he'd been friends with for a very long time had let him believe a bunch of untrue things, and had successfully hidden the one true thing. *It's not about me.* He sighed, sat down, composed himself. "I'm ready." Charlie hit the pause button. Gary was sure Tony hit his, too. "Okay. My name is Gary Fisher. I worked as a writers' agent in Los Angeles from nineteen seventy-five to two thousand sixteen. I first met Jerry Morgenstern at a screening in nineteen eighty. A client of mine was the head writer on the project, and Jerry was an associate producer on it. We met, we hit it off. Over the next few years, we kept running into each other, we got friendly. We weren't in competition." He paused, glanced away for a second, half-laughed. "That's a thing in Hollywood," he said when he returned his gaze to the primary camera. "Everybody is basically self-employed. So everywhere you go, you're trying to get a job. Everyone around you is trying to get a job. Sometimes they're trying to get *your* job. But Jerry and I didn't do the same thing, so it was okay for us to be pals." He cleared his throat. "Anyway, I was around when his first marriage was breaking up, and he was around when mine was breaking up. We had dinner here and there after he got married again. We were at the same parties fairly often. Awards shows, whatever. I liked him a lot. I thought he did good work. But there was always a little bit of a, I don't

203

even know how to describe it. He kept his private self private. And in twenty fifteen we all found out why." He had a sip of water. "In two thousand, Jerry was in a bad car accident. His back was broken. His second wife left him, you don't want to know what I think about that. He dropped out of sight for a little while. They said he wouldn't walk again. He told me later he was determined to prove them wrong, and he did. The next time I see him it's two years later, and he's out of the wheelchair. Still using a cane, but back on the set making people crazy, bitching about the budget, criticizing the script. Was I glad to see him? Even though my client wrote the script in question." Gary saw Charlie smile. "He never stopped working, but while he was in rehab he basically stayed with that TV series. It was on the air from two years before the accident, real solid performance, steady. He was able to manage that. Then once he was on his feet again he was a tiger. He started going out again, and we saw him with different women from time to time. When people asked him if he wanted to get married he said never again. And then he shows up at the Emmys in two thousand three with this absolute knockout. Acting like they've known each other forever. Acting like lovers. Everybody after the thing was like, Jerry, dude, who is this? He says this is Maggie Eisenstein. Tells us this story about how they met. It all made sense, and I mean if you saw her you didn't question it. And basically every time he's out after that, awards show, gala, whatever, Maggie is there." Gary couldn't help smiling, remembering. "Anyway. So in twenty fourteen, Jerry turned sixty-nine. He had a party at the Beverly Hills Hotel, and Maggie was there. I've never told anyone this. I got him alone and asked, are you ever going to marry her? He said, I would if I could."

He saw Charlie's eyes go wide. *Yeah, I know.* "I had no idea what he meant. I thought he must mean that she was already married, maybe always had been. Maybe that was why she never talked to the press. I mean never, and that takes some doing. She always managed to exit a conversation before it got too personal. We don't really get too personal at these things. An industry party, even somebody's birthday party, it's always about doing business." Another sip of water, because from here on out it was going to get rough. "Not long after that Jerry started dropping out. Passing on invitations, skipping some events. At the Emmys that year he shows up in a wheelchair and everybody's like dude, what. He said where his back broke before, the therapy couldn't keep up with it anymore. It was a good cover story. We all bought it. He still went to a few big things, and Maggie was still there with him. She never got less gorgeous, let me tell you. But we saw less and less of him. He kind of let people know he'd rather not see them. I tried to stay in touch, but if someone doesn't go out and doesn't want you to come in, there's only so much you can do. I still regret not trying harder." He blew out a breath. "Anyway. He died a couple of days before the Emmys in twenty fifteen. They scrambled together one of those tribute reels. And the hospital gave a statement, Jerry's assistant gave permission, to say he'd had cancer. He'd had it for a year and a half. He knew he was going to die. That's why he dropped out. So we all go to his memorial and tell stories about Jerry, and I for one expected Maggie Eisenstein to be there. But nobody ever saw her again." Another sip of water, it felt like he'd been talking forever. God knew if they would want to use all this. "Then his will is made public and we find out he's leaving most of his estate to a person nobody ever heard of. Sacha Lebedev. Everybody's like, who the hell is that. Is it a woman? A few people start looking. Oh, it's this guy. A *guy*. The story is he's known Jerry since two thousand three. Nothing coming from the inside. Nothing but speculation, the gossip press is crucifying this guy. Everybody's like but Jerry wasn't gay! Was Jerry gay? Why the hell is he leaving all this money – it was a lot of money – to this guy? He must have been gay. Lebedev never speaks. Almost three months later there's finally a statement from the executor. Jerry and Lebedev were in a relationship all that time. The lawyers are satisfied, the executor is satisfied, it's a done deal." Gary sat back, sighed. Did a 'still don't understand' thing with face and hands. "Two months after that, I get a letter from Sacha Lebedev. Now I still feel like shit about Jerry being sick and me not knowing, about Jerry being gay and me not knowing – I thought we were friends, I thought I must have been a bad friend – anyway, he says he could really use some advice, some contacts. I agreed to meet because of Jerry. So I'm at the meeting place and in walks Maggie Eisenstein. And all I think is wow! Still looks great! I tell her I'm sorry. I missed seeing her at the memorial, where was she. She says, I was there." Now a 'what the fuck' thing for the camera. "And all of a sudden I got it. The person I was there to meet, Sacha Lebedev, was Maggie Eisenstein. All that time." He shook his head, knocked out all over again by the memory. "Practically the first thing I think is, what kind of loyalty, what kind of *devotion*, does it take to keep a secret like that for so long. Since then I've gotten to know Sacha very well. I am trying to be a better friend to him than I was to Jerry. Let me say this one last thing." He paused to put the rehearsed

206

words in order. "I couldn't care less about straight or gay. That is so totally irrelevant to me. People are people, and love is love. I believe that Sacha loved Jerry. Jerry himself called Sacha the love of his life. I am so glad he had that." Voice shaky, eyes wet. Gary turned away and held up a hand, the gesture saying 'that's enough.'

"Thanks Gary," Charlie said softly. "Camera's off. You okay?"

"Yeah, I'm okay. Jesus. That was a lot, huh?"

"It was perfect," said Tony. "I know exactly how to use it." He was packing up the cameras already, no follow-up questions to ask.

Gary heaved a sigh. "Is it too early in the day for a drink? We have a truckload of hooch down in the conference room. Some things in Hollywood never change." He stood up, went around the desk, and accepted a hug from Charlie. "What did that come to, anyway? It felt like I was talking for an hour."

"Less than ten minutes," Tony said. Gary made a disbelieving noise. "I don't think you missed a single point."

"Fuck, in ten minutes, I hope not. The last time I spoke for ten minutes it was a commencement thing at my son's college. All set there?"

"Yeah." Charlie patted his back. "Let's go raid the conference room."

"Sacha, honey," Charlie said when she got home. "I have to warn you about something Gary said in this tape. I'm pretty sure Tony's going to use all of it, obviously you'll have a chance to see it when we go in to review the next stage, but there was one thing."

"Tell me." She'd found him in the den, watching another of Jerry's movies with a notebook open on the

207

side table. Taking notes for the book. "I could use a break from this."

"Not all of them were good, huh."

Sacha smiled. "Most of them made money anyway. So what did Gary say?"

She sat down beside him. "It was so organized, he must have rehearsed at least part of it, we didn't have to prompt him a single time. Anyway. He was talking about Jerry's sixty-ninth birthday party. You were there." Sacha nodded. "Gary said he pinned Jerry down and asked if he was ever going to marry Maggie." She stalled.

"What did Jerry say?"

"He said, I would if I could." Sacha inhaled sharply and closed his eyes. Charlie set her hand on his leg. "He obviously didn't tell you about that."

"No." Sacha opened his eyes again. "I wonder sometimes. Just like Jerry in his letter. Do you think if I had been gay, he would have asked me to marry him?"

"Oh, sweetheart, I don't know." She thought about it for another minute, because of course she'd been thinking about it all the way home. "I doubt it. He didn't have to marry you to give you what he wanted to give you. If he married you he couldn't have Maggie anymore, because Maggie would have become a notorious sideshow. He would have had to come out, and he didn't want to. Sacha." He made eye contact. "You really were perfect for him. You made it possible for him to be as honest with a partner as he could be, and to live the life he wanted to live, which was not the life of an openly gay man."

"He didn't mean he wished I was gay, then." Sacha thought about it. "He meant he wished he was different."

"Yeah, sort of. I think he meant he wished he was straight, and Maggie was a woman. But that didn't stop him from loving you just the way you are."

"I know." He sighed, then kissed her. "Thanks for telling me about that. How was Gary?"

"He suggested raiding their conference room booze stash. Which is why I was so late getting back, because then we had to order some pizza, and then some other people who were in the office caught on, and the next thing you know Tony and I were schmoozing with all these development people. It was bizarre."

A couple of days later, Charlie was in her office reviewing all the photos she'd gotten for the yogi series when Sacha came in. "Hi honey. How was your thing with Mandy today?"

"Great." He bent to kiss her. "Like what you have so far?"

"Oh yeah. One of these days I'll get you to model for me."

"I'm not a pro like all these people." He was smiling. He knew Charlie just liked to take pictures of him.

"Yeah, but your body is beautiful." She swiveled around to look up at him. "What's on your agenda today?"

"Want to go for a walk? I had a why-not moment and drove up the street a little ways before turning around to come home, and I noticed a front garden I never noticed before. You know Salvador has been after me to do something different in front."

"I think he thought you were ready to go as soon as you told him to strip out the old stuff. You liked this other yard? Sure, I'll go for a walk. Did you eat something?"

"Not yet."

"Go do that while I get ready." She switched off the monitor, stood up, kissed him again. *Jeans, sneakers, camera.* She looked out the window; the day was brightly sunny. She'd need her sunglasses too. Or better yet, a hat.

It was a nearly two hours later when they finally got home again. The garden Sacha liked – which met with Charlie's complete approval – belonged to an actress, close to their own age, named Jenny Wilson. She'd come out to talk to them. They now had her landscaper's contact information, and her promise to come by for cocktails later that week.

"She was so nice," Charlie said. "You never met before?"

"Not that I can recall. I'm going to have to look her up on IMDb and see what she's been in."

"And find out who she was married to. I guess a divorce is almost never a good thing, but at least she got that house. Are you going to tell Salvador 'do that' in front?"

Sacha laughed under his breath. "I'm going to have to get more people in. Salvador's great, but it's going to take a whole team. Electrical, plumbing. We'll need a contractor."

"Well, if that designer can take charge of the job she'll probably handle all that." Charlie studied their naked yard. There was nothing but mulch, to keep the dirt from drying out and blowing away. "God, it would look so much better than this."

"Water feature under our big tree, meadow and small trees inside the driveway to hide the wall?"

"If there were a few of them, it would be like a miniature woodland thing. Bird feeders could go there. I'd be on the window seat all the time taking pictures."

Sacha could tell she already loved the idea. "Then that's what we'll do." He kissed her before they went inside. They found Natalie in the kitchen with Cecilia and told both women all about meeting their neighbor. "She's going to drop by for a cocktail later this week. And we decided what to do with the front yard. There'll be some commotion once that starts. Natalie, it'll probably be best to bring Moses with you when you come in so he doesn't let himself out of your place. Salvador doesn't scare him but who knows what all will be going on out there for a while."

"Okay," she said. "He's in here half the time anyway now that it's hot."

"He likes the view," Cecilia said. Moses usually claimed a spot on the cool tile in front of the kitchen's sliding glass doors. None of them pointed out that he also scammed Cecilia for treats. "I'm going to the market now, see you later."

"Thanks Cecilia." They got themselves snacks and water, then went their separate ways: Charlie into her office, Sacha into his, and Natalie into hers. They'd refurnished the third bedroom so she had space to work with all those scripts and notes and books, filling in the timeline from Jerry's work journal. She'd already warned Sacha that they might actually have two books here: the Jerry story, and a film history. Sacha told her to talk to whoever she needed to talk to in those departments at UCLA and USC. She was out of the house half the time, doing interviews or other research. The rest of her 'work' time was split between reading film histories and dealing with Sacha's giving program.

Sacha used Jerry's old office for most of his reading and correspondence. Now that Natalie had him organized, he was able to keep up with everything. He checked his calendar again, looking for a few possibly-good days to suggest to the landscaper for a consultation. Then he sent her an email describing what they'd liked about Jenny's garden, with a picture of their own currently-denuded front yard labeled simply 'clean slate.'

Charlie went back to her office, read an email from the gallery about her upcoming teachers show, and then another from Tony with a schedule of upcoming interviews for the documentary. *Wow he's got a lot of people*, she thought with surprise. Somehow she hadn't thought that many people would want to participate. But, she reminded herself, this was Los Angeles; everyone wanted to be in a movie.

CHAPTER 11

The landscaper came the following Monday to meet Sacha and look at the property. Charlie was working in her office again; she watched them, for a few minutes, walking around. Sacha had asked her if she wanted to participate and she said no because her gallery opening was imminent. She was obsessively proofreading the histories that were going on the wall with the portraits. It would not do to have a typo in something about a teacher. The mounted prints had all been inspected, approved, and delivered to the gallery. The books had been printed – hardcover and paperback – and the opening-night catering menu set. She couldn't believe it was happening. Once she finalized the histories, all that remained was sending out invitations.

When she looked up again, the landscaper's car and Cecilia's were gone. Natalie was out all day, she knew, doing some research at the UCLA library. That meant she and Sacha were alone, a thing that did not happen very often during the day. She immediately wondered if she could talk him into doing some modeling. She hadn't yet taken any pictures or video of him in dance mode. He would come in to see her, she knew, after checking his own messages. The floor was clear, the camera was on its tripod, and a few other things were ready whenever he did.

"You look like you're open for business," he said not too much later. Charlie looked up; he was standing in the doorway. *God you are beautiful*, she thought. He may have read her mind. He smiled and came over to her, lifted her out of her task chair, and kissed her.

"That was nice," she said after a minute or two. "Why'd you do that?"

"The way you were looking at me, I thought you wanted me to."

"Well, I did." She kissed him again, put her arms around his neck, and smiled up at him. "I had this idea that we might have the place to ourselves for a while."

"I believe we do. Cecilia's taking the rest of the day off."

"Good for her. So I wondered if maybe I could take a few pictures of you."

"What kind of pictures?"

"I haven't taken any of you dancing. You're seeing Mandy tomorrow, right?" He nodded. "Would you be up for giving me a little demo of what you're doing with her?"

"It's mostly exercises still. But we are doing a short piece of choreography. Nothing fancy." Sacha gazed at Charlie, thinking about other ways they could use this precious time alone. But the piece really was short, and it would be good for him to run it before his lesson the next day. "Let me get my phone. I've got the music on there." He kissed her once more, then went back out.

Charlie woke up her camera, set it to video mode, and made sure the field of view was clear. When she was working with a model, she used the pocket doors – with drapery all the way across like a theater curtain – as a backdrop. She pulled the sheers across the big picture window. As soon as Sacha returned she closed the doors, then the drapery, tweaking the fabric so that the pleats were optimal. He plugged his phone into the sound system, did a few stretches. She waited by the camera without speaking. When he was ready, he

214

went out into the middle of the room. He'd changed clothes: out of his jeans and tee shirt, into dance trunks and Dance Paws. The trunks were a tan color slightly darker than his skin. *That body, my God.* Charlie took a breath as he got into position. "Ready?" He nodded. She un-paused her camera, then his cued music. She didn't recognize the piece; it looked almost like yoga, ending in a position similar to boat pose but prettier. She stopped the camera when the music ended and he went flat on the floor. "What was that?"

He sat up, draped his arms over his knees, and smiled at her. "That's a solo from the musical 'Cats.' Usually a girl does it, a character called Victoria. Did you like it?"

"It was beautiful. You are incredibly sexy. Can I take a few stills?"

"Where do you want me?" His voice was soft. He saw her react, knew she was turned on. He was too. He stripped off the Dance Paws and tossed them over by her desk.

"On the slipper chair." She had two seats for models. One was a chaise longue, like the one in Maggie's room. They'd used that before for a few photographs, and for other purposes. It was in the corner by the shelves of cinema-arts books. The other seat was in the opposite corner. Sacha went over to get it, sliding it on its felt feet to a position in front of the doors. He felt her eyes on him all the way. Was tempted to go over to her, stroke her hair off her neck and put his mouth there. He knew before they left this room they would make love. He hooked his thumbs in the waistband of his trunks and raised his eyebrows, asking the question: on or off? She swallowed. "On, for the moment."

Sacha sat down. Unless and until she said something specific, he could do whatever he wanted. So he used the chair as a prop, draping himself over and across it in various ways. The click and hum of the camera told him she liked what he was doing. The chair was covered with leather; the sweat on his skin made it feel cold. Knowing Charlie was watching him so closely made him feel hot. He loved knowing she thought he was beautiful. Loved knowing she wanted him. Loved her. He was upside-down on the chair, legs hooked over the back, arms and head hanging down in front, eyes closed. He heard her crossing the floor. A pillow hit the floor by his head with a soft thump, and then she was kneeling beside him, kissing him. "Mmm."

"Jesus, Sacha." She gave him a hand and he reversed himself, sitting up, leaning forward to kiss her again. Then her fingers were under that waistband and tugging off his trunks. "Oh my God." He was completely aroused. She wrapped her hand around him and he huffed out a vocal breath. She ran her other hand up his thigh and he leaned back, head resting on the top of the chair, eyes drifting shut as her mouth closed over him.

"Charlie," he said, a few minutes later, when it was almost too late. Then she did something with her tongue and he surged against her with a gasp. She made a ravenous sound and he was coming. She held him in her mouth till the end. "Oh *Jesus*." He needed a few seconds to catch his breath. "I wanted to be in you."

"I wanted that too but I wanted to feel you come like that. God almighty." She was up off the floor, then sitting astride him, drenched and hungry, kissing him. He spared a glance across the room; her jeans were in a heap by the camera. Its light was on.

He laughed under his breath. "Are we making a porno?"

"Maybe." Charlie felt his hand, sweeping down her back and that oh-so-sensitive skin even lower, hooking under the top of her thigh for a moment to pull her close against him, then around in front. "Oh *fuck*." He was kissing her again, fingers sliding in, the base of his thumb pressing lightly. She rode his hand, panting, whimpering, and finally crying out into his mouth. She felt his smile as he slowly withdrew those fingers, petting her. Leaned her forehead against his, stroked the soft tawny hair on his chest. Ran a fingernail around his nipples. "That always works," she said with satisfaction, feeling him twitch.

He spoke softly against her throat. "Do you want more?" They didn't go twice very often. When they made love at bedtime, they usually fell asleep after. If they made love in the morning, one or the other of them usually had someplace to be. An encounter like this was very rare. Sacha had a hand under her top, on her body. Brushing the backs of his fingers across her belly, around her breasts. She wasn't wearing a bra. He teased those sensitive areas he'd discovered, mouth still against her throat. Feathered his lips across her face to her mouth. That wonderful hot mouth, open against his, her hands in his hair. She tipped her hips against him with a muffled sound. "More," he said again, very softly, because he was ready and she was so wet. When she moved again they both sucked in a breath.

"More." She moved one more time. Enough to take him in.

"Holy wow," she said a little while later. "That was kind of epic." She peeled herself off Sacha, tottered over to the wet bar and opened a drawer to get out a few tea towels. Sacha peeled himself off the slipper chair and they wiped everything down, giggling. "I'll hit that with the saddle soap later," she said, and he laughed out loud. "Seriously wow. Oh." She turned off the camera. "I promise I will not save that, but I do want to watch it sometime."

"So do I." He went over to the coat rack on the wall by the wet bar, selected a cotton kimono, and pulled it on. "That thing you have on is awfully cute." A sleeveless cotton gauze tunic, long enough to cover her bottom. Barely. With jeans, it was very company-ready.

"Have anything you need to do, or can we hang out for a few minutes?"

"There's always something to do. But let's hang out." He stretched out on the chaise, feeling extremely relaxed. "What do you have to drink in here?"

Charlie opened the mini fridge. "Pellegrino, Sofia, Not Your Father's Root Beer."

"Sofia, please."

"Yeah, that sounds good." She got two cans out and took them over to the chaise. Nudged him over so she could squeeze in next to him. "Maybe we should have gotten a double in here."

He held her close against his side. "We both fit." One more kiss, because she was right there and he loved her so much.

"I love you so much," she said. "It's so nice to have moments like this. Does all this help make up for last winter?"

"It definitely does." They were quiet for a while.

Charlie was thinking about watching him dance, even that little bit. Watching him get turned on by posing for her. She set her empty can on the floor. "Did you ever get turned on when you were dancing?"

"Oh yeah," he said, sounding amused. "When I was a teenager it was bad, for all of us guys. The teachers pretended it wasn't happening, so we all tried to pretend it wasn't happening. In college the teachers were better about addressing it. They were like, this is natural. Your bodies have minds of their own, don't freak out, it doesn't mean anything. Still, this one time I was partnered with this girl I really didn't like. And she kind of hated me. But I got turned on. I was all, but I don't even like you."

Charlie laughed. "What did she say?"

"Oh thank God, I can't stand you either, I thought I was losing my mind. She got turned on too. Must have been something in the air. We never did really get along, but we laughed like idiots that day." Sacha finished his wine, set the can down. "It was good I had that experience. Otherwise some of the stuff before Jerry would have blown my mind. The first time I responded to a man I thought wait, what? No."

Charlie turned her head to look at him. "What did you do?"

"Talked myself off the ledge. Ran it down in my head, you're young, you're lonely. The body sees and hears and smells something like sex and it wants sex. You don't want this man, but that's your brain. This is everything else. Don't freak out."

She straightened up again, thinking about this. "And so you didn't freak out."

"Yeah. It was never okay, exactly, but." He stopped for a second. "I never let it cost me money."

"Sweetheart."

"There was this one guy," he said, then stopped again. Sighed. "Should I tell you this stuff?"

219

She patted his leg. "Yes." If he was talking about it, he needed to talk.

"Okay. This one guy, kind of a regular. All he wanted was to give me head. He would get off from that. Always in his car. He would come to this club where I was working, and on my break we'd go outside and do that. He had this SUV with tinted second-row windows. We'd get in that back seat. The more I seemed to like it, the more he would pay me."

"How did you deal with that?" she asked quietly.

After a moment he said, "I tried to pretend he was a woman, I played along. I stayed outside it as much as I could, kept my focus. Then one time it had been a really good night, nothing bad happened, some of the other dancers and I were laughing before I went out with this guy. I was a little bit high. And." He stopped again. Charlie didn't say anything. Sacha went on as if compelled. "And I had an orgasm. Then I was sitting there with my eyes closed, not even breathing, trying not to throw up or cry or fucking hit him, and he came so hard I thought he was going to hurt himself. He was all oh my God, that was so good. He gave me a hundred dollars. I hadn't seen that much money at once since the last time I got paid from an extra gig. I stared at it, and tried to smile at him, and thought, maybe now is when I get out on the street side. I could turn my back and take a couple extra steps, and it would be over. The buses just flew by on that stretch of road."

"Jesus, Sacha." She pressed close, one arm across his ribs, feeling the shallow breath, the slight tremor. Wondering if he'd spoken to his shrink about this. He obviously wasn't completely over it. How would a person get over it? "Oh honey. My poor baby. What did you do?"

A deep steadying breath. "I got over it. I didn't really want to die. I was brought up that way, you know, where there's life there's hope. And even though that club was where guys went after they'd gotten kicked out of all the nice ones, I could still tell myself things could get better. I went back inside and bummed a joint from somebody. And the next time I saw him I let him get going. I made the right noises. Talked about how I'd been waiting to see him again, how much I wanted him. He wanted to believe it. He wanted that to happen again, so he got off faster. And I didn't, but he paid me almost as much. After that I knew how to handle it."

Charlie was thinking, *Never knew men could fake it.* She'd never thought about any of this. She'd faked it herself plenty of times. Never had an orgasm when she didn't want to. "Was he still in the picture when Jerry came around?"

"No. Couple of months before that, I'd gotten so thin. He saw me at the bar and said, are you sick? And I wasn't, not the way he meant, but I wasn't exactly healthy either. Anyway, that was it for him, he didn't want to touch me. I never saw him after that."

"I *hate* him." Charlie couldn't believe it. "He could have at least tried to help you."

"He didn't care. He didn't even know my name. None of them did. None of them cared. Nobody cared till Jerry." She didn't ask, but he answered. "Yeah, I responded to Jerry. I never let him know. That would have been too much."

"Even the first time?"

"God, the first time, he was so panicked. I could have come like that," he nodded toward the slipper chair, "and he wouldn't have noticed. I didn't come," he added. "Not even close. It was only a reaction. I never did come with him, unless I was masturbating. Then I could think about a woman."

"Who did you think about?" Charlie had no idea why she was asking.

"My college girlfriend, mostly. She was my go-to for a long time. We had a good relationship. I would pretend I never came out here, that we'd gone into the city together to be stars on Broadway, and we'd go home to our little apartment somewhere and make love with the city lights shining through our window. It was a good fantasy."

"Yeah. I had fantasies like that sometimes. After I met Maggie, I had fantasies about you." That was true, and it made Charlie smile. She turned her head again and Sacha was smiling too. "I'll bet a lot of people did. But I knew you were a man. I wondered why you were doing that, except even then I could tell there was something real between you and Jerry. So I figured you were gay. It was not the first time I had a little mental fling with a guy I thought was gay."

Sacha laughed under his breath. "I thought about you. After last May." He held her a little bit tighter. "I thought about the way you touched my hand."

I thought about that a lot. "I love you, Sacha."

"I love you too." The tension had gone out of his body. "You know when we make love I don't think about what happened before. You look at me, you say my name, you kiss me. I know you love me. And I love you so much."

"I know you do." She laid her head on his shoulder.

October 2016

Charlie looked around the packed gallery and tried to breathe. She didn't really have much to do; she was only there to answer questions, if there were any, but this was the first time in her life that she'd been The Artist. Thank God for Sacha, who'd taken her shopping. Even she thought she looked great in an above-the-knee sleeveless purple sheath dress and gray peep-toe pumps. Her long, lightweight sweater was a blend of purples and grays. He'd retrieved a set of jewelry from the safe-deposit box. This one was almost casual: silver, set with amethysts. It was modern in style, and didn't look obnoxiously rich. She wore the ring and bracelet on her right hand so they wouldn't clash with her ruby ring. Sacha himself looked stunning in a gray pinstripe suit.

Their new publicist had made a list of potential donors, people known to support education and the arts in Los Angeles, and invited them. Natalie already had a list of people Sacha had been corresponding with, plus their own slowly-growing circle of friends, and all of the teachers featured in the book.

Some of the teachers whose portraits were on the walls seemed as nervous as Charlie; others were having a great time, laughing, talking to everyone, telling stories. Natalie (in a long black and white dress) was circulating with Gary (in black tie). The catering staff was weaving through the crowd. Charlie's own glass was empty, but she didn't dare have more champagne. She could have all the drinks after they were home. She set the glass on a passing tray and looked around again. Sacha was talking to their neighbor Jenny, and somebody else who had his back to Charlie. She started working her way over there.

"Hi Charlie." She looked over and up; it was Andy Martin, tall, dark and handsome as ever. "The show is great, congratulations. Want to meet Victor?"

"God, yes," she said. He laughed. They finished crossing the room. Apparently Victor was the man talking to Sacha and Jenny.

"Victor, this is the artist." Andy's boyfriend turned around and smiled.

Oh my God what a fox. Charlie did not usually like facial hair, but she would make an exception for Victor's mustache. She tried not to swoon, aware that Sacha was watching, and probably trying not to laugh. "Mr. Garcia. Thank you so much for coming tonight. Both of you."

"Call me Victor." He shook her hand. "Jenny and I were getting nostalgic about a project we did together, a few years back."

"I haven't seen Victor since then," Jenny said, smiling. "I got a job in New York, and then I was getting a divorce, and it was a mess." Charlie asked about the project they'd done together, and they both went into the story. They made it funny – it was about putting on a world premiere musical play on a low budget in a hundred-year-old theater with a tiny crew – but there were some distinctly non-funny parts to it.

"What a minute, this person *killed* somebody?"

"She was a piece of work," Victor said. "Had this idea her boyfriend would get moved up in the cast if she took this one guy out, I guess. Did some other stuff too. Called in a bomb threat to my apartment building, sabotaged the set, vandalized a car. Pushed Jenny in front of a taxi."

"Holy crap!"

"That's a very mild version of what I said," Jenny remarked. "And that's not even all. She set fire to her

224

boyfriend's apartment and went after our ingénue with a vodka bottle." Charlie was speechless. "Yeah, when you say it all at once it's like, what the what."

Sacha laughed under his breath. "But the show came together great. You were both terrific." He hadn't recognized her at first, when they met in the neighborhood, because the play was set in the 1980s and she'd been costumed accordingly. All he'd really remembered about her look was the big hair.

"Oh, you saw it?" Jenny looked gratified. Sacha didn't tell her he'd been there as Maggie. "It was a fun experience in spite of everything. I need to remind my agent I did that. See what else might be coming around. Of course," she said ruefully, "I'm squarely in the mom zone now."

"Our friend Dana used to say that's all there is between thirty and fifty," Andy said. "But look at her now."

Jenny looked thoughtful. "I am not sure I could pull off a police captain."

"You could play the bad guy," Victor suggested. "Be Annie Wilkes." Jenny made an 'oh my God no' face.

"Be Mrs. Lovett," Sacha said.

Andy made a *pfft* sound. "Be Sweeney Todd." Jenny was laughing. Sacha made their excuses then, because he'd spotted some people who looked like they had questions. They all said 'Call me, let's get together,' and he steered Charlie away.

"Having a good time?" he asked softly as they headed for a group near one of the portraits.

"This is so, so bizarre. But yes, I think so. After the fact I'm sure I'll look back and say, what a great time! Right now I'm still half petrified."

"You look beautiful. Your photos are fantastic. Everyone is impressed." He kissed her cheek. "And I think the foundation is going to get a nice boost from this."

"I hope so."

The gallery show was going to stay up all month. For that among several other reasons, Brittany the publicist had talked Sacha into finally doing a press conference. "Is anyone even interested anymore?" he asked, without much hope that the answer would be 'no."

"You know perfectly well I've been getting inquiries ever since the Emmys. People were like, oh yeah, that thing last year, whatever happened about that. And all I have to give them is those clips and pictures that popped up in July, and then that bit from Pop Quiz after the dance thing in Hollywood. You two don't go out much."

"Not to the obvious places, no." They went out fairly often now, but to the theater or ballet or opera, or dinners with friends. Not to nightclubs or galas or industry events. They'd been invited, by Gary, to a post-Emmys party. Sacha wasn't ready to get that up-close-and-personal with people who might have known Maggie; he'd said 'maybe next year.' He sighed. "If you think I should, I will. The documentary is on schedule, but until that's finished and some kind of deal is made, I want to keep that side of things under the radar. The content of it at least. Is there a way to keep the questions focused on Jerry? I mean me and Jerry."

"Yeah, I get it. And yes, of course, we can require them to submit questions in advance, tell them what kinds of questions you absolutely will not answer, tell them what you're there to talk about. That's not unusual at all. You have an NDA with your filmmaker and your assistant, right?"

He didn't, actually, and said so. "We're working on trust."

"Um, Sacha."

He laughed under his breath. "Tony Benedetti has talked to a lot of people doing his series. Not one of them has ever gone around saying he can't keep his mouth shut. I know what kinds of things have come out in some of his interviews, things that don't make it to the rough cut."

"You've seen some of his raw material?"

"He volunteered, when we were first talking about the documentary." And they had now seen the entire series.

"Okay. Okay, then. I'll send you parameters for this thing, you give me your comments, we'll get this rolling."

"Okay, Brittany. Thanks." He disconnected, still strongly disinclined to do this at all. But it was best to try and control the outcome, if they possibly could. The longer he went without speaking the more people were going to think he really did have something to hide. *Of course I do.* He went to warn Charlie and Natalie, then sent a text to Tony: *Planning a press conference. Will be mentioning existence of documentary project but not subject matter. OK if I give your name?*

Tony got right back to him: *Quite okay, if anyone contacts me I will refer them back to your publicist*

Great, thanks. They were going to show the rough cut to Gary, when it was done. Tony thought that was going to be before the end of December.

Once a deal was made – if Gary's team decided to acquire the film – they would have to decide if any part of the Maggie story was going to come out in advance. The working title was 'The Role of a Lifetime.' It wouldn't take long for people to make the connection. They needed to start working on their strategy now.

Brittany had the press conference scheduled a week later. She sent Sacha a list of the journalists who'd confirmed; it was much longer than he'd expected. He took it to Natalie and she said, "Yikes." He laughed under his breath. She looked up at him from her desk, studied his face, reached for his hand. "You're going to be fine. You've dealt with much worse than this."

"Yeah. And at least it's a controlled setting. If things blow up I can walk away."

"Do not do that. Sit there with that face you have, the one that says 'you have no power over me,' and wait it out. Remember they need you a lot more than you need them."

"Do I have that face?" He was smiling now.

"Of course you do. You go still, and you get this kind of clinical expression, like hmm, what an interesting specimen. I tried it myself on Gary and he said hey wait a minute." Sacha laughed. Natalie said, "It's not that different from what I used to do in difficult classes, actually. Teenagers aren't used to being really seen. They are all, always, trying to put on an act. A lot of them totally freak out at full eye contact. I'll bet a lot of these reporters do too."

"Thanks, Natalie. I'll remember that."

"And also." She stopped for a second. "Remember that no part of your relationship with

Jerry was wrong. And that you have people who love you." He still had her hand, so he pulled her up from her chair for a hug.

Sacha thought about that conversation as he sat behind the table in the e-suite, gazing across it to the rows of reporters. Some were sitting, some were standing, some had cameras, others had voice recorders. A few had old-fashioned steno pads. Video cameras on tripods stood to each side of the mob. There was a lot of noise at first. He waited for people to settle down. "Good morning," he said. "My name is Sacha Lebedev. A little over a year ago, Jerry Morgenstern died and left me the bulk of his estate. I didn't speak to the press at that time, and I've avoided doing so since."

"Why are you speaking out now?"

"It's time." He paused, listening to the click and buzz of cameras, listening to various other questions. He was going to say what he wanted to say. If there were any questions at the end that he wanted to answer, he would. They all knew that. "Jerry and I were in a relationship for a dozen years. We met by chance. He was out with his assistant and his driver. He liked to see the city at night. Said it was the best way to see how people really behave. How people drive, how they park, how they walk down the street. He used a lot of that in his work. Anyway, his assistant saw me getting mugged, and they pulled over to help." A skirmish of questions. Sacha waited. There was only one that led to the next thing.

"You went to live with him?"

"Yes," he said, looking directly at that reporter. "I was living in pretty bad conditions. I was broke. I was injured. He had a guest house. I lived there for two years while I was getting my professional training. I learned to help with his physical therapy. His back was broken three years before." A slight rustle of reaction; a lot of people had forgotten that. It was a long time ago. "He and his assistant taught me how to help with his business, with the paperwork and research. Our personal relationship began about seven months after we met."

There were a lot of questions now, and most of them were about Sacha's personal history. They knew he wasn't going to answer those. He simply waited until they were quiet again. "Jerry was gay. He did not want to be gay. He wasn't a homophobe, but there were things in his past, in his history, that shaped him. He didn't want to come out. He lived his life as a straight man." Questions about their sex life. The underlying assumption was, of course, that they must have had a sex life.

Sacha abruptly went off script. "Jerry and I had an almost completely non-sexual relationship. I'd had a previous experience with a man, but I am straight. He was thirty-five years older than me. He did not want to be gay. Think about that." Sounds of noncomprehension. "Jerry never touched me beyond a hug." An outburst. Everyone wanted to know what 'previous experience' meant. They wanted to know what 'almost completely' meant. He wasn't going to tell them. Let them think what they liked. Everything would be clear when the film came out, when they saw the touches and kisses between Jerry and Maggie.

He gazed at them all as if they were not-especially-interesting animals in a zoo. Gradually the commotion abated. "I know that wasn't on the agenda. I also know that was the thing you were most curious about. My relationship with Jerry was really not about sex. He was my mentor and my best friend. I was the one person he could be honest with." He had to take a moment, and of course a flurry of questions filled the pause.

There was one answerable question. "Why did he trust you?"

It all came down to one thing. "He loved me. And I loved him. I miss him to this day. My team and I are working on two biographical projects. We're writing a book, about Jerry's life and work. And we're making a documentary film."

"Who's your team?"

"Charlotte Montgomery, my fiancée. Natalie Sanders, my assistant. Tony Benedetti, our director and editor. Questions about either of these projects, for any of these people, should be directed to my publicist." He didn't invite people to ask questions now, but of course they did anyway.

And one of them asked a question he'd actually hoped for. "Will we hear from Jerry at all in this film?"

"Yes. I'm glad to say we will. We're talking to a lot of people who knew him, we have some archival footage, and we're using a letter he wrote to me. It's very personal, he would never have wanted it read while he was alive. He made sure I didn't find it until long after he died. It was," he paused to steady his breath, "the greatest of the many gifts he left me."

More questions, everyone looking at the clock, knowing their time was almost up. Sacha finally heard another one he wanted to answer. "When did you and Ms. Montgomery meet?"

"We met in February of last year."

"Did Jerry know about her?"

"Yes, of course."

"When did you start dating?"

"In May of last year. We weren't in touch after Jerry died, for a lot of reasons, until the estate was settled. Charlie is wonderful. I love her completely. We're getting married in January." He glanced at his watch, the Patek Philippe that he wore any time he went out in public. "And we're out of time. If there are any follow-up questions, please direct them to my publicist. Thank you." He stood up, gave them a little bow, and stepped through the room's back door. Brittany was in there; she'd been watching on a closed-circuit monitor connected to a discreet camera in the adjoining room. She gave him a thumbs-up. He could hear more commotion from the reporters. "I jumped the tracks."

She laughed. "You were right, though, that's the one thing most of them wanted to know. Did you have sex, what kind of sex, how much sex. Whatever. They're still curious and now they are also confused." She eyed him for a moment. "I'm confused, for that matter. I just assumed." She shrugged.

"Everybody does. Everybody will. The best thing I can do is keep saying, he did not want to be gay. He knew I was straight. He wished he were straight. There are things gay men do together that he absolutely did not want to do, because that's not how he wanted to be." Sacha waited to see if she got it. From the enlightened expression that dawned, she did. "If people push you, you can tell them that."

"Right." Brittany listened for a moment, then glanced up at the monitor. The outer room was almost empty. "We can leave in a minute, I think. That was good. That's going to set you up nicely for the wedding, and when the film gets picked up. Jeez, I'm tired, it's like I was out there myself. You must be exhausted."

Sacha nodded. "Want to go get lunch?"

"Absolutely. Thanks." She made sure her tablet and phone were in her bag. "Did Jerry really know about Charlie?"

"He really did. Before we ever went on a date he said, tell her everything. If she sticks, she's the one. I said Jerry, what about you. He said Sacha, I'll be dead, I won't care. I just want you to be happy." He blinked away tears. "And then I told her everything on our very first date, when he was still alive, and I was so scared."

Brittany patted his back. "But she stuck. I knew I liked her." Sacha coughed out a laugh. "Come on."

CHAPTER 12

The press conference made all the entertainment news outlets, though it appeared in full only on the locally-based Pop Quiz. Brittany sent Sacha regular updates on feedback and fielded follow-up questions. Paparazzi haunted the house for a while; they didn't get anything juicy. The front yard was a work site, but clearly not in a 'tearing down lover's house to build a McMansion' way. All four people in the house were now experts at not responding, no matter how offensive a question was. Sacha and Charlie continued with their regular daytime activities – ballet and guitar lessons for him, visits to Tony and photo shoots for her – and stayed with the car service that, so far, had kept them unhassled when they went out at night. Before long, the new burst of interest waned, to the point that they decided to invite some people over for dinner.

"The landscaper says the installation is going to be finished by Halloween," Sacha said. He was leaning on the kitchen counter, a cup of coffee in one hand, toes in Moses' belly fur.

"You spoil that cat," Natalie said. "Look how chubby he is."

"It's not me, it's Cecilia."

"I can't say no," Cecilia admitted. "He gives me the hungry face. I know he's a liar. Mentirosito, gato gordito. No más, Moses," she told the cat. "You on a diet from today."

Charlie came into the kitchen. "Who's on a diet? Oh. He is looking a little bit round. Honey, would you

234

believe I've already got eighteen subjects for the yogis thing?"

"Of course I would. I was just saying to Natalie, the landscaper says the yard will be company-ready by the end of the month. We should have some people over. It's been a while."

"Yeah it has. Fine with me. Our list is a little longer these days." Charlie was smiling. They weren't making a real effort to add people to their circle, but it was getting bigger anyway. "Maybe we can empty out one of those bar cabinets in back."

"Maybe we should pour some of it down the drain," Sacha said, watching her. "Like that butterscotch schnapps."

"Do not touch my butterscotch schnapps." She leaned in to kiss his laughing mouth. "Want to see what I got yesterday? It was that guy who teaches paddleboard yoga."

"Were you out at the beach?" He followed her out.

"In the Marina, and I was severely overdressed. I've been watching through the window. This is going to be so cool." She looked out the picture window again. "What did Salvador say about it?"

"He doesn't get it yet. I walked with him up to Jenny's and told him that's what we were aiming for. He thought it was messy."

"Well, he's really a turf and roses guy. The backyard always looks great, but it is a lot more formal than this is going to be."

"It's great for sunbathing and cocktail parties. Which is what a backyard should be for."

"It's perfect for you, that's for sure. Did you have a pool growing up?" Charlie sat down at the computer and woke up the screen, then activated a slide show of the images from the previous day's shoot. Sacha stood behind her to watch.

"Not our own. There was a YMCA pool we could walk to. And we could get to the beach in a few minutes."

Charlie hadn't ever asked where, exactly, in New York his family was based. "Which beach?"

"We lived in Brighton Beach, it connects to all the Coney Island stuff. Rockaway was close, too. Those are great pictures. How does he even do that?"

"I have no idea. The idea of standing up on one of those things blows my mind, much less doing a backbend. So my mother called again about Christmas."

"What did you tell her?"

"I told her we weren't traveling till we go on our honeymoon, there's too much to do. She didn't throw a fit this time." Charlie glanced up. "She didn't ask for money, either."

He patted her shoulder. "Good. But you know if you ever think there's a genuine need, we can help them out."

"Yeah. I'll probably go over there next spring to take a look at things. See how my siblings are coping with their offspring." She didn't really need to go to Indiana to find that out. Facebook told her all she needed to know. But if she stayed away too long she knew what kind of parental bitchery she'd have to deal with. Her siblings hadn't asked for money. They'd barely commented on her new work, home, and romantic circumstances. Maybe they thought none of this would last. "Any news from your people?"

Sacha was still watching the slideshow. He shook his head. Charlie leaned against him. He stroked her hair. "On the plus side, I haven't gotten any more hate mail." All communication, in fact, had stopped after the press conference. They must have seen some of it; he wondered which part. He wondered how long it would take before they could be a family again. *It's been so long already*, he thought. Then shook it off, and focused on Charlie's work.

About a week later they were in the den, watching a movie after dinner, when Sacha's cell phone rang. He rarely got calls at this time of night; he glanced over at it, frowning, then picked it up. "Mama?" Charlie paused the movie. It was almost midnight in New York. She immediately thought *something's wrong*. Sacha's next words confirmed it. His voice was sharp with concern. "When? Where is he now? Yes, of course I'll come."

Charlie stood up, jogged down the hall, retrieved one of the laptops from the office and brought it back. She had it open to Expedia within a minute, half-listening. Sacha's father, apparently. In the hospital. She touched Sacha's hand; he glanced over. "La Guardia?" He shook his head, then returned his attention to the phone. Charlie searched for flights into JFK.

"Charlie's finding us a flight right now. No, we'll get ourselves to the house. When can we see Papa? After nine tomorrow, okay. We'll go straight there. Yes, Mama. We're on our way. I love you too." He disconnected, scrubbed a hand over his face, and said, "He had a heart attack. Mama says, I always told him this would happen someday."

"But he's alive. He's doing okay?"

Sacha made a 'not sure' face. "Mama's too upset to know how bad it is."

"How's this one." A nonstop flight leaving at eleven. They should be able to get to LAX in time.

"Fine. Get first class. I'm going to pack."

"Right behind you." She started the booking process, trying to ignore the ticket price. Thought *oh dammit* anyway, and then said "Thanks honey" when Sacha came back in with their passports and his credit card. He touched her shoulder and went out again. She finished booking the flight, checked them in, printed boarding passes, called the car service. "We'll be ready to go in ten minutes. Thanks."

They went out the door with an overnight bag apiece, Charlie's camera, and their phones. Charlie sent a message to all the people they'd invited for dinner, saying *At the moment we're still on but we've had to dash over to NYC for a family thing. Will let you know ASAP if plans change.* Sacha was on his phone too, cancelling lessons, postponing appointments, assuming that they'd be gone for several days. By the time they reached LAX Natalie had pinged back with a *Take care and don't worry, I'll hold the fort.* They put away their devices and headed for Departures.

Charlie had never taken a red-eye flight before. She'd also never flown in first class. She dozed, off and on. When they landed, it was morning. The flight attendants told them it was cold outside. Welcomed them to New York. Said 'thank you for flying with us.' Charlie shuffled up the rampway beside Sacha. She didn't know if he'd slept.

"Are you hungry?" he said. "I know it's not even five in the morning for us, but we should eat. And have some coffee."

"Coffee sounds good. Yeah, let's eat."

He steered them into the first place that seemed to offer both a hot breakfast and coffee. "Thank you for coming with me." Charlie gave him an incredulous look and he almost laughed. "I know. I love you too." She smiled, shaking her head, and followed the hostess to a table. They both felt better after eating. Sacha sent a text to his mother and got back an answer saying his dad was hanging in there. He confirmed that they would meet her at the hospital, and signed off looking relieved. "This is not how I wanted to see them again."

"How long has it been?"

"Not that long. I came two and a half years ago. Before Jerry got his diagnosis, but after we knew there was something wrong. I wanted to see my family because I thought I might not want to leave him for a while." He sipped coffee. "It was really hard not to tell them, that time. Not to say, my best friend is sick and I'm afraid it's serious. Just, I'm afraid. All I ever told them about Jerry is that he gave me a job, while I was getting the massage training."

"Well, that was true." Charlie looked around for the server. She wanted more coffee, and some milk to soften it. Fatigue had her feeling hollow inside, sore, almost like she had the flu. "For the record, not a fan of red-eye flights."

"Oh I know, they're awful. It's better to try and stay up till close to a normal bedtime. But if you need a nap, take one."

"I know you won't. Iron Man." The server was there with more of the stuff of life, returning swiftly with cream. "Should we move out, after we finish this?"

"Yes." He sat back, tried to stretch his shoulders, gave up. "Mama said Pavel had a job today and wouldn't see us till dinnertime. He'll probably make jokes. They won't be funny. His idea of a joke is to call me the ballerina."

"Oh lord. Is he a big guy like your dad?" Sacha nodded. Charlie sighed. "Did your dad give you hell about not joining the moving company?"

"No, he knew I was never going to be any good for the company. I wasn't strong enough." Charlie made a confused sound. "I'm a lot stronger now than I was then. They didn't trust me to carry or lift things. I couldn't even help in the office because of all the numbers. That's why they sent me to college. It was like, please God, let them teach him some way to earn a living."

"Am I going to get mad at these people?"

Sacha laughed under his breath. "You don't have to. They did the best they could."

Charlie didn't really mean to take a nap, but it happened anyway. One minute she was sitting up on the couch in Oleg Lebedev's hospital room, talking to Sacha's mother Marian, and the next she was looking at the side of the bed. *I am lying on the couch. I am in the patriarch's room. It has not been very long. I could go back to sleep.* She didn't. She might have, if she hadn't heard Sacha say, "Oh Mama. Was I the young man who was going to say, you were right. It was a mistake to come out here. I'm giving up. After less than a year? You know all I had was pride."

"You had talent," Marian said. "Everyone said so. Where were you, when he found you?"

There was a short silence. "You wouldn't like the answer."

"Tell us anyway." A man's voice, deep, solid Brooklyn. It must be Oleg, he was awake, that was good.

"You know we love you no matter what. This thing, we were confused, and then there was the money. Was I going to say, hey son who is a bazillionaire, for some reason I don't understand, come home and see how we're still moving people's moldy old sofas?"

"Papa." It was almost a laugh, but not a happy one. "You remember what you told me?"

"I was wrong." It was gruff.

"You said, he might as well have been a girl." Sacha didn't even sound like himself. His voice was hard, like the blow that sentence must have been, however long ago. Charlie bit her lip, feeling a little sick. *Why this, why now, did you mean to say that.*

"Oh Sacha, oh God, I never knew you heard that." Marian, sounding distressed.

"It's not that big a house, Mama." A pause. When he spoke again, his voice was closer to normal. There was still an edge. "Then it was, these people have turned your head and now you think you're too good for us. This was never good enough for you. So go be a star, maybe we'll see you on TV. You know that to me, knowing I was useless to you, that sounded like don't come home. So was I going to say, Papa, I've failed, can I please come home?"

Charlie squeezed her eyes shut, tried not to sniffle. She'd always thought there must be more to the story, had never pushed, had always known there was some deep pain. Something that would have made Sacha turn to Jerry so wholeheartedly when he so desperately needed help. A father figure, and one who needed Sacha exactly as he was.

"I was wrong," Oleg said again. "And I'm sorry."

"I'm sorry too." Another pause. A sigh. "I don't think I should tell you everything that happened. I'm

241

not proud of what happened before I met Jerry. And what happened after is strange, and confusing. We're making a film, and that will tell you what happened in a way that's easier to understand." A few seconds of silence. "I'm happy now. I'm in love with a wonderful woman, and thanks to Jerry none of us need to worry about money again. And I'm so glad you're all right."

"He's a stubborn old man," Marian said. "How many times have I said leave those things to the young men, you don't have to do that now, why do we pay them if you're going to lift washing machines by yourself all day. Will you stop now?"

"Yes, my wife, I will stop now. This is God telling me to stop with the goddamned washing machines. I'll walk to the Y with Pavel and swim, and when you tell me to lay off the danish I will lay off." There was a pause, with some minor rustling and an 'mmm' noise. Charlie deduced a kiss. "Maybe they'll let me go home tonight."

"I doubt it," Sacha said. He sounded amused now. "But we can ask."

They didn't let Oleg go home that night, but he was home the next day. Charlie and Sacha stayed for three days. Marian filled the house with his family. His brother Pavel, his wife and their kids were there the first night; the next, it was uncle Boris and his wife; then a cousin or two, a few kids on that side. Charlie didn't even try to get all the names straight. Everyone was mostly interested in Sacha. Everyone was slightly hesitant, slightly tentative. There were no jokes about ballerinas. There were hugs, kisses, and variations on 'we missed you.'

242

Lying in bed the night before they meant to return to California, Charlie said, "Was that the cousin who sent you the hateful email?"

"No, that one didn't come. But this one told me what that was about."

"Oh really." Charlie turned to her side. There was some light in the room thanks to a streetlamp. Sacha's face was calm. "Was it excusable?"

"Almost. That cousin's fifteen-year-old son recently came out."

"Oh. And that's bad?" Charlie didn't think that was excusable at all. "And it's somehow your fault?"

"Well, he didn't come out until after the news broke last year."

"He's *fifteen*."

Sacha laughed silently. "I know. Anyway, this cousin asked if I would talk to the kid. I said, you know I'm not gay, right? And he said yeah, I get it, but you're the closest thing we have."

"Oh my actual God." She couldn't help laughing too, even though she still wanted to smack that other guy if she ever met him.

"So of course I said sure, you have my email, he can get in touch anytime."

"He'll probably end up in your guest house after Natalie moves in with Gary."

"You think she will?"

"I think he's going to ask her to marry him, so yeah." Charlie pressed close and draped an arm over Sacha's chest. "You're going to have to get your own cat." She was glad they were going home. She'd taken hundreds of pictures of the family, and pictures of pictures in the photo albums Marian pulled out. She was going to put off any more work on the yogis project until she had a family book made. As those thoughts wound up she realized Sacha was still awake too. So she said, "You look so much like them. Your dad and your brother."

"A smaller version."

She made an annoyed sound and he laughed. "More refined. You have your mother's bones."

"And now you know what's going to happen to my hair." On Oleg and Boris the hairline had retreated. The older men both wore their light-gray hair brushed straight back from a widow's peak. Sacha's was the same length as theirs now, longer than he'd worn it when he was being Maggie on a regular basis. His time in the sun kept it more brightly blond.

"Your hair is and will be fine."

"I would never have made it as a ballet dancer," he said, almost out of nowhere. "I had the bare minimum of pas de deux training. Too slight, too short. Not original enough to break out in jazz or contemporary. I realized that almost as soon as I got to Los Angeles, and saw the other people working at the studio. I was so far out of their league. I wondered why the advisor steered me that way. I mean, it doesn't matter. Everything that happened would still have happened."

"Maybe you should ask her. Him. Whatever."

"It's too late now, he died five years ago. For the longest time I thought, you know, my best chance really was on Broadway. Why didn't he tell me that." Another quiet minute. "Papa would never have said he was wrong if he hadn't been scared."

"He thought he almost missed his chance. But he did say it. He said he was sorry, he said he loved you. And now because he's a guy he will probably never say those things again."

"It's good we both said those things. I'm so glad we finally cleared it up. And that they've met you now. My mother loves you."

"She knows I love you."

Sacha turned to her, burying his face in her hair. "I love you too."

The front garden was finished when the car service dropped them off late the next day. Cecilia had gone home, and Natalie was out with Gary. As soon as they dumped their bags in the house they went back outside to walk through the yard in the twilight. "This looks promising," Charlie said. "Of course you want it to be all mature and perfect immediately, but I can see how it will be."

"It'll be beautiful." Sacha wandered over to the new artificial creek. It ran from near the house to a water garden in the outside corner of the yard. "We could put a bench under the tree. Sit out here and listen to the water."

"That would be great." Charlie joined him. Wrapped an arm around his waist, and leaned her head on his shoulder. "Do you like our mini forest?"

"I love it." The landscaper had installed five six-foot-tall manzanitas, spaced from the entry gate to the exit. Two birdfeeders were already being visited. The arrangement made the high wall by the street much less obvious. "It doesn't look like a prison yard anymore."

Charlie laughed under her breath. "Think what it'll be like next summer."

"I'll be parked on your window seat, watching the birds." He kissed her. "It looks like our house now. I can't wait to show everybody at dinner."

"Jenny will be so happy." They turned around and went back inside.

November 2016

Tony called the week after their dinner party to say they needed to choose a date to meet at the recording studio. "Jonathan Morris has agreed to record the letter. And we need to know about this song. We have the license."

Sacha said, "Valerie knows?"

"She knows which song. She needs to hear you."

"Is there any downside to going straight in to record it? If she doesn't like how I do it, we still have time to get another singer."

Tony made a dubious sound. "You don't have any other recordings?"

"Well, nothing serious. We have a thing of me singing to Natalie's cat." Tony laughed. Sacha was smiling, thinking *don't be a diva.* "I mean, what do you think. The alternatives are me meeting with Valerie in advance or singing to her over the phone. And I'll do either of those, if she wants me to."

"I'll speak with her and let you know. Ciao."

"Ciao Tony." Sacha disconnected, and went to practice. He had a feeling he'd be singing over the phone pretty soon. And the singing part he wasn't worried about, but the guitar part wasn't as simple as it sounded. His teacher said 'you're doing great,' as did Charlie. He knew she would tell him if it was honestly no good. Still, he wanted to do justice to the project.

Tony texted back the next day with *phone audition please,* a time, and a number. Sacha blocked out the time, thought about where and how to do the call, tested the acoustics in a couple of rooms. The best turned out to be the dining room. When he told Charlie what was going on she said "Can I take video?" and even though he was getting more nervous by the minute, he said yes. She was all set up when he went in to make the call.

Valerie picked up right away. "Hi, is this Sacha? Great. Look, I want to say something. This is your project and ultimately what you want is what we'll do. But my name goes on it, which is why I want to know what I'm getting into."

"Hi Valerie. I understand completely. It's good we're doing this. I wanted to speak with you before we meet for Jonathan's thing anyway. Get acquainted." He was smiling, intentionally softening his voice so she would know he wasn't annoyed about doing this.

"Yes. So. Are you ready to go?"

"Let me put this on speaker. We're in the dining room, it seemed to have the best acoustics. How does this sound at your end?"

"Not bad at all. Whenever you're ready."

Sacha picked up the guitar, took a deep breath, let it out slowly. Charlie pressed her camera's 'record' button, admiring him all over again. She knew how nervous he was. He started to play, and then to sing. She closed her eyes to listen, afraid if she watched him she'd start to cry. Of course, she cried anyway, so she opened her eyes.

When he finished Sacha didn't say anything for a second. Charlie stopped the camera. Valerie filled the pause. "Have you been playing guitar for long?"

"Since this summer. This is the only song I know."

She uttered something; they couldn't tell whether it was a word. "Okay. We'll record that the same day we get Jonathan in. Do you want only guitar, or do you want me to get some strings? A violin, a cello? I know some good people."

Sacha and Charlie were staring at each other. She made an 'I'm clueless' face and he almost laughed. "Maybe we could record it with only the guitar and then with the other instruments, and you could decide which you like better?"

"We can do that. Schedule pretty open?"

"We'll move anything we have to."

"Great. Thanks. Tony will let you know after he's got me and Jonathan squared away." She disconnected.

Sacha put his phone to sleep, then laid the guitar on the table. Stared at Charlie for another few seconds. "Do you want to send that tape to Tony?"

"Oh my God, he will have a fit. Can I? Yes. You are so, so beautiful. I can't believe I'm the first person in the world to ever see that." She stopped, struck by a thought. "Except your teacher?"

"No, he hasn't seen me sing. I've been humming along. Too shy." Sacha laughed at himself. "Maybe we should send it to him, too. Barry's a good teacher."

"Yeah, obviously. Holy crap. Oh shit."

"What?"

Now she made an 'eek' face. "Speaking of teachers. If we're going to learn Viennese waltz we'd better get a move on."

Sacha came around the table and kissed her. "Set up some lessons. As soon as we're done with this recording, I can get in there too. And can you organize our officiant?"

"Yes. I completely lost track of that for a couple of months. It was like we had the conversation with Elena and then it felt like we were done planning, you know?"

"There's plenty of time. It's only a backyard party. We can do it whenever we're ready." He kissed her again, taking some time over it. "God, I love you."

"I love you so, so much. I wish I could have met Jerry. I wish I could thank him, for saving you." She wrapped her arms around Sacha and hung on.

Charlie made the short trip to West Hollywood the next day, after checking in with Tony. She sent him a text to say she'd swing by after going to the dance studio. When she got there, things were only slightly less crazy than they'd been that summer. She sidled along the wall, staying out of the way of all those flying bodies, went to the office, and poked her head in. "Hi Elena. Oh! Hi Dmitri. I was coming to see you. Both of you. Remember a while back when you said Viennese waltz was not hard?" Dmitri nodded, almost smiling. Charlie knew that on most people that would be a laugh. "Well we were thinking of learning it. Not to go to Vienna. We're getting married in January. We're going to have a backyard party, you and Patrick are invited of course, but is two months enough time to get me to a point where I will not actually fall in the pool if I try dancing?" Elena was laughing.

Dmitri said, "Two months is good. You will have dance floor?"

"We will have a dance floor. We've got a lot of space back there."

"Yes. Excellent. We make schedule. Sacha will come?"

"Sacha will join us as soon as he's done with this other thing for this documentary we're making. Jeez, one year ago today I thought I would have exactly one thing to do in twenty sixteen, which was work." They scheduled a half-dozen lessons. Then Dmitri glanced at the clock and excused himself. Charlie huffed out a breath and perched on the edge of the desk. "Did Tony show you that video I took?"

"Oh my God. He was so amazed. You know there are a lot of people in Los Angeles who think they can sing."

Charlie laughed. "It's such a simple melody."

"But there's so much more to it than hitting the notes. Anyway, yes, and I'm so glad you took that. If he doesn't find some way to use it in the film I'll be astonished. Are you heading over there now?"

"Yes I am. But I wanted to see if you could hook me up with that person, the one you said was ordained. I kind of forgot about it with the other things we had happening."

"Sure, of course. Rory lives right in this neighborhood. Let me ping her." Elena sent a quick text. They chatted for a few minutes while waiting for a reply. When her phone buzzed Elena glanced at it and said, "Oh. She's not at home. She's over at Andy's place. She uses his studio sometimes when she's working on a routine. You know where that is, right? Could you go over there?" Charlie nodded. Elena sent another text. The reply came fast. "Okay. She's cool with that. You're going to love her. I'll tell Tony to expect you a little later. Is Sacha busy this evening or could he join us for dinner?"

"I'm pretty sure he could join. I'll text him before I head over to Andy's. Thanks Elena!"

"You are welcome. See you later." Elena waved as Charlie went out. She went through the studio's back door again, out to the parking lot, opened up her car. Sent a text to Sacha, then sat in the driver's seat and checked her calendar. Nothing much in the way of commitments, aside from the new dance lessons on the schedule. She'd have plenty of time to get the Lebedev family book done.

There was still no security guard at Andy Martin's house, and again Charlie thought *these guys are insane*. She could hear music coming from the studio. After she hit the buzzer it took a minute until the door opened. The person standing there was wearing a sports bra and trunks, and was covered with tattoos of feathers. Charlie blinked. "Hi, I'm Charlie Montgomery."

"I'm Rory Atwood. Come on in." She headed back up the stairs. Charlie shut the door behind her and tried not to trip over her own feet as she went up. Rory's back had wings. A lot of wings, and some scattered feathers that had spots like eyes.

"Are you a cherubim?" The question escaped her.

"Holy shit! Yes! You are the second person on planet Earth who ever got that without me telling them! Well, hell, now I know I want to do your wedding." Rory was grinning when Charlie made it into the studio. She was several inches shorter than Charlie, with thick black hair cut in something close to a Mohawk, and a cute Pacific Islander face. "I hear you're marrying a millionaire. Good for you. I'm shacked up with one, it's the greatest. Dana Richardson, she's on one of those stupid cop shows."

Charlie laughed. "Was she a millionaire when you shacked up?"

"Only on paper. She owns a house in Los Angeles, that pretty much pushes you over the threshold. Anyway I'm here re-working a thing I did almost ten years ago and I'm buggin' out. Tell me about you and your wedding."

"We're going to do it in our backyard, in January. Dmitri will try to teach us Viennese waltz. Elena and Tony are two of our best friends. Tony's making a documentary for us, about Sacha's previous relationship."

"I saw the press conference thing on Pop Quiz. Dana knew that guy, Jerry Morgenstern. She worked on a project he produced ten years ago."

"What did she think of him?"

"Never got to know him personally. She said, as a producer, he took no crap and had a lot of creativity. She liked him. Now. Because I am a kept woman my schedule is hella easy." Rory picked up a phone that was lying on Andy's desk.

"Mine too."

"That said, I'm a principal in this wacko dance company and we do a show at Chrome every month so there are always days that are not possible for me. We have the schedule for next year." She pulled up her calendar. "This particular Sunday is dress rehearsal for our show the next weekend."

"That dress rehearsal day is one of the days we talked about. Is your thing at night?"

"No, we do it early in the day because the club is open after five. January evening is going to be on the chilly side."

"We have four heat lamps."

"Then you're probably good unless it rains. If you get a canopy thing over the dance floor that'll keep people warm. Do you want to do it that day?"

"Six o'clock?"

"Works for me." They both updated their calendars, then grinned at each other. "Want to see this nutball thing I did a million years ago?"

"Sure." While Rory was pulling up her old video, Charlie sent Sacha a text to let him know the wedding date was set. Then she leaned in to watch. It was the same music she'd heard from outside, 'Zoot Suit Riot.' Rory was doing a striptease routine, starting from a pinstripe suit with fedora, necktie, and pocket watch on a chain. Charlie started snickering right away. On 'now you sailors know where your women come for love,' she laughed out loud. At the end she held up her hand for a high five. "You are hilarious. And very sexy. Are you doing it just like that this time?"

"Eh, not exactly. The show this month is all swing so the music is fine. I still have the costume. But this month's show is also partner dance, so I want to do some actual swing before I start taking my clothes off. Or in between taking my clothes off. I may make Dmitri dance with me."

"Oh my God I would love to see that. We've only been to one thing at Chrome, that big show this summer. You weren't in that."

"No." Rory looked slightly grumpy. "All that martial-arts stuff, I really wanted to, but I would have been starting from nothing and I'm so goddamned short. Whatever. All those whippety fuckers throwing that 540 at the end, I wanted to kneecap every one of them."

Charlie laughed again. "What's a 540?" Rory told her about the big ballet jump that some of the dancers had done as a relay. Charlie stored it away. Sacha must have known what that was. "Do they ever put those shows on DVD?"

"Oh yeah. Go to Underground Cabaret Dance Theater online and there's a whole backlist. I've been doing it forever, we started doing DVDs in, let's see, wow it's five years ago. These guys?" Rory indicated the studio and the main house. Charlie nodded comprehension. "They did two shows last year. Andy's one of our best friends so we adopted Victor too."

"It's good to have friends. I had kind of a dry spell when I was working so much. There wasn't time to have friends."

"I feel ya. I was there before I met Dana. This is better, huh?"

"It's so much better. Sometimes I feel like I should be guilty about it, not working. Then I think, well, all it means is someone who needs the money more is getting those jobs." Charlie shrugged. She was still a little uncomfortable with it, still not used to her time being her own. Not having to hustle. Being able to do exactly and only what she wanted. Barely having to remember about the insurance bills that someone else was paying now.

"Yeah, me too. I still feel like, gotta have some kind of job. But the amount I was bringing in was only worth the hassle after I got an office job, and then it was like, no time to do anything else. Dana said, please stop this nonsense."

"Exactly. My average income was so average." They both laughed. "And I still get to take pictures. I'd love to take yours." She was suddenly struck by a memory. "You were Andy's model, weren't you? For City of Angels? Those photos were so amazing."

Rory looked pleased. "It was a first for both of us. Are you coming to his new show? It's going up this weekend." She indicated the two dozen framed pieces

254

leaning against the window wall of the studio. "It's from his chorus boys thing. He's hanging it here, says he can't be bothered to get a gallery."

Charlie added that to her calendar. "I definitely want Sacha to see those. I got a sneak peek when I met Andy, in August." She sighed, smiling. "I could stay here talking to you all day, but you have stuff to do and I have an appointment with Tony. So I will let you do your thing. I really enjoyed meeting you. And thanks," she added, offering a hand. Rory shook it. "I'll see you around."

"Tell that millionaire of yours I will wear clothes for the wedding."

"He wouldn't mind if you don't!" Charlie heard Rory laughing as she went down the stairs.

CHAPTER 13

Back in West Hollywood, Charlie parked at the dance studio again and walked the short distance to Tony's apartment. He met her downstairs and they went up. "Elena told me you liked that video."

"Charlie, I was never so surprised," he said as they went in. "I shouldn't say so."

"Well, I was surprised, and I've heard him sing before." She was smiling. Tony offered coffee; this time she declined. "Water, please and thank you. I've been over at Andy's place talking to Rory about officiating at our wedding. Before that I was setting up dance lessons with Dmitri. I can't believe this is my life."

"It's quite a change, eh? So. I have all the interviews. The primary assembly, I think it's done. Now to begin tightening up, trimming back, as soon as we have the song and the voice-over recorded. And then you send this video and I want to use it." He blew out a breath, half exasperated and half amused. "I think, maybe the credits. The way when he finished, he laid his hand on the strings and looked up. He was looking at you?"

"Yes. I was a mess."

"Everyone will be. Shall we go through it? You have time?"

"I have time." Charlie sent Sacha one more text, to let him know she was at Tony's whenever he got free, then settled in to watch.

Sacha was increasingly entertained by Charlie's series of texts. He sent her one to confirm everything

256

and tell her he'd be on his way to West Hollywood as soon as he was done with a meeting at the lawyer's office. He got to Tony's place before five o'clock and instantly knew something was up. "Problem?" he said.

Tony said, "Eh," and stalled.

Charlie rescued him. "There's this big hole in the middle, honey. Even when the voice-over goes in, even with the song, there's going to be a hole. At that point we've seen Maggie come apart, we've heard from Gary, some of the other interviews where people are like yeah, I always thought Jerry was crazy about Maggie, we never did know where she came from."

Sacha sat on the arm of the couch, studying both of them for a minute. "You think I need to speak."

"Only for a minute or two," said Tony. "It's the *why* of the whole thing that's missing. Why he needed it, why you were willing to do it."

It was true. Sacha knew it. He'd thought that himself at the beginning. And he'd seen it himself, the last time they'd gone through the assembly. Hearing from him was as important as hearing from Jerry. The voice-over would communicate Jerry's side of their strange love story. If he didn't say anything, it would be a failure to answer Jerry's 'I love you,' and that wasn't acceptable. "Okay. I'll work on something. Can we tape it at home?"

Tony said, "Of course," with open relief. They looked at their schedules, and decided on two days after their date with Valerie and Jonathan. Then he changed the subject, talking about what was happening with his day job and with his personal film project – negotiations were complete between a new ballroom couple he wanted to follow – until Elena called to say she was ready to meet them for dinner.

Tony sent a text, nodded at the quick reply. "Our sitter will be here in a few minutes."

"That child of yours is so quiet," Charlie said. "I forget he's here sometimes."

"Gio is quiet when people are talking. He's like a little cat, sleeping in the day and then at two in the morning he wants to run." Tony shrugged, smiling. "It's good I can work from home. I can take naps with him."

Charlie and Sacha had their first Viennese waltz lesson on Friday morning. After saying goodbye to Dmitri and walking out to the car, they looked at each other. Charlie had been close to cracking up for the entire lesson, because she was so lamentably bad. Sacha said, "You'll get it."

Now she did laugh. "If anyone can teach me, I'm sure it's Dmitri, and thank God you have talent. But oh my lord. I definitely need a distracting dress because I do not want anyone to notice what my feet are doing."

"Well, should we go and see about this ballgown?" He was smiling. Elena had given them the number and said, 'text to make sure someone's in the office,' because it wasn't a conventional storefront.

Charlie nodded. "Yes please. If I know I'm going to look fabulous, it'll help motivate me."

"You always look fabulous." Sacha got his phone out and sent the text. "Let's go get coffee." They walked down the alley. There had been a very brief moment of time when it seemed one or more tabloids had eyes on Sacha's car; he would go somewhere and a photographer would show up before he left. Whether it was the press conference or the low news value of their usual activities – 'Morgenstern heir goes to accountant's office' wasn't going to get many hits - neither of them usually felt pursued. They were in West Hollywood so often that nobody even noticed them anymore. By the time they got back to the car with their coffees, Sacha had received a reply text. "We can go over now." He entered the address in the car's navigation system and they rolled out.

The dancewear company was based in a private home west of the 405 freeway. They parked in the driveway, as instructed, and walked up to the door. A pretty Filipina woman answered the buzzer. "Hi, you must be Sacha and Charlie. Come on in. I'm Kristine, I do most of the bridal design."

"Well, we have got a challenge for you," Charlie said. "I lived in jeans for thirty-three years and still don't know how to dress. Sacha has all the fashion sense. If he didn't shop with me I'd be screwed." They talked nonstop for the next quarter hour, while flipping through a style book. Sacha waited, enjoying the chatter.

Eventually Kristine said, "Okay. Winter, outdoors, danceable. Is this a glam sort of thing or casual?"

"Well." Charlie glanced at Sacha. "None of our friends are super posh, but we have noticed that everybody likes to dress up. Is there such a thing as casual glam?"

"Sure! Now, do you want to wear white?" Kristine waited while Charlie and Sacha stared at each other.

Charlie no longer owned a single white garment, didn't much like the thought of something so obviously single-purpose, and realized the answer was "No."

"She looks beautiful in red," Sacha said. "Any tint or shade of red."

"But is it possible to make a red dress that still sort of looks like a wedding dress? I mean, I don't want to look like Carmen or something." That led into some more discussion.

Kristine was eyeing her thoughtfully, fiddling with her glasses. Then she put them on again and said, "Let me show you something. I'll be right back." Charlie stood up, restless, and paced a little. Sacha watched. He'd had an idea that this might be the toughest decision. The party itself was going to be simple, thanks to Cecilia and Natalie. When Kristine returned she was lugging a bolt of fabric. It seemed to be wound inside-out. "This was a special order for someone who changed her mind. Kenji kept the fabric because he liked it." She laid the bolt down on a table, flipped it a few times, and then unfolded the fabric to show the outside. They both went over to look.

"Holy wow." Charlie stared at it. She'd never seen anything like it. "Honey, is that what they call couture fabric?"

"That's exactly what it is." Sacha touched the very edge. It was a sheer pink mesh embroidered with a variety of crimson flowers. Not an all-over pattern, but heavy near the selvage, the flowers three-dimensional with applied fabric petals. The design became more open and delicate toward the top. Sequins and beads sparkled. "Over a darker red?" he asked. Kristine nodded enthusiastically. "Honey, I think this is it."

Charlie wasn't so sure, but he'd never been wrong. "Well, you're the expert. What happens now?"

"Now I take your measurements, and next I draw you a sketch. I'll send that with an image of the fabric

I think would work best underneath. There are a lot of styles that simply won't work with a surface design like this. But this isn't far off some of the ballgown embellishment I do. I could get back to you next week."

"Okay." Charlie checked in with Sacha again. He was smiling. She did too. "Okay."

When they got back in the car to go home Charlie said, "If that looks as good as you think it will, I could wear it sometime for a Christmas party. With that first jewelry Jerry gave you."

Sacha laughed, then leaned over to kiss her. "I would love to see you in that. But I think you'll need something of your very own for the wedding." He touched her face, traced a finger down, all the way to her cleavage. "I think you need something long." He put his mouth where his fingertip had been. Kissed his way up to her collarbone, then her neck, hearing her breath catch when his lips teased the sensitive skin on the side of her face. Kissed her mouth again. "I think we should go home right now."

"Yes," she said. "I think so too."

Andy had a valet service on duty for his gallery show on Sunday. They drove in through the alley, the car was taken somewhere, and they walked through the open gate to the open studio door. "He is completely out of his mind," Charlie said. "They both are. Still no guard."

"At least they have the valet people out here. Maybe they're so used to it they can't be bothered. I hardly even remember now, unless someone's being really obvious."

"Yeah, but it's going on a year since anyone said anything truly scary about you. These guys get death

261

threats every week." They walked up the studio steps. A few other people were there, but nobody they knew except Andy himself. "Andy. I was here earlier this week to talk to Rory. She told me this was going up and I had to make sure Sacha saw your gorgeous pictures."

"Thank you! Nice to see you both again. How did your show do?"

"From my point of view, it was amazing. A lot of the books were sold. A lot of donations were made. I gave all the prints to those subjects, and had enough books that everyone got one of those. It was really cool. Great experience, and thank you again for your help. Did you not do a book for this show?"

"No." Andy performed a gesture that said 'too much trouble' and Charlie remembered everything else he had going on. "I did one for a different tango thing last year, a show at Chrome. There are still a few of those up for sale. This was something I threw together in a couple of weeks, mostly for fun because that one guy was in town for a minute. Anyway. Enjoy, if you have any questions you know where to find me." He went to mingle.

Charlie and Sacha took a slow lap around the studio. The twenty-four prints included a portrait of each of Andy's nine subjects, eight vignettes, and a series of seven. Those – according to the captions – were about the tall guy, the one with the butterfly tattoos, teaching a cabaret sequence to the others. Charlie's favorite was one where the tall guy was standing off to one side and Dmitri off to the other, while the other seven guys cracked up. "I would love to know what happened right before this."

"I love that picture," Sacha said. "That's what it was like sometimes, preparing a show. I only got to do a few. But there would be the choreographer looking patient like Dmitri, and the director looking like that guy. Like, would you idiots get yourselves together so we can go on. Don't make me turn this car around." Charlie laughed. "I might have to get this print."

"You should see if we can get one in a bigger size. We could hang it in the dining room."

"And take down the Lempicka?"

"I never did like that," she confessed. "I mean, it's not ugly, but it seems like something Jerry got because it was expected of him." It was stylish, moody, and faintly erotic. "We could put it somewhere else."

"Or give it away." Sacha was smiling. "I don't think it's an original. You don't want to hang one of your own pictures in there?"

"Ugh, no." He laughed. Charlie added, "My favorite pictures are all of you, and mostly they are not appropriate for mixed company, so no. Thanks. Let's get this one instead." Sacha was still smiling when he went to talk to Andy.

Meeting at the recording studio felt like crossing a finish line, even though there was still so much to do. These recordings were the last big pieces of the puzzle. Valerie greeted Sacha and Charlie in the studio lobby, saying, "Tony got here about ten minutes ago. He said he'd never been involved with soundtracking, and could he come in and see what happens. I said sure. My musicians are due in an hour. We're waiting for Jonathan now."

"You're doing his thing first, right?"

"That was the idea, yeah. That still okay?"

"Yes, that's good." Sacha glanced at Charlie. "I've never been in a recording studio before. Are we allowed to sit in the booth?"

"Sure. The engineer and I will have headphones on so you won't be able to talk to us. You can talk to each other as long as you keep it down." She studied them. "You don't seem like loud people."

"Quiet as mice," Charlie said, mouselike. Valerie grinned. "That letter is going to take a while to read, isn't it?"

She took them into the main space. Tony waved from the other side; he was setting up to record Jonathan on video. "I'm guessing close to ten minutes for each take. We'll take it twice at least, I'll listen to the first one while he's doing the second. Then a break while I listen to the second." They were in the booth. Sacha set his guitar case by the wall. Valerie introduced them to the engineer, then said, "Tony said he's going to use this voice-over scattered throughout the film. The way it's written kind of lends itself to that, those short paragraphs. Anyway, Jonathan is going to take a beat after each paragraph to make it easier to cut. He's been studying that archival footage Tony found, of the producers' round table, to get Jerry's speech pattern down. Though as far as I could tell, he wrote exactly the way he talked." Her phone buzzed. She pulled it out of her pocket and glanced at the screen. "He's parking. I'm going out to the front. If you want some coffee or whatever, it's out there too."

She went out. Charlie and Sacha looked around the recording booth. Then by tacit agreement they followed her, in search of coffee. It would be at least half an hour, by the sound of it, before Sacha needed to get settled, warmed up, and into performance mode.

He was glad they wouldn't be able to hear Jonathan. Hearing the letter was going to be tough, if he really sounded that much like Jerry.

And he did. Charlie could tell, from Sacha's physical reaction. She set her hand on his back, offering silent support as they all introduced themselves. "Sacha. I know this is a really personal project for you," Jonathan said. "Thanks for trusting me with it."

"Have you done something like this before?" Sacha managed.

"I voiced an animated character one time. Not quite like this. It was a comedy, and there were no F words."

Charlie patted Sacha and said, "How about your movie this summer? Any F words in that?" There had certainly been a few in that behind-the-scenes goofing-off video Andy had.

"No, they were going for the PG-13 rating. You know, want to get those teenagers in." He was smiling. "But I think the boss wants to move. Let me get some water, and we'll get this rolling." He went down to the water cooler, then followed Valerie into the main room.

"Okay, honey?" Charlie still had her hand on his back.

Sacha was steady now. He'd kept his gaze on Jonathan, consciously connecting the painfully-similar voice with the new face. A different person, who looked nothing like Jerry, though he was the same height. *Quit looking for equivalencies.* "I'm okay. Let's go in."

There wasn't much to see from the booth. Jonathan was in a small enclosure on the far side of the main space. A monitor camera in there fed to a screen in the booth; they could tell when he was reading, they could tell when he stopped. They could tell when he said something to Valerie, and heard her reply. "Whenever you're ready." He nodded, rolled his neck, and began again. The engineer was listening to the new live feed while Valerie listened to the first take.

Then the second take was done. Valerie told Jonathan to take a load off. He went out to the lobby again. Charlie and Sacha glanced at each other. The musicians were due soon. Charlie said, "I'm going to the bathroom, then I'm getting some water, then I'll come back here."

"And I'll do two of those things and take the guitar in there to warm up a little."

"Nervous?"

Sacha huffed out a laugh. "So nervous. I don't know why. You and Tony and Valerie have all heard this already."

"Well, it's your first time. For what it's worth, I'm nervous and I'm not even singing." She kissed him and they went out.

Sacha was at the water cooler when he heard that voice say "Hey." He turned around. Jonathan was looking a little bit apologetic. "Valerie might want to take it again. I got kind of emotional the second time."

"It's heavy, I know."

"Tony didn't tell me much about the story." He was studying Sacha. "Any chance I could see it at rough cut?"

Sacha smiled. It took some effort. "I'm sure that could be arranged. Are you in town through the end of the year?"

"Yeah, I live here now. Got a place downtown. Convenient for getting to the ball games." He looked around, as if to make sure nobody was listening. "And Disney Hall. Don't tell anybody. Wrestlers aren't supposed to like classical music."

"It's a wonderful venue. Charlie and I went recently." They discovered they'd been to the same concert, which led into such a comfortable conversation that Sacha forgot about the voice. They were laughing together when Valerie found them.

"Oh hey Valerie," Jonathan said. "Did the second take sound all right? I could go again if you want me to."

"Actually I think the second take was ideal. It's going to grab people by the throat. Word perfect, crystal clear, and really heartfelt. Excellent work. You might want to put a clip in your reel if the filmmakers will give permission."

Jonathan looked at Sacha with his eyebrows up. After a moment Sacha said, "Once we have a deal." Jonathan smiled.

"Okay then." Valerie glanced at her phone, which she had in her hand. "My strings should be here any minute. Mr. Morris, I think you're done for the day. Thanks for joining us."

"My pleasure. Let me know when, you know. Nice meeting you, Sacha."

"You too, Jonathan." They shook hands. Sacha watched him go, then turned to Valerie. "I should go warm up."

"Yeah. I'll send the fiddlers in when they get here. Charlie's already in the booth again," she said, pointing. Sacha looked, smiled, then went to get his guitar.

"Andy said he was a nice guy," Charlie said when Sacha stepped into the booth.

"He is. I had kind of a bad moment at first."

"I know. Okay now?"

"Okay now. I love you." He leaned over for a kiss.

"I love you too. Go be a rock star." Sacha snorted. "Hey, imagine the stories you're going to have for your brother's kids next time we see them." Charlie was grinning when he went out. She'd been worried for a minute there. Whatever that conversation had been, it seemed to have helped Sacha. And she thought he hadn't noticed her scooting past behind Jonathan's back, which was good.

They did two takes of his solo version. Then Valerie brought him out of the main space and left the violin and cello players to rehearse with the second take before sending him back in to do it with them live. "One more time," she said through the board mic after a ten-minute break for review. Sacha spent that time chatting with Tony and the musicians, getting comfortable again. He was able to enjoy it, to feel like he almost knew what he was doing, during that last take. He asked Valerie, when they were done, if there was any difference in his voice. "Between the first take and the last one? Oh yeah. In fact, if you want to go again with just the guitar, we still have some time." He nodded. She told the string players to hang out till he was done, then set up the new take.

Charlie heard that whole conversation. Sacha and the others were out on the floor, and the booth glass wasn't soundproof. She'd been able to hear all the music. She was glad Sacha wanted to go again. They hadn't even discussed whether he might want to pursue this music thing. If today's session was as positive an experience as it seemed to be, he might decide yes.

On their way out, Valerie handed Sacha something. Charlie was saying thank you to the string players, so she missed the exchange. When they got to the car, he popped the trunk to put the guitar back there. Then he pulled something out of his jacket pocket and handed it Charlie. An unlabeled CD in a Tyvek sleeve. "What's this?"

"Songs Valerie wants me to learn." He went around to the passenger door and opened it for her. She stared at him. He laughed. "Come on, honey. Let's go home." He waited until they were back out on Ventura Boulevard to ask her about her moment of avoiding the actor. "I couldn't help noticing you weren't all that comfortable with Jonathan."

Charlie sighed. "I hope he didn't notice. It's not his fault."

"Is it his size?" He was watching the road, but he could tell she'd turned to look at him. "I realized almost all of our guy friends are on the smaller side of average. From Tony to Dmitri. Andy's the only six-footer."

"And he's gay." That slipped out. *For God's sake just tell him.* "I had two really bad experiences with big guys. Both football players. One in high school, and the other in college." She was testing her readiness to talk about this, positive Sacha wouldn't push, also positive he wouldn't make her feel like everything was her fault, the way her parents – and almost everybody else – had before. "For the longest time I believed it must have been my own fault. I led them on, or I wore the wrong thing, or I shouldn't have done this or that. Anyway the right name for it, both times, is date rape." Now that she said that, everything else was easier. "Neither of them used force. The high school guy just wore me down, wore me out. I was like whatever, get it over with and let me go home." She thought about that, hearing it. "I guess there are degrees of force, huh."

"Yes, there are." Sacha knew all about those too.

Charlie nodded. "I figured you would understand. Anyway the college guy, it was over at my shitty little apartment and I'd had too much to drink."

"I'm surprised you were okay with my family. All those big guys."

"There were a lot of women around. And you were there." Charlie patted his thigh. "And now you know one of the reasons why I love your body so much."

"I love yours too."

"That's another reason." She smiled. "You have all those years of mingling with all those Hollywood beauty queens and I'm the one you looked at. You have no idea how that makes me feel." She glanced over at him. "Or actually I guess you do." He was smiling too. "So that's also one of the reasons I thought I'd never get married. Because I was always attracted to athletes, but then I had those two experiences and I was like, your judgement stinks, and these guys are gross, and no. And then there was you."

"Not a football player."

"No, thank God. Jeez, if I'd only met some dancers before." He laughed. Charlie left her hand on his thigh.

Sacha's interview happened toward the end of that week, in the rose garden. It was a brightly sunny day, so they took a chair outside and set Sacha up under one of the shade trees. He did the same minimal makeup he'd used that time they went out with the yogis, and wore the same clothes. Tony had a wireless mic for him, and they got two cameras ready. Of course, as soon as Moses saw people outside he came to investigate. "Do you mind?" Sacha asked, when the cat jumped onto his lap.

"Of course not. He'll help you relax."

Sacha nodded. They'd already agreed that he would give them a cue when he was ready to begin. He sat and thought for another minute, about what he'd decided to say. *It's for Jerry*, he reminded himself. "Let's go." Two camera lights went on. He waited a couple more seconds. "I hadn't been in Los Angeles very long before I knew I was going to fail," he said. "It's a terrible feeling. To spend all those years training, doing everything right, following all the expert advice, and then look around and realize you're never going to make it. Whatever talent you have isn't good enough, or maybe not the talent people want at that moment in time, or maybe it's not really about talent at all. There was a long moment of feeling betrayed, of such total bewilderment. Not knowing what to do. Jerry found me at the very bottom. He gave me a safe place to think and learn. And while I was climbing up out of that hole things changed between us." He petted the cat for a moment, looking away as if to gather his thoughts, a calculated pause. "There was a day when we had a very important conversation. He told me things he never told anyone. Then I kissed him, and he hugged me, and he said he wanted to take me to the Emmys. And I said Jerry, if you do that," he shook his head. "And he said, I know, but." He shrugged. "He was willing to do that. He was scared to death. I said, what if I were a woman." A tiny smile, that half-shrug. "He said, eh?" A full smile. "So confused. But I'd done drag before. This wouldn't be that. This would have to be so subtle, so realistic, that nobody would guess. The idea was exciting, for me. It was a chance to do a unique kind of performance, something no one would ever expect. To create and truly embody a character. The whole idea was that no one would ever know, but that was how I would know I'd done it right. And it would be a way I could show him I loved him. A way he could accept."

Sacha petted Moses for another breath or two, then returned his gaze to Charlie. "I said, let me try it for you, and you can decide if you want it to leave this room. He said okay. He gave me some money, some cash. His driver took me out, in his own car, not Jerry's. We went to a few consignment places until I found the right dress. I could wear a women's size ten. I have this light bone structure, and my muscle development was consistent with a female athlete. We came up with a whole story for that. Anyway, that was the first dress. I could wear a bra with it. We created our own style after we knew it would work. I found shoes, and a good wig. I got all the stuff for the makeup. Picked up some costume jewelry. After Jerry saw the presentation he said, I'll get some good stuff, people will think they're looking at Sophia Loren. The first thing he said, though, when I said okay open your eyes, was holy shit." Another full smile. "I did the voice. I said," now in Maggie's voice, "How do I look, honey? Ready to go?" Then his natural voice again. "And he laughed."

He stopped then. After a few seconds Charlie and Tony turned off the cameras. Charlie said, "I wish you could have recorded that moment. Was his face like Patrick's, that first time he met you?"

"Pretty much," Sacha said, smiling again at the memory. "Obviously he knew it was me, he just kind of couldn't believe it was me for a second. God, how he laughed. He was like, this is the greatest mind-fuck of all time." Tony stifled a laugh. "Yeah, didn't want to say that on tape."

"This was good," Tony said. "It's enough. Thank you."

CHAPTER 14

Once that interview was done, the documentary was truly out of their hands. Charlie left Tony alone to get on with it when he could. Elena and her partner were competing at the end of the month; it was a big deal and they were all anxious. Tony would go with them to Ohio. He said he was well ahead of his work on the Ovation series and would be able to finish the rough cut of the Jerry project on schedule.

Charlie and Sacha found themselves with plenty of time for dance lessons. Charlie got better. Kristine sent a sketch that she loved, a glamorous but informal dress design inspired by the 1930s RKO musicals. It would show the fabulous embroidered mesh to full advantage on the flowing skirt and fluttery sleeves. Natalie located a vendor for their outdoor dance floor and a freestanding, semi-enclosed canopy to cover it. "They'll even provide a chandelier," she said, looking excited. "I had to get it."

"Of course you did," said Sacha. "It'll be great." Then he looked pointedly at her.

"What?" Now he looked at her bare left hand. Natalie laughed. "No."

"Not now, or not ever?"

"Not now. Let's get you kids squared away."

"Is that what you told Gary?"

"Yes."

"And did he agree?" Sacha thought that he probably had not.

Natalie hedged. "Not exactly." Sacha didn't pursue it, but he did go to his office and send a text to Gary: *You're not getting any younger*

A reply came back within the hour: *Believe me, I've noticed*

I happen to know where there will be a nice wedding party in January

Bahaha

I'll bet our officiant wouldn't mind making it a twofer

Sacha you're a nut

Gary in all seriousness we would love to share that day with you and Natalie, if you're ever going to do it why not now?

You make an excellent point

Meet us at Chrome next Sunday. Show at 8. Dress to impress

I always do

Sacha almost added 'bring a ring' but figured he'd pushed it as far as he reasonably could. Then he went to find Charlie and warn her. "You really are a nut," she said, smiling. "But you're right, I would love to share that day. Think he'll do it?" Sacha made a 'don't know' face. "Did you tell him at least one of the numbers in the show will include some striptease?"

"No I did not. But somehow I don't think he'll mind."

Sacha arranged for their usual car service to take him, Charlie and Natalie to Hollywood. They arrived a half hour before showtime and went to the pair of loveseats Sacha had reserved. Charlie took a moment to take phone pictures of Sacha (in gray jeans, a black silk shirt, and a gray alligator blazer with matching cowboy boots) and Natalie (in a 1940s-styled dress). Natalie then took her phone to get a picture of Charlie in her scarlet pencil dress with a zoot-suit-inspired

275

jacket, black with a red pinstripe. The high-heeled black and red booties got their own picture. They took their seats, and Charlie picked up a table talker that had a miniature show poster and the list of performances. "The Underground Cabaret presents Mating Dance: Swing It," she read. "That's Rory. 'Zoot Suit Riot.' Closing the show, with Dmitri. It's going to be funny," she told Natalie. "She showed me the original version she did nine years ago."

Then a server was there asking if they wanted the night's special cocktails. One of them was called a Cab Calloway. "Plum wine with a scoop of cabernet sorbet," Sacha repeated, giving Charlie a sideways look. "I think that might be sweet enough even for you."

"I agree! One of those, please," Charlie said. Natalie was giggling. "Actually, two of those, because I know somebody else who likes the sweet stuff."

"And the other is our Jitterbug," said the server, smiling at Sacha. "Cherry-lime vodka, lime-twisted gin, et cetera. A classic."

"Fine, one of those." The drinks came back a few minutes later. Sacha took a sip. "It's good. Not too sweet. How are yours?"

"Very sweet. Delicious," said Charlie. "Now all we need is Gary."

"And you have Gary," he said, sitting beside Natalie. "Hi there." He gave her a kiss. "So it's been quite a month! You got your recording things done. We're on schedule for final cut in January?"

"Right on schedule," Charlie said. "How are things down your way?"

"Well, we have been acquiring like maniacs and thank God most of it is finished product, or mostly-finished. We also snagged a really strong pilot out from under those other guys and ordered thirteen episodes of that, we'll see what happens there. Anything new at the house?"

"We took down the Lempicka print in the dining room and put up one of Andy's. Aside from that, nothing since you were there last month. Gary, if you like lime, I recommend this Jitterbug," Sacha said. "It's strong, though."

"One of those, and only one, then. I drove myself up here unlike some people. Do they have anything to eat? Oh yes they do." Gary picked up the little menu. "Black and white bowtie pasta with chicken and Alfredo sauce, okay. Or pinstripe lasagna? Portobello mushroom, beef tenderloin, caramelized onion, béchamel. This I've gotta try."

Charlie made a yummy sound. "God that sounds good. You want that, honey? Okay, I think we all want that." The server was there a minute later, and before the curtain went up they all had their food.

Sacha thought if Gary was going to make any kind of scene he might make it at intermission. The first act closed with a jazzy foxtrot danced to 'Harlem Nocturne.' "That guy was in Andy's pictures," Charlie remarked when the lights came up. "And they were both in the thing this summer."

"Talented," Sacha said. "It must be a lot of fun to work with this company."

Charlie gave him a sideways look. "I'll bet you could, if you wanted to. But not till we finish this wedding dance, please." He laughed. "Oh hey, speaking of weddings." She nudged Natalie, who set down her water glass abruptly.

"What?" She wasn't making eye contact.

Charlie made big 'now please' eyes at Gary, who made a 'give me a minute' face and excused himself. "Oh, you know. I get to go have my dress fitted in a couple of weeks. Do you want to come with me? Sacha has all this homework from Valerie."

"That is true. My guitar teacher was like, what the hell." Sacha pretended nothing else was going on. "He's having to actually teach me how to play the guitar now, not just learn one song."

Natalie had recovered somewhat. "You know, that's a common problem. You establish that you're competent and all of a sudden people give you all the work."

"Well, you would know about that." Charlie looked sadly at the bottom of her empty cocktail glass. "That was delicious."

"You can have another," Sacha suggested. "As someone pointed out, we didn't drive ourselves here."

"You two are awfully frisky." Natalie looked suspicious. Then she looked dumbfounded because Gary was back, and he was kneeling in front of her. "What."

"Natalie. You sweet lady. I love you. I would really like to marry you. Even though I am older than dirt, would you marry me? These kids are not going to give us a moment's peace until you say you'll marry me." Gary was holding an open ring box, with a significant diamond ring inside.

Natalie gazed at the ring, then at Gary's hopeful face. Her eyes were glistening. "You didn't have to get me a ring, you know."

He looked insulted. "What kind of bullshit proposal would that be?" Sacha and Charlie both laughed. Gary glared at them and said, "Is that a yes or a no?"

278

"That's a yes. I love you too. Do you need a hand up?" Natalie took the ring from the box, biting her lip at the open outrage on Gary's face now. Sacha and Charlie were cracking up.

"My God." Gary waited until the ring was safely on Natalie's finger, then got halfway to his feet, leaned over to kiss her, and sat beside her again. "I work out every day, I'll have you know."

"Yes, you've mentioned that. In other contexts."

"Mayday! TMI alert!" Charlie was still laughing. Sacha had his hand over his face, shoulders shaking. Gary wrapped Natalie in his arms and hugged her. Three out of four of them had fresh cocktails, half of them were still giggling, and other half were still kissing when the lights went down for Act Two. The giggles were mostly under control by the second number. They were all in sufficient command of themselves to fully appreciate Rory's closing routine. "That's our dance teacher," Charlie announced to the room during the curtain call, brandishing her empty glass. "Dmitri foxypants Vasko."

"You did not just say that," Natalie said admiringly. "That's exactly what I was thinking."

"My God," Gary said to Sacha, "what was in those cocktails? Spanish fly?"

"Maybe," Sacha said gravely. "Maybe Natalie should go home with you."

"You know what, maybe she should." Gary shook his head, smiling. "Good idea, kid. Want to help me get her off this loveseat?"

"I will do that." Sacha stood up, Gary stood up, and the two men assisted Natalie to her feet. "Gary's taking you home now," Sacha said. "You have the day off tomorrow." He kissed her. "Congratulations." Gary was giving him a narrow-eyed look. "What?"

"You're taller." Sacha indicated his feet. Gary looked down, noticed the cowboy boots, and sighed. "Asshole." Sacha laughed.

Natalie missed all this while she was retrieving her handbag. "Thanks Sacha. See you ... sometime." She reached out for Charlie's hand. "Get home safe. Love you both."

Charlie said, "We love you too." Sacha helped her up as the older couple headed for the exit stairs. "Wow those were strong cocktails. I thought plum wine was, like, wine."

"Want to hang out for a little while? Say something to Rory, maybe? Warn her about the possibility of a double wedding?"

"Oh lord." Charlie giggled all over again. "I think I'd better put that in a text. I do not think that is a conversation to have immediately after a striptease swing routine."

"If you say so." Sacha got his phone out and sent a quick text, then put his arm around her and started steering her toward the stairs. "We're going to have the house to ourselves tomorrow," he murmured. "I just gave Cecilia the day off, too."

"You have a guitar lesson. We have a dance lesson."

"Guitar at two and dance at four. We could do a lot of damage by two o'clock." He paused before setting a foot on the bottom step, because he couldn't wait another second to kiss her.

"If we do too much damage we won't be able to dance at all." Charlie would have been concerned about the people trying to squeeze past them if Sacha hadn't been kissing her neck. He raised his head, smiling, and they started up the stairs.

December 2016

Sacha studied his calendar for December and January and almost couldn't believe how much his life had changed. A year ago, he'd been virtually housebound. Isolated, confused, grieving, and completely out of his depth. Now he knew what he was doing. He had friends, family, and freedom. They were going to tell the world about Jerry, and his own twelve-year secret identity would be a secret no more. It was scary, but it was exciting.

He was doing two ballet lessons and two guitar lessons a week. He and Charlie saw Dmitri three times a week for Viennese waltz. They were getting good. His lawyer – the original lawyer, the one who'd worked with Jerry – had mentioned a client looking for a real-estate investor. Sacha had his financial team reviewing that possibility.

He'd booked their honeymoon trip to New Zealand. They would fly in and out of Sydney, adding a few days in Australia at each end of the trip. Charlie was already compiling an itinerary of things to do and see. The wedding party plans were nearly complete. The only remaining question was whether it was going to be a single or a double ceremony. They weren't pestering Natalie or Gary. Not yet, anyway. They were planning a New Year's Eve party and if there wasn't an update by then, they would pester.

An email notification pinged in. Test results from the clinic. Sacha went to find Charlie and give her the news. She was in her office, frowning at her computer screen. "What is that?"

"That," she said, sitting back and turning her head to look at him, "is my attempt to get artsy and fartsy with Karen the yogi and Moses." Sacha leaned in for a

281

closer look at the black and white image. Karen was tied in some kind of knot. She was wearing a hooded, long-sleeved bodysuit, posed in front of the drapery-covered pocket doors. Moses was inside the knot.

Sacha tilted his head. "How did Moses get in there?"

"Gumby girl folded herself up and invited him over. He was all, seriously? That is not a lap. She got a hand free and kind of scooped him in. And then he was all oh okay." Sacha was laughing. "There are six of these, all different shapes but between us we got him in there every time. I really love them but I can't imagine how to use them."

"Nothing like the rest of your series," Sacha agreed. "It seems like there's some kind of metaphor."

"Maybe I should hire a writer to do captions, and put them out as greeting cards. Oh hey! Would that be a good party game? Get people to write captions, and then we can all vote on them, and the winning caption gets a prize?"

"What's the prize?"

She thought for a second, then went for the obvious. "Bottle of champagne? We're going to have tons of it anyway." Sacha laughed again. "We could get six really good bottles. Yeah, let's do that. I'll send these off to the printer." She made herself a note. "Now I'm sure you had a reason for coming in here."

"Well, I came to see you." He leaned down to kiss her. "But also to tell you the clinic says you're clear to stop taking the pill if you want to."

"Oh, the count came back! I still can't believe you did that for me." Charlie tipped her head back, inviting another kiss, which Sacha promptly delivered. She smiled. "For us, I guess."

"It made a lot more sense for me to do it. Simpler, faster, less chance of complications."

"You did have a couple of uncomfortable days there." Charlie put her hand on his leg, slid it up the inside of his thigh. "Thank you."

"You're welcome." He took a moment to enjoy what she was doing. "If you keep doing that I'm going to have to interrupt your work for a while longer."

"I was hoping you'd say that." Charlie turned her chair, put both hands to work unbuttoning Sacha's jeans, and said, "Could you take that sweater off please?"

Now that they were within a single-digit number of weeks to the wedding, Charlie was getting nervous. Not about marrying Sacha, only about everything else. Natalie was trying to talk her down all the way to West L.A. for the first dress fitting. "You know, sweetie, Cecilia and I will take care of everything on the day. Sacha's booked that person to do your hair and makeup. You say the dance is going to be fine. What's really freaking you out?"

"I'm getting married!"

Natalie laughed. "It's not much different from the way you are now," she pointed out. "You're already living together. Everybody knows you're together, everybody knows you're in love. Is it your family?"

"Eh." It probably was, Charlie realized. She'd invited her parents and her siblings, and didn't know yet if any of them were going to come out. "I told them we'd pay for their travel. I thought that would get them out here for sure. But this is Sodom and Gomorrah, so maybe not."

"Maybe they have to pray about it first." Natalie's voice was a bit dry.

"They can pray about it all they want as long as they let me know one way or another by the RSVP date." Charlie was exasperated. That date was two weeks off; everyone from out of town was reminded that it might be a backyard wedding but they still needed to know how many people would be there. Everyone who already lived in L.A. knew all about trying to get caterers and parking squared away. "Ugh, let's talk about Sacha's family. I was so pleased his parents are coming. I figured they would, after the way they were in October, but, you know."

"That was a nice letter," Natalie said. "And it was nice what Pavel said, about having you both up to the summer house next year." Sacha's brother was staying in New York to manage the moving business while Oleg and Marian were away for the week of the wedding. "Sacha said he'd never been there before."

"Yeah, they only got that five years ago." Sacha's father Oleg and uncle Boris, who had his own successful business as a plumber, had gone in together to buy a house on the North Fork of Long Island. "If the documentary gets picked up, and if it gets a good response, we might end up hiding out there for a while before the Emmy nominations come out. If it gets nominated we'll need to be here to do press." Gary had already given them very clear instructions about that.

"You know it's going to get picked up." Natalie sounded amused now. "A little bit of advance publicity, and there'll probably be a bidding war. Jerry was a big name for a lot of years. He worked with somebody at every one of the streaming platforms, and most of the cable channels." She turned south on Sawtelle. "Almost there. That picture Kristine sent was a dream."

"Oh, I know. Never in my life have I worn a dress like that. The closest was this bridesmaid dress when I was twenty." Charlie made a face. "Pale blue, and this really hot itchy chiffon stuff. The color of sadness and the texture of a yeast infection." Natalie cracked up. A few minutes later they pulled up at the Matsumoto house. "You know one of the things I love about Kristine?"

"What's that," Natalie said as they got out of the car.

"She never gives me that look like why don't you have a perfect body."

"You do have a perfect body. The perfect body is the one the person you love wants." Natalie took a second. "That sentence construction was not the best, but you know what I mean." Charlie gave her a fond look. "Let's go in and see this perfect dress."

Sacha was on his way out of his guitar lesson when the text came in from Natalie: *This dress is a showstopper on Charlie. Want a sneak peek?*

No thank you. I mean yes but I can wait a few weeks. Does she like it? Sacha was pretty sure she would.

She says OMG I feel like Ginger Rogers
PERFECT

Yes. Want me to get a measurement for a necklace

Yes please and if you could get a detail pic so I can have the designer match the colors that would be great

Will do, hang on. Sacha waited by his car, aware of a paparazzo hanging around about thirty feet away. When the picture came in with a number he sent back a 'thank you' and then looked over. He didn't say anything, but the fact that he didn't get in the car clearly sent a message.

The photographer came closer. "Hi, my name is Steve Mitchell. I've noticed you around here a few times. Sacha Lebedev, right?"

"That's right."

"Would you be meeting up with Barry Teller?"

The guitar case leaning against the car was a dead giveaway. Sacha nodded. "I started lessons this summer. He's an excellent teacher."

"Yeah, he is, he's actually a friend of mine. I live down the street. Didn't want you to think I was, like, stalking you. I usually do the Hollywood route, the Pantages to the Chinese theater."

Now that he thought about it, Sacha recognized the guy; they'd seen him outside the Pantages. He was wondering why they were even having this conversation. "Did you want to get a picture?"

"Well, actually. Barry's doing a gig in a couple of weeks, did he tell you?" Sacha nodded again. "Would you mind if I took a picture of you with your guitar and used it on his social media? I try to help him promote."

Now it made sense. "Sure, no problem. My fiancée is producing a documentary and I was learning guitar for that." Sacha opened up the case and lifted out the instrument. He connected the strap, wrapped his hand around the fretboard, and couldn't help strumming the strings. "I like it." He was smiling when he looked up at Steve. The camera was making those familiar noises. He focused on his hands, playing a little bit of the song he was learning now.

"That's really nice," Steve said. "Billy Joel, right? Always a Woman? Good job. Thanks very much. I'll let you go now. I know Barry will appreciate it."

Sacha looked up again. "For the record, the lyrics to that song bear no resemblance to my relationship with Charlie."

"Jesus, I hope not. Thanks again." Steve waved and walked away. Sacha put the guitar in its case, loaded it into the trunk, and got into the driver's seat. Then he locked the doors, out of habit, and stayed a minute to send another text: *Hi honey just did an intentional few minutes with a paparazzo who's a friend of Barry's. Who knew. Still want to go to his show?*

Charlie's answer came back fast: *That's a yes. Now I suppose I have to go to FB and find those pictures*

LOL might take a few minutes

Oh like I'm going to forget. What's next for you?

Going to the jewelry designer. I hear there is a perfect dress for my perfect bride

God that WORD

Sacha laughed for real. *It's better than groom*

You have a point. See you at home. Love you!

Love you too. Sacha put the car in gear and rolled out. He was taking a chance on this designer, but she'd been recommended by Kristine. And if they didn't click, there was still time to find a different solution.

Two weeks later, they had answers to some important questions, the most important being: were any of Charlie's family coming to the wedding. "Thank God," she said, "they're staying home."

Sacha wasn't fully convinced by her show of relief. "You're sure you don't mind?"

"Honey, I am sure. I would not put it past them to turn the party into a prayer meeting. They would be all, the music is too loud, people are drinking too much, and oh by the way you couldn't really wear a white dress, could you, but did it have to be red." She rolled her eyes. "This way they can see the pictures and pick us apart with their friends, and then when I go in the spring they can tell me how I should have done it, and you will never have to hear any of that bullshit. Or any of their other bullshit." Charlie was genuinely relieved, but it was still nice when Sacha hugged her. She leaned into that solid comforting embrace and said, "There was a time when all I wanted was their approval. And then a moment came when I realized I would never get it, no matter what I did. I was the cuckoo in their tiny little intolerant nest. They probably wonder every day if I'm some kind of judgement on them."

"I doubt that." Sacha kissed her forehead. "That would mean examining their own behavior." He changed the subject. "I picked up your necklace today. Do you want to see it?"

Charlie stood back, making an 'are you kidding' face. "It's casual glam, right?" Sacha made an 'I think so' face. Charlie laughed. "I'm sure it's perfect. Yes, I want to see it."

He took her hand and led her to the master. "After the honeymoon, we'll do this room."

"We've had a lot to do this year. Come on, show me." Sacha picked up a white box from his nightstand and handed it over. Charlie took off the lid. The necklace inside was arranged on a shaped platform. "Oh. Wow. How did they, wow." It was beadwork, but like nothing she'd ever seen. A strand of rose-pink freshwater pearls spaced between gold cubes. A gold filigree clasp, set with what looked a lot like diamonds. Two beaded tassels in back, hanging two and three inches below the clasp, each topped with one of the pearls. Beaded fringe in front, in shades of pink and red, that would fall from the points of her collarbones down to her cleavage. More of the pearls, accented with gold, were worked into the fringe. "Fringe," she said, smiling up at Sacha. "And tassels."

"There are more tassels." Sacha picked up another box, much smaller. Charlie set down the big box, took the other one from his hand, opened it, and laughed. Earrings, of course; gold filigree set with more of those sparkly things, with beaded tassels.

"Are those real diamonds?"

"What do you think." Sacha was smiling too. "Lucy said if you hadn't decided on your hairstyle she hoped you were wearing it up." Lucy was the jewelry designer.

"Well, I hadn't decided, and I have no idea how to put it up but since you're getting me professional help with that, I think I'll wear it up. Not all princess perfect, though. A little messy. It's going to get messy at some point anyway." Sacha retrieved the little box, set it with the other one, plunged his hand into her hair, and kissed her. "Mmm. Yes. Like when you do that." It was quite a while before she remembered to tell him she liked the jewelry. By that time he was pretty sure she did.

On the Monday before Christmas, they got the word from Tony: the rough cut was ready to view. Sacha read the text, went to find Charlie, and found her reading it too. She looked up and said, "Eek."

Sacha smiled. "Okay. The question is, if we go to see it alone will we be instantly throttled by certain people when they find out?"

"I don't think there's much doubt about the answer to that, do you?" He gave her a few seconds. "Jonathan asked if he could see it. So he would know what it was all about."

"Once it's being marketed, people are going to ask him about it, so we probably should have him there. Natalie and Gary, obviously. Valerie?" Sacha nodded. "Cecilia? We should have her, too. So she knows. And because she's part of the family."

"Yes. Will nine adults fit in that little apartment?"

"Ugh." Charlie thought for a minute. "How about this. Do it here. Get a big screen, wow I'm getting good at spending your money."

"Jerry's money."

"Whatever. Big screen in my office? We could play it on my computer. Bring in the chairs from the dining room. Would that work?"

"That sounds great. I'll get back to Tony, see what day works best for him. Did you finish your book?" Sacha knew she'd been working on his family pictures, off and on, ever since October. He hadn't seen a proof come in.

"Barely." Charlie hunched her shoulders. "I wanted to get it done in time for Christmas. The proof will be here later this week. If it's clean I can order the copies and at least send an e-card that says your present is on its way."

He was leaning on the door frame, smiling at her. "It was really nice of you to do that. Mama has no idea that's why you were taking all those pictures."

"I couldn't not take pictures. Put me in a room with humans, I want to take pictures. And, while you were by far the most beautiful person in the room, none of your family members are unsightly." Sacha laughed. "So I enjoyed the hell out of Barry's show. Why does he not have a big fat recording contract?"

"No idea. There are so many musicians."

"Maybe that's a project for me next year. A series on undiscovered musicians of Los Angeles. We could do a show with a concert, package a CD with the book." Charlie was only thinking out loud, but Sacha's face said he thought it was a great idea. "You know, when I realized I was going to have to stop working, I thought what will I do with my time." He laughed again. "Yeah, I know, you too. I'm going to obsessively proofread this thing again so I can order another proof if I have to fix anything."

"Okay honey. I'll see you at dinner." Sacha went out, sent the text to Tony, and very shortly received two proposed days. He wrote back *Either is fine for us, pretty sure we can get Gary here, can you check with Valerie and Jonathan?* It took a little more back and forth, but they eventually settled on that Thursday night. Cecilia was leaving on Friday to spend the holiday with her sister in Sacramento. She was very excited about the film, more than Sacha would have expected. But when he thought about it, he remembered how long she'd been with Jerry. And she'd stuck with Sacha through that transition, which had to have been troubling, even upsetting. He got online and ordered the screen they would need, then went to the kitchen, where she was putting the finishing touches on dinner. "Hola amiga," he said, leaning on the counter, as out of the way as he could be. He said nothing about the fact that Moses was also on the counter, supervising things. A little cat hair wasn't going to hurt anybody.

291

"Hola Mr. Swan. You nervous about that movie?"

"Not really. I'm excited. Okay, yes, a little nervous. Once it goes public, the title and the marketing, we'll probably have the press outside again. Definitely when it gets picked up. I'm sorry you'll have to deal with that."

Cecilia made a *pfft* sound. "It don't bother me. It's good you can tell the truth now."

"What did you think about it all? Truly."

She dried her hands, studying him. "I never understood it. But it didn't matter. Mr. Jerry, he was a good man. He wasn't easy but he was good. He took care of people who were straight with him. He took care of me and Jesús, he took care of you. And you," she shrugged. "Lo amabas. Anybody could see. So whatever, you and him, that was none of my business."

"I'm grateful for you. Grateful to you. You've always been kind to me."

"You're a good man too." She turned away and got back to work. "Now go pick your wine, this is ready soon."

"Sí, sí." He kissed her cheek as he passed.

Charlie thought it was a good thing the dining-room chairs were fully upholstered. That was a thing she never thought about before she started having dinner with people who would stay at the table for hours, talking and laughing. Her parents stuck to a strict routine: sit, pray, eat, get up. Their chairs were unforgiving, uncushioned wood. Since leaving home, she'd either lived alone or with roommates who hadn't worked the same hours she did. Well, hardly anybody worked the same hours she did. Her living-alone dinner routine was to throw something in the microwave, and eat it while sitting at the computer. Now every night they were home, she ate with Sacha at the table. When Natalie was also home, the three of them ate together. Being able to sit in comfort while somebody (sometimes Charlie) told a long story about what they'd been doing was a fine thing. And having ten of those chairs was superb.

The new giant screen was standing on her layout table. Her task chair was pushed out of the way behind it; her own work screens were shoved to the back of her desktop. The upholstered chairs were arranged in three slightly staggered rows facing the screen. They discussed bringing in small tables from here and there, and decided against it. If people wanted to set a drink on the floor that was fine. If someone knocked one over, no biggie; there were the tea towels over at the bar. Cecilia had prepared an array of finger food. The plan was a drink first, then the film, then talk and eat.

Everyone was there before the suggested rendezvous time. "Does being early mean people really want to see this thing?" Charlie asked Sacha in the butler's pantry, where he was opening a couple of bottles of wine. She was so nervous. "I keep having these moments where I think, I can't believe you let me start this, I can't believe you helped me do this, I can't imagine what it's been like for you. I keep second-guessing it."

"Honey." He set down the wine opener and put his hands on her shoulders. "If I really didn't want this to happen, I would have said something. You know I can say no when I want to."

After a moment she nodded. She knew that was true. "But you've never said no to me."

"That would be because you've never suggested something I couldn't deal with. This was so gradual. I had a chance to get used to each thing. It wasn't something you forced on me. And it really wasn't long before I thought it was the best possible way to tell the story. So stop worrying. Take these out to the kitchen?"

"Yes. Okay. I love you."

"I love you too." He kissed her, watched her go, and thought *I am still such a good liar.* He was petrified.

Jonathan didn't seem like such a big guy in a room full of talking, laughing people. There was a half-hour of catching up, everyone talking about what they'd been up to, or what they were doing next. Cecilia mentioned her imminent trip north. Elena talked about her competition season, Gary talked about his acquisitions, Natalie talked about the progress she and Sacha had made on the biography. Tony talked about the next round of episodes of 'Live Work Dance,' and about the new couple he was working with for his personal film project. Jonathan said that a sequel to the movie he worked on with Victor Garcia over the summer had just been green-lit. Valerie talked about two albums she produced that year, one for a jazz singer and the other for Andy and Victor. Sacha confirmed he was still taking ballet and guitar lessons. "And we've got this Viennese waltz thing in the bag," he said, giving Charlie a sideways look. She made an 'oh yeah right' face. "Dmitri even added a fleckerl."

"I saw that!" Elena looked delighted. "Did he tell you most American-style competition couples never even learn that?"

"No he did not." Charlie looked impressed. "Is it hard? Because once I figured out how not to trip poor Sacha in the natural turns the fleckerl seemed easy."

"Well, then I won't tell you it's hard. What music are you using?"

"That's a thing our New Year's Eve guests will be voting on," Charlie said. "I do have a favorite from among the options, but I'm not going to say what it is."

Sacha said, "That'll be party game number two. But I guess we should proceed to the main event?"

"Yes." Tony looked nervous too. "Before we go in, I would like to say something." Everybody paid attention. "This is my first time as a solo director on a feature-length project. Shaping the entire thing. So if there is any part of it that you think, ugh, please blame me and not Sacha or Charlie. Charlie gave me beautiful footage. They have both been," he made a very Italian gesture, "wonderful to work with."

"Thanks Tony." Charlie patted his back. "You've been great too." She took a deep breath, blew it out. "Let's do this." They all trooped into her office. Tony gave Charlie the media. She loaded it into her computer and stood aside. "Ride 'em, cowboy." Tony laughed under his breath. Charlie went to sit in the back row beside Sacha, reaching for his hand. Tony activated the media, then sat down beside his wife. Charlie saw Elena take his hand. *Glad I'm not the only one.*

The film faded in on the title: THE ROLE OF A LIFETIME. They heard Sacha's guitar, then his voice. The first verse of the song, over a short crawl of text that Sacha and Natalie had written:

> This is a true story about Jerry
> Morgenstern, a man who wanted to be
> something other than what he was.
>
> It's a story about Sacha Lebedev, a
> man who invented a way for Jerry to
> have the life he wanted.
>
> This is a love story.

Tony began with a clip, Jerry and Maggie on a red carpet, Jerry looking sly and happy as he told a reporter it was going to be a great night. Then the scene dissolved to Gary, and the story began. Charlie's tape of Sacha began when Gary said "And in twenty fifteen we all found out why." Tony's use of Sacha's vocal recording was subtle. Clips and the other interviews were woven through Gary's. When Jonathan's voice came in, about two thirds of the way through the Maggie disassembly and right after Gary said "All that time," everyone reacted. It was such a strong voice, and by then they'd heard Jerry's voice several times. It really seemed they were hearing him again. Charlie glanced at Sacha, squeezed his hand. His face was expressionless, but he squeezed back.

At the turning point, sixty-five minutes into the film, there was a quiet moment showing Sacha at the vanity, face bare. Charlie had let the cameras run for thirty seconds after he finished, after he went silent. Tony included ten seconds of it, blending the three camera angles, before dissolving to the short segment of Sacha under the tree, talking about himself and the genesis of Maggie.

Then it was into the creation. More of Jonathan-as-Jerry in this part. Gary's part had finished before the midpoint, and there were no further interviews. Sacha's recording was heard again, alternating with Jonathan's. Tony had created a montage for each year, capturing a still from a clip when he hadn't been able to find a good photo, and worked them into the creation tape. Maggie always beside Jerry as he grew visibly older, then visibly less well. Jerry in the wheelchair, and their final appearance in April of 2015. Jonathan's voice, the last paragraph of the letter, ending with "I love you. Jerry."

Charlie was crying. Everyone else might have been crying too, but Charlie didn't try to see. The film ended with a short clip of Maggie in 'her' room, glamorous and beautiful in a dark-green gown with those diamonds sparkling. She stood up and walked from the vanity to the adjacent wall, turning like a model on the catwalk before giving Charlie a quarter profile. As the image froze, Sacha's recording was heard again, a chorus. Then it was a dissolve to Charlie's video of him singing, a perfect segue to the last few bars of the song. He stopped singing, stopped playing, and looked up. Tony had somehow made that slow motion, and then he froze it for a few seconds. The screen went black and the credits rolled.

CHAPTER 15

Tony took a minute after the film stopped before he stood up to turn off the screen and eject the media. Charlie sniffed, wiped her face, gave herself silent congratulations for having the sense not to wear makeup, and turned her head. Sacha had his eyes closed. Jonathan was leaning forward with his elbows on his knees. He had one hand over his mouth, and his eyes were wet. *If we can make an action hero cry we may have something here.* Charlie leaned in a little to bump her shoulder against Sacha's, still looking at Jonathan.

He must have seen her move; he turned his head. "Fucking wow," he said. "I was at a couple of those things. I saw you," he said to Sacha. "That was fucking amazing."

Sacha had his eyes open now. He scrubbed a hand over his face, made a move that was something between a nod and a shrug. He didn't try to speak. Valerie was on her feet, talking in a low voice with Tony. Elena was leaning over talking to Cecilia in Spanish. Gary and Natalie were up, his arm around her waist, head close to hers; she was saying something.

Charlie finally let go of Sacha and stood up. She went over to Valerie and Tony, hugged Tony, then said, "Well, Valerie? What's your professional opinion?"

"My professional opinion is that you had a great story to tell and this guy has put it together really well for you. Congratulations. I will need to see that again before I can write your title and credits music."

"We can get you a copy," Tony said. "I still have a little bit of cleanup to do."

"Don't do too much. I know it's tempting to keep fiddling with it, but it's a good length at a hundred and ten. I don't think you had much fat in there. Maybe a couple of the interviews in the first sixty minutes, we might not need to hear from all those people. Don't cut anything from Gary, or any more of the transformations."

"No, I won't."

"How much of that did you have, anyway?"

"The construction took more than two hours," Charlie said. "Deconstruction obviously a lot less. About thirty minutes."

"That little clip at the end, where he – she - stood up and did the walk? Amazing. I can't walk like that."

"Neither can I." Charlie smiled. "Though I'm getting better. These dance classes are carrying over." She felt another person and looked over, then up; it was Jonathan. He put himself between Valerie and Tony. She thought *oops, he can tell, oh well*. "So you still want some of that for your reel?"

He gave her a 'hell yeah' look and said, "Yes please. I'm so glad it worked. At first I really didn't get what the whole thing was about. All that about thank you for Maggie, I was like what does this even mean. I had to think it through, do a little Googling. Then I was like does this really mean that? But it couldn't have been anything else."

"You read it perfectly." It was Sacha, standing beside Charlie, putting his arm around her. "You read it like a man who's been in love."

"Yeah, well." Jonathan made an uncomfortable movement. "There's a big difference between being in love and staying in love. Seems like you're a guy who knows about how to stay."

"He is." Charlie was leaning on Sacha again. "Lucky for me. Jeez, I'm exhausted, and I'm starving. Anybody else hungry?"

"It's funny," Sacha said later, when everyone was gone and they were private. He was sitting cross-legged on the bed the way he had their very first time, wearing a short cotton robe. Charlie was sitting in front of him, in her nightgown and robe. Unlike the first time, they each had a coffee mug in hand. Decaf with Bailey's had been Charlie's prescription, and something sweet had appealed to Sacha too.

"What's funny."

"I was really, really nervous. Even though Gary and Natalie knew the story, Tony and Elena had already seen the footage, Cecilia knew me and Jerry. The only people who didn't know for sure what was going on were Valerie and Jonathan. Why was I scared?"

Charlie spared a moment to think *and you pretended you were fine, you liar. You actor.* It made her smile. "Because of what I've been saying all along. This is super personal, super important. Non-trivial shit." She sipped coffee while he snickered. "It got to Jonathan."

"Yeah. I couldn't tell about Valerie."

"I think the fact that she basically said don't cut it is encouraging." Charlie watched him drink, wondering what was going on in his head. She was positive that he was happy with the film. There was a still a long way to go before they were done with it. Months when they'd have to talk about it. "Did you hear Gary say he thought it should get a theatrical release?"

Sacha looked startled. "No."

"Tony just about dropped his wineglass. If it goes into theaters, it's eligible for a lot of stuff beyond the Emmys. But if that happens – which I only know because I've been reading up on this crap – we could conceivably not be done with it until the Oscars, which would be more than thirteen months from now." Charlie finished her coffee, leaned over to put the mug on her nightstand. "That's a long time to not be done with it."

Sacha also set his mug aside. "It is a long time. On the other hand, if it really went that long, we would really be done. We could go into year two of being married as Sacha and Charlie, not Sacha and Jerry and Charlie." He had another thought. "And think of all those red carpets." Charlie giggled. "If we had to go to the Oscars, you could wear those diamonds."

"Oh my God, I'd be afraid to. My neck's not as long as yours. I won't look as slim as you did. Ugh, no."

"You'll look beautiful. You always look beautiful. I would dress you in nothing but diamonds if I could." He leaned in for a kiss. Put a hand on the side of her neck, stroking with his thumb, then brushing his fingertips around where the necklace would lie. Still kissing her. Taking his mouth away to say, "You would have a dress to show this beautiful shape." Fingers brushing into her cleavage now, his lips on Charlie's face. Hearing her breath catch when his hand went to her breast, sliding over the silk. He pushed up onto his knees, leaning in, bearing her down.

Charlie stretched out and felt his weight come down on her. Felt his arousal through the thin nightgown. Her hands were on his body and his mouth was on her neck. She stroked down his naked sides under that robe, down his hips. Took one hand off him to tug her skirt up, wriggling a little. He made a sound of hungry amusement and shifted to help. Then she had him in her hand, stroking, bringing him to her. "Oh God." That tease, that enticement. Sliding through wetness. She raised a knee and he was inside her, with a deeper, hungrier sound. "Sacha. I love you."

"I love you." Then he was propped on his elbows, hands in her hair, kissing her. Moving in her, with her, until she clutched him and cried out. One more kiss and then he braced himself on his hands, going deeper and harder with her legs wrapped around him. Arching back and going still, "Jesus!" His orgasm seemed to go on forever. One more thrust, an aftershock, a gasp from Charlie. He felt her, that new pulse, an echo. He tried not to completely collapse onto her. His face was against hers. He could tell she was smiling. He kissed her cheek, slid off to the side, rolled onto his back. "Charlie. Yours," he said lazily, "is a perfect body."

At that moment, she had to agree.

Sacha was positive he knew which of the possible wedding-dance songs Charlie liked best. He'd overheard her listening to it more than any of the others. It was the one suggested by Tony's friend Vince, half of the new couple he was following for his ballroom documentary. So he did his best to make sure their New Year's Eve guests voted for that one. Evidently his best was good enough. When Natalie tallied up the votes and announced, "It is You I Have Loved," Charlie's face was eloquent. Also slightly suspicious when Natalie added, "By a landslide."

Since all of their guests that night had been invited to the wedding too, there were some requests for a sneak preview of the dance. Sacha shook his head, pointed to the glass in his hand – not his first – and said, "No drinking and dancing. Also the only clear space is in Charlie's office, and it's not big enough. You'll have to wait, I'm afraid."

"And for those of you who can't be here, cough Jonathan cough, there's a very strong possibility the dance will end up on the internet." Charlie was perched on the edge of the dining table, also with a glass in hand. "Besides, we haven't voted on captions yet and it's almost midnight. We have shit to do."

Many of the captions proposed for the photographs of Karen and Moses were not suitable for the mass market. They got through five of the images, with one 'suitable' caption and one 'totally not' caption selected for each. Then Jenny was reading them out for the last image, trying not to crack up. None of them were suitable. "Jeez, you guys, who *wrote* these things? Would you send that card to your mother?"

"It was probably all Jonathan," Charlie told her. "He's got a blue streak a mile wide. I saw this backstage video I wasn't supposed to see, and wow." Jenny was giggling. She read the next caption, shook her head, handed it to Charlie. "Oh my *God*." Everyone laughed. Charlie handed it to Sacha.

His eyebrows shot up. "Jonathan, was that you?" Jonathan leaned over to see, made a 'maybe' face. "The only other person it could possibly be is Gary."

Gary crossed the room to see. "Nope. Not me. And I must say I am gratified that you thought it might be me." Jonathan laughed. People started asking to hear the caption. Sacha handed it back to Jenny.

"I am not reading that out loud," she said. "Nothing that filthy is coming out of my mouth unless I'm getting paid for it." She handed it to Jonathan.

"It's not that bad, come on," he said. "It's practically a movie quote!"

"It is not!" Jenny made a 'seriously!' face at the room full of people now demanding to hear the caption.

"Okay." Jonathan struck a pose and said, "I have HAD IT with this motherfucking cat on my motherfucking ass!" The whole room cracked up.

A few minutes later, when she could hear herself, Charlie said, "You know, the irony is that if we used that caption, we would sell a million copies." Jenny laughed all over again. Then the timer went off. "Oh hey! That's five minutes to midnight. Everybody who isn't a designated driver, get yourself a refill." Sacha came around with a bottle. Charlie turned up the audio from the screen in her office, showing a local event where they were on the final countdown. People arranged themselves next to the person they wanted to kiss first. Charlie couldn't help noticing that Jonathan was next to Jenny. Then Sacha was next to her, arm around her shoulders, smiling at her. Everyone was listening, then counting down with the program on-screen. "Three, two, one, happy new year!" Sacha kissed her. "Mmm," she said after a minute. He gave her some space. She peeked around him. Yep, Jonathan was kissing Jenny. "Okay. More please." Sacha delivered.

Eventually, everyone voted for the 'not suitable' captions. Charlie rolled her eyes and accepted the inevitable. "Poor Karen," she said. "When she gets back from Costa Rica I'm going to have to tell her what she and Moses inspired."

"What's she doing in Costa Rica?" Natalie said.

"Yoga retreat. Yoga in the jungle. Yoga with giant bugs in the jungle. That's so far down the list of things I want to do, I won't get to it until I'm about a hundred and never." Charlie shuddered. "Anyway, okay, this depraved group has selected the blue captions. Who wrote them? We know the last one was you, Jonathan." It didn't come as much of a surprise to find that Gary was responsible for two, Jonathan for three. The last winning caption came from Elena. "Elena!" Charlie made a shocked face. "I am shocked."

"Eh." Tony shrugged. "She works with Mateo." Elena was giggling.

Sacha started handing out bottles of champagne. "You need another hand, Jonathan."

"No I don't." He handed one of the bottles to Jenny. "Thanks for a great party, guys. I'd better whistle up the wagon, though. Got a flight to catch tomorrow." That was the signal for everybody else. It hadn't been a huge party, so it broke up fast. Charlie hugged everybody, including Jonathan. Sacha offered to walk Jenny home.

By the time he got back, Charlie had the worst of the debris cleared and was sitting in the den with Moses on her lap and a cup of decaf on the side table. "I noticed Gary's car is still here," he said.

"Natalie seems to have convinced him that driving home was a less attractive option than crashing with her." Charlie leaned her head on the back of the couch. "I'm not sure how it came to be that Moses is still in here with us." Sacha smiled, leaned on the back of the couch and kissed her. "Better than last year, sweetheart?"

"So much better. What did you do last year?"

"I was working. I did get a bottle of champagne to take home at the end of the night, at least."

"Was it good champagne?"

"Nope. I didn't have to work the next day so I made mimosas. All day." Charlie regarded him for a moment. "What did you do last year? Things had started to look up a little, hadn't they?"

"A little. I didn't stay up till midnight. Cecilia left me dinner. I took it back to the guest house and listened to some music for a while. Tried not to think about the year before." There had been a party, with Jerry. "Thought about you instead. I wished I could call you. I thought it was still too early. I should have called you." Sacha was still leaning on the couch.

"I would have been happy to see the call the next day. I would have called you back. Might have invited you over for mimosas."

"I wish I had. We could have had a couple more months together." The more time he spent with Charlie, the more Sacha thought there would never be enough. "I could have kissed you so much sooner." He kissed her again to make up for that.

"We'll have plenty of months. And plenty of kisses." Charlie addressed the cat. "Moses. Mighty Mooch. It's time for bed." She got her hands underneath him and transferred him to the couch. He grumbled a protest. "God, can you believe that Jonathan?" She snickered, pushed herself forward, laboriously stood up. "Oh, yeah. A little champagne." Sacha was there, arm around her waist, to steer her down the hall.

January 2017

Tony kept Charlie and Sacha updated. When he finished the final cut, when he sent it to Valerie, and when he heard from Gary's assistant that the streaming platform wanted to see it. Then he sent them a copy – with an apology that he couldn't hand deliver it; he was heading out of town for an episode of 'Live Work Dance' and wouldn't be back until the day before their wedding – and they sat down to watch it again.

"Well," Charlie said after the credits rolled, "it still makes me cry. So I am either a total sap or this is a good film, or possibly both."

Sacha didn't cry this time. Jonathan's voice sounded like Jonathan now, not Jerry. He'd found himself paying attention to the sound design, noticing where Valerie had cleaned up the clips, where she'd added echoes of their leitmotif song, where she'd enhanced the audio on Charlie's footage. "Valerie's good at this," he said. "It's never obvious, like some movies, where the soundtrack music is beating you over the head with how you're supposed to feel."

"Oh my God, I know. Hey audience, be scared! Hey this is funny! Hey we're tearjerking here! I never really paid attention to that stuff," she admitted. "Not till I started watching movies with you."

"Jerry was a holy terror on soundtracks." Sacha was smiling. "He said, if you need music to tell the audience what's happening, you're doing it wrong. He said it should be used to reinforce, not to dictate. So he would have liked this."

Charlie nudged him. "He would have liked it anyway. Now what happens?"

"Well, now we call up our agent and say it's ready to put on the market." Tony's agent had agreed to represent the project. "And then we get married." He was still smiling at her. "Is the dress ready?"

"I can pick it up any time. Kristine and her elves are doing some matching shoes." She eyed him for a moment. "What are you going to wear? I can't believe I haven't asked before."

"Well, we told everybody casual glam, but I'm wearing my tux."

Charlie was pleased. "Good, I love how you look in a tuxedo." *I love how you look in anything.* "You know I got you a ring."

"Natalie kind of let that slip, yeah." He was grinning now. "You know I got you a ring too."

"I knew you would. Are you going to go photo-ready for me?"

"You mean am I going to wear makeup? I will if you want me to." Sacha was a little surprised. And intrigued.

Charlie could hear it in his voice. She gave him a sideways look. "Okay, true confession. It may be a little twisted but I've always liked it when a good-looking guy wears makeup. I did some photo shoots for bands, way back. High school and college, when I was learning how to do it, deciding that's what I wanted to do. For most of them if they did hair and makeup it was kind of a gag, you know? Oh, we're pretending to be rock stars, let's be Ace Frehley or whoever. They knew they were going to be working at Costco or Home Depot. Some of them really dug it though. It was more of a lifestyle. There wasn't

308

anything close to a gay scene, much less a drag scene, where I went to school. But there were enough other girls who liked it that if a guy wanted to learn how to do it right, they could learn. I think a couple of those guys did eventually get to work in media. Local TV, that kind of thing, even if they didn't stay in music. Anyway, it never seemed like an aberrant thing to me. It seemed like, this is part of working in media. Which you still do."

"Sort of." Sacha thought about this. "Well, I did say I liked looking that way. And that was true. Though I don't think I'll ever go full drag again."

"Unless someone pays you to. Imagine the press if you went on RuPaul's show." Sacha laughed. Charlie was grinning. "Anyway yes. This is probably as glam as I will ever be unless we actually end up going to awards shows, and if we do that I'm going to be too nervous to bend the rules."

"There aren't any rules, sweetheart." He kissed her. "So I should be at least as glam as you?"

"Oh, at least. Be so glam that when our friends post pictures on the internet and hashtag them with Role of a Lifetime, they will instantly be trending. All the channels will be falling over themselves to get their hands on our little film. Someone from, like, Fox Searchlight will call our agent and say we want to launch it at Cannes."

"Be Keyser Söze?" he said, then giggled because this all seemed so impossible. "We're both insane."

"Hey. If we're going to do it, we might as well go all the way. Right? Like Jerry with those diamonds?"

Sacha sobered up. "Yeah. You're right." He studied her for a few seconds. She didn't look scared at all. In fact, she looked excited. "Okay. It's a deal. And if we go to Cannes, I will wear those diamonds."

Oleg and Marian Lebedev arrived a week before the wedding. Sacha put them up at a hotel not far away, with the car service on call. They had a long list of things to do and see in Los Angeles. Sacha also wanted them to see the film. They settled in to watch it on their second night, after a day doing an architecture tour and then dinner with Sacha and Charlie at home.

"You know a little of this already," Sacha said, when they were all assembled in Charlie's office, with the film ready to start and drinks in hand. "This is the part I never told you. This is about how Jerry and I had a relationship that no one ever knew about."

"For so long," Marian said. "A lot of marriages don't last that long."

"Neither of Jerry's did. But then, he was married for the wrong reasons." Sacha could say that now. One of the many things he'd had to come to terms with was Jerry's lifetime of deception. The fact that he'd been a willing partner in it was only excused – he thought – by the fact that they hadn't hurt anybody else. Jerry's second wife didn't concern him. She was married for the wrong reasons too. Brooke, though, had put in ten years in good faith. "Anyway, this is about how we were able to be together." He started the media and sat down. He found himself watching his parents, rather than the screen. They got it early in the deconstruction of Maggie, when the wig came off. Then his mother turned to stare at him. He did that half-a-shrug thing, with half a smile. She turned back to the screen.

Neither of them said anything for a minute after the film ended. Oleg finished his drink and leaned over to put it on Charlie's desk. Then he turned

310

sideways to look at his son, and sighed. "I don't know that I understand it. But I feel better about it. Is that what you wanted?"

"That'll do, Papa."

"So that, what do you call it, cross-dressing? How did you learn to do that? Was that all from college?"

"Most of it. Still, I had to study, and practice, a lot. It had to look right up close."

Marian said, "Would you have gotten in trouble if somebody figured it out?"

"Not in trouble with the law. What we were doing wasn't illegal. But in trouble for business, yes, for a while. Jerry could have laughed it off, said it was only a joke, putting one over on everybody. He had so much power already by the time I met him. As for me," he shrugged again. "It would have been a story for a minute. Then I could have moved away, maybe changed my name. It's possible nobody would even have learned my real name. Nobody would remember before long anyway. There's always a new story."

"And he would have taken care of you, wouldn't he." Marian was staring at him again. "As if you were his wife. Or his son."

"I was closer to that. Being his son. It was a very strange relationship, I know. But if I could have pretended to be someone else in order to make Papa happy, I would have. I still would."

"Sacha, please." Oleg shifted uncomfortably. "It's not a son's job to make his father happy."

"Then if I could have done it to make you proud." Sacha was giving him that steady look.

Charlie was sitting beside him, quiet as a mouse, afraid to say anything. This still could go wrong in so many ways. She knew that this - getting things right

311

with his parents - was more important to Sacha than almost anything else. Marian looked upset; Oleg's expression was unreadable. She didn't know him well enough. She couldn't stop hearing what Sacha had said back in the hospital, in October: 'he might as well have been a girl.' She hadn't asked Sacha how old he was when Oleg said that. How long he'd been carrying that. She wondered if his father was hearing that again now and thinking, well he sure showed me.

Then, finally, when she was starting to think none of them had anything else to say, Oleg sighed again and said, "I am proud of you. You did something difficult, and you did it well, and you did it for a good reason. You helped someone. I would never in a million years have thought that was possible, what you did. And I don't understand everything but I know he helped you when nobody else did, including me. So him and you, whatever that was, I'll try to get used to that. But I am proud of you." He stood up and held out a hand. Sacha stood too, took the offered hand for a second, then flung himself into his father's arms.

The day of the wedding, Sacha and Charlie were more or less under house arrest (as was Moses). Natalie and Cecilia were busy outside, making sure the floor and then the canopy were properly installed. Bossing the caterers around, when they came at four. Greeting the guests who started arriving soon after five. Gary was among the first to arrive, and since he and Natalie weren't going to share the ceremony after all, he took charge of the cocktail hour. He also took charge of Oleg and Marian when they arrived not much later, introducing them to everyone and getting them to talk about what they'd done and seen during their week in the city.

The canopy sparkled with the rented chandelier and with strips of LED lights. Flower arrangements stood on pedestals in each corner of the dance floor. The outdoor speakers were live, with a playlist of guitar-based music from all over the world. Rory arrived at five-thirty, wearing a casually-glamorous purple jumpsuit under a white haori jacket embroidered with gold cranes. She checked in with Gary about the license, accepted a drink and an introduction to Sacha's parents, and before long was the center of a laughing circle.

Charlie was in the master bedroom, getting buffed and polished and dressed and made up by an expert. Sacha was in Maggie's room by himself. He did his makeup, briefly wondered if his parents were going to freak out, then remembered he'd warned them. His hair was styled with a slightly metallic gel and diamond studs were in his ears. His shirt was spotless; his tie was perfect. He pulled on the tuxedo jacket, buttoned it, and gave himself one last look in the mirror. He couldn't help smiling. He knew Charlie was going to like it. He went outside at ten till six. Heads turned as he passed people. He didn't stop, going straight to the dance floor and then to join Rory at the far end.

Charlie's phone buzzed at five minutes to six. It was a text from Natalie: *Everyone is here, ready and waiting. Good to go?*

Charlie texted back *I'M SO NERVOUS OMG but yes. On my way out now TYVM and OXO.* She was not exactly shaking but also not exactly not. Remembering what Sacha told her, she took a couple of slow deep breaths, telling herself everyone there

313

was a friend. Then Cecilia and Elena were there to walk with her. "Oh my God. Thank you."

"You look amazing," Elena said. "And wait till you see Sacha."

"Did he do it?"

"I think so."

"Perdoname," Cecilia said, and people stood aside. Charlie walked out behind her. There was scattered applause. There were sounds of appreciation. Charlie thought *Oh my God everybody's looking at me* and wished for a veil, but everyone was smiling. It felt as though she were moving in slow motion. She tried to smile, tried to breathe. Then they were at the edge of the dance floor, with what looked like a thousand people on the dainty gold chairs, a few more taking their seats, and she could see Sacha and Rory. "Está muy bonita, querida," Cecilia said, and kissed her cheek. Charlie clung to her hand for a moment and then Cecilia stepped away.

Elena stayed with her all the way down the aisle, holding her hand. "It's awful, isn't it," she said very softly. "But look who's waiting for you."

"Thank you," Charlie said. Elena kissed her cheek, put her hand in Sacha's, and stepped away. Charlie gazed at him for a moment. He looked sensational: handsome and beautiful, male and female, the best of both. Darkened eyebrows and highlighted cheekbones framed those incredible eyes. Some kind of eyelash enhancement, too. It was much more theatrical than his makeup as Maggie. The colors were soft and subtle, but the effect was of a mask, almost like butterfly wings. He was smiling. "You look like a fucking rock star," she said, and he laughed. Rory was stifling laughter, one hand over her mouth, and Charlie abruptly remembered where they were.

Sacha had watched her all the way, since she stepped out of the kitchen door. Her hair was up in a loose-looking knot, with wavy tendrils hanging free to bounce against her neck. Her makeup was perfect. The jewelry shimmered, reflecting the soft lights like the beads and sequins on her dress. "You look like a movie star," he said. "I can't wait to kiss you." Now she was smiling.

Rory said, "Dearly beloved!" and they began.

Charlie didn't remember much, or rather remembered a lot but not very distinctly, about the ceremony and what immediately followed. She kept being surprised by the new ring – rings - nestled against the Bulgari. Two narrow gold bands with channel-set diamonds, framing the ruby. She kept remembering Sacha's kiss, which felt almost like their very first kiss, as if something new and wonderful was beginning. She kept remembering his smile when she slid the ring onto his finger. A rock-star ring, almost an inch wide on top. Not plain gold but *mokume gane* made with three colors of gold, and set with a triangular champagne diamond. He was holding her right hand with his left as they mingled. They had glasses of champagne, and then their hands were empty. There was food, and more champagne. There was some business with a cake, after a while. There were informal pictures, posing for everybody. Sacha remembered to tell people what hashtag to use.

Then suddenly the dance floor was clear again. Charlie focused in. All of the ballroom chairs were scattered around the patio. Gary was standing in the middle of the floor, saying, "They've been working on this for a couple of months now and I hope you people didn't give them too many glasses of champagne, because the last time we asked to see it they said no drinking and dancing. You're not going to give us that nonsense tonight, are you?"

"No," said Sacha. "Why aren't you married yet?" Half of the people there laughed.

Gary looked mildly embarrassed. "We're going to Vegas as soon as you kids get back from Down Under. Now get out here and do your thing."

Sacha took Charlie out to the center of the dance floor, led her in a circle so everyone could get another good look at that dress (and take more pictures), then brought her into dance position. "Ready, sweetheart?" She made a 'God I hope so' face. He kissed her. Gary, or Natalie, or somebody cued the music.

They were dancing the whole song, because Charlie insisted on including the part about 'your perfect face.' They'd practiced at Dmitri's studio the day before. This floor felt a little different, it wasn't the same size, there weren't mirrors. But their routine wasn't complicated, or at least if it was Charlie hadn't let anybody tell her so. What made it look ravishing – they agreed, later, seeing it on video – was the way Sacha led, and the way Charlie followed, and the way her dress swirled through the swooping turns. And then the way he sang along with the last line as he brought her into their ending position before kissing her one more time.

They were in Australia before Charlie felt like she really had a handle on things again. She got out of the shower, pulled on a robe, looked at herself in the mirror, thought *we are on our honeymoon*, and went into the bedroom part of their suite. "That was surreal," she told Sacha. "I was in a dissociated state or something for going on three days. Did I manage to

316

behave more or less normally, or does the whole world think I'm a dope fiend?"

He was lounging on the couch, also in a robe, looking perfect as usual, and probably trying not to laugh. "You behaved just fine," he said. "Though I did occasionally have to say something more than once."

"Well most of a day was on that flight, and nobody would be sane on that flight, so." She flopped down beside him, then remembered she wanted coffee. She got up again and went to find that. "What's the news of the world."

"I don't know. I was only checking email. Gary says there's a bidding war, and if they can't get the film he's going to at least push the price as high as he can."

"Aw, he's so sweet. What's on our agenda today?"

"Limo to airstrip, private plane to Hunter Valley, winetasting and some sort of food all part of the package. Back here in plenty of time for the opera house."

Charlie took a moment. "Did I plan that?"

"Almost." Her version involved driving themselves in a rented car, and going to the opera house on another day. "I tweaked your itinerary a little."

"Yeah, I guess." She sat down beside him again. "You're figuring all this out, aren't you?"

He leaned over to kiss her. "We aren't big spenders at home. And there's only one honeymoon."

"True. Kiss me again." She set her coffee cup down so she could get her arms around him. It didn't take him long to get his hands under the robe. Soon after, their robes were off, she was on her back, and he had his mouth on her breast. "Mmm. I love you. How much time before I have to get dressed?"

THE END

317

About the Author

Alexandra Caluen lives in a small purple house with her husband, a bottle of Laphroaig, a lot of books, and nine pairs of ballroom shoes. She works in patent law and has enough hair for three people.

www.thelastories.com

www.ingramcontent.com/pod-product-compliance
Lightning Source LLC
Chambersburg PA
CBHW031657170626
46808CB00005B/1489